New
4.95

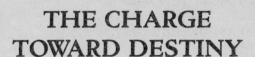

THE CHARGE
TOWARD DESTINY

Daoud slung his bow across his back and drew his long, curving saif from the scabbard. The noonday sun flashed on it as he held it high. His men roamed and brandished their own swords.

The band had caught up with them, and the trumpets and hautboys screamed death to the enemy while the kettledrums rumbled.

There was nothing left to protect Charles d'Anjou now. There was not even time for the French leader to run. He seemed to know it. He had his sword out and he held up a white shield with a red cross.

Urging the Arabian on, shouting the name of God, Daoud raced toward triumph. . . .

THE SARACEN: THE HOLY WAR

ROBERT SHEA

BALLANTINE BOOKS · NEW YORK

Library of Congress Catalog Card Number: 88-92181

ISBN: 0-345-35933-X

Manufactured in the United States of America

First Edition: April 1989

PROLOGUE

A summary of *The Saracen*
Book One, *Land of the Infidel*

A.D. *April 12, 1264 / 4th day of Jumada*, A.H. *662*

FEVERISH, HIS ARROW-WOUNDED LEG THROBBING, DAOUD IBN AB-
dallah lies in bed after a night of battle and defeat. As dawn lights
the eggshell-white windowpanes in his room, he recalls the events
that led him to this bitter hour.

Daoud was born to an English crusading family that had settled
in Palestine. Captured by Muslims as a child, he was taken to El
Kahira, Cairo, chief city of Egypt, and selected for the Mamelukes,
the elite corps of slave warriors gathered from all parts of the Middle East to serve the sultans of El Kahira.

He became a favorite of a leading Mameluke emir, Baibars.
Young and in need of comfort, he converted to Islam. He came to
love the faith of Muhammad, totally and humbly dedicating himself
to its tenets and to the welfare of the Muslim people. He studied
with Sheikh Saadi, a Sufi mystic, and with the Hashishiyya, the
dreaded sect known in Europe as the Assassins.

In those years the Tartars, invincible legions of mounted barbarians, had come out of Asia, invading the Islamic world. A huge
army led by Hulagu, grandson of the Tartar conqueror, Genghis
Khan, had already conquered Persia and Syria and was poised to
attack Egypt. And Hulagu was sending ambassadors to the pope to
urge Christian Europe to join with the Tartars in destroying the
Muslims.

Should Tartars and crusaders strike at Egypt simultaneously, the
people and faith Daoud has come to love would perish. Daoud has
seen with his own eyes how the Tartars obliterated Baghdad, its
200,000 men, women, and children slaughtered to the last soul,
the city leveled, a wasteland. He is determined that the same fate
not befall his adopted El Kahira.

Baibars—having made himself Sultan of El Kahira—sent Daoud
into the land of the infidel. Because Daoud is blond and gray-eyed,

1

no one would ever suspect him to be a Saracen, as Christians call all Muslims.

Daoud's mission was to go to the court of the pope and use every means necessary—from intrigue and bribery to assassination and outright war—to stop Christians and Tartars from forming an alliance against Islam.

He went first to Manfred, king of southern Italy and Sicily. King Manfred's family, the imperial German house of Hohenstaufen, had been at war with the popes for generations, and Manfred had among his subjects many Sicilian Muslims. Manfred agreed to help Daoud. But to protect his own interests Manfred insisted that Daoud take with him Lorenzo Celino, a middle-aged Sicilian warrior, and Sophia Karaiannides, a beautiful Byzantine woman. Lorenzo brought along his huge, formidable dog, Scipio. Journeying northward, the three rescued Rachel, a Jewish girl, from tavern ruffians. Daoud agreed, with misgivings, to let her travel with them.

The pope, threatened by political violence in Rome, had moved his residence to Orvieto, a strongly walled town built on a huge flat-topped rock. Here, Cardinal Adelberto Ugolini, a Sicilian churchman who had long been secretly sending information to Baibars, was horrified to find Baibars's agent on his doorstep expecting hospitality. But the cardinal reluctantly agreed to help.

Hulagu Khan's ambassadors to the pope, Christianized Tartars named John Chagan and Philip Uzbek, arrived in Orvieto two weeks after Daoud. A young French nobleman, Count Simon de Gobignon, commanded their military escort. Daoud had arranged for garbage-throwing hecklers to mar the ambassadors' procession. The arrogant Cardinal Paulus de Verceuil, accompanying the Tartars, was hit by excrement. He ordered the hired Venetian crossbowmen to fire into the crowd, killing two innocent bystanders.

Calling himself David of Trebizond, a merchant from the eastern shore of the Black Sea, Daoud appeared publicly for the first time at a council of Church leaders called by Pope Urban. He spoke from firsthand knowledge of the horrors committed by the Tartars. But Friar Mathieu d'Alcon, the Tartars' interpreter, testified that in his opinion the Tartar empire was no longer a danger to Europe.

The Tartar ambassadors and their entourage were guests at the palace of Orvieto's most powerful family, the Monaldeschi. When Contessa Elvira di Monaldeschi gave a reception for the emissaries, Daoud drew them into drunken gloating over their atrocities and boasting of their plans for world conquest. Pope Urban and many other Church dignitaries were appalled listeners.

With Ugolini's help, Daoud was able to persuade the influential

Dominican philosopher Fra Tomasso d'Aquino to write and preach against the alliance. But then, subjected to unknown pressures, Fra Tomasso suddenly changed his position.

Daoud now felt that he could do no more through intrigue. He had been in contact with the Filippeschi, an Orvieto clan who were hereditary enemies of the Monaldeschi family. And through Lorenzo he had been quietly recruiting a company of bravos—armed adventurers. Offering the help of his mercenaries, he persuaded the Filippeschi to attack the Monaldeschi palace. With de Gobignon and the Tartars' other guards diverted, he could enter the palace and kill the ambassadors.

While the Filippeschi prepared for the attack, Daoud discovered that Andrea Sordello, one of his hired bravos, had been set to spy on him by Simon de Gobignon. In Tilia's brothel, Daoud subjected Sordello to a Hashishiyya initiation, using drugs and women to make the spy his slave. He implanted in Sordello's mind a command that if he should see a silver locket that Daoud keeps on his person, he would immediately kill Simon de Gobignon. And henceforth Sordello was to give Simon only the information Daoud wanted him to have.

After the initiation Daoud was troubled. He had been taught how to do this, but had never done it before. Had he truly and completely subjugated Sordello's soul?

On the night of the attack he was dismayed to discover the Monaldeschi ready for a siege. But, garbed in black as a Hashishiyya fighter, Daoud went ahead and slipped into the Monaldeschi palace.

The Tartars, with Simon de Gobignon, Friar Mathieu, and four guards, were in the most secure room in the palace, the cellar pantry, where costly spices from the East were kept behind a thick door with a strong lock.

Trained by the Hashishiyya to use his senses other than sight to fight in the dark, Daoud forced his way into the spice pantry and put out the lantern. He struggled with Simon in pitch blackness and came close to killing him. Swords thrust at him from all directions. He had the Tartars' lives almost in his grasp, but de Gobignon was thwarting him. He tried frantically to kill de Gobignon and was no more able to do it than if the man were a djinn.

Then the old priest escaped from the cellar and came back with a lighted candle. Gripped by the terrible fear that he would be caught and exposed, Daoud raced up the cellar stairs. Despair almost killed him when he felt the searing pain of a Tartar arrow in his leg.

He felt terror when he saw the white-bearded friar on the stairs blocking his way, even though the old man held no weapon in his outstretched arms.

He had been about to stab the friar, who was too useful to the Tartars and the Christians to be allowed to live. But his arm could not move. It was as if a powerful hand held it, and he seemed to hear a voice booming in his head, *You dare to murder a priest?*

In his dread he hesitated, but if he did not escape Sophia would die. The moment of paralysis passed, and instead of killing Friar Mathieu, he thrust him aside, to fall from the banisterless stairs.

As he lies in bed the following morning in Ugolini's mansion, Daoud forces himself to think. He has extended himself to the limit of his powers and failed, but he must try again. He has to find a new plan, lest his faith and his people, his whole world, meet annihilation.

In a room near Daoud's, Sophia Karaiannides kneels before an icon of Saint Simon Stylites that she herself painted. She is thankful that Daoud escaped alive from the Monaldeschi palace. She is glad that Simon, who coincidentally shares the name of her favorite saint, is alive, too. But how much longer, she wonders, will she have to live here in the midst of enemies with the fear of a hideous death as a spy and an enemy of the Church dogging her day and night?

Sophia was born in Constantinople during the years when it was ruled by French invaders. As a very young woman she had seen her parents and her lover slaughtered by rampaging French troops. She went on to serve the Byzantine general Michael Paleologos, who drove out the French and became the Basileus, Emperor of Constantinople.

Michael sent Sophia as a confidential envoy to his ally, Manfred, and she and Manfred became lovers. But when the blond Saracen who called himself David of Trebizond arrived at Manfred's court, Manfred told her she must help David in his mission of preventing the Christian-Tartar alliance. Manfred hinted at danger to her if she stayed with him. Though heartbroken at being sent away by Manfred, Sophia accepted the undertaking because another French crusade might well lead to another French attack on "the Polis," her beloved home city.

When Rachel joined their party, Sophia, remembering her own orphan girlhood, befriended her. But Daoud insisted, to protect the secrecy of the mission, that after they arrived in Orvieto, Rachel be sent to the brothel run by Tilia Caballo, Cardinal Ugolini's mistress.

After a few months in Daoud's company, Sophia felt powerfully attracted him. The Saracen admitted that he was likewise drawn to her, but insisted that they deny any loving feelings, because he must use Sophia to corrupt and defeat the advocates of the Tartar-Christian alliance.

And he did so at the Contessa di Monaldeschi's reception for the Tartars, sending Sophia to lure Simon de Gobignon away from the great hall of the palace while he tempted the Tartars to discredit themselves. Sophia and Simon went for a walk in the atrium, and in a dark corner she let him kiss her.

A month after the reception Simon and she had a clandestine tryst in her room at Ugolini's. Though she was ready to take him to bed, Simon insisted that they remain chaste, according to the customs of courtly love, thereby endearing himself to her all the more.

She is surprised to realize that she has come to care deeply for the idealistic, innocent young Frenchman. But her feeling for the Saracen is stronger. More than once the ruthless things Daoud has done in pursuit of his mission have made her almost hate him. Even so, when Sophia is with Daoud she feels a fire building in herself to match the fire she perceives behind those gray eyes.

She glances at an hourglass, sighs, and rises from where she has been kneeling before the saint's icon. It is time to prepare a fresh poultice for Daoud's wound.

Morning at the Palazzo Monaldeschi. The dead are laid out and wept over, the debris of the siege cleared away, repairs begun on the damaged walls. Simon de Gobignon strips off his mail shirt, about to step into a hot bath. He is profoundly grateful to be alive and relieved that he successfully protected the Tartar ambassadors from being murdered by the man in black. But relief turns to anguish each time he is reminded that his friend and adviser, Friar Mathieu, has been cruelly hurt by his fall and may yet die.

Count Charles d'Anjou, brother of King Louis of France, commissioned Simon to guard the Tartar ambassadors. King Louis wants to go on crusade to win back the Holy Land with the help of the Tartars. Pope Urban, however, is not interested in a crusade in the Middle East, but wants the help of the French in wresting southern Italy and Sicily away from Manfred von Hohenstaufen. He has offered Manfred's crown to Count Charles, but King Louis so far has not agreed to let his brother make the attempt. So the two strongest leaders in Christendom are stalemated.

Simon is desperately determined that the alliance of Tartars and Christians succeed. As he has confessed to Friar Mathieu, he bears a double dishonor. The world despises him as the son of Count Amalric de Gobignon, whose treachery caused the disastrous defeat of his king and the death of thousands of his comrades on crusade in Egypt fourteen years earlier. But only Simon and his parents know that Simon is in truth the offspring of an adulterous affair between his mother, Nicolette de Gobignon, and the troubadour Roland de Vency. Ultimately Roland killed Amalric in a duel and Nicolette married him. And Simon, though not Amalric's son, inherited the title and the domain of the Count de Gobignon. Simon has undertaken the task of guarding the Tartars as a way of restoring the honor of the name de Gobignon and proving to himself his right to bear that name.

The cause of the alliance has met with many setbacks in Orvieto, and Simon suspects a secret enemy is behind them. But in recent months the influential Fra Tomasso became a vigorous supporter of the alliance. And Sophia, Cardinal Ugolini's lovely niece from Sicily, responded favorably to Simon's attentions. Events seemed to be taking a turn for the better.

But then Sordello warned Simon that the Filippeschi were planning to attack the Monaldeschi palace. Preparing to defend his hostess, the contessa, Simon insisted that the Tartars, despite their desire to fight, be kept safe in the spice pantry. Directing the defense of the palace from its tower, Simon suddenly sensed that the attack must be only a diversion, that the Tartars were the real target of whoever was behind the Filippeschi. He abruptly left the tower and rushed down to the spice pantry.

He had barely gotten there when a man all in black forced his way in and doused the lights. In darkness the stalker killed two of the Tartars' guards and almost strangled Simon.

Simon fought off the killer long enough to give Friar Mathieu time to open doors and let in light. One of the Tartars managed to wound the man in black with an arrow. The attacker threw Friar Mathieu from the stairs and vanished into the maze of rooms on the first floor of the palace.

Now, Simon thinks as he eases himself into his bath, he has met the hidden enemy whose presence he felt ever since coming to Orvieto. Evil as Satan, powerful enough to throw an army against a fortified palace, subtle enough to strike at victims no matter how well protected. A being of almost inhuman strength and skill. Cruel and pitiless, ready to murder anyone who stands in his way.

Certain as the judgment of God it is that Simon and the man in black will fight again. This is war to the death.

BOOK TWO

THE HOLY WAR

Anno Domini 1264–1266
Year of the Hegira 662–664

"That which striketh!
What is that which striketh?
Ah, who will convey to thee what the Striking is?"
— The Koran, Surah CI

"How many men have slept in happiness, unaware that sudden death
was about to strike them?"
— Hulagu Khan

XLV

DAOUD DRIFTED IN AND OUT OF CONSCIOUSNESS FOR TWO DAYS after the fight at the Monaldeschi palace. Sleeping was much better than being awake and remembering failure.

In dreams he rode once again with his khushdashiya, his brother Mamelukes.

A yellow silk banner rippled in the breeze before them, declaring, WAGE WAR UTTERLY ON THE IDOLATORS, AS THEY WAGE WAR UTTERLY ON YOU.

Dust clouds swirled around them as they thundered down upon a row of Frankish knights. From a distance Daoud sent bolt after bolt from his compound bow whistling into the dark line of mail-clad men. He saw men clutch at their throats and topple from the saddle.

Screaming, he charged into the midst of the Franks, whirling his saif over his head, his lance in his left hand. A knight galloped into his path, holding up a shield white as an eggshell, emblazoned with a red cross. Daoud brought the saif down, and the knight raised his shield to fend off the blow. That left the crusader momentarily blind, and Daoud thrust under the shield with his lance.

The lance went in as if the knight wore no mail. As the Frank fell backward from his horse, Daoud saw that it was Simon de Gobignon.

Sophia's light touch on his shoulder woke Daoud. He was lying on his stomach. He propped himself up on his elbows and saw the glowing, diamond-shaped windowpanes and the familiar white walls of his room on the upper floor of Cardinal Ugolini's mansion. He turned his head to look at Sophia. Her dark eyes comforted him.

"Time for your poultice," she said.

He tried to smile at her. "And something to drink. My mouth tastes dry and foul."

"Wine?"

"By the Archangel, no! The juice of oranges, and later kaviyeh."

Sophia laughed. "Oranges? In April? You must be dreaming.

11

Trees do not bear fruit all year round in this part of the world, David. Your bitter beverage I can supply. But let me see to your wound first.'' She raised the blanket that covered his body. He felt his skin grow hot from scalp to toes. She was gazing upon his nude body. He was glad he was lying on his stomach rather than on his back.

Did his nakedness mean anything to her? Among Christians, he knew, men and women often saw each other naked. Not only did women go through the streets with their faces uncovered, but in warm weather the common folk, men and women both, walked to the public baths with barely a bit of cloth wrapped around their loins. And all Christians slept naked. When Sophia saw his body like this, was it just another unclothed body, like the many she had doubtless seen in her lifetime? Did she feel any embarrassment? Or desire? As for himself, his sense of helplessness made him feel only embarrassed, nothing more.

He turned his head again to look at her. She was intent on administering the poultice, and that doubtless took her mind off his nakedness. She had lifted off the old cloth, stained an ugly yellow-brown, and dropped it to the floor. He got a glimpse of the wound, a red slit about half a finger's length with black knots of thread in it in the back of his right leg, halfway between knee and buttock. Gently she patted and stroked on the wound a paste made of ground rose petals, lime water, and egg white, the Sufi remedy he had taught her to make.

Lorenzo had used his knife to open the hole made by the arrow so that he would not tear Daoud's flesh pulling the barbed head out. While Lorenzo worked over him, Daoud drew upon Saadi's final teaching to him to defend himself against the pain. In his mind he began to create the drug called Soma. He envisioned it as a bowl of glowing, silver-colored liquid, and he believed it could form a capsule around any part of his body where there was pain and wall it off from the rest of himself, at the same time filling him with a feeling of well being.

Once you have experienced the effects of material drugs on your body and learned to master them, Saadi said to him, *you have the knowledge you need to create a drug of the mind, Soma. This is more powerful and more reliable, and it will not harm your body in any way. Indeed, Soma will make your body stronger. It will calm your mind, fill you with peace, sometimes give you visions. But if you should suddenly need all your faculties, they are yours at once. The drug is gone in an instant.*

It was Saadi's teaching that whatever a man could accomplish with drugs, he could accomplish more effectively and reliably with his mind alone. A trained man could envision a drug that would serve any desired purpose. And thus a man could transcend the Hashishiyya reliance on administered drugs.

While he had drunk from the bowl of Soma and it had flooded through his body, Daoud's fingers had gripped the little leather case hung around his neck that contained the Sufi tawidh, the numerological invocation that he believed would speed his healing. A river of blood had poured out of his leg when Lorenzo drew out the arrow, and he had fainted. Sophia had stitched the wound with cotton thread that was now black with congealed blood.

Now Sophia laid a clean, folded linen cloth over the wound, used another strip of linen to tie the poultice to his leg, and then pulled the blanket up over him. Their eyes had not met once during the time she was caring for him. He found to his surprise that he had to know what she was thinking and feeling.

As if sensing his need, she spoke. "I have wanted to tell you, but you were too sick to understand me. D'Ucello, the podesta, came here the night of the uprising, looking for you and Lorenzo. As we planned, I told him you had both gone to Perugia."

Daoud's body went cold. He felt as if he were being stalked, and the hunter was closing in.

"Did he believe you?" he asked.

She shrugged. "He blustered some, but the cardinal ordered him off in the end. I think he must have hoped to find you among the dead or wounded at the Monaldeschi palace."

Daoud rolled over in bed, the wooden frame creaking, and the pain tore through his leg like the slash of a scimitar. He groaned through clenched teeth. Despite his ability to shield his mind from pain when it took him unexpectedly like this, it could hurt like the torments of the damned.

"What are you doing?"

He gasped. "Trying to get up. D'Ucello will be back, and he must not see me wounded." He tried to sit up, and she laid her hand, firm and cool, on his forehead and pushed him back against the pillows.

"You are in more danger from fever than you are from d'Ucello," she said, letting her hand rest on his forehead.

"You will be surprised at how quickly the wound heals," he said, touching the tawidh at his neck. "As for fever, it is healthy. It burns out impurities." He laughed bitterly. "I hope it is burning the stupidity out of me."

"You—stupid?" She laughed.

He did not join her. It pleased him a little, in the midst of his anguish and self-disgust, to see that she thought well of him. But she was wrong about him—and her life depended on him, and that thought made him feel worse.

"De Gobignon was waiting for me. He knew I was coming for the Tartars. He *knew*."

"How much could he have known?" she asked. "No one knew what your plans were."

"Sophia, if de Gobignon had not been there, I would have been able to kill those two barbarian pigs easily. I did my best, with all my skill, all my training, all my experience, and it went for nothing."

That was a pain Soma would not shield him from, the pain of failure. It felt like a mace blow to his chest every time he remembered the fight in the blackness of the spice pantry.

To drive away the damnable memory of being routed by the Christians, he had to concentrate on the present and the future.

"Send someone to fetch Sordello to me."

"You should be resting."

He laughed and touched her hand lightly. "Resting! Our enemies are not resting." She sighed, but went.

When Sordello entered Daoud's room, Lorenzo followed him closely, eyes boring into the back of the mercenary's skull. Sophia entered behind Lorenzo.

Trembling, Sordello knelt by Daoud's bed. "I feared for you, Messer David. I am happy to see you looking so well."

Would Sordello give up the pleasures of hashish and the promise of a paradise with beautiful women? What reward could Simon de Gobignon offer him that could be more enticing?

Yet, I have always known that this man was a two-edged sword that could turn in my hand.

"The Monaldeschi were prepared for us," said Daoud. "They were armed and on their battlements when we came. Someone warned them."

"You do not suspect me, Messer David?" Sordello, crouched on the floor by Daoud's bed, looked up slyly sideways at him. "I would be a fool to injure one who has been so great a benefactor to me."

Daoud felt rage boil up inside him at Sordello's false abjectness. He glared at the old bravo and saw a faint tremor in his jaw.

Propping himself up on one elbow, he leaned toward Sordello. "Your fawning insults me. I think you lie."

Hatred briefly twisted Sordello's face. Then a knowing smile made it even uglier.

"Messer David, if I had told the Count de Gobignon what I know about you, you would surely be dead by now."

Daoud forced himself to his feet. The pain shot through him like a lightning bolt, but in his fury he ignored it. He bent down and seized Sordello's throat with his right hand. He fell back sitting on the bed, pulling the popeyed bravo toward him so that his good knee pressed into the Sordello's chest.

Somewhere, nearby, he heard Sophia cry out in protest, but he paid no attention.

"Confess that it was you, and I will kill you quickly," Daoud whispered. "I have shown you paradise, and I can show you hell. If you do not give yourself up now, and I find out later that it was you, I will inflict torments of mind and body on you beyond your imagining."

"David, stop, you will kill him!" Sophia screamed. She gripped Daoud's arm, digging her nails into his muscle.

Gradually Daoud released his hold on the corded throat. With his eyes alone, employing the Hashishiyya "look that imprisons," he held Sordello fast. The bravo's eyes were bloodshot and red-rimmed.

He was glad Sophia had stopped him. She must have realized that he would regret it if he killed Sordello in a fit of rage. If Sordello had not betrayed them, his false reports to Simon de Gobignon would still be useful. And in any case his sudden disappearance immediately after the attack on the Monaldeschi palace would draw de Gobignon's attention.

"If it is not you, then there is another among us who told Simon de Gobignon about my plans. If you want to save your life, you will find out who it is."

"I promise you, messere." Sordello's voice was a hoarse croak. "Whoever the escremento is, I will deliver his life into your hands."

Sordello stood up, then turned to Sophia and bowed.

"Madonna," Sordello gasped. "My eternal gratitude—"

"Just get out," Sophia snapped.

Was there a suggestion of a leer in Sordello's lumpy face as he stared at Sophia? But pain spread from the wound in Daoud's leg in great ripples through him, and he lay back and concentrated on the Sufi exercise that detached him from his body.

The heavy oak door closed behind Sordello. They were all three silent for a moment. Then Lorenzo jerked the door open and looked out into the corridor. He nodded, indicating Sordello had truly gone.

"It might have been wiser to strangle him," said Lorenzo. "He has all our lives in his hands."

Daoud held up his hand. "What he said was true. He could have delivered us to our enemies before the attack, I believe he is still in my power."

When alone with Sophia, Daoud lay back on his cushions. She stood looking down at him, and he wondered if that was pity he saw in her face.

"You are in such pain," she said.

He shook his head. "It is nothing."

"I do not mean the pain of the body."

She understood, then, what he was feeling. He smiled at her and shut his eyes.

She sat in silence on the edge of the bed while he lay there, brooding. Again he escaped into drowsiness. His mind drifted back to the sands of Egypt. He dreamed again of riding as a Mameluke.

When he woke, a short time had passed, and Sophia was still sitting there, gazing down at him.

Hints of a new plan began to come together in his mind. As fever purged him of poison, it had brought him dreams of battle. Not of intrigues with the priests and bishops around the pope. Not of ambushes in narrow streets. Rather, open war.

That was the meaning of those dreams. Perhaps God Himself had sent them. He was called upon to wage jihad against the enemies of Islam as a Mameluke, on horseback, at the head of an army.

He held out his arm to Sophia. "Help me up. You and Lorenzo and I must meet with Ugolini."

Later that morning, a heavy spring rain hammered on the windows of Ugolini's cabinet. The storm had so darkened the room that the cardinal's servants had lit extra candles. Daoud, Lorenzo, and Sophia sat in a semicircle across from Ugolini's worktable.

The painted glass eyes of Ugolini's stuffed owl glared disapprovingly down from the bookshelves at Daoud, who had a sense that the cardinal felt as the owl looked. The skull on the table seemed to be laughing at him.

He understood now what he had to do, but would the others, especially Ugolini, go along with it? Over Ugolini's frantic protests he had insisted on inciting the Filippeschi to attack the Palazzo Monaldeschi. That attack having failed of its purpose, would the three of them still accept Daoud's authority? Ugolini, surely, would think that events had proved him right about the futility of the attack on the Monaldeschi. How could he be won over to the idea of a wider war? *Make war utterly on the idolators*—that, he had decided, was the meaning of his dream.

"Manfred's supporters, the Ghibellini, must take the pope captive," he said. "I know that you would prefer peace to war, but now that I have tried to kill the Tartars and failed, we do not have that choice." It was best, he thought, to admit his failure openly before Ugolini threw it in his face.

The cardinal's eyes were almost as wide and as stark as the owl's. "You would plunge the whole of Italy into war?"

"No," said Daoud, "but that is what is going to happen. The one thing that has kept the French out of Italy is the pope's refusal to give the Christian kings, especially the king of France, permission to ally themselves with the Tartars. But now that Urban is ill, he may give King Louis what he wants. When the pope allows the alliance, Louis will give his brother Charles permission to attack Manfred. It is not I who will plunge Italy into war. I am proposing only that we act before the French do."

Ugolini shook his head. "What do you mean, take the pope captive?"

"The Papal States are surrounded by cities ruled by Manfred's Ghibellino supporters. The nearest is Siena. With gold and with timely warnings about the danger from the French, we can persuade Siena to move against the pope." He held up his fist. "And then we can make sure that the next pope elected is favorable to Manfred. And through him, well disposed toward peace with Islam."

It was the same sort of plan, Daoud thought, as inciting the Filippeschi against the Monaldeschi. But Lorenzo had already visited Siena and made sure that the Ghibellini of Siena, with Daoud's help, could raise a far greater army than the pope could muster in Orvieto. This time he would succeed.

"Impossible!" Ugolini cried. "No king can control the Papacy. The Hohenstaufen have been trying to rule over the popes for centuries, and for centuries they have failed."

"Perhaps it takes a stranger to see that where the Hohenstaufen failed, the French are about to succeed," said Daoud. "France is now the strongest kingdom in Europe. If Manfred does not get control of the pope and the cardinals, the next pope will be under the protection of the French, and will have to do whatever they want."

"Urban is a sick man," said Ugolini. "There is not a cardinal who would risk a wager that he will live to see the year 1265. He will not call for the French to save him when he knows the angels are coming to get him."

"No, there I must disagree with Your Eminence," said Lorenzo, lounging in a large chair facing Ugolini's table. "Urban is a Frenchman, and he will work to bring the French into Italy until the moment the angels knock at his door."

Sophia, who had been sitting quietly in an armless straight-back chair with her hands folded in her lap, said, "The pope will blame the Ghibellini for the attack on the Monaldeschi. He will want help, and he will ask it from the French even if it means Christians joining the Tartars in a crusade the pope does not really want."

"Very shrewd," said Daoud with a smile in her direction. "Except that the pope had decided before the attack on the Monaldeschi to approve the alliance with the Tartars. As we know from his persuading Fra Tomasso to switch sides. It was because the pope had clearly turned against us that I planned to kill the Tartars."

Daoud was tired of sitting. Despite the pain in his leg, he used his stick to push himself to his feet and stepped out of the window recess. He limped over to Ugolini's table.

"We must send Lorenzo to Siena with enough of our precious stones to raise an army big enough to overwhelm the papal soldiery and the Orvieto militia. It may take time to persuade the Sienese to act. It will take more time to muster an army and march on Orvieto. We must begin as quickly as we can. With the pope in Ghibellino hands, with the Ghibellini in a position to sway the outcome of the next papal election, we may yet keep the French out of Italy."

And that, he thought, would keep crusaders and Tartars out of the Dar al-Islam.

Ugolini's shrug spoke more of despair than of acquiescence. "Certainly the French will come if we do nothing. You are right about that. Do as you will. It is a miracle we have survived this long."

Strange, Daoud thought. Ugolini saw their mere survival as miraculous. To Daoud, failure so far to put a final stop to the alliance of Christians and Tartars made him wonder whether God disapproved of him.

Once he accepted the fact that he had to go, Lorenzo had hoped the rain would continue. Under its cover his leaving the city was less likely to be noticed or impeded. But by mid-afternoon, the hour of None, when he was packed and mounted, a spare horse trotting behind him, a bright, hot sun had come out, and the puddles in the narrow streets were turning to steam.

At the Porta Maggiore he stopped when he saw two clerks seated at tables on either side of the gateway, one questioning each person entering the town, the other examining those leaving. A dozen of the podesta's men in yellow and blue stood by to keep people in line. Each clerk consulted what appeared to be a list on a scroll and on another scroll wrote down the names of those he questioned.

Only two days ago Sophia had told d'Ucello that David of Trebizond and his man Giancarlo were in Perugia. Now, Lorenzo thought, those damned clerks were probably watching for their return. They could have been set at the gate the morning after the attack on the Monaldeschi palace.

He smiled ironically as he remembered how, last summer, he had sat as these clerks did now, at the gateway to Lucera waiting to catch a certain Saracen newly arrived from Egypt.

Now, thought Lorenzo, if he tried to leave Orvieto he would not only be stopped and possibly arrested, he would be as good as telling the podesta that he and David had never been out of the town at all.

Lorenzo clenched his fists. He felt like a tuna caught in a net.

And if I stand here much longer staring they'll notice me and haul me in.

He quickly turned his horses away from the gate and headed back to Ugolini's mansion.

At the beginning of the third Nocturn, Lorenzo, David, and a servant of Ugolini's named Riccardo, whom they had chosen for his size and strength, emerged from an alley near the north side of the city wall.

David wore a hood pulled low over his face. He limped and walked with a stick. Lorenzo had advised against his being out in the street at all, but David had answered that the watch did not know he was in Orvieto and would not be looking for him.

Lorenzo was amazed at how rapidly David had gotten better. He had never seen a man walking only two days after taking a bad arrow wound in the leg. The Muslims who taught David the art of healing must be even better than Jewish physicians.

As they walked, Lorenzo made David recite the names of half a dozen prominent Perugian merchants who were supporters of King Manfred. If the podesta were to question David about his whereabouts the night of the Filippeschi uprising, these men would bear witness that David and Lorenzo had been in Perugia.

"If d'Ucello does question you, how will you explain that you are back in Orvieto without having been seen entering through the gate?" Lorenzo asked him.

"I will tell him—with the greatest reluctance—that the line was very long when I arrived and that I was in haste to enter, so I bribed the men on duty to let me by. The more time passes before he discovers my presence in Orvieto, the more believable that will be."

"If he suspects you of anything, he will arrest you no matter how good a story you tell him," Lorenzo said.

David stopped walking and rested his hand on Lorenzo's shoulder. "That is why you must go tonight, my friend. And come back quickly with an army from Siena."

Lorenzo had a pack over his shoulder and wore a long traveling cloak. Riccardo carried a coil of rope. Ahead of them was a small stone shed built against the wall, beside one of the round guard towers.

Lorenzo was not particularly frightened by the ordeal ahead. He had done enough climbing in his younger days. But he was repelled by the thought that through the large opening in the floor of the little house the people of this quarter dumped, not only their garbage, but also the contents of their chamber pots.

They went quietly to the door of the shed. There was a guard in the tower above them, though he would have no reason to watch the garbage chute.

Riccardo put a meaty hand on the rough-hewn door. It gave without a struggle. Not even locked, thought Lorenzo. He supposed the podesta, may his ballocks wrinkle up like prunes, had not thought that anyone would choose this ignominious way to escape from the city.

"Sophia told me to tell you she would miss you," David said.

"Kiss her for me," said Lorenzo.

Wonder if David has bedded Sophia yet.

Riccardo filled the little room so that Lorenzo felt himself being crowded to the edge of the chute.

"Hey! Riccardo! Push me down *after* you have the rope around me."

"Sorry, messere." The burly man tied the rope tightly around Lorenzo's waist, just above the belt that held the jewels, and they both pulled hard on the knot to test it. Tying the knots in the dark, they had to be doubly careful. Then Riccardo tied the other end of the rope around his own waist and donned heavy oxhide gloves.

It was a warm April night, and Lorenzo smelled a horrid odor of garbage and excrement coming up from the pit. It was not actually a pit, but a crevice in the face of the cliff on which Orvieto was built. Lorenzo had hoped the day's heavy rain would have washed the cliffside clean. But the people of Orvieto had been dumping offal here for centuries.

"Your final instructions?" he said to David.

"Ugolini's servant Guglielmo seems to have gotten safely out of the city with your horses and baggage," said David. "He must not have been on any list. He will meet you at the shrine of Saint Sebastian on the road to Siena. From there you know what you have to do."

David grasped him by the shoulders and then patted his back. They had become good friends, Lorenzo realized. Look how David was trusting him to ride with a fortune in gems to Siena, meet the right parties, bargain with them, deliver the gems to them and come back to Orvieto with a Ghibellino army. That was much to expect of a man. Yet David seemed not to doubt that Lorenzo would do it.

Lorenzo felt warm when he thought how much David meant to him. He had come on this mission as King Manfred's man, but he was going to Siena just as much for David as for Manfred. Bringing the Sienese into the struggle might keep the French away, though, and that would help Manfred as much as it would the Muslims.

"Lower away, then," Lorenzo said to Riccardo.

David stepped back. Riccardo and Lorenzo both took hold of the rope. Lorenzo stepped over the edge of the chute. His legs dangled, and he tried not to think about how much empty space was between him and the rocks at the base of Orvieto's mountain. The rope cut painfully into his waist and back. He gripped it tightly with his gloved hands and wrapped his legs around it to take some of the strain off the loop around his waist.

Grunting, Riccardo slowly lowered Lorenzo through the chute. David was standing beside Ugolini's man and had laid a protective hand on the rope. The hole in the floor was just wide enough for Lorenzo's shoulders to pass through. Then he was hanging free below the city wall, his back to the cliff, staring out at a starry black sky and the silhouettes of distant hillsides. He felt dizzy and shut his eyes.

"Turn me," he whispered hoarsely up at the opening above him.

After a moment he felt his body rotating, and again he had to fight dizziness. He was facing in toward the smelly crevice, and he drew up his legs and planted his feet firmly on its walls. With the help of the rope he could walk down the cliffside. Riccardo let out the rope a little more, and Lorenzo's boot sole scraped loudly against the crumbling tufa surface, releasing a shower of pebbles.

"Who's down there?" a distant voice shouted, and Lorenzo felt as if someone had dumped a bucket of cold water over him. That was the guard in the tower high above. He wondered if the guard could see him down here. He tried to grip the sides of the crevice with his feet and pull himself closer to the cliff face.

"I am taking a piss, buon'amico!" Riccardo called up to the guard. "Do you mind?"

"That place is not for pissing," the guard called back.

"Would you rather I sprinkled your tower?"

There was no answer this time, and Riccardo began whistling loudly to cover any further noises Lorenzo might make. Lorenzo hoped the guard would not come down to investigate. What if he did, and Riccardo felt he must let go of the rope?

Riccardo must have had the same thought, because he began paying out the rope more rapidly, and Lorenzo's feet flew over the crackling rock. He was like a man running furiously backward. It would be comical, he thought, were he not in danger of breaking his neck.

This was a time when he wished he had clung to a religion of some sort rather than abandoning the faith of his fathers and replacing it with nothing. It would be so comforting to pray to an all-powerful being who might be kind enough to protect him. Just *hoping* not to get hurt seemed stupid and futile.

He felt the cliff wall beginning to slant outward a bit under his feet. The whistling from the shed had stopped. He looked up and saw that he was halfway down the side of the cliff. The backs of his legs ached from the strain of supporting his weight, and his shoulders and arms hurt too. He began to worry, not so much about whether he would fall as what he might land in when he reached the bottom.

And the smell of rot and filth all around him might choke him before he ever got down. He saw directly below him a pit of blackness surrounded by trees that were only a little less dark. The muck might be over his head; he might just sink into it.

As he reached the level of the trees he drew his knees up and then straightened them hard, giving himself a push away from the cliff. He was still being lowered, so that when he swung back to the cliff he was much farther down. This time his boots hit a coating of soft stuff on the rock, and the smell was unbearable.

I'd rather break my neck than smother in shit.

He kicked again with his legs, and when he hit the end of the outward swing, the rope feeling as if it would cut him in two, he grabbed for a tree branch, barely visible in the darkness. It hit him in the stomach and knocked all the wind out of him, but he clung to it desperately.

Bent double over the tree limb, he looked down and saw shadows that might be forest floor as far below him as his own height. Then again, he might be seeing the tops of other trees. He drew his dagger and cut the rope around his middle but held it with one hand. He took deep, relieved breaths when the constraint was gone. He gave three sharp jerks on the rope, the signal that he was down. After a moment all tension left the rope, and he felt it falling in the darkness. Another moment and he heard rustlings, thumps, and splashes as the rope landed at the bottom of the crevice. Tomorrow's dumping, he thought, would quite conceal it.

He wondered briefly if David and Riccardo had safely left the dumping shed and were on their way back to Ugolini's. He looked down again into the darkness, realizing that if he jumped from here he might fall far enough to kill himself. Having swung away from the pile of offal, he was now more worried about breaking his neck. He pulled himself up, straddling the tree and facing in toward the trunk. He slid down to the trunk, then tried to feel about with his foot for another branch.

His feet met nothing. He swung over the side of the branch, feeling the trunk with one hand and the space below him with his feet. Still nothing. Now he was dangling from the limb, holding on with two aching hands. If he had not worn gloves, he would have no skin left on his palms.

Well, here goes one hopeful atheist. He let go.

He fell a short distance, feetfirst, into a pool of water. It came up over his low boots, soaking his hose. There was no smell; apparently it was a pure forest pool, probably a puddle enlarged by the recent rain. Sighing, he sloshed out of it. Small creatures hopped and scurried away from him.

It could have been much, much worse.

Glad to feel his feet on the ground, he hoped the rest of his journey to Siena would be less exciting than the beginning.

XLVI

FRIAR MATHIEU SAT IN A CUSHION-LINED ARMCHAIR IN THE CLOIS-
tered garden of the Hospital of Santa Clara, the white wisps of his
beard ruffling like feathers in the morning breeze. The dappled
shade of a pear tree protected him from the June sun.

A young Franciscan, his tonsured head a gleaming pink spot
surrounded by a wreath of close-cropped black hair, stood at a tall
desk beside Friar Mathieu, writing on a piece of parchment.

"All things lead to good if one looks at them aright," Friar
Mathieu said with a chuckle. "That murderer in black gave me the
time I needed to do something needful—get the story of my journey
among the Tartars written before it is lost in my failing memory. A
good thing I did not land on my head."

Despite the pain he felt at Friar Mathieu's injuries, Simon had to
smile at the old Franciscan's little joke. And indeed, he might look
small and fragile huddled in his chair, but he was showing energy
and zest for life. He was pulling through.

"And behold," Friar Mathieu went on, lifting his bandaged right
arm, "I myself am exempted from writing. Friar Giuseppe must
do the work while I sit here and explore my memory. And when I
grow tired of even that little bit of work, Friar Giuseppe reads to
me from the newly arrived manuscript on mathematics, called *De
Computo Naturali*, by our gifted brother Friar Bacon of Oxford. I
could almost be grateful to that Assassin."

Simon stood awkwardly, looking unhappily down at him, till
Friar Mathieu motioned him to sit on the ground beside him. To
make room for himself, Simon moved a pair of crutches out of the
way. It was worrisome that so soon—only a few weeks after the fall
that had almost killed him—Friar Mathieu had started hobbling
about on crutches and had begun dictating, sitting painfully upright, to Friar Giuseppe. Even though one leg was certainly broken
and there were probably a dozen other cracks in his arms and ribs,
Friar Mathieu insisted that he was more likely to die if he remained
in bed than if he was up and moving about.

"You are looking well today, Father." He had to admit it, even though the old priest was not taking proper care of himself.

"I am lucky this happened to me in the spring," said Friar Mathieu. "The sun and air help me mend. But I fear you will not see my complete recovery, since you will have to leave Orvieto shortly."

"Leave? Why, Father? Has something gone wrong?" His first thought, as always, was for the safety of the Tartars. Ever since that terrible night in April, he dreaded leaving them out of his sight.

Instead of answering, Friar Mathieu asked Friar Giuseppe for privacy. The young priest bowed deeply and touched the old man's hand reverently before gathering up his writing materials and turning to go.

"You have not heard, then? A courier brought the news to the pope's palace last night. All through the north, the Ghibellini are on the move. Siena, it seems, has been quietly raising an army to send against Orvieto. And the Ghibellino party has taken power in Pisa and Lucca. It appears the Ghibellini have decided to seize all of Italy before the French come in and take it."

But we are French, thought Simon, *and we have no ambitions in Italy.*

Uncle Charles does.

In this quiet garden it was hard to believe that an army could be preparing to march against Orvieto. Or even that the attack on the Palazzo Monaldeschi had happened in the same city. Simon watched a friar in his brown robe serenely weeding. The rows of plants were already tall and thick—peas, haricots, lettuce, cabbage, carrots. At Gobignon this time of year the seedlings would not be half as high.

"Will the Sienese besiege Orvieto?" he asked.

Another battle? And another attempt on the Tartars?

"Pope Urban will not wait to see what they do," said Friar Mathieu. "He feels threatened from both north and south, and intends to move away from here as soon as possible. There is a rumor that Manfred of Sicily himself may invade the Papal States this summer."

Simon sprang to his feet and threw his arms wide in astonishment. "And what about the Tartars?"

"They will certainly go where His Holiness goes."

"God's blood!" Simon struck his forehead with his hand. "Forgive me, Father. But if the pope has not enough troops to keep him safe in Orvieto, surely he is in even more danger on the road. And if the Tartars are with him, we could lose everything."

Friar Mathieu shook his head, absently rubbing his bound right arm with his left hand. "We can gain everything. His Holiness needs help desperately. Now he can be persuaded to give King Louis permission to join with the Tartars." The old Franciscan's eyes fixed on Simon's. "You must go to the pope."

Simon felt the palms of his hands grow cold. "The pope will not listen to me, Father."

Friar Mathieu chuckled. "Is he more likely to listen to that fool—God forgive me—de Verceuil?"

"Yes," said Simon after a moment's thought. "De Verceuil is a cardinal. And is it not his task to treat with the pope? Mine is to guard the ambassadors."

"Are you not close to King Louis, Simon? Almost a foster son?"

Simon hesitated. "That is putting it a bit strongly. But he knows me well."

Friar Mathieu gestured with his left hand. "Then you are the person to carry His Holiness' appeal for help to King Louis."

The suggestion dismayed Simon. It meant he would have to leave the Tartars for months. And just when they would be much more vulnerable to attack, following the pope from one city to another.

"No, Father," he said. "I cannot leave the Tartars."

Friar Mathieu shook his head patiently. "Do you not see, Simon? If the pope does decide to approve an alliance with the Tartars, John and Philip's work is done."

Standing on the gravel walk of the Franciscan cloister garden, Simon felt as if the earth were shaking under him. He could not picture himself speaking to the pope as one statesman to another. Persuade the pope suddenly to take a stand, when he had vacillated for nearly a year? And yet, he told himself, he was the Count de Gobignon, and the lands he held were larger than some kingdoms.

But that only reminded him that he held the title through a lie.

The courtyard before the papal palace was crowded with covered wagons and open carts, horses and donkeys, men carrying crates and bales. Here and there, mailed papal archers in gold and white surcoats strode, crossbows on their shoulders, alert for pilfering. Simon asked a series of servants for the pope's majordomo and was directed to that official, clad in a glittering embroidered tunic, who stood at the center of the papal library overseeing the packing of books and scrolls. Simon summoned up all his confidence and presented himself to the man.

"The Count de Gobignon of France?" the horse-faced major-domo repeated. "I will try to find His Holiness for you, Your Signory."

They found Pope Urban in a tiny chamber on the second floor of the palace, writing furiously at a desk that faced a window opposite the door. He was wearing a white cassock with a white linen hood drawn up over his head. On his desk Simon saw a jar of ink, a sheaf of quills, and a stack of parchment sheets. A wrought-iron stand held a black earthenware pitcher over a candle flame.

"Holy Father—" the majordomo began, addressing the pope's back. Simon watched with fascination the rapid movements of Pope Urban's right arm as his quill raced over the parchment, leaping after each line to the ink jar and back again.

"Maledizione!" the pope exclaimed. "Not now, Ludovico. God's pity, let me get at least one letter done without you interrupting me. The Archangel Michael run you through if you speak another word to me."

Simon was momentarily shocked, but then recalled that the pope was a shoemaker's son. Once a bourgeois, always a bourgeois, he thought, even if one becomes God's vicar on earth. But, by God's robe, the man could write fast. In a moment he had filled a sheet of parchment with the short, unadorned black strokes of a chancery hand. Simon estimated it would take him the better part of a morning to write that much. Of course Pope Urban, being a churchman all his life, had a good deal more practice at writing.

Urban folded the parchment and poured melted red wax from the black pitcher to seal it. He took the large gold ring from his finger and stamped it into the wax. Without looking around, he handed the letter to his majordomo.

"To Duke Alberto Baglione at Perugia by our best horses," said Pope Urban. "Have Pietro Pettorini carry it; he is our fastest man."

"Holiness," said the majordomo diffidently, taking the letter, "the Count de Gobignon wishes to see you."

"Ah!" Urban half turned in his chair to look at Simon. Simon saw that the pope's wrinkled face was a deep pink, and his eyes glittered. Loose strands of gray hair escaping from under his hood quivered as his head shook with a slight, constant tremor. Simon had heard that men sometimes rallied in the final stages of an illness, before the slide into darkness. That, perhaps, accounted for the pope's color and energy. Simon's heart ached for the old man. This was the spiritual father of the world, and his troubles, troubles Simon had in part brought to him, were aiding whatever disease was destroying him.

"Simon de Gobignon!" Urban cried, raising bony hands in benediction. "If you had not come to me, I should have sent for you." His pale blue eyes shifted from side to side, and Simon felt even more pain for him.

This man should not think of traveling. It will kill him.

Urban half stood, and his majordomo rushed past Simon to turn his chair so that the pope could face his visitor. He was sitting in a simple straight-back chair without arms.

Simon stepped into the room and dropped to one knee. The pope extended his trembling right hand, and Simon kissed his gold Fisherman's Ring. On its circular face was an engraving of a bearded man whom Simon guessed must to be Saint Peter, casting a net from the stern of a boat.

Seen close at hand and without the tall tiara and the crozier and the heavy robes of office, Urban was very short. Simon wondered whether he had always been a little man or whether age and the strains of his office had shrunk him.

"Stand up, Monseigneur le Comte, s'il vous plaît," said the pope, changing to French. "I am sorry there is no chair, but this is where I do all my real work, and it is best not to encourage visitors to sit. Ludovico, leave us and shut the door behind you. And do not hang about in the corridor eavesdropping."

Simon rose, and found himself looking down at the skullcap on top of the pope's head. Feeling awkward, he took a few steps backward until his back was against the door of the tiny chamber.

Urban said, "I have long wanted to hear from your own lips what happened at the Palazzo Monaldeschi."

Simon gave the pope a detailed account of the battle. He ended with his fight with the man in black. Urban's eyes widened, and the trembling of his head grew more pronounced. When Simon told how the enemy had escaped, throwing Friar Mathieu from the cellar stairs, the pope winced in pain.

"So," Urban mused, "this murderer—doubtless sent by Manfred von Hohenstaufen—still lurks somewhere in Orvieto."

"We have tried to track him down," said Simon. "But the Filippeschi deny any knowledge of him, and the podesta, it seems, has not the power to make them answer our questions." He allowed the contempt he felt for d'Ucello to creep into his voice.

"Open the door and see if that sneaking Ludovico is listening outside," Pope Urban said. His lips twitched under his flowing gray beard in what was probably a smile.

Simon went to the door, and saw no one in the corridor but a helmeted man-at-arms standing about ten paces away. Servants with a huge bed frame struggled past. He closed the door and turned again to the pope.

"Yes," said Urban. "What was I saying? Ah, yes—Simon, I expect to be in my grave before the year is out."

"God forbid, Your Holiness!"

"God do me that kindness, you mean." Urban raised a depre-
cating hand. "I am worn out. I am ready to go home. But I have a
last task to do before I die. I must insure the destruction of the
odious Manfred. I must not let him kill me before my work is done,
and I must not fall into the hands of the Ghibellini. So, though it
will shorten my life even more, I must leave Orvieto. Now that the
Ghibellini have stirred up the Filippeschi to make civil war, I am
no longer safe on this mountaintop. Perugia is more secure. It has
a big army, and it is surrounded by a strong ring of other Guelfo
cities and castles. After I am gone, the cardinals will be safe there
while they elect a new pope."

Simon realized that he was indeed looking at a dying man. From
here to Perugia was a journey of at least two weeks, through difficult, mountainous country. Urban might get there safely, but he
would not live there long. The election of a new pope would take
months; it had been known to take years. And Urban's successor
might be even more reluctant to join forces with the Tartars than
Urban had been. What if it were Cardinal Ugolini—he was as eli-
gible as anyone—or someone under his influence? The little they
had accomplished so far might be wholly undone.

Time. Time was the most terrible enemy of all. The more time
passed, the less likely that the alliance would be formed, the joint
attack on the Saracens launched. Simon saw time as a black river
in flood, sweeping away everything he had worked and fought for.

*I must prevail upon him to give his permission—now. But how
can I sway a man three times my age—the pope himself?*

The only way to keep from giving in to despair was to plunge in,
as if this were a tournament, or a fight to the death. Simon plunged
in.

"Your Holiness, before you leave Orvieto, I beg you to recognize
that we must join with the Tartars to crush the infidel."

Urban sighed. "You think just as your King Louis does." He
held up an admonitory finger. "Europe first, Simon. The Church
must be strong in Europe before our princes go adventuring in
Outremer."

"But it was the popes who preached the Crusades in the first
place," Simon answered, baffled.

Urban's eyes grew wide and he leaned forward. "And I will
preach yet another crusade, Simon. Against Manfred the Anti-
christ. That is why I would have sent for you if you had not come
here. You must make the journey to King Louis and tell him that
this crusade that I will preach is the most important war of his

lifetime. He must come to my aid. I will make his brother Charles king of southern Italy and Sicily. I will write the letter to King Louis, and you will carry it to him.''

Now I must make my effort.

''He will heed your appeal if you give him what he wants, Your Holiness. Write that letter. But in it give your permission for King Louis to ally himself with the Tartars and begin preparations for a new crusade.''

Urban looked slyly up at Simon. ''Surely you suspect that it was I who persuaded Fra Tomasso d'Aquino to change his colors where the Tartars are concerned. I saw to it that the possibility of an alliance was kept alive, so that I might have something Louis and I could haggle over. Louis is the most stubborn man in the world. If I simply give him whatever he wants, there is no guarantee that he will give me what I want.''

Simon took a deep breath. What he was about to say might offend the pope deeply.

''Your Holiness, you have said it yourself. There is no more time for haggling. You must make your best offer and hope it is enough.''

The pope shut his eyes and slumped in his chair. Simon's heart went cold, thinking for a moment that the old man had suffered a seizure.

But then Urban said very softly, ''Help me to turn my chair around.''

Now Simon's heart beat faster as he moved the pope's chair so that it faced his desk. Urban took a gleaming blank sheet of parchment from the pile on his desk, dipped a quill, shook it, and began to write.

Simon stood by the wall, his heart pounding with exhilaration. Could it actually be that his words had moved the pope himself? It seemed impossible, as if he had stood in the path of a mighty river and diverted its course.

''The Tartars,'' the old man said with a sigh sometime later, when he had covered two sheets of parchment. ''I hope I am not making a terrible mistake. I still think Fra Tomasso was right in what he first said about them.'' He dropped wax at the bottom of the letter, stamped it with his ring, and blew on the wax to cool it. Then he folded the parchment and sealed it again.

''Ride to King Louis as quickly as possible.'' Urban turned, again half rising from his chair, and handed Simon the letter.

''Shall I carry the king's answer to Perugia, Holy Father?''

Urban shrugged. ''Oh, yes, I shall surely be in Perugia by the time you come back. But God will take me before the first of Charles d'Anjou's knights sets foot in Italy." He raised a pale hand to silence Simon's polite protest, and there was actually a twinkle in his eye. "Whatever my successor thinks, he will have a hard time undoing the decisions I have made today. By the time the next pope is elected, he will have a French army to help him destroy the Hohenstaufen. Whether he wants to or not."

"What of the Tartar ambassadors, Your Holiness?" Simon asked, thinking that it would be best to hasten those negotiations, too, lest the next pope disapprove of them. "Should I take them with me to the king?"

"No," said Urban firmly. "Then you would have to take a troop with you to guard them. You may have to travel far to find King Louis. He is setting out on a royal progress through his kingdom. I had a report of him just two days ago. That is one great benefit of this office—" His gray beard twitched again, and Simon knew that he was smiling. "News comes to us from everywhere." Then his eyelids lowered. "That is also what makes being the Holy Father so wearisome."

Yes, of course, King Louis made a journey of inspection through some portion of his realm nearly every summer. It might be months, Simon thought with a sinking heart, before he could find the king, deliver the pope's letter, and get back to the papal court. So much could happen.

But the most important thing of all has already happened. We have won. We have the alliance!

Triumph rang like cathedral bells in his ears. He was bringing victory to the king and to Count Charles. And his success would restore honor to the house of Gobignon.

Simon knelt once again, kissing the Fisherman's Ring and thinking that the hand that wore it would soon be cold.

But as he hurried down a corridor in the Palazzo Papale, already planning his route to France, the bells of triumph stopped ringing and in the silence a face appeared before his mind's eye. Amber eyes, olive skin, and wine-colored lips.

Sophia! By all the angels and saints, I may never see her again!

For a moment he felt torn. Duty and honor demanded that he leave Orvieto at once. But what of love? Sophia's image smiled, and he decided. He would need at least a day to prepare for his journey anyway. Before he left Orvieto he must see Sophia and make sure that the meeting would not be their last.

XLVII

Fat gray clouds hung low over the Umbrian hills, and Sophia thought she heard thunder rumbling in the west. As Simon's message had promised, he was waiting for her by the shrine of the Virgin on the road leading north from Orvieto. But what was he doing here, she wondered, with spare horses and a loaded baggage mule?

He waved to her and dismounted, and his scudiero—the same man who had yesterday delivered Simon's note to her—took charge of the beasts.

Clearly Simon was beginning a journey. He had not simply come out here to meet her. But he would not go anywhere far with no more company than one squire. And how could he leave the Tartars when hardly two months ago he had nearly lost his life protecting them?

Trying to puzzle out what was afoot, she rode with Ugolini's man Riccardo beside her to the shed-covered shrine where a blue-robed Mary held a smiling baby Jesus. Riccardo helped her down from her horse and Simon came forward.

She took Simon's arm, and he led her into the pine forest beside the road. She studied his face, trying to guess what thoughts were passing behind his somber blue eyes.

As soon as they were out of sight of their companions, she asked him, "Are you going to Perugia ahead of the pope?"

He did not answer her at once, so she kept her gaze on him.

Sophia enjoyed looking at Simon as she enjoyed looking at beautiful icons, jewels, sculptures. Yet his body did not have the fine proportions she had seen in statues made by Greeks of old. He was very tall and slender, all sharp lines pointing to heaven. His head, framed by long dark brown hair, was narrow, the nose and chin angular. His eyes, set in deep hollows, were bright with candor and intelligence, though at times she saw in them a haunted look.

She even found his barbaric Frankish garb pleasing. From Simon's narrow shoulders hung a cloak of rich crimson silk, and he wore a soft maroon cap adorned with a bloodred feather. The purple surcoat that extended below his knees sparkled with dozens of embroidered repetitions of a design of three gold crowns. In Constantinople only the Basileus and his consort were permitted to wear purple. From Simon's black leather belt, decorated with silver plates, hung a curving Saracen sword. Precious stones twinkled in its handle.

Now that she considered it, she recalled that she had always seen Simon in more subdued colors.

He dressed this way to please me, she thought fondly.

He looked away from her, but there was nowhere for him to look. They were walled in on all sides by a thick growth of pines. The lower trunks of the trees were straight and clean, like the poles of a palisade, their branches, which started higher than she could reach, putting out the bright green needles of new summer growth. Somewhere far above them was the cloudy, rain-heavy sky, but here they were enveloped in deep shadow under interlocked pine branches. The forest was so dark and soundless that she began to feel a little frightened. Simon and she were enemies, after all, even though she hoped he would never realize it. She often forgot it herself, when she was with him, liking him as much as she did.

"I am not going to Perugia," he said.

"Did you have me ride all the way out here to tell me no more than that?" she demanded.

"I wanted to tell you that I love you," he said hoarsely. He turned toward her, and his face glowed with adoration.

Oh, the boy! The dear, beautiful boy! He loves me, and he means it with every fiber of his being.

She felt a wave of warmth, not love but surely a kindliness, going out from her to him. He turned and took her shoulders in his big hands. She liked the feel of his hands on her. If only she could forget about David, she could happily give herself to him.

But she *was* acting for David, and she was here to find out what this Frank was planning. She must make some guesses, and then see if she could get him to confirm them. Such as, where was he going, and why was he leaving the Tartars behind?

She had to tilt her head back to look into his troubled face. "Come, let us sit down," she said. She took his hand and led him to a tree whose trunk was wide enough to let them rest their backs against it. Her silk skirt formed a dark green semicircle around her, bordered by an embroidered orange and red design of flowers.

There was a grace in the way he sat down, despite his long arms and legs. With a practiced movement he swept his sword back behind him, out of his way.

"Where were David of Trebizond and Giancarlo the night of the attack on the Monaldeschi palace?" he asked suddenly. She went cold. Did he suspect them, and her too? Had d'Ucello told him of his unsuccessful effort to see David and Lorenzo that very night?

"They had both left the city," she said. "They went to Perugia and Assisi. David wished to see the wonder-working body of San Francesco at Assisi."

"I thought he was interested in silk, not saints." Simon glowered at her.

She made herself laugh. "Surely you do not think David the merchant was in the streets, fighting, the night the Monaldeschi were attacked?"

She heard a bell ring somewhere in the distance. Some little hillside church ringing out the hour of Tierce. The chiming sounded clear and peaceful.

Dear God, sometimes I wish I could have become a nun.

Simon sighed and took her hand gently and held it resting on his thigh. "Why does it have to be Cardinal Ugolini who is your uncle?"

"If not for my Uncle Adelberto I would not be here and we would never have met," she said.

"You are so beautiful," he said.

The adoration in his eyes was like a dagger in her heart. She wanted so much for it to be for her, and it was for a woman who did not exist.

I am so far from what he thinks I am. Michael and Manfred treated me like a whore. David sends me to seduce this man who is his enemy.

And that, she thought, was why she so much hated to see what had happened to Rachel, and to know that David had done it and that she herself had a hand in it.

"You will never come back to Orvieto, will you?" she said disconsolately.

His grip on her hand tightened. "No. That is why I wanted to meet you today. Tell me—if your uncle goes to Perugia to follow the pope, will you go with him?"

She let her body lean sideways till she was pressed against him. "Oh, I am sure my uncle will go. He is the cardinal camerlengo, after all. As for me, I would go if I thought I would see you there."

His head drew down toward hers. "Do you care for me that much?"

"I have never known love like this, Simon. My husband was kind to me, and I was sorry when he died, but the way I feel about

you is different. I think I will die if I do not know when I can
see you again.''

Joy lit up his thin face, and she despised herself. ''I will find
you, Sophia. I will be gone for months. But I will ride like the
wind, and when I come back it will be to Perugia.''

He must be going to France! He was traveling with but one man,
so as to go faster. The Tartars had nearly been killed in the Filippeschi uprising, but he would be leaving them for *months*.

Only one thing could be more important to Simon than the lives
of the two Tartars, and that was what the Tartars represented.

The pope must be offering to approve the alliance. Simon must
be carrying the message.

*When I tell David about this, he will ride after Simon and kill
him.*

Her thoughts began to race. Even if Simon were stopped, was it
not still too late to keep the Franks and the Tartars from joining
forces? No, probably not, because the pope was dying. If this alliance were not settled now, the talking and deciding would have
to begin all over again, with a new pope.

Could she seduce Simon into abandoning his mission altogether,
running off with her? No, he would never betray so great a trust,
not even for love of her.

''I swear to you, I will find you, I will see you again, Sophia,''
he was saying. ''Believe me.''

You will not live long enough.

''I do believe you, Simon.'' Her loathing for herself grew
stronger.

Now his arms were around her, and he was pressing her back,
away from the tree trunk and down onto the soft bed of pine needles.

His open mouth was against hers, his lips devouring hers. His
hands caressed her shoulders and her back, moving ceaselessly.
One hand slid around and held her breast, and she heard his little
indrawn breath of pleasure. It must feel good to him, she thought.
It felt good to be touched there, and she pushed back against his
hand. She felt her body relax and grow warm. It had been so long—
nearly a year—since a man had held her in his arms.

*I need this as much as any man does. Men can go to whores, but
where can I go?*

She loved the feel of his strong arms around her as she lay beside
him. He moved so that his whole length was pressed against her,
and now he did not seem any taller than she was. She felt the

hardness at his groin that he pressed against her leg, and she felt an answering heat within herself.

No!

I cannot let this man make love to me and then send David after him to kill him. I cannot, I cannot. I would hate myself forever.

She felt her body opening to him, felt her bone-deep need of him. If they came together now, it would be love, not the love she felt for David, but love even so. And if she condemned him to death then, she would destroy herself. But if she did not tell David where Simon was going, she would betray him, and bring ruin down on his people and her own. If she let Simon make love to her, she would be so torn that afterward she would probably go mad.

He was already partly on top of her, and she wriggled away from him, pushing at him.

"Stop it!" There was a power in her voice that she had not intended to unleash. She was no longer Cardinal Ugolini's sweet little niece, Sophia Orfali from Sicily, but Sophia Karaiannides, the woman of Byzantium.

A hand's width of space separated their faces. Her voice seemed to freeze him. He stared at her as if he were seeing a stranger.

Then anger blazed up in his eyes. His arms tightened. Those arms seemed so lean, but the strength in them was like steel chains drawn tight. She clenched her fists and locked her bent arms in front of her to keep him away. His lips drew back from his teeth and she felt his hot breath on her face.

Frankish barbarian! she thought. Where only a moment ago she had wanted him, now she hated him. He was just like all those mail-clad savages who had destroyed Constantinople, stolen, raped, murdered her parents. Yes, and she had helped the Basileus Michael to drive them out, and she would kill this one too. Never would a union of Frankish and Tartar barbarians threaten her people. By this one man's death she could guarantee that.

With all the strength her anger gave her, she straightened her arms, pushing him away. Her right arm free, she thrust her open palm against his jaw, forcing his head back.

"Let me go!" And again it was the powerful voice of Sophia Karaiannides.

"God's blood!" His eyes were wide, and there was amazement in them, no longer anger. He released her so suddenly she fell back, hard, against the floor of the forest.

Immediately he reached for her, but his hands were gentle once more, helping her to sit up.

He knelt before her. "Please forgive me." He sounded on the verge of tears. "Please. I lost command of myself."

Standing up, she brushed pine needles from the back of her skirt and her shawl. He moved to help her, and she pulled away.

"Sophia, I have never loved any woman as much as I love you."

"Nonsense. Simon, you have far to ride."

He moved around so that he was facing her, his usually pale face flushed, his chest heaving.

"Marry me, Sophia."

If he had struck her, she could not have been more astonished. But she quickly recovered herself. He thought he could have his way with her by offering marriage.

"Simon, I am not a woman whose legs can be parted by a promise of marriage." The note she heard in her voice distressed her. She was being too much her true, worldly self with him. If he were not deaf to everything but his own passion, he would hear it, and he would suspect that she was not what she seemed to be.

She reminded herself: *I must seem to be awed that this great nobleman speaks to me of marriage.*

"You put it crudely," he said, his eyes narrowed with warmth. "To shock me, I suppose. But you defend your honor, and you speak plainly. I speak plainly too—I love you."

The sight of him standing there gazing at her with such yearning in his eyes was too painful. She kept thinking of herself telling David what she had learned today. She kept seeing this tall, handsome man lying dead in a ditch. She had to get away from him.

"The morning is well along," she said. "You had better get started if you want to cover much distance by nightfall. Where do you plan to spend this night?" She despised herself because she had asked the question to make it easier for David to trail him.

He frowned at her. "Sophia, I must have your answer. I mean what I say. I love you. I want to marry you."

Holy Virgin, would the fellow never give in? Did he really think her foolish enough to believe he was sincerely proposing to her? Yes, perhaps he did think that of the Sophia she pretended to be. She must answer him as that girl would. She cast her eyes down, her hands clasped before her.

"Simon, do not torment me. I know that you cannot marry me. My uncle has told me who you are—your ancient noble house, your vast holdings. Perhaps you mean to be kind to me by speaking of marriage, but a man of your rank has too many obligations. You cannot marry as you choose. So, please, speak of it no more."

But what if we could get married?

The thought arose unbidden in her mind as she stared down at the brown pine needles. She wanted to drive it out again, but could not stop herself from seeing what it might be like.

Marriage, a home, a fixed, secure abode where she might live out her life in serene, peaceful occupations. Raising children, spinning, embroidering, managing a household. What so many women, rich and poor, had. What she had not known since she was a young girl—a *place*, a *family*. And to be the wife of a man like Simon—kind, brave, handsome, well spoken.

She understood suddenly why it was always so easy for her to forget Sophia Karaiannides and become Sophia Orfali. She did what was given her to do, but in the core of her heart what she longed for was to be someone like Sophia Orfali, who truly had a place in the world. Sophia Orfali, for all that she was a mask, was more real than Sophia Karaiannides.

It was too painful for her, the unexpected longing for the love she could never have, the grief for Simon, whom she was going to murder.

"Let us get back, you to your scudiero and I to my escort," she said. She started walking toward the road.

He stepped in front of her. "Sophia, wait."

She felt something in her chest like a ball of iron. She had her tears well under control for the moment, but she had to get away from him. Otherwise she would not be able to stop herself from crying.

"Please," he said again. She felt herself forced to look up at him. His thin face, so grave, so intelligent.

"I beg you to believe me. I do want you desperately. Love is of the spirit, and it is of the body too. But I am not proposing marriage just to possess you. I want to marry you because I love you."

She stood looking at this handsome young man and breathing the fragrance of pine-scented air, and she thought of David. What she felt for David drew no line between body and spirit. If she had all the things she had just been longing for—a husband, a family, a home—and David appeared out of nowhere and looked at her with those glowing eyes of his and told her to come with him, she would abandon everything for him. When she looked at David, she saw a pillar of pure fire burning inside him. There was a power in him that called out to everything that was strong in her and demanded that she accept no other man for her mate.

"You think that my title, my family, is an obstacle to our marrying," Simon said. "But it is not. If you knew who I really am, you might not want to marry *me*."

She laughed a little at the thought of him not being who he so obviously was. "Are you some peasant lad who stole the place of the true Simon de Gobignon, then?"

"It is something like that."

"In God's name, Simon, what are you talking about?"

His nostrils flared. He drew air in a great gulp through his mouth. He took a step toward her, and she tensed, lest he seize her again, but he kept his hands at his sides.

"The last Count de Gobignon was a traitor to his king, to his countrymen, to his own vassals. He betrayed a whole army of crusaders into the hands of the Saracens. He died in disgrace. His grave is unmarked. So foul was his treachery that no man of good family in France will permit his daughter to marry me."

Sophia found that hard to believe. There must be many great barons in France who would forget the crime of the father, no matter how horrible, when the son was so attractive and, especially, so rich.

"Simon, you have so much to offer a wife." She would have laughed at the absurdity of all this, but the tortured expression clearly mirrored a tortured soul.

"Oh, surely, there are barons who would sell their daughters to the devil for a bit of land," he agreed. "I meant that I could not marry the women I chose. But there is worse, Sophia. I could lose everything if what I am about to tell you were known, but that is the least of it. It puts my life in your hands and the lives of my mother and—my father."

Your life is already in my hands, she thought, her eyes hurting from looking so intensely into his. But then the full meaning of what he had said bore in on her.

His father?

"Simon, are you telling me that you are not—"

"I am not the son of the Count de Gobignon. My father was a troubadour, the Sire Roland de Vency, with whom my mother fell in love while Amalric de Gobignon was still alive. She succeeded in passing me off as the count's son, but we three, my mother, Roland, and I, know the secret. And my confessor. And now you."

She shook her head, bewildered. She felt no doubt that what he was telling her was true. The pain in his face was like that of a man who had stripped his very skin off to reveal himself to her. It tore at her heart to see him suffering so much.

"But how could this happen, Simon?"

"It is too long a tale for today. Perhaps one day I can tell you all of it. But do you believe me now? Truly there is no barrier of family between you and me, Sophia. Unless you set one there, knowing that I am—I am a bastard and an impostor. Could you think of marrying me?''

The tears she had been holding back, for an hour it seemed, burst suddenly from her eyes, as sobs welled up in her throat. And yet, she wanted to laugh as well, at the irony of it. To think that he was ashamed of his pretense. If he had any idea of *her* pretense, and David's, he would probably kill her on the spot.

His face, coming nearer and nearer. All his finery was a red and purple blur before her tear-filled eyes. His hands were reaching for her.

He loves me. He really loves me. He really does want to marry me.

If he had taken that strange Saracen sword of his out and run her through with it, he could not have hurt her more. She had been thinking about sending David to kill him, and he had just entrusted all of himself, his family, everything he possessed, his body and his soul, to her.

If David went after him, this time one of them—Simon or David—would surely die. The luck of the Monaldeschi palace encounter could not protect both a second time.

She felt Simon's hands on her shoulders. She pulled away from him.

''Sophia!'' She heard the anguish in his voice.

Tartars and Muslims were a thousand leagues away. If Christians and Tartars were destined to join forces and destroy Islam, it would happen. She willed herself to believe that. And if it was not destined, it would not happen.

David and Simon were here. To say anything to David about Simon's mission to France was to doom one man, perhaps both. It might be the man who loved her, or it might be the man she loved. And she did not want either to die.

''Sophia, I beg you, speak to me! Are you turning against me?''

She wiped her streaming eyes to see Simon standing before her, his arms hanging at his sides, his face agonized.

I cannot doom this young man.

She took deep breaths to calm herself enough to speak to him.

''Simon, I pray that God will bless and protect you.'' She stifled a sob. ''I cannot marry you. You must forget me.''

He scrambled to his feet, his arms outstretched. ''Do not turn from me, Sophia. I would rather have you kill me.''

''No!'' It came out of her as a scream. She turned and started to run, holding up the hem of her long skirt to keep from tripping.

Her anguish was like a giant's hand that had seized her heart and was crushing it.

She ran like a hunted animal, tripping on rocks, turning her ankle in hollow places. She could only hope she was running toward the road.

"Sophia!"

She looked back over her shoulder. He was following her out of the forest, but at a distance. He was walking, staggering like a wounded man.

"Forgive me, Simon!" She ran on.

A pine branch struck her across the face, and she cried out in pain. But she felt that she deserved it. She ducked under the branch and kept running, seeing brighter light among the dark rows of tree trunks now. The road must be that way.

She forced her way through a tangle of shrubbery and was out on the road. Simon's scudiero, standing with their string of horses, stared at her wide-eyed. The huge Riccardo, Sophia's escort, was with him, talking. They were standing with their backs to a roadside statue of the Virgin in a little protective shed.

At the sight of Sophia, Riccardo rushed to her, looming over her protectively. "Madonna! What has happened to you? Dio mio! Did he—"

His eyes were wide with outrage, but there was anxiety in his face too. He must be wondering whether he would have to fight a nobleman.

"I am not hurt—he did nothing. He did nothing!" Sophia babbled, choking down sobs. "Mount quickly, Riccardo, and let us go from here."

He held her horse, and she threw herself into the saddle. She spurred on without waiting to see if Riccardo was ready to follow.

When they came to a turning in the road, she looked back once. The scudiero stood alone with the horses. Simon had not yet emerged from the pine forest. She started to cry again. The pain in her chest was worse than ever. She silenced Riccardo's questions.

"I cannot talk about it. He did no wrong to me. No harm. That is all you need to know."

I cannot talk to anyone about it, ever. I am going to betray David. I pray God I never see Simon de Gobignon again.

XLVIII

Just as Sophia and Riccardo arrived at the Porta Maggiore
in the city wall of Orvieto, the air around them seemed to glow and
crackle. A cold wind blew across the road leading up to the gate.
Sophia spurred her bay, but the horse hardly needed encouragement
to gallop the last few paces to the shelter of the gatehouse. A shaft
of lightning dazzled Sophia, and a mighty thunderclap, loud enough
to shake the rock on which Orvieto stood, deafened her. She and
Riccardo were in the shelter of the gatehouse before the first fat
drops began to fall, making craters in the dust of the road.

They identified themselves to the guards without dismounting.
Clerks were no longer posted at the gates to interrogate and record
the name of every person entering and leaving Orvieto. Evidently
the podesta had given up on that.

Sophia, Daoud, and Ugolini had, even so, been chilled by a
polite letter from d'Ucello to Ugolini requesting that "His Eminence's distinguished guest from Trebizond" not leave Orvieto
without the podesta's permission. Sophia, on the other hand,
seemed free to come and go as she pleased.

The thought crossed Sophia's mind that she would be soaked as
she rode from the gate to Ugolini's mansion. But the meeting with
Simon had left her in misery, and the storm suited her mood. David
knew that she was meeting Simon outside the town. Now what
would she tell David about where Simon was going?

She was about to ride on into the city streets when a man stepped
out of the crowd that had gathered for shelter under the gateway
arch. He raised a hand.

"Madonna!" It was Sordello. "A private word, I beg of you."

She saw fear in his face, but in his bloodshot eyes burned another
feeling she could not identify. She disliked the man and did not
want to talk to him, especially not now, carrying secrets as she
was. But he served David, and his disturbed look suggested that
what he had to say might be important. Sighing, she dismounted,

42

gave the reins of her horse to Riccardo, and walked beside Sordello to an unoccupied corner of the gatehouse.

"You know that Messer David has set me to find the informer among us, and he says he will kill me if I fail." He had backed her into the corner and pressed uncomfortably close to her. His breath smelled of onions, and he was altogether repellent.

"What do you want of me?"

"The one person who might give me a clue is the Count de Gobignon, and he has disappeared. No one at the Monaldeschi palace will tell me anything about why he left."

Does he know that I just met with Simon?

"Why ask me?"

"I know that it is Messer David's wish that you allow de Gobignon to court you. If he has left Orvieto, perhaps you have heard where he is going." He smiled, showing a gap in his upper front teeth. And now she realized what the hidden feeling was. It was lust. She was disgusted, and pushed past him to give herself room.

He said, "I saw you ride out earlier today, and I waited here at the gatehouse for you to come back. You must have met with the count. Madonna, I do not know what to do. And Messer David will kill me if I do not tell him something."

She desperately wanted to get away. "I am going to Messer David myself to tell him that Count Simon has left for Perugia. Where the pope is going. He is recruiting more guards and preparing a refuge for the Tartar ambassadors. You'll gain nothing with Messer David by telling him the same thing."

Sordello frowned thoughtfully. "No, but I might try to catch Count Simon on the road and talk to him."

Sophia's heart leapt with alarm and seemed to lodge in her throat. What if Sordello followed Simon and discovered he was on his way to France and came back and reported *that* to Daoud?

"You needn't go to all that trouble," she said, keeping a grip on her voice. "We will all be going to Perugia shortly, and you can question Count Simon there."

He nodded, as if satisfied with that, and she felt a little better.

He bowed again and again. "Thank you, Madonna, thank you."

In a moment she was on her horse again and riding into the rain. She wanted nothing more to do with Sordello.

But the encounter had helped her in one way, and now she felt more confident about talking to David about Simon. Rehearsing the lie with Sordello had helped.

* * *

"He is leaving the Tartars behind? After I came so close to killing them?"

"They will be closely guarded. I do not think you will be able to get at them again."

There was a bitterness in the small smile that quirked David's thin lips. "I do not intend to try until the Sienese arrive here. When I seek their lives again, a whole army of guards will not be enough to stop me."

What would David do, Sophia wondered, if he learned that the alliance he had fought so hard to prevent would soon be sealed in France by Simon de Gobignon?

She looked at David's eyes, the color of the thunderclouds outside. Her hatred for herself struck her heart with hammer blows.

He stood by the window of his room, straight and broad-shouldered, wearing a belted gown of black silk with a broad red stripe at the bottom. His wound no longer required a poultice, and it was almost healed. The strange Saracen treatment he had prescribed for himself had worked.

She saw pain in his eyes, a pain of the heart. "No doubt you will miss the count," he said in a low voice. He turned to look out the window.

He had pulled the leaded pane of glass slightly inward on its hinge, letting into the room the cold breeze stirred up by the storm. Locks of his blond hair fluttered around his forehead. She studied his profile, the nose long and straight, the chin sharp, the brows seeming to frown even when relaxed.

"You wanted me to make love to him," she said softly.

He kept his face turned. "Yes."

"You did not want me to make love to him."

"Yes."

She stood in the center of the room, about ten paces from him, her hands clasped before her. Her shawl and her gown were cold and wet. A net of small pearls held her hair in place, but her hair, too, was sodden with rain. She felt on the verge of shivering, but she held herself very still.

White light filled the room. David's body jerked, and his lips tightened. A long, rolling peal of thunder followed the lightning, ending in a crash so loud it hurt her head.

He was afraid of thunderstorms. She had noticed that before. There was little rain in the part of the world where he had grown up. He was afraid of nothing else, as far as she could see. There was nothing he would not do, nothing he *could* not do. If only he were Greek, what a fighter for the Polis he would be.

But when he winced away from the lightning, she wanted to cradle his blond head against her breasts.

The rain beat down on the walls and roof of Ugolini's mansion with redoubled intensity. She saw a small pool of water on the wood floor, rain blown in through the open window.

"I never did make love to him," she said, raising her voice to be heard over the wind and rain.

"I know that." He took a step toward her.

I am doing worse than that now, she thought with a stab of guilt. *I am keeping from David something he would badly want to know.*

"He put his arms around me and kissed me many times," she said.

David turned fully to look at her, saying nothing.

"Whenever he took me in his arms, I thought of you."

He closed his eyes.

When she was with David she never grieved over the turns her life had taken. She never felt sorry for herself, as she did with Simon, because she had not married and could not marry. Simon had actually said he wanted to marry her, and in the end she had believed him. That seemed like a dream now. A pleasant dream, but an impossible one.

For an instant she tried to picture herself, a woman of Constantinople wed to a Frankish lord and living in a castle in the north of France. If such a preposterous thing should come about, she would be enormously wealthy and powerful—though she had not really thought about that when she was with Simon. She was not herself when she was with Simon. And now, when she *was* herself and able to see things clearly, the wealth and power still did not matter, because they would give her no pleasure if she had to live among barbarians.

When she was with David she never worried or even thought about her future, what life would be like for her when she was older. With David she thought only of now.

He had opened his eyes and was staring at her. She looked at him, standing tall and fair.

I love you, David. I want you so.

Why had it not happened? Soon it would be a year since they had met at Lucera, and she had long known that she wanted him, and believed that he wanted her as well. But something had always held him back.

Her body grew warm inside her cold garments.

It is not because of me that we have waited this long.

There was a question in his eyes, and she felt something inside her pulling her toward him. She took a faltering step across the tile floor. Then another, surer one.

He held out his arms, his harsh mouth softening as his lips parted slightly.

"Come to me," he said.

He watched her walking toward him one step at a time, and he thought she looked like a woman in a trance. Her head was lifted to receive his kiss.

"How like rose petals your lips are," he said in Greek. He had never spoken Greek to her before. She stopped her slow march toward him and gave a long, shuddering sigh.

Then she ran the last few steps and threw herself into his arms. Joy flooded his chest as he pulled her against him.

At last, at last, at last!

He had wanted to hold her like this for so long, and much of the time had not even been aware that he wanted it.

He had not wanted to be aware of it, he thought, knowing that he must use her against his enemy. And how he had hated Simon de Gobignon simply because Simon was to have Sophia.

I should have known then that my hatred for de Gobignon was a measure of my love for her.

But he had not wanted to know that either, because Blossoming Reed, the daughter of the sultan, awaited him in El Kahira, and he had sworn to be faithful to her all his life.

Take as many women as you like. But love always and only me.

He felt a chill, and realized that he was feeling cold not merely because of the memory of Blossoming Reed's warning, but because Sophia was rain-wet against him. She had ridden through the storm still thundering away outside, and he felt a cold dampness soaking through his gown.

"Your clothes are wet," he said, continuing to speak Greek.

She rubbed herself against him. "I am wet to the skin. I need to take these clothes off.'

"Yes. Why not do that?"

Without hesitation she stepped out of the circle of his arms and undid the brooch that held her printed shawl around her shoulders. She would not be shy, he realized. There had not been time, in the life she had led, for hesitation with men. Only, he hoped that she would not, like some of the experienced women he had known, show little feeling herself while she let him use her in any way that pleased him.

She is not that sort. I know it.

Foolish of him to even think it. But some part of him needed to doubt. This moment was too good to be true.

And too frightening. Because what they were about to do was not just satisfy their bodies' hungers; it would seal the bond of love between them. And then he would not be able to send Sophia like a falcon to strike at his enemies. He would not be the same man when he went back to Blossoming Reed. What they were about to do would change both their lives.

Standing in the crumpled heap of orange and green silk that was her shawl, she turned her back to him.

"Help me with the laces," she said. He saw that her gown laced down the back.

"One small moment," he said, running his hand caressingly over her back. He walked to the door. There was still pain in his right thigh when he moved quickly, but now it was overwhelmed by his body's yearning to have this woman. He felt the swelling and pressure of arousal in his loins.

He opened the door of his room partway and looked up and down the shadowy corridor. There was no one in sight. He closed the door firmly and slid home the heavy iron bolt that would guarantee their privacy.

She was standing where he had left her, watching him, her amber eyes warm. He went quickly to her and untied the knot in the laces at her back, marveling at the slenderness of her neck. She could have unlaced the dress herself, he saw, but she wanted him to.

She wore no belt, and the dress fell away. Under it was a white silk chemise without sleeves. Still standing behind her, he dropped his hands gently on her small, square shoulders and slid the chemise down. His eyes followed its fall, savoring her delicate shoulder blades, the shadowed hollow of her back. All that remained now were light green hose attached to a wisp of silk that girdled her hips.

Sophia shivered, and he knew it was not the cold, though the storm was blowing a strong, moist breeze through the partly opened window.

He put his hands on her shoulders, firmly now, and turned her around. She threw back her head and laughed as he stared at her breasts and bit his lower lip.

What Daoud carried under his black gown felt as big and heavy as a mace.

He dropped to one knee before her. He reached around to her buttocks, his palms tingling at their cool firmness, and he slid down the last of her garments. She stood, all exposed, before him.

"Will I not see you naked?" she said with a throaty chuckle. "Is that the Turkish way, for the man to remain clothed?"

"You will soon learn what the Turkish way is, my lady." He leaned forward, still genuflecting, and dropped a dozen light kisses on her belly and thighs, and then buried his face in the rich triangle of hair between her legs and kissed her deeply.

She cried out in surprise and pleasure.

Suddenly he stood up and swung her up in his arms like a Bedouin chieftain carrying his bride to his tent. She laughed delightedly. She felt as light as a child. He strode across the room to the bed and laid her down.

He wrestled his black silk gown over his head and threw it off. Quickly he pulled off the locket Blossoming Reed had given him and dropped it on the gown. He stood over her, looking down at her, and letting her look her fill at him.

"The blond Turk," she said in Greek with a small smile, and moved her hips from side to side.

Slowly she reached up to her head and pulled free the net of pearls woven into her hair. Long locks, black as raven's wings, spread out around her head on the pillow.

"I must look like Medusa," she said.

"Who?"

"A woman with snakes for hair. Men who saw her were turned to stone."

He remembered now: In a bazaar at El Kahira he had listened to the story of the she-monster.

"The sight of you would bring a stone to life," he said.

"Ah, but part of you is already hard as stone. How long are you going to stand there? I want you." The yearning in her voice made something vibrate inside him, as if she had plucked a taut string in his very soul. He was seized by a violent urge to throw himself upon her and take her at once. And she would welcome it, too, he knew.

But this moment was too precious to be allowed to pass so quickly.

He sank to his knees and reached out to pull her hips to the edge of the bed. She squirmed across the bed to help him.

Just after he grew out of boyhood, when he was very wild and afraid of nothing, Ayesha, the youngest wife of Emir Faruk abu Husain, discovered that he existed, and showed him a way to come to her in abu Husain's harem. He knew he would die writhing on a spike if the emir's slaves caught him, but he was also quite certain that such a thing could never really happen to him.

With a boy's eagerness and excitability, he had spent himself an instant after he joined Ayesha in the darkness on her couch.

"The emir is very old and has many wives," she purred. "Rarely can we slip a beautiful young man like you past the harem guards. So we must learn how to pleasure each other. There are many things that will delight a woman's body besides a man's rumh. Shall I show you?"

He was curious, and at his whispered agreement she pushed his head down between her legs and told him what to do.

"And put your fingers *here* at the same time. Ah, that feels very good."

He looked at Sophia lying open before him and said again, "How like a flower." He saw dew on this flower, and he bent to taste.

He did to her the things he had learned from Ayesha and later on from other harem women.

As he worked upon Sophia the magic of the harem, he listened to her breathing as it grew faster and faster. He watched her breasts rise and fall, her chestnut-color nipples standing up.

She groaned and tossed her head from side to side, the groans turnings to screams as she reached a pinnacle. He brought her to another, and another.

Panting, almost crying, she put her hand on his head. "No more. This way of the Turks is wonderful, but I want you inside me now."

He stretched himself full length beside her, put his face, wet with her own sweet liquor, against hers and kissed her with lips and tongue. She seized his shoulders, her nails digging into his muscles, and pulled him over on top of her.

The way was so well prepared that he was within her in an instant. He knew that he could not hold himself back very long, and he gave himself up to the floodtide of pleasure. He raised his head a little so that he could look down into her wide amber eyes, and so that she could see into his soul at the moment when he gave all his force to her.

Almost at the same moment the muscles in her face tensed and her neck corded. Through clenched teeth she cried out again and again and again.

Their bodies relaxed together. Daoud felt that now, in the aftermath of frenzy, their flesh was melting and flowing together and becoming one.

They lay in silence, and a distant growl of thunder told him that the storm outside had passed. He had not noticed its dying away. He felt a cool breeze blowing through the windows.

It seemed as if hours passed while they lay there in silence, arms around each other, legs entwined, and he listened to her breathing slowly grow calmer.

She stroked his cheek and played with the blond hairs on his chest. "Is anything changed now?"

"For us, I think, much is changed."

She kissed him lightly on the cheek. "I love you. Does love mean anything to you Muslims?"

He laughed softly. "Of course it does. *In this world, women and perfume are dearest to me.* So spoke our Prophet, may God commend and salute him."

She shook her head and ran her finger down his forehead and nose. "I am glad I am as dear to you as perfume. You say 'our Prophet,' lying there looking more French than Simon de Gobignon. Of course, that is why your sultan sent you here. If I, who know what you are, still find it hard to accept you as a Saracen, those who do not know would never suspect."

As she spoke the name de Gobignon, he felt a twinge of anger. Just his name, mentioned in their bed, was an intrusion. Her eyes flickered momentarily away from his, as if she, too, realized it was an error. Best, he thought, to say nothing about it.

"Yes, I am truly a Muslim, and Muslims know more of love, I believe, than most Christians." But now he thought of Blossoming Reed.

Why must these ghosts hover over us?

She reached out to touch the little leather capsule tied by a thong around his neck, the only thing he was wearing at the moment. "What is that?"

"It is called a tawidh. Inside are numbers written on a scroll. It protects me from death by wounding and causes any wounds I do receive to heal quickly."

"Tawidh?" She mimicked exactly the Arabic pronunciation. "How can numbers on a scroll protect from wounds?"

He did not fully understand himself the Sufi belief that all things are number, and that numbers written by a holy man could control objects and events.

"One must be of my faith to understand it," he said briefly.

She looked at him earnestly. "It is so hard to think of you as a Mohammedan, David."

"Not Mohammedan—Muslim. And David is not my name. My true name is Arabic. Shall I tell it to you?"

"Oh, yes, please. I will use it with you when we are alone together."

"I am called Daoud ibn Abdallah. Daoud is Arabic for David."

"Then your name *is* David."

"No, it is Daoud," he said. "The sound matters a great deal. It is the sound that God hears."

"You believe that God speaks Arabic?"

"It is the language most pleasing to Him. Did He not give His message to the Prophet—may God praise and salute him—in Arabic?"

She pulled herself closer to him. "Ah, David—Daoud—do not talk to me of religion now. Here and now, let us think not of religions and empires and wars, but only of you and me." She paused and looked at him a little anxiously. "Do you think the servants or anyone else heard me screaming?"

"I saw no one outside. Most of them probably suspect that we have been lovers for a long time. But suspicion is one thing. To confirm it by our outward behavior could be dangerous. We must continue to act as if this never happened."

"We will do this again, will we not?"

He touched her dark red lips with his fingertips and said:

> After suffering the joy of love
> I have no abiding place.
> I live only to be
> With the one I love.

"Yes, we will do it again. Very soon now. I feel my strength returning." He curved his hand around the softness of her breast.

"Ah, good! I did not want it to be over yet—Daoud."

In the first days of the Christian month of July the sun grew very strong, and above the narrow streets and tiny gardens, dust rose. Daoud found the climate more to his liking. Although he believed he would never have a true home or enjoy peace in this life, he felt a happiness such as he had never known before. And this was strange, because Hulagu Khan's emissaries to the Christians still lived, and al-Islam was still threatened with destruction, and while he turned many plans over in his mind, he was not sure what to do next.

But when he and Sophia were together he was able almost entirely to forget those threats. And when he was not with her, he carried her image in his heart, and his heart was the lighter for it.

His leg had healed, and it was safe for him to walk the streets now. He knew the podesta's men must be watching him, but he feared them less now, because they would not see him limp. They might wonder when he had returned to Orvieto from Perguia, but they would have to suppose it was after the podesta took the clerks away from the gates. Each day he wandered through the town, forming plans, observing.

He sensed a tension in the air, growing a little stronger each day, like the summer's heat. Around the palace of the Filippeschi on the south side of the town, in its windows and on its battlements, men stood watchful, holding crossbows, hands on their sword hilts. They were not as strong as they had been last April. The bravos Lorenzo had gathered and Daoud had lent to their cause had quietly left Orvieto. The Filippeschi had lost many men and were thrown back on their own resources now. Their grim apprehension was obvious.

Daoud did not speak directly to the Filippeschi. Aside from his one meeting with their leader, Marco, he had avoided any contact with them that might compromise him. He wondered whether Marco had given any thought to a suggestion Lorenzo had made to him: that aid might be forthcoming if the Filippeschi switched their allegiance to the Ghibellino cause. Apparently Filippeschi loyalty to the pope went back centuries, and was not easily changed. That was something to be discussed when Lorenzo returned.

At the Palazzo Monaldeschi Daoud saw an air of preparation, of forces gathering, of confidence. One afternoon Vittorio de Monaldeschi, aged eleven, in full mail—a child's mail shirt and hose must cost as much as a man's, and be usable for only a short time—wearing an orange and green surcoat, rode slowly along the length of the Corso with a dozen horsemen, orange and green pennons on their lances. A show to intimidate his enemies.

Both sides seemed to be awaiting something, and the air of the city felt to Daoud as it did when a thunderstorm was approaching.

The petty street wars of Orvieto would mean nothing to him soon, Daoud thought. Lorenzo had managed to send two messages by way of Ghibellino merchants passing through Orvieto. He had made his way safely to Siena, was negotiating with Rinaldo di Stefano, Duke of Siena, and was recruiting bravos by the hundred. But all was not going quickly enough for Daoud. With the pope on the verge of leaving Orvieto, it appeared the Sienese would not come quickly enough. Unless Lorenzo and the Sienese arrived in time to trap the pope and the Tartars here, he would have to follow them to Perugia.

Or he could go to Manfred and urge him to make immediate war on the pope. Every rumormonger in Orvieto claimed that Manfred was on the brink of marching out of southern Italy to make the whole peninsula his. But Daoud doubted it. It would probably be difficult to persuade Manfred to take any action against the pope, unless the French actually invaded Italy.

Every day he and Sophia spent hours together, sometimes in his chamber, sometimes in hers. They chose different times of the day, hoping to make their meetings less obvious.

The best times were the afternoons. Most Orvietans slept an hour or two after their noon meal, just as most Egyptians did. Sophia and Daoud would draw the curtains to hold out the heat and dust. They would make love, their bodies slippery with sweat. Then they would lie side by side and let themselves cool, talking of what they felt about each other, of the world, of the mission they had come to Orvieto to accomplish.

They never spent an entire night together. This would cause too much gossip among Ugolini's servants. For the benefit of the podesta and whoever else might be watching them, Daoud wanted to maintain the fiction that he was a trader from Trebizond, far to the east, and Sophia a Sicilian girl from Siracusa, and they had very little to do with each other. Alone in his bed at night, Daoud sometimes lay awake thinking about what Sophia had come to mean to him. He had fallen in love with her, he realized now, long before he first possessed her body.

If it was their fate to die here in Italy, at least they would have known this happiness first. But if he succeeded in his mission, and if he and Sophia were still alive after that, what then? Return to his emir's palace in El Kahira, to Blossoming Reed, bringing Sophia with him? A Greek Christian woman entering a Mameluke's harem? And even if Sophia were willing, Blossoming Reed would try to kill her. But Sophia would make a formidable enemy for Blossoming Reed.

No, he could not subject either of them to that. Or himself.

But for him what else was there? El Kahira was the only home he knew. He had left it only to protect it. He must return.

All this thinking, he decided, was foolishness. What would happen was written in the book of God, and one could be sure only that it would be very different from what he expected. Let him concentrate on following the path as far ahead as he could see clearly, and the next stage would be revealed when God turned the page.

An orange radiance suffused Cardinal Ugolini's dining hall, gilding dust motes that hung in the air. A stout maidservant cleared away the trenchers, the round slices of bread on which Ugolini had served spring lamb to Daoud and Sophia. She bundled up the knives and forks in her apron. Daoud's fork was clean. He preferred, among friends, not to use the strange implement, which seemed to him a bida, an undesirable innovation. He ate with the fingers of his right hand.

"His Holiness takes the road for Perugia a week from tomorrow," said Ugolini. "You have not told me what you intend to do, David."

"We must await Lorenzo's coming. He and the Sienese may be here before the pope leaves."

"I assure you that if that were possible, the pope would be galloping out of town right now," said Ugolini. "His information is better than ours."

Sophia daintily wiped her hands and lips with the linen cloth that covered the table. "Your Eminence, Messer David, I want to use these long July hours of daylight for painting. I beg to be excused."

She refused more wine and genially overrode Ugolini's protests. Carefully keeping his face blank, Daoud watched her walk out of the room, tall and straight in a cherry-red gown. He found himself picturing the things they had done not long ago, while Orvieto rested at midday. He turned back to Ugolini to see the little cardinal was also, with a lubricious smile, watching Sophia.

Ugolini's long nose twitched with amusement as he turned to Daoud. "There have been times when I thought there was a chamber of torment on the top floor of my mansion. The groans, the screams—"

"I have heard nothing, Your Eminence," said Daoud, keeping his face expressionless.

"I should have been concerned for the lovely lady, except that she is obviously so healthy and serene. Much more serene, I believe, than when she first came here. What do you suppose accounts for that?"

Daoud shrugged. "In silence is security from error."

"Is that a saying of one of your Muslim philosophers?"

"Yes," said Daoud, allowing himself the faintest of smiles. "The Princess Sheherazade."

The sun had set by the time Daoud left Cardinal Ugolini, and the third-floor corridor was nearly dark. Servants had placed small candles on tables at each end of the corridor. Daoud had allowed himself a cup of wine with the cardinal because there was nothing else to drink, and now his face felt slightly numb.

A large figure walked slowly toward him from the opposite end of the corridor as he approached his room. With the candlelight behind him, the man's face was in darkness, and Daoud tensed himself.

"Messer David, it is Riccardo."

Now they stood face-to-face, Daoud having to look up a little.

"I searched everywhere. Questioned everyone I know. I would stake my life that Sordello is not in Orvieto. He went out the Perugia gate after talking to Madonna Sophia. I do not think he ever came back."

Dismissing Riccardo, Daoud went into his room to think and to pray. He felt baffled. He would have staked *his* life that no man bound by the powers of the Hashishiyya would ever turn against the one who showed him the delights of paradise.

But I did threaten him with death, and he saw that I wanted to kill him. That might have been enough to break the bond.

And I did wonder, even when I initiated him, whether there might not be some part of him that remained free.

Daoud bolted the door of his room. He needed to be alone, to think and to refresh his mind.

He faced the charcoal-marked spot on his wall that marked the direction of Mecca and, with care and thought, went through the sequence of the salat, standing, bowing, kneeling, striking his head on the floor again and again until he was done. He asked God, as he did every night, to favor his efforts here in Italy with success, out of His love for the people of Islam.

I place all in Your hands.

After he was finished praying, he unlocked his traveling chest and began to take things from it. First came a small grinder box he had bought from an Orvieto ironsmith, a grinder such as women used to make small amounts of flour. Next, from a cotton bag he took two handfuls of roasted kaviyeh beans given him by Ugolini and put them in the top of the grinder box. He ran the beans through the grinder, rapidly turning the crank on the box until they were a coarse powder.

He took his old pack out of the chest and found in it the brick of hashish wrapped in oiled parchment. It nestled in the palm of his hand, and he weighed it, wondering whether he deserved this pleasure. For that matter, did he deserve Sophia? His attempt to kill the Tartars had failed, and now they might be slipping out of his grasp.

With money and the threat of a French invasion, Lorenzo should be able to persuade the Ghibellino leaders of Siena to follow their natural inclination and send an army against Orvieto. But that army would not be enough to counter the forces the pope could gather around himself at Perugia.

I must get Manfred to march.

With Manfred's help he could capture the pope and kill the Tartars. And he saw an even larger vision. Under Manfred, Italy could become a bulwark against the crusaders from northern Europe. Manfred was not just friendly to Egypt. He had Muslim officials and soldiers and was not far from being a Muslim himself.

There was so much to be done. Daoud wanted to go to Siena to hasten the Ghibellino attack on Orvieto. He wanted to ride to Manfred and urge him to invade the Papal States. But he had to remain here as long as the Tartars were here. Were it not for Sophia, these months of inactivity since that night at the Monaldeschi palace would be driving him mad.

He held the black hashish cake over the grinder, using his dagger to shave small, coiling peels into the ground kaviyeh beans. Then he filled a small iron pot from his water jar. He poured the mixture of water, kaviyeh, and hashish into the pot and set it to boil on a rack over the flame of short, fat candle.

He smiled and inhaled deeply as the rich, burnt smell filled the room. Just the smell of kaviyeh could give him visions, making him think of the gaily lighted streets of El Kahira, of the dome of the Gray Mosque, of the white arms of Blossoming Reed.

When his brew was ready he poured it into an Orvieto porcelain cup painted with bright flowers. He carried the cup to his window and pulled the window open. Even though Orvieto was atop a great rock, the starry sky seemed much farther away here than when he lay on his back and looked up at the stars in the desert. He wondered how far it was to the crystalline sphere in which the stars were set, like jewels. Was it farther than the distance between Orvieto and El Kahira?

He recited to himself the invocation, *In the name of the Voice comes the Light*.

Standing at the window, he drank his hashish-laced kaviyeh in slow sips. When he knew, by a peculiar intensity in the starlight, that the magic horse had begun its flight to paradise, he started to walk to his bed. A sudden impulse took him, and he went to his pack again.

Folded inside a square of blue silk he found the silver locket Blossoming Red had given him. Since he had started lying with Sophia he had stopped wearing it. He remembered the suggestion he had planted in Sordello's mind, that at the sight of the locket he would kill Simon de Gobignon. With Sordello and Simon both gone, the locket was useless for that purpose.

As he held it in his hands, he remembered what Baibars's daughter had said to him:

I will always know if you are well or ill, alive or dead, and how you fare and what you feel. And if you would know how it is with me, seek me in this.

He lay in bed propped up on one elbow and turned the tiny screw that held the locket closed. He had meant to think about Manfred and Sophia, to try to catch some glimpse of the future. It troubled him that he had taken this bypath. He remembered now how troubled he had been when last he looked into the locket. He had not meant to use it again.

Now, though, it was somehow too late for him to stop. He seemed to have no will of his own. He raised the lid of the locket and looked down into it, at the design incised on rock crystal that looked like an interweaving of Arabic letters with circles and triangles. He waited to see what visions the locket would give him tonight.

The knowledge you run from is the most precious of all.

He gasped.

A pool of darkness opened in the center of the design. The network of straight and curved lines seemed to crumble into it as the pool spread. And it began to rotate, slowly at first, then faster. He was looking into a whirlpool of blackness.

It drew him in. He felt as if his eyes were spinning, then his head; then he fell into the whirlpool and it sucked him down. He could not breathe. He was drowning in blackness.

At the last moment, when he thought he would die, suffocated, the black pool released him and flung him back on his bed, contemptuously rejecting him.

He lay there, gasping, terrified.

Take as many women as you like. But love always and only me. For if you do love another, I promise you that your love will destroy both her and you.

Had he truly heard the voice of Blossoming Reed, burning and cruel in his mind, coming from as far off as the stars? The locket fell to the floor with a crash that seemed to shake the stone building in which he lay. He remained motionless, paralyzed with dread.

XLIX

FEELING AS IF HE WOULD BURST INTO FLAMES WITH ANGER, SIMON stood under a bright blue sky dappled with high white clouds on a wooden quay at Livorno, two weeks after leaving Orvieto. The masts of small boats lined the waterfront like a forest of tree trunks stripped of their leaves.

If I were traveling with a proper entourage, a few knights and a troop of archers, by God's wounds they'd carry me. These shipmasters are too damned independent.

One large ship, anchored midway between the shore and the arm of the harbor, looked to Simon like his last chance. Leaving Thierry on the quay, he dropped a silver denaro into the callused palm of a man with a dinghy and had himself rowed out to the big ship.

From what he knew of ships, this was a middle-size buss, sitting high in the water, with rounded prow and stern. The name *Constanza* was painted on the stern. Human muscle moved it; Simon counted ten oarholes on each side.

As he trod the catwalk from the prow of the ship to the stern castle where the captain stood, Simon saw no one sitting at the oars and no chains. So the ship must be rowed by its crew, free mariners. A square sail, furled at present, mounted on a single mast amidships would help the rowers when the wind was right.

The captain, whose bald scalp was brown as well-tanned leather, bowed deeply when Simon presented himself. He was half Simon's height, twice as broad, and all muscle. He smiled, showing a full set of bright white teeth when Simon explained that he needed passage to Marseilles.

"Bon seigner, you must understand that it is not a simple matter to engage a ship of this size to carry you wherever you wish to go." The language the captain spoke was neither French nor Italian. Simon recognized it at once, and he felt a little inner leap, because it was the tongue his parents spoke, the Langue d'Oc, the speech of Aquitaine, Toulouse, and Provence.

"Of course I understand that," Simon replied in the same tongue. "But if you—"

"Bon seigner," the captain interrupted, "there are no words to describe how honored I would be to carry you. And no words to describe my grief that I cannot take you." That could be taken two ways, Simon thought.

"I am prepared to pay prodigiously, Captain," said Simon with sinking heart.

If the captain noticed that Simon was speaking in his own tongue, he did not remark on it. "I do not own this ship. That is the point, you see, bon seigner. The owners have instructed me to wait here for a cargo of olive oil, which I must take to Cyprus. So I cannot leave now, and when I do leave, I must sail away from France."

The captain was respectful enough, but Simon sensed a hidden glee in his refusal.

"But you have not heard how much I will offer you," he said, desperate.

The bald man shut his eyes as if in pain. "It does not matter. Merce vos quier, forgive me, but I have a duty to those who have entrusted this ship to me. Surely there must be some other captain in this harbor who will let you make him wealthy."

"I have been to every other captain," said Simon. "All have refused me for one reason or another. Yours is the only ship left."

The captain of the *Constanza* spread his hands. "Ah, well, Pisa is only a little farther north, and there are many more ships docked at its quays along the Arno. You are bound to find one that will carry you. Or, failing that, this is the best time of the year to make the journey to France overland. The roads are good."

Simon knew that Pisa had been a Ghibellino city for generations. Word of his coming might even have reached enemies in Pisa. He was sure that he and Thierry had been followed along the road they had taken up the Tyrrhenean seacoast. The Pisans would be only too glad to put an end to his mission, and quite possibly to him. And following the endlessly winding coastal road—which would require him to pass dangerously close to Pisa—it would take him a month or more to get to French territory. He decided that this captain meant him nothing but ill. He broke off abruptly and made his way back to the rowboat.

A shout of laughter came floating across the water from the *Constanza* as the boatman rowed him back, putting Simon in an even fouler mood.

Looking toward shore, he saw a man in a short, dark cape standing on the dock with Thierry.

The boat tied up at a piling, and Simon gave the rower a second denaro and climbed up a short ladder to the quay. With a jolt of anger he recognized the man talking to Thierry as Sordello.

What the devil is he doing here?

Instantly Sordello was kneeling at Simon's feet, clutching at his hand and kissing it and weeping copiously.

"I followed you all the way from Orvieto, Your Signory. I did not make myself known to you before this because I feared you would send me away."

"Get up," said Simon impatiently. "We thought we were being followed by enemies. We took unnecessary precautions, thanks to you." This utterly unwelcome encounter with Sordello, added to the impossibility of finding a ship, filled him with an almost uncontrollable rage.

"Your Signory, on the roads of Italy there are no unnecessary precautions." The man's expression shifted in the blink of an eye from fawning tears to a cocksure grin showing his missing teeth.

"What are you doing here?" Simon demanded. "I did not give you leave to stop watching Cardinal Ugolini's household."

"Circumstances gave me leave, Your Signory, as I was just explaining to my good friend Thierry here." Thierry looked startled at being so described. "The woman Ana who carried my reports to you betrayed me. She told Giancarlo, the henchman of the merchant from Trebizond, that I was in your service. That Giancarlo is the sort who opens a second mouth in your throat before you can explain yourself with the first one."

"Does anyone else in Orvieto know where I am going?"

Good God, was he lurking about when I was with Sophia?

Sordello looked at him out of the corners of his eyes. "No one knew, Your Signory. I had to think it out for myself. I heard you had gone to Perugia. But, I asked myself, whyever would you do that? There is nothing in Perugia until the pope moves there. What, then, would be important enough to make you leave off watching over the Tartars? A message for Count Charles, I guessed—or perhaps for your king—too important to be carried by anyone but yourself. Then I had to decide which road you'd take. Directly north would lead to Siena, and we have all heard that an army of Ghibellini is gathering in Siena to attack Orvieto. So, you must be headed for the coast. And, as we see, my guesses all turned out right." He finished up with a broad, self-satisfied grin.

How could a man so often foolish also be so shrewd? Simon turned and stared out at the water of the harbor, a deeper blue than the sky. What a nuisance this fellow was! Turning up now, when

Simon had problem enough trying to find a way to get to France. Simon momentarily saw himself running Sordello through with his scimitar and kicking the body into the harbor.

And that story about Ana betraying him is almost surely a lie. She is not at all the sort who would do such a thing. Probably he himself did something stupid that gave him away.

Sordello broke in on his thoughts. "Thierry tells me you want to sail to Marseilles, Your Signory." He pointed to the high-sided, round-hulled ship that Simon had just left. "That buss you were on out there, is that not the *Constanza*? I think I know the master—his name is Guibert. Did you arrange passage with him?"

Grudgingly Simon told Sordello of his failure with the captain of the big ship. Sordello grunted.

"It is not right that a man of your distinction and wealth and gentle birth should have to go up and down the dockside begging for a ship." Simon despised the flattery but could not help agreeing with it. His situation was indeed embarrassing.

"It is past midday, Your Signory," Sordello continued. "Thierry tells me you are staying at the Hare. A good inn, I know it well. You can get a decent noonday meal there for a denier or two. Meanwhile, let me try my luck. I warrant I will find a ship for you before you finish your last cup of wine."

Tired, hungry, and discouraged, Simon thought: *At least it will give me an excuse to rest.*

And Sordello had not yet asked him for money or employment. That was a relief, but Simon told himself to be ready; the begging would start soon enough.

Feeling more relaxed, Simon was draining his third cup of red wine when Sordello reappeared. Bread, cheese, and a stew of goose, onions, and cabbage for Simon and Thierry had cost twelve denari. Simon suspected the price had gone up when the host saw the scarlet silk cape and gold-embroidered purple surcoat he had worn in the vain hope of impressing the ships' captains.

"Being cheated and lied to is a normal part of traveling," he told Thierry. "If you wish to avoid it, stay home. One must be philosophical about it."

"Your Signory!" Simon saw Sordello's burly figure silhouetted against the blue sky in the open doorway of the inn. He waved him in.

"Success!" Sordello sat down at their table without asking permission. "We have passage on a large ship sailing north and west along the coast, and stopping not just at Marseilles, but at Aigues-

Mortes, whence we can travel north through the Rhone valley."
Simon noticed the "we" but said nothing. "It takes on a cargo of
woolen cloth and silk and spices this afternoon, and it leaves tomorrow at sunup. We can board our animals and sleep on the ship
tonight."

"How much will this cost—us—Sordello?" said Simon, his improved mood making him feel a bit like joking.

A quick glance from Sordello's bloodshot eyes showed he understood that Simon understood. "Thirty florins, Your Signory.
Oh, and I promised him an additional forty-five florins when we
get to Aigues-Mortes. That little extra after the passage helps guarantee that you get where you want to go."

Thierry whistled. "Seventy-five florins! We could buy five more
horses for that."

Sordello shrugged. "But more horses would not get you as far
and as fast as that ship will. And it is no more than Count Simon
would have had to pay if he had done the bargaining himself."

"Less," Simon admitted. In his desperation he had actually been
thinking of offering Guibert a flat hundred florins.

Wait! What is happening here? he asked himself suddenly. When
he had first seen Sordello this morning, he had fully intended to
turn him away here in Livorno. Now he was paying his passage to
France. Again he was being taken advantage of.

He leaned forward suddenly, planting his folded arms on the
table.

"But why must I take you, Sordello, eh? What further use are
you to me? Can I not save some florins if I leave you on the dock
here?"

Sordello looked pained, brushing the curly gray hair back from
his forehead. "What I have just accomplished shows Your Signory
how useful I can be."

"Thus far you have nearly ruined my mission by attempting to
murder an Armenian prince—"

"That was more than a year ago, Your Signory."

"And you have failed to learn anything useful as my agent in
Ugolini's household."

"Your Signory! If not for me, you would have been totally un-
prepared for the attack on the Monaldeschi palace."

Simon saw that Sordello's rough skin was reddening. His bad
temper was threatening to break through.

It was true, though, that Sordello's warning about the Filippeschi
attack by itself made up for all the man's misdeeds.

The mention of Ugolini's household brought back the pain of that parting from Sophia. He pictured again that dizzying moment when he almost possessed her, remembered how he had poured out all his secrets to her. He saw again her tears and remembered his own, that he had shed after she ran from him. The memory made him feel like weeping now.

Hoping to sound casual, Simon said, "The cardinal's niece—I believe her name is Sophia. Did you see her before you left Orvieto?"

Sordello's discolored eyes met Simon's. "No, Your Signory. I have seen little of her since the night of the Filippeschi uprising."

Damn this gap-toothed brigand!

Simon continued to pretend to be casual. He stood up and yawned. The wine made him feel less in control of his feelings than he liked.

"Let us go and see this ship you have found for us."

"Your Signory, you have not told me whether you will take me back into your service."

Simon shook his head, as if tormented by gnats. "After we see the ship."

Sordello sighed and led the way out of the inn. They crossed the cobble-paved roadway that led along Livorno's waterfront, Simon breathing deeply of the salt-smelling air to clear his head.

Sordello pointed. "There it is."

He was pointing toward the same big, ungainly buss that Simon had visited earlier, whose captain had refused Simon.

"But he said he was going to Cyprus!"

"He lied to you," said Sordello. "I know the man. Guibert was shipmaster for a boatload of us mercenaries in the last war between Pisa and Genoa. He feared that if you were to travel on his ship, you might find him out."

"Find out what?"

"He is one of those Languedoc heretics who hate the Church and the French nobility, a follower of the Waldensian heresy. He was imprisoned once and sentenced to death in Montpellier. He recanted his heresy and was released after signing over all that he possessed to the Church. But then he came to Italy, made a new start, and backslid to Waldensianism. If the Inquisition got him now, he would go to the stake even if he recanted a thousand times."

"Then why has he agreed to carry us?" To think, the man had seen Simon as an enemy. Simon, who had inherited his Languedoc parents' loathing of the persecution of heretics.

"I told him that if he did not take us where we wanted to go, I would tell the officers of the Inquisition here in Livorno about him," said Sordello blandly.

"What!" Simon was outraged.

Sordello looked hurt. "Surely, Your Signory does not see any wrong in forcing a heretic to do a good turn for the pope and the king. Especially when it means he gets to go unpunished. So we do our duty, but with a leavening of charity."

For Simon to say more would reveal too much about himself and his family. Fuming, he bit his lip. But another objection came to him.

"We will have to take turns standing guard the whole voyage," he said. "That captain will want to slit our throats to make sure his secret is safe."

"We would have to stand guard anyway, Your Signory. A sea captain knows no law but his own greed as soon as he puts out from shore. If you can pay him seventy-five florins, that tells him you must be carrying a great deal more money. But I have insured our safety another way. I have told him that an old friend of mine here in Livorno knows his secret, and if that friend does not receive a message from me in due course assuring him of our safety, he will report Guibert to the Inquisition. Guibert would never be able to come back to Livorno, his home base, and he would not really be safe anywhere in Italy."

Simon shook his head angrily. "I like none of it."

"Even the greatest barons, even kings, must put up with much they do not like," said Sordello sententiously, "if they are to get anything done."

"As you said before, Monseigneur," said Thierry in a comforting tone, "a man must be philosophical."

"Philosophical, yes," said Simon wearily. He could, he supposed, afford to be philosophical. If the heretic sea captain did not manage to kill them, in three or four days he would be in France, on his way to find King Louis. All these unsavory doings, indignities, and discomforts would mean nothing if his mission ended in triumph.

The thought of the king's gratitude, of Uncle Charles's respect, of the way the tale would spread among the noblesse of France, bringing him new honor, sent a thrill of pride through him.

At last he would have proven himself.

L

THE SKY WAS IRON-GRAY, AND A COLD WIND, UNSEASONABLY COLD for August, blew down from the north. Daoud stood near the entrance to the courtyard of the Palazzo Papale, facing a row of the podesta's guards, in yellow and blue, who held back the watching crowd. A troop of mounted lancers clattered out under the gateway arch. Then, in mule-borne litters, came the nine cardinals who had elected to go with the pope to Perugia. Each had his own small procession of clergy and guards. In a sedan chair borne by six burly men rode Fra Tomasso d'Aquino, reading a small leather-bound book. Then came a hundred mounted archers, their conical helmets gleaming dully under the overcast sky.

Finally, as the people threw themselves to their knees, some crying out and stretching their arms wide, Urban himself, on a litter carried by eight men-at-arms, with a column of priests on either side, came through the open gate of the palace. He wore white gloves on the trembling hands that he raised to bless the people. He was bundled up in a white wool cloak, and his head was covered by a hood of fur so white that it made his own hair and his beard look yellowish.

Reluctantly, but knowing it would be dangerous not to do so, Daoud dropped to his knees as Urban passed him.

"Do not leave us, Holy Father!" a man next to him cried out.

Daoud thought of the whispers he had been hearing in his wanderings through the streets and marketplaces. People were frightened. Some said that terrible things would happen after Urban left. There would be new bloodshed between the Monaldeschi and the Filippeschi. The Sienese would beseige Orvieto and massacre its people.

Daoud himself believed d'Ucello, the podesta, would use the pope's departure to try to increase his own power over the city.

And that bodes ill for me.

The podesta was a clever man. Daoud felt certain d'Ucello suspected him of the killing of the French knight and of involvement in the Filippeschi uprising.

Daoud followed the procession along the curving street to the Porta Maggiore, intending to watch it follow the road to the north, wishing the Sienese army might appear suddenly in the distance and intercept it. But at the gate a sergente in yellow and blue stepped into his path.

"I am not leaving," Daoud said, staring at the man. "I want to stand just outside the gate."

The sergente shrugged. He was a broad-shouldered man with a square brown face and a mustache cut straight across. As they stood talking, he darted little glances at Daoud's hands and feet, half smiling. Daoud sensed that he was ready for a fight, perhaps even wanted one. The sergente thought, of course, that he was dealing with a merchant, who would not be as skilled in combat as a professional soldier.

Daoud felt a chill along his spine. D'Ucello was still determined to keep him prisoner in Orvieto. That confirmed Daoud's suspicions that the podesta might soon move against him.

"You can watch the procession from the top of the wall," the podesta's man said. "The view is better from up there anyway. You may not go beyond the gate, Messer David."

Angered by the feeling of confinement, Daoud thought about throwing the guard, disarming him, and walking through the gate just to teach him a lesson. But that was hardly what a trader would do. That would only bring more suspicion down on him. He nodded curtly and walked away.

The following Sunday, Daoud stood at the front of the cathedral, reluctantly hearing Mass, bodies pressing him from all sides. Four of Ugolini's men-at-arms, including the massive Riccardo, stood with Daoud. The little cardinal, required by the etiquette of the Sacred College to attend but made fearful by the rumors of fighting and killing to come, had begged Daoud to come with him and stay near him. The noonday heat together with the heat of packed human flesh turned the interior of the cathedral into an oven. The reek of sweat mixed with the heavy smell of incense rendered the air almost unbreathable.

A gilded screen standing on the altar displayed the miraculous linen cloth of Bolsena, lighted candles massed around it. The pope, at least, had left that to Orvieto. Ugolini was one of six red-robed cardinals, half hidden under their huge, circular red hats, who sat in chairs in a row before the altar. Each one had a cluster of assistants and guards behind him. Cardinal de Verceuil was among them. Daoud recognized him from the rear because he was the tallest of the six.

That meant the Tartars were still in Orvieto. If Lorenzo and the Ghibellino army from Siena arrived in time, there would be a chance to kill the Tartars before they rejoined the pope in Perugia. It was maddening, not knowing what Lorenzo had accomplished or where he was. This was one time he wished Christian armies could move with the speed and decisiveness of Muslims. Or Tartars.

The elderly Cardinal Piacenza, his arms supported by priest-assistants, held up the gold cup of wine which Christians believed, in a sense that Daoud had never been able to understand, to be the blood of Jesus the Messiah. The cathedral was filled with a reverent quiet.

A burst of angry men's voices from the rear of the cathedral broke the silence. Shouts echoed against the heavy stone walls. Daoud heard thuds, scuffling, the clash of steel. A jolt of alarm went through him, and his hand went to his sword.

Everyone, including Piacenza, turned to stare. The last time there had been a clash of arms in the cathedral it had been the Count de Gobignon and that heretic preacher, Daoud thought.

Daoud was amazed that Christians would interrupt the most sacred moment of their Mass. He tried to see over the heads of the people around him. One voice, roaring in protest, was raised over the others. It sounded familiar to Daoud.

People were passing word back from the middle of the nave, where the struggle was. "It is Marco di Filippeschi," a man near Daoud cried. "They have come to kill him."

Daoud's body went cold. Might whoever was coming after Marco attack him too?

The fighting seemed to be moving toward the doors, and the crowd flowed after it. Mass was forgotten as the congregation, cardinals and bishops included, rushed to see.

Ugolini hurried to Daoud and took his arm. The two of them were carried with the crowd toward the rear of the cathedral. Ugolini clutched at Daoud so tightly that his fingers hurt. The servants, Daoud noticed, managed to stay with them.

"Stay close to me," Ugolini said.

"You might be safer in the cathedral," said Daoud.

"Outside there is more room to run."

The short-legged Ugolini could not run very far, thought Daoud. He steeled himself. If they were attacked by a large number of enemies, they were dead men.

Daoud and Ugolini came through the main door of the cathedral together and stood on the crowded steps.

"I cannot see!" Ugolini cried. People on the steps below him were blocking his view.

Daoud was tall enough to see quite well. His heart, beating rapidly, seemed to be rising from his chest to his throat. Marco di Filippeschi, his long black hair flying as he jerked his body from side to side, was struggling with four men who held him, while a fifth wrapped a rope around his arms. Other men used pikes to push back the crowd, forming a ring of space around the young Filippeschi leader and his captors.

Marco is going to die, Daoud thought, feeling cold sweat all over his skin.

He looked to the edges of the piazza and the mansions that overlooked it. He saw crossbowmen in the orange and green livery of the Monaldeschi on rooftops and in windows, and mounted lancers in the outlets to the square.

The Filippeschi should have missed Mass today.

"God damn your puzzolenti souls, you bastards!" Marco roared as he fought. "May your mothers and fathers burn in Hell!"

Some men were trying to help Marco; Daoud saw little knots of struggle as his eyes traveled over the crowd. But no one could reach Marco because the orange Monaldeschi tunics were everywhere.

"What is *happening*?" Ugolini demanded.

"They are killing Marco di Filippeschi," said Daoud, thinking: *He helped me. He needs help now.* His hand gripped the hilt of his sword tightly, and he wanted to draw it and rush down the stairs to fight beside Marco.

But the knowledge that anyone who went to Marco's aid would die with him held him motionless. Daoud was not free to draw his sword for Marco, not while the Tartar ambassadors lived and the pope might yet proclaim a new crusade.

Marco was shouting obscenities so rapidly that Daoud's Italian failed him and he could not understand. The Filippeschi chieftain was tightly bound and helpless, and the men around him pushed him to his knees.

God be merciful to him, Daoud prayed.

"Lift me up so I can see!" Ugolini cried to his men-at-arms.

"You do not want to see," said Daoud, but Riccardo obediently hoisted him up to sit on his shoulders. The cardinal looked ridiculous, Daoud thought, like an overdressed child being carried by his father.

A man holding a long two-handed sword stepped out of the empty space surrounding Marco di Filippeschi. Daoud drew in a breath. The crowd gasped. The blade flashed in the sun like a mirror as he swung it up. Marco struggled, shouting curses, twisting and thrashing to escape the sword. Blood splashed over the gray-black paving stones as the sword came down. Marco cried out in agony. It took three strokes to behead him.

As much death as Daoud had seen, this sickened him. He felt bile flooding his stomach and rising in his throat.

After Marco's head lay apart from his still-trembling body in a rapidly spreading pool of blood, the silence was shocking in the piazza that had an instant before rung with his cries. As shocking as the look of the bound body without its head.

A woman's piercing scream broke the silence. Holding a baby in her arms, she burst out of the ring of men who had cordoned off the beheading. She knelt, screaming and sobbing, and reached out with one hand to touch Marco's severed head.

Another woman ran out of the crowd with a dagger in her hand. She pounced on the mother and baby and stabbed and stabbed. A pikeman in an orange tunic dragged the baby from its mother's arms, tossed it in the air, and caught it on the end of his pike, spitting it. Some in the crowd screamed with horror. Others cheered and laughed.

Daoud's stomach lurched. He pressed his hand against his middle and hoped the mother had not lived to see what had been done to her baby.

He wanted desperately to be away from there, not just because he himself might be in danger, but because he could not stand to watch.

He looked up at Ugolini. The little cardinal sat rigid on Riccardo's shoulders, his face white and blank, his whiskers quivering. How foolish he had been to want to see.

Not far away, de Verceuil's dark face under his wide-brimmed red hat stood out above the other faces in the crowd on the steps. The little mouth was set in a satisfied smile. Daoud wished he could slash that smug face with his sword.

Another Monaldeschi man-at-arms set Marco di Filippeschi's head on the end of his pike and waved it in the air for all to see. The mob in the piazza began to boil. It was a chaos that Daoud's eyes could take in only piecemeal. Men and women fought with swords and daggers and clubs; masses of people shrieking with terror surged toward the streets leading off the piazza where mounted Monaldeschi retainers slashed at them with swords and drove lances into them; crossbowmen fired into the crowd from balconies.

Now Daoud's heart was beating so hard that the booming of his blood in his ears almost drowned out the noise in the piazza. This was a war breaking out all around him.

A continuation, he reminded himself guiltily, of the war he had started.

No, he need not blame himself. He had not started this. These people had been slaughtering one another long before he came to Orvieto.

How could the Monaldeschi tell their friends, or the innocent, from their enemies, Daoud wondered. Perhaps, he thought, it did not matter to them.

He now made out, on a balcony opposite the cathedral steps, the stooped figure of the Contessa di Monaldeschi. Her cloak glittered with gold embroidery, and on her gray hair she wore a small silver coronet. She rested one hand on the shoulder of a boy, her grand-nephew Vittorio.

What a monster that child must be!

Daoud heard Ugolini's choking whisper from above him: "Get me out of here."

There was only one way to escape, back into the cathedral and out one of the side doors. Daoud helped Ugolini down from Riccardo's back, and they hurried through the center doorway, followed by his men-at-arms.

"Do not draw your weapons," Daoud said to Riccardo and the others. "Or you might get pulled into the fighting. But be ready to stand and fight if we must."

The din of the massacre in the piazza echoed within the cathedral, which was now mostly emptied out. Cardinal Piacenza had brought his Mass to a quick end. He was sitting in a chair near the altar, looking stricken, and a young priest was mopping the old cardinal's forehead with a white cloth. On one side of the nave stood the podesta, d'Ucello, surrounded by a group of his sergentes in yellow and blue.

There is murder in the piazza, and the keeper of public order hides in the cathedral, Daoud thought.

The podesta's eyes met Daoud's as Ugolini's retinue hurried past him toward the rear doors of the cathedral. There was a menace in d'Ucello's set face, but he said nothing as Daoud strode by.

The look in d'Ucello's eyes told Daoud that the moment when the podesta would strike at him was not far away. Daoud felt as if a ghost had gripped the back of his neck with an icy hand.

Ugolini, muttering to himself, led the way to the north transept. A half-dozen men in orange and green tunics, swords drawn, barred the door.

"Stand aside in the name of God!" Ugolini cried as he approached the Monaldeschi men-at-arms. "Your damned bloody quarrels have nothing to do with me."

Daoud was surprised. He had often seen Ugolini frightened, but now fear seemed to have given him sudden strength. The men guarding the door stepped aside. The cardinal's servants held the door for him, and in a moment they were in the narrow street running along the north side of the cathedral, where they joined a crowd of weeping, shouting people who had managed to break loose from the piazza. There were splashes of blood, Daoud saw, on the tunics of many men and the dresses of many women. Ugolini's servants formed a wedge around him, and in stunned silence they walked back to his mansion.

Daoud felt shaken and sick. His hands were trembling.

The Filippeschi could have been allies for Daoud against the podesta. Now he was alone.

Ugolini's small contingent of armed retainers could not resist the town militia. A cold feeling of helplessness settled over Daoud. If only Lorenzo would come back.

Bars of afternoon sunlight slanted through the windows of Ugolini's cabinet, giving a fiery tinge to his red rug and glistening in the eyes of his stuffed owl. Ugolini sat behind his table, holding the painted skull in both hands and staring intently at it, as if it held the explanation of what had happened at the cathedral this morning. Sophia sat in a chair on the other side of the table, and Daoud stood by the window.

"The Monaldeschi and the Filippeschi are both Guelfo families, and the Filippeschi have high connections with the Church," Ugolini said. "That is why the contessa waited until the pope left before taking her revenge."

"I have seen Christians slaughter Muslims and Muslims massacre Christians," Daoud said. "But today Christians were killing mothers and infants that could have been their own. Women were doing some of the killing."

Ugolini smiled at the skull, but there was no laughter in his round eyes. "Are not family quarrels the cruelest of all?"

Daoud noticed that Ugolini's hands, fingertips pressed against the smooth curve of the skull's cranium, were still quivering. As for Daoud himself, he was quite calm now.

The last time I was really terrified was when I looked into the locket and saw whirling blackness.

He was still angry with himself about that, knowing what a foolish thing it had been to partake of hashish when he was already in a dark mood. The fear he had felt a month earlier after taking the drug and looking into the locket remained with him, clinging to his mind like some parasitic insect. It rose to confront him now, as he looked at Sophia. Would something horrible happen to her because of him? Blossoming Reed had threatened just that, and so far Blossoming Reed's magic had worked well. Since that vision, the joy he felt with Sophia had been chilled somewhat by fear for her.

"How safe are *we* now, with the Monaldeschi rampaging through the streets?" Sophia asked.

Ugolini shuddered. "And the Filippeschi. Those who are left will be striking back. This city will destroy itself, like a rat eating its own innards. I say leave now. All of us."

Leave? Daoud thought. He would be less afraid for Sophia if she were in a safer place. But where should he go?

"Where do you want to go?" he asked Ugolini.

The little cardinal drew himself up. "I am still the cardinal camerlengo, and will be as long as Urban is alive. I am obliged to follow the pope as quickly as I can to Perugia. There is peace and order in Perugia." He looked at Daoud uneasily. "What do *you* want to do? Stay here?"

He is hoping to be rid of me. Daoud considered Perugia, but there he would have everything against him and no forces to help him.

He must go to Manfred. Once the pope and the Tartars were safely in Perugia, only Manfred's army would be powerful enough to get at them. Manfred might not want to go to war, but war was inevitable. Clearly the pope was no longer neutral. He favored the Tartar-Christian alliance and was waiting only for the right moment to announce it. When the pope came out for the alliance, the French would come into Italy.

The time for Manfred to act was now. If he marched north and seized all of Italy, including the person of the pope and as many cardinals as he could capture, the French never *would* invade, because a Ghibellino pope would not approve a joint campaign of Christians and Tartars against Muslims. Then, for certain, there would be no alliance.

"Now that the pope has moved to a place of safety," he said aloud, "only King Manfred can dislodge him."

Ugolini wrung his hands. "First you incite the Filippeschi against the Monaldeschi. Then Siena against Orvieto. Now Manfred against the Papal States? Sometimes I think you are like one of the horsemen of the Apocalypse, spreading war wherever you go.''

All too true, Daoud thought. He turned to Sophia to see whether she agreed with the accusation. She looked at him somberly, did not speak.

He sighed. ''I am fighting for my people. For my God.''

''I, too, for *my* people,'' said Sophia quietly. Her tone told Daoud she sided with him, and he felt an inner warmth.

''And what have your people to do with this?'' Ugolini cried. ''Have you forgotten that you are not Sicilian but Greek?''

''Not at all,'' said Sophia. ''I want to see Manfred in control of Italy. He is a friend of Byzantium. The Franks are our enemies.''

Ugolini shook his head. ''I am the only Italian in this room. And I weep for *my* people.''

Daoud strode over to Ugolini's table, pressed his hands flat on it, and stared into his eyes.

''Be *strong* for your people,'' he said. The hairs on the back of his neck rose with excitement as he spoke. He had wanted to try to put strength into Ugolini for such a long time.

Ugolini looked bewildered. ''What do you mean?''

''Think what Italy would be with Manfred von Hohenstaufen ruling from the Alps to Sicily and a pope who supports him.''

''A Ghibellino pope?'' Ugolini looked surprised, then nodded. ''Why not? As a Ghibellino myself, I would rejoice at that. But it will happen only if Manfred has the College of Cardinals in his power.''

''Yes,'' said Daoud. ''And that is why I must go all the way south to Lucera, where Sophia and Lorenzo and I started from.'' Ugolini's eyes were brighter, and Daoud felt with pleasure that he had breathed new life into the little man.

''But the podesta won't let you leave the city!'' Sophia exclaimed.

Again Daoud felt that cold hand grasp his neck. Perhaps he should have left long ago. He turned from Sophia to Ugolini.

''You must demand that he let me leave, Cardinal,'' said Daoud, feeling less confident than he tried to sound.

Or, he thought, he could escape the way Lorenzo did. He had never truly been a prisoner here.

''I will order the servants to start packing for me,'' Ugolini said. ''Of course, I must make arrangements for Tilia to move, too, and that might take time. Although many of her best clients are gone now.'' He sounded like a man who knew what he was doing and Daoud was relieved to hear it.

Daoud turned from Ugolini to Sophia. The knowledge that he would soon leave Orvieto, where he had seen too much of defeat and slaughter, lifted his spirits. He smiled at Sophia, and she smiled back. He knew she was thinking the same thought he was—that they had hours to spend together this afternoon.

Daoud and Sophia lay naked in her bed, legs entwined, her head resting on his bare chest.

''What about me?'' Sophia asked. ''Will I go south with you to Manfred, or north to Perugia with Ugolini?''

''With me, of course,'' said Daoud. At the mention of leaving her, he felt as if a cold wind had blown across his naked body. He was surprised that she was even considering staying with Ugolini.

''I want to be with you,'' she said, caressing his chest with a circular movement of her palm. ''I hate the thought of our being apart. But with the pope and the Tartars in Perugia, you need someone there besides Ugolini. Someone who has an aim in common with yours. I can help him and make sure that what he does helps you. Helps us.''

He ran his fingers through her long, unbound hair. ''I will think about what you've said. But I do not like it.''

''Neither do I. But it may be necessary.''

A loud knock at Sophia's door interrupted them.

Something in the urgency of the knock made Daoud spring out of bed and reach for his sword, hanging from a peg on the wall. Putting a finger to her lips, Sophia got out of bed more slowly and went to the door.

''It is I,'' the cardinal called through the door in answer to her question. ''I know David is there with you. Let me in. The podesta is here.''

The ghost that haunted him whenever he thought of himself and d'Ucello seized Daoud's entire body in a cold, paralyzing embrace. His first thought was of escape. But d'Ucello probably had the mansion surrounded.

Sophia and Daoud dressed quickly and opened the door for the cardinal.

''D'Ucello has come here with twenty or more men-at-arms,'' Ugolini said. ''He demands that you go with him to the Palazzo del Podesta, David.''

''Can you not order him away?'' Sophia demanded. ''You are a prince of the Church. You did that before.''

"He waited until most of the power of the Church had left Orvieto," said Ugolini.

"And until the Filippeschi had been crushed, thinking I might call upon them for help," Daoud said.

"You must try to escape," said Sophia.

"Then what would happen to you?"

"We will escape together!"

Daoud looked at her drawn face, and at that moment he loved her more than ever. His love warmed him, and freed him from the grip of fear. This woman—who had spoken a short time ago so calmly of separation—was ready to run, to dodge arrows, to hide in ditches, to climb walls, to do whatever she had to, to be near him.

"If he finds out what you are, we are all doomed," said Ugolini. Daoud saw that the small body was aquiver with fear.

He could imagine what Ugolini was thinking, that the evil he had dreaded since Daoud came to Orvieto had come upon them at last. Just when he thought he was about to escape it.

"He will learn nothing," said Daoud.

"He will torture you." Ugolini sat down on Sophia's bed and wrapped his arms around his stomach. "We will all die horribly—me, Sophia, Tilia—everyone who helped you." He raised hands curved like claws and shook them at Daoud. "Oh, God, how I wish you had never come here!"

Sophia sat beside Ugolini and put her hand on his knee. "If we can stay calm, dear Eminence, we can think of a way out of this."

"Even if he tortures me, I will tell him nothing, except that I am David, the trader from Trebizond," said Daoud. The methods of resisting pain that he had learned from the Hashishiyya would serve him now.

"You must not think of going with him!" Sophia cried.

"It is the only way. If I cooperate, it shows my innocence. The cardinal can use his influence to get me freed."

She jumped up and threw herself against him, weeping. "You are going to your death!" He held her tightly.

"D'Ucello has nothing to gain by killing me," he said. "And surrendering to him is the only thing I can do." He looked at Ugolini. "Do you agree?"

Ugolini sighed and shook his head. "I cannot think."

Gently Daoud freed himself from Sophia's embrace. "Insh'Allah, God willing, I will return to you."

He turned to the door. Every muscle in his body screamed at him to run, or to draw his sword and try to fight his way out. He cringed inwardly from the thought of imprisonment and torture. He remembered the poor madman whose body they had torn apart with red-hot pincers. He forced himself not to tremble. He took the first step toward the door, then another.

God, make me strong in the face of my enemies.

LI

"MANY THINK I HAVE LITTLE POWER IN THIS CITY," SAID FRES-cobaldo d'Ucello. He sat in a dark window recess with one foot up on the ledge and the other dangling, his fingers tapping the raised knee. Lashed to a chair in the center of the long, narrow chamber, Daoud had to turn his head to look at him. Daoud's back ached from being held rigid by the back of the chair, and the ropes bit into the muscles of his arms and legs.

At the end of the room, a clerk with scalp shaved in the clerical tonsure sat in the podesta's high-back chair behind a heavy black table, writing down what was said on a scroll with a feather pen. Four tall candles set in brass stands formed a square around Daoud, casting a bright light on him. A row of candles burned in a wrought-iron candelabrum beside the clerk, lighting a wall hanging behind him that depicted some idolatrous Christian religious scene. D'Ucello sat in the shadows that lay upon the rest of the chamber.

Daoud sensed that d'Ucello meant what he had just said as a sort of challenge.

"All I know is that for my part I have very little power in this city, Signore," Daoud said with a smile. "I depend altogether on those who have befriended me." That was the way David of Trebizond should respond. Not very frightened, because not guilty of anything. Humble, ingratiating, but retaining some scrap of dignity.

D'Ucello stood up suddenly, strode briskly across the room to Daoud, and stood over him.

"Do you think your friends will save you from this?" he said tonelessly. His eyes had an unfocused look, as though they were made of glass.

"Save me from what, Signore?" Daoud put bewilderment and a shade of anger into his voice.

D'Ucello swung his hand. Daoud felt the sting of a hard palm against his jaw, and the crack of flesh slapping flesh made his ear ring. The blow jolted his head to one side.

It was not very painful. It was meant to insult more than to hurt. To test. And rage did erupt in Daoud like a fountain of fire. His muscles tensed, the bindings cutting deeper, and the chair creaked.

D'Ucello was trying to break through the Mask of Clay. But the mask held firm, because the Face of Steel, Daoud's spiritual armor, was beneath it. The fury of Daoud the Mameluke, who yearned to tear d'Ucello apart, remained hidden. It was David of Trebizond who blustered at the indignity of being slapped without cause.

"How dare you strike me, Signore!" he protested. "I have done nothing to deserve that, nothing to deserve being dragged here in the night and tied up. I demand to know—what do you want of me?"

D'Ucello sighed like a chess player whose opponent had escaped check, and went back to his seat in the window recess. Daoud saw the flickering glow of heat lightning through the thick leaded-glass window behind the podesta.

"I dislike intensely being made to waste time," said d'Ucello, drumming his fingers on his knee. "Listen carefully: Every time you force me to tell you something we both already know, I will prolong your suffering another hour."

Daoud allowed a note of fear to creep into his voice. "Suffering? I beg you, Signore, believe me. Even if you torture me, I still cannot tell you anything different from what I will freely tell you. Ask me whatever you want."

The Mask of Clay was useless with this man, Daoud saw. The podesta's mind had pierced it. How had he been able to do that? Because he was a man who observed much and thought much, unlike most men Daoud had met in Orvieto, who let their passions rule them.

Yet d'Ucello had passions. He was a proud man, who must hate standing by helplessly, holding the supreme office in Orvieto, watching the two great families bespatter his city with blood. If he could not stop the Filippeschi and the Monaldeschi from murdering each other, at least he could do *something*.

D'Ucello had seen enough of Daoud's comings and goings to make him suspicious. Like a hawk soaring above a plain, the podesta might be too high up to know exactly what he saw below, but he knew when he sighted prey. And perhaps d'Ucello saw that this prey, if hunted rightly, would lead him to others.

D'Ucello leaned forward, out of the shadow of the window recess.

"There was a man in black who tried to kill the Tartars the night of the Filippeschi uprising. What do you know about him?"

"I know little about the uprising, Signore, since I was not here. I was in Perugia."

"Why Perugia?"

"To speak with several silk merchants."

"Are there those in Perugia who will vouch for you?"

"Certainly," said Daoud, feeling uneasily that d'Ucello was not deceived.

"I will write to the podesta of Perugia and ask that your witnesses be examined," said d'Ucello. "Give me their names."

Daoud had a struggle to remember the names of the witnesses. Lorenzo had given them to him months before, members of the Ghibellino network who were willing to perform this service for Manfred. The clerk's pen scratched rapidly as he haltingly brought out the names of five men.

"When did you return from Perugia?"

The clerks, Daoud recalled, had been removed from the town gates at the end of May.

"Sometime in June," Daoud said. "Forgive me, I did not think to bring my journal with me, and I cannot tell you the exact date." He tried a weak smile.

"Where is your man Giancarlo?"

On his way here from Siena with an army, Insh'Allah.

"I sent him on from Perugia," Daoud said. "He travels to Rimini, then Ravenna, eventually to Venice, looking for those who would be interested in receiving shipments of silks and spices from Trebizond. He had not been punctilious about writing to me, or perhaps his letters have been lost, so I do not know exactly where he is now."

"I thought you were in competition with the Venetians."

Daoud essayed another smile. "That is why I sent Giancarlo."

"And where were you the night the French cavaliere was murdered?" d'Ucello asked.

"I was with a woman."

"What was her name?"

"I do not think I ever knew it." He tried a flash of sarcasm. "If I had known there was to be a murder that night, I would have asked her name."

"Everyone was with a nameless woman that night," D'Ucello sighed. "Yes, you should have taken more care to arrange for proof of your innocence, messere."

He gestured to the clerk, who picked up a small bell on the table beside his ink pot and shook it, a silvery clangor.

Two broad, leather-faced men in the yellow and blue tunics of the watch came into the room. They took a few steps toward d'Ucello and stood awaiting orders like a pair of mastiffs.

"Take him down," said d'Ucello.

"Wait! Will you torture me? I have tried to tell you the truth. Do not do this, I beg you."

D'Ucello slid off the window ledge. "I am the sort of man who would rather spend hours picking a lock than break it open." The smile that stretched his thin mustache was genuine. "But, as we both know, the Ghibellini of Siena may be upon us at any moment, and I must break you open quickly. So now I will sleep. And while I am restoring my strength, my men will prepare you for our next talk."

Daoud tried to keep the Face of Steel firmly in place while with the Mask of Clay he feigned helpless terror. But his defense against feeling seemed to have flaws. Genuine terror of what he was about to suffer kept seeping through. When d'Ucello's guards untied him and forced him to stand, his knees nearly buckled under him.

The steps Daoud descended must have been hollowed out by the feet of hundreds of hapless prisoners and their guards. The wall of the circular stairwell, which Daoud brushed with his fingertips to steady himself, was of rough-hewn black stone.

His heart was thudding heavily as he descended the stairs, preceded by one guard, followed by the other and by d'Ucello's clerk. The thought of hours, perhaps days, of pain he must undergo made every muscle in his body tremble. The stairwell, lit at long intervals by torches held by wrought iron cressets, went down so far it seemed to have no bottom. Many a prisoner must have felt the temptation to throw himself down from the stairs and escape suffering.

The chamber he entered through a door of thick oak planks had been carved from the yellow-gray rock of Orvieto's mesa. The room smelled of fire, blood, rot, and excrement.

A man slid down from a chair when Daoud entered with his guards. Standing, his head would have come to Daoud's waist. But he was bent double and held his arms out from his sides to keep his fingers from touching the ground, so his head was not even as high as Daoud's knees.

Memories flashed through Daoud's mind: The woodcutter who

had blessed himself when Daoud was arrested at Lucera. The executioner who had tossed the heretic's cod into the air to the delight of the crowd before Orvieto's cathedral. Daoud had always wondered how the little man had come to appear in two such different places. The skin crawled on the back of Daoud's neck. This creature was uncanny.

"You are to keep him awake all night, Erculio," said the guard who had followed Daoud into the room.

"Did I not sleep all day today, so that I would be able to properly entertain our guest tonight?" The little man bustled forward to Daoud, rubbing his hands. His head was as big as that of a full-grown man, but his hands and feet were small. His mustache bristled in spikes of black hair, like a portcullis over his mouth.

"Please, in the name of the mercy of God," Daoud pleaded. "I am a merchant. I am rich. Do not hurt me. I will pay you well."

"We want to hear nothing from you except frequent screams and answers to the questions the podesta wants me to put to you," said Erculio in a cold voice. "What do we want to know, Vincenzo?"

D'Ucello's clerk said, "The podesta believes he is a Ghibellino spy sent here by the bastard King Manfred. He thinks he incited the Filippeschi uprising. Also he may have killed the French cavaliere."

Erculio nodded vigorously. "Well, then, messere. Are you prepared to admit your guilt, now that you see where you are and realize what is about to happen to you?"

"These accusations are false!" Daoud cried. "I swear it!"

The tonsured clerk, carrying a handful of quills, a bundle of scrolls, and his ink pot, seated himself at a table in one corner of the room and began to write.

To gain time, Daoud looked around Erculio's domain, remembering the similar room in Tilia's brothel where he had subjected Sordello to the Hashishiyya initiation. This place was starker and more frightful. It was large, perhaps fifty paces on a side, divided by two rows of thick columns holding up the weight of the great stone building above it. Despite its size, the chamber was well lit. The candle sconces were lined with sheets of tin to throw extra light.

Daoud recognized most of the implements of torment around the room. A rack, a tilted wooden table with chains and winches. A sharp-pointed wooden pyramid over which a victim could be suspended. A chair with spikes protruding at the joints. A coffin lined with spikes. A brazier full of pokers and branding irons of various sizes. Weights and pulleys. Whips and cudgels, hung neatly from pegs that lined the walls. A cage full of rats. A number of smaller devices to crush fingers or limbs—or even skulls—laid out neatly on tables beside rows of long needles.

Daoud visualized himself drinking from a bowl of liquid light and felt the mind-created drug Soma pouring down into his stomach and spreading to his heart and lungs, through all his veins.

But still he must keep up the Mask of Clay.

"I can say no other than what is true," he cried. "I am David of Trebizond. I came here to sell silk. I have harmed no one. Please be merciful."

Erculio grunted. "Strip him and string him up."

Daoud protested weakly, letting his voice tremble as the guards pulled the clothes from his body. He felt the cool, dank air of the cellar on his bare skin.

"Be careful," Erculio said. "That is a good embroidered tunic. The hose and boots are new. Those clothes are my property now." Fussily, he folded the garments as they fell away from Daoud and laid them on a chair.

"Will you not return them to me—afterward?" Daoud quavered.

"Afterward?" Erculio laughed.

"What is this?" said one guard as he used his dagger to cut the thong that held the leather capsule around Daoud's neck. The tawidh, that healed his wounds and protected him from death.

Daoud said nothing.

Now they can truly destroy my body.

The guard handed the tawidh to Erculio, who glanced at it and threw it on his low chair. He frowned at Daoud.

"Put a loincloth on him, fools," he growled. "Did I say to strip him stark naked? Are we not decent fellows here?" He fumbled about in a pile of rags and threw one to a guard.

"That's the first time you've complained about a prisoner being naked, Erculio," the guard grumbled as he wrapped the cloth around Daoud's hips and passed it between his legs. "Don't you need to be able to get at his cock?"

"Do not try to teach me my craft," Erculio said snappishly. "Up with him now."

The guards grabbed Daoud by the arms and pushed him under dangling chains. They lifted his arms over his head and bound his wrists with thick leather cuffs. Then they went to a winch with a crank on each side, next to the wall, and began to turn in unison.

Daoud cried out in pain as his body was jerked into the air. The leather cuffs cut into his wrists. His shoulders felt as if his arms were being torn out of their sockets.

He pictured the Soma cascading through his body, and the pain receded. But he continued to cry out as if in unbearable agony until the two guards stopped raising him. He hung there, the Mask of Clay sobbing and whimpering.

Erculio scuttled over to stand under him, holding a thick stick as long as a man's arm. Daoud's feet were just level with Erculio's head. Leaning on the stick, Erculio looked up at Daoud, appraising his body, and a pink tongue tip flickered under the bristling mustache.

"You have a beautiful body, messere. Well-proportioned, with powerful muscles. You are un bello pezzo di carne, a fine piece of meat." Erculio walked around behind him and stopped there for a moment, where Daoud could not see him.

"Scars from old wounds, too, I see," the little man said.

Perhaps in this light the scar left by the Tartar's arrow looks old.

Erculio stood before him again. "You look able to endure much, so you will last longer. You may think when a guest comes down here I just pick the first instrument that comes to mind. Not so. I follow a strict order. You will get to know every instrument here, if you live long enough. This will be very educational for you."

"I have been telling you the truth," Daoud moaned. "Will you not believe me?"

"Bugiardo! Liar!" Erculio struck him hard on the shin with the stick. Pain blazed through his leg. Daoud could have remained silent, but he shrieked loudly, knowing that fear, as much as pain, would make the man he was pretending to be cry out.

Turning to the others, Erculio said, "What will you wager against these handsome clothes of his that I get this pezzo di carne to speak the words our honorable podesta wants to hear? A bet makes this game more interesting. What say you, any takers?"

"The man is quivering like a frumenty now," said one guard. "He would have been talking long ago if he had anything to say."

"You think so?" Erculio snapped his fingers. "Good. Bet with me, then."

The guard fumbled in a purse at his belt and drew out a glittering coin. "There you are. A gold florin, not ten years old and barely worn. I won it dicing last night."

Erculio examined the coin. "Twenty years old, and the lilies are a bit wilted. But it's heavy enough, I suppose. Done! Now, Messer Pezzo-di-Carne—I call you that because I do not know your real name—you had better tell us what we want to know, or I will *really* make you suffer." He dropped the coin on top of Daoud's clothing.

Erculio brought the stick against Daoud's shin, in the spot he had struck a moment ago. The pain shot through Daoud. But Soma turned the pain to a tingling, and Daoud visualized it as a glow that spread from toe to hip. He screamed, as he knew he should, but behind the Face of Steel he felt at peace.

Erculio let out a laugh that sounded more like the clucking of a chicken. "You see, we do not need elaborate instruments. We can inflict unbearable pain with the simplest means—like this!" And he swung the stick to hit precisely the same spot on Daoud's shin he had struck twice before.

Daoud bellowed and felt the tingling and saw the glow in his leg, and the Soma, the drug created by his spirit, preserved his sanity.

How small Erculio looked, crouched down on the stone floor. So man must look to God. God was so infinitely far above man, the miracle was that God was mindful of man at all. But God was inside of man—inside of each human being—as well as above him.

It is blasphemy to liken myself to God.

He called to mind the Koran's admonition, *There is none like unto Him.*

His mind occupied with God, he barely noticed the activities of the spiderlike creature that crawled about on the floor below him as he hung like a trapped fly. Erculio worked on his legs for a long time, bruising the shins with his heavy stick until Daoud thought both legs must be broken. Then the torturer pressed a red-hot poker against the soles of his feet.

Erculio had the guards let Daoud down and force him to walk on his burned feet to the rack table, where they chained him face-down and stretched him till the ligaments that held his bones together were ready to snap.

The Mask of Clay screamed and pleaded for mercy and insisted he had already told them everything. But the pain lay as far from his consciousness as the sea lies from the desert tent of a Bedouin.

Erculio applied more instruments to Daoud's body, inflicting many kinds of pain—burning, stabbing, bruising, crushing. He kept Daoud awake, and Daoud knew that hours must have gone by, perhaps the whole night.

Daoud's outcries grew hoarser and weaker, and at last Erculio's efforts brought forth nothing from him but soft groans and whimpers.

Daoud saw the clerk, Vincenzo, rise yawning and leave as another clerk, also shaven-headed, but with a short brown beard, came in to replace him. He saw the two guards in yellow and blue sit down on the floor, their backs to the wall, and doze off. He saw after a time the second clerk lower his head on his folded arms. He saw all this while Erculio pranced about him, hurting him and hurting him.

Erculio looked around at the others in the chamber. He left off pushing a needle into Daoud's ankle and rushed over to the guards and shouted at them to wake up. He poked them with his stick. They cursed him and kicked at him and went back to sleep. He scurried to the sleeping clerk.

"You are supposed to be writing down everything the prisoner says. Come now, wake up! Indolento! The podesta will hear of this, I promise you."

The clerk mumbled something without raising his head from his arms. Erculio nodded with satisfaction and hurried across the chamber to Daoud. He stood by Daoud's head.

"As-salaam aleikem, Daoud ibn Abdallah," the torturer whispered.

For a moment Daoud could not believe he had really heard it. The drug that he had brewed in his mind had taken control of his ears. Or else this was their way of tricking him into talking freely.

But if they knew my Muslim name and that I speak Arabic, they would not waste time accusing me of being a Ghibellino.

"Wa aleikem salaam," he replied. The uprush of joy he felt at finding a friend here in this terrible cellar momentarily shattered the Face of Steel. What madness this was, that the friend should be the source of all his torment? He bit back hysterical laughter.

"Like you, I serve El Malik Dahir," Erculio said in Arabic. Hearing that title, Daoud thought it even less likely that the little man was trying to trick him.

"I have been watching you since Lucera, My Lord," Erculio went on. "You have done well, even if it has been God's will that you should not succeed. You have been clever. But you should have taken the tawidh off before you surrendered. Do you think there are no Christians who can recognize Arabic numerals?"

Now Daoud was sure the little man was an ally of some sort. In Arabic he said, "Does the scar on the back of my leg look fresh?"

"It has healed so completely that no one would believe you got it a few months ago. They know nothing of our Islamic medicine. You bear another wound, though, that would have much to say to the observant—your circumcision. That was why I had them put a loincloth on you and lay you facedown on this rack."

"Lucky for me you were here," Daoud said.

"Not luck," said Erculio. "El Malik deemed it wise that, should you be made a prisoner, one of his men ought to be among your captors."

Even here, Baibars's hand reaches out to me, thought Daoud, feeling a rush of gratitude.

"Help me to escape," said Daoud. "The guards and the clerk are asleep."

Erculio brought his small hand downward in a gesture of flat rejection. "There are a hundred men-at-arms on duty up above. The podesta himself will be down here in an hour. Why can you not make up a story that will satisfy him? Say you are a Ghibellino. That is what he believes, and since it is not true, it will not help him. In a thousand years he would never guess the truth."

"No. The only way I can protect those close to me is to admit nothing."

Erculio shook his head, and his black eyes were liquid with sadness. "What a pity. Your case is hopeless, then. Ever since I saw you in Lucera I have felt sorry for you. How can El Malik expect one man to change the course of nations? You are like a man trying to hold apart two ships about to collide." He sighed. "I have done all I can for you. I have hurt you as much as I can without doing you permanent injury—so far. There is only one other service I can perform for you."

"What is that?" said Daoud, though he felt sure he already knew the answer.

"You would not want to reveal under torture that you are an agent of the Sultan of El Kahira, and provoke the very crusade you were sent here to prevent. You would not want to give your friends away. If you break, I will see to it that you die before you might speak."

"I will not break," said Daoud. "And when it is all over, and d'Ucello has killed me, he will at last come to believe that I was telling the truth. Because he believes that no one can hold out against torture to the very end. But promise me one thing."

"Insh'Allah, anything."

"If you must cripple me, see that I do not leave this dungeon alive."

Understanding and respect glowed in the black eyes peering at Daoud over the edge of the rack. "As you wish, My Lord."

He knew he should be grateful that he had this man here to guarantee him a decent death. But a great sadness came over him at the thought that his life must end miserably in this dungeon. He had always hoped that he would meet his fate amid the glory of jihad, holy war.

Well, this is jihad of a kind.

* * *

The respite was over. Erculio fell upon Daoud with renewed
vigor, driving needles under his toenails and fingernails and beating
him with a whip of knotted rawhide cords that tore open his back.
Daoud felt the blood running down his sides and pooling underneath him. The little man took a red-hot poker and pressed it,
hissing, against the scar made by the Tartar's arrow and Lorenzo's
knife. That, Daoud realized, would make it impossible to tell what
sort of wound it had been.

The pain seemed to be happening to someone miles away as
Daoud converted it to ripples of light passing through his body. He
understood that Erculio was applying tortures whose effects could
be seen. The podesta would be satisfied that Erculio had done his
work well.

Daoud did his part too. The rest had restored his strength, and
now Daoud screamed so loudly he woke the guards and the clerk.
Erculio set the guards to work replacing the burned-down candles
in the sconces around the dungeon. When Daoud turned his throbbing head to look at the candles, he saw hazy rings around them
and rays radiating from them. Sweat stung his eyes.

The thick wooden door of the cellar swung inward, and d'Ucello
entered. He walked over to where Daoud lay on the rack, and stood
staring at him with his peculiar, glazed expression. D'Ucello's face
was more sour than usual, and his eyelids were puffed. He looked
just awakened from a sleep that had given him little refreshment.
His mouth twitched under the thin mustache.

Daoud noticed that in one hand d'Ucello held a small silver flask
with a narrow neck and a glass stopper. D'Ucello clenched his
hand around it tightly, as if he feared to drop it.

"What has he said?" he demanded, turning to Erculio.

"Just much screaming, Signore." Erculio looked across the room
at the bearded clerk, who nodded vigorously.

"You have not hurt him enough, then, Erculio," said the podesta. "He should be offering us *something* by now. To withstand
torture for so long almost smacks of sorcery."

"Perhaps he really has nothing to tell," Erculio ventured.

"Nonsense!" D'Ucello glared at the dwarf. "Even an innocent
man would make the torture stop, if he had to lie to do it. And this
man is not innocent."

By that one remark Erculio risks much for me, thought Daoud,
praying the little man would not again endanger himself.

"Attenzione," said d'Ucello, coming close to Daoud's head and
holding the flask so Daoud could see it. He withdrew the stopper,

a long icicle of glass. He held the flask low over the rack table and
tilted it momentarily. A few drops of dark brown liquid splashed
onto the wood. At once d'Ucello righted and stopped the flask.

A white flash, bright as lightning, burst before Daoud's face,
blinding him.

He jerked his head back and squeezed his eyes shut. He heard
Erculio curse in Italian and the clerk and the guards cry out.

Smoke burned Daoud's nostrils and throat. As he coughed, he
opened his eyes and saw a small fire burning its way into the wood
a hand's breadth from his face. He felt a wave of heat. D'Ucello
and his men watched in silence as the fire ate through the thick
planking of the rack table. Gradually the blaze lost its intensity as
the liquid that started it was used up. It ended in a hole a man could
pass his fist through, with glowing, smoking edges.

"What *is* that?" said the clerk, tugging nervously at his brown
beard.

"Witchcraft," said d'Ucello with a grim chuckle. The clerk and
the guards stared at him. Erculio was expressionless.

In spite of Soma, in spite of his years of training, Daoud felt a
scream of horror rising inside him at the thought of what d'Ucello
was threatening.

"Not witchcraft, but just as evil," d'Ucello went on. "It is a
weapon devised by the Byzantines."

"Ah!" said the clerk. "This must be that Greek Fire I have heard
crusaders tell of. I always thought it another of their lies about the
East."

"It is real," said d'Ucello. "Perhaps our guest, being from the
East, has seen it before. The Turks stole the secret from the Byzantines and have been using it against the crusaders. It starts burning the moment it is exposed to air. It clings to whatever it touches,
and its flames cannot be put out. Maligno."

The podesta turned to Daoud. "But in this case we will be using
it for a good purpose. Messer David, do you love your organs of
manhood?"

"What are you saying to me?" Daoud cried, determined that he
would be David of Trebizond to the very end. His real terror now
matched his pretended terror, but he managed to keep them two
separate feelings. The scream trying to escape him battered itself
like a trapped animal against the inner wall of the Face of Steel.

D'Ucello bent closer to Daoud, and from his painful position,
belly down, arms and legs stretched taut, Daoud lifted his head to
look at the podesta. D'Ucello glowered at him, his lips tight under
his thin mustache.

"I mean that if you do not tell me who you really are and what you are doing in Orvieto, I will apply this healing potion to your male member. It should not take more than a drop to burn away everything you have there." D'Ucello feinted at Daoud's face with the flask, and Daoud flinched back and cried out. He strained desperately against the chains that held him.

Greek Fire—what a cruel turn of fate that a thing invented by Sophia's people should destroy him. Grief swelled in his throat as he mourned the end of those hours of delight they had passed together.

But, Daoud thought, d'Ucello did not need Greek Fire to destroy his manhood. He could burn it with oil and a torch, or he could order Erculio to slash it away with a knife. The podesta had chosen Greek Fire because it was strange, hinted of magic—maligno. Daoud remembered what d'Ucello had said, an eon ago, when they were talking upstairs: that he would prefer picking a lock to forcing it. Even now the podesta was trying to use fear rather than pain to make Daoud tell him what he wanted to know. D'Ucello himself did not really relish inflicting physical pain; he preferred to work on men's emotions.

D'Ucello peered at him. "Under the appearance of a helpless and terrified merchant, there is bravado. But now you know what a terrible thing is going to happen to you if you persist. I will give that understanding time to ripen."

He drew away and turned to Erculio. "I will return at midday, after my morning audiences. See that he thinks about what is going to happen to him."

Erculio bowed. "Signore."

The podesta left the dungeon, still holding the silver flask.

He has to put off carrying out his threat, Daoud thought. *Once he has poured that Greek Fire on my loins, he has done his worst. If the fear does not force me to speak, the deed is pointless. After it is done I will have little more to lose. If he were a true torturer, he would have begun with my toes.*

Even so, Daoud was sure d'Ucello would carry out his threat. *Therefore, I must prepare myself for death.*

If d'Ucello used the Greek Fire on him, Daoud would want Erculio to kill him. And he was sure Erculio would do it.

He turned his mind again to thoughts of God. Soon he would be face-to-face with God in paradise.

He heard Erculio talking to the guards, making preparations for some new torment. Rather than wallow in fear, Daoud visualized a fresh flood of Soma coursing through his heart and mind and limbs. Saadi had explained that there was no limit to how much of a spiritual drug a man could take.

This time, as Soma detached his spirit from his body, something happened to him unlike anything he had never known before. He was looking down at himself. He saw himself lying facedown, nearly nude on the rack, his blond hair darkened and plastered down with sweat. He saw the bloody slashes across his back, the blackened burn mark on his leg.

He was floating near the ceiling of the dungeon. He looked down at the spider shape of Erculio, talking with the guards and the clerk. Amazing that they did not look up here and see him. They thought he was still on the rack.

He rose through solid stone, a space of lightlessness. Then he was moving over tiled floors through the upper levels of the Palazzo del Podesta, and he was out through its iron-sheathed oak door.

The vault of the sky over him was as black and heavy as the stones of the dungeon where his body lay. It must be the final hour of night. Even though he was a spirit, he sensed that the air was hot and damp.

He rose higher and higher over Orvieto, and amazingly he was able to see despite the absence of light. He could see the entire oval shape of the city from end to end, and the deep valleys that surrounded it. There at the west end was the cathedral of San Giovenale, with the great piazza where public events took place. There was Cardinal Ugolini's mansion, near the palace where the pope had lived. On the north side of the town, the Palazzo Monaldeschi, where he had hoped to end the threat to Islam with swift blows of his dagger. And there—

From such a height—and since it was not yet dawn—he should not have been able to recognize her, but he saw and knew at once the small figure of a cloaked and hooded woman striding purposefully through a twisting street. She was walking through the eastern side of the town, in the direction of Tilia's house, which he could see from up here, with the dovecote on its roof and its crenellated balconies, though Sophia could not. Beside Sophia, a hulking figure carried a torch to light their way. Ugolini's man-at-arms Riccardo.

Without knowing how he did it, Daoud was down from the sky in an instant and walking invisibly beside her. Her black brows were drawn together in a frown, her nose and mouth covered by a silk scarf. She looked almost like a Muslim woman. She was full of fear for him, he knew. He wanted to tell her not to be afraid, but how could he, knowing he was going to die?

He thanked God for letting him see Sophia one last time.
I love you, Sophia. Remember our joy.

LII

FIGHTING BILLOWS OF TERROR THAT THREATENED TO ENGULF HER,
Sophia pulled her veil aside so that Tilia's servant Cassio could
recognize her. Yawning, Cassio led Sophia and Riccardo into the
large, column-lined reception room and left them. Ugolini's man
threw himself down on a padded bench. Sophia, too agitated to sit
still, unpinned her hooded cloak and dropped it beside Riccardo.
Even though she had just walked halfway across town, she paced
the carpeted floor, twisting her fingers.

Would Tilia be able to help, or would she be as powerless as
Ugolini? This journey across the city might be utterly futile, but
Sophia, unable to sleep and tormented by demon-inspired visions
of what was happening to Daoud, had to do something.

Tilia quickly appeared on the landing of the second floor gallery,
followed by Cassio, who held a candle. Despite her bulk, she
seemed to flow down the stairs in her trailing red silk gown.

"Quickly, tell me what has happened," she said. "For you to
come this late it must be disastroso." Her voice was calm but
hoarse. Her face was puffy and creased with deep wrinkles. She
wore one piece of jewelry, her bishop's cross.

"We had better talk alone," Sophia said. Tilia nodded. Riccardo
was already sitting on a couch in the entry hall with his eyes shut.
Cassio looked inquiringly at Tilia. His shoulder-length black hair,
usually well-combed and glossy, was a nest of unruly locks pointing every which way.

"Give me the candle, Cassio," said Tilia. "Come up to my
room, Sophia. Your escort can wait here." She sighed. "A few
weeks ago there would have been clients waiting in this room even
at this hour. Since the pope left—" She waved a hand at the emp-
tiness of the great chamber.

Sophia felt herself wanting to cling to Tilia, as if the short, fat
woman were her mother. A few months before she had felt nothing

but hatred for the brothelkeeper because she had introduced Rachel into whoredom. Now she prayed only that Tilia could help her.

Her bedroom was cool, the shutters of a large double window having been swung open to let in the night air. Tilia sat on her wide bed, which was covered with embroidered cushions and silk sheets that draped over the four posts. Sophia went to the window and drew back the curtain to look out. The street outside was dark and empty.

What was happening to Daoud in the Palazzo del Podesta? Were they crippling his beautiful body? Was he dying? Dead? She felt like crying at the thought of how they might be hurting him. But she could not help him unless she kept her head.

Sophia quickly told Tilia about Daoud's arrest. Tilia lay back on the bed, her beady eyes fixed on Sophia, and fingered the cross on her ample bosom. Every so often she nodded, as if this were just what she she had expected.

She covered her eyes momentarily with her hand. "May God be kind to Daoud ibn Abdallah. He is worth ten of any ordinary men."

She knows Daoud's Muslim name!

But Sophia had no time to pursue the thought. Tilia had quickly wiped her tears away and turned to Sophia expectantly.

"With Lorenzo away you are the only one who might be able to do something," Sophia said.

"What do you expect of me, if David lets himself be taken away and the cardinal does nothing?" Tilia asked. "Have I more power than they?" Clearly her use of "Daoud" was a momentary indiscretion.

"We need someone who can think," Sophia said, realizing how vague she sounded in her desperation.

"How is Adelberto taking it?" Tilia asked.

"He is almost speechless with terror. He just moans and weeps and wrings his hands. I am afraid he may try to run away, or confess everything or do something equally foolish."

Tilia nodded again, grimly. "He is picturing all the things they will do to him if he is found guilty of conspiring with the enemies of Christendom." She looked at Sophia keenly. "What about you? Are you not afraid for yourself?"

"I am dying of fear."

Tilia reached over and squeezed her hand. "I am frightened too. Who would not be? But you're right—giving way to panic just leaves us helpless. Let us go back to Adelberto's mansion. He is a changeable man. I may be able to get him to think sensibly. I will see what I can do with him."

A wave of relief swept over Sophia. At least she was no longer struggling alone.

Sophia could see a bluish light on the tile roofs of the houses across from Tilia's window. It would soon be morning.

God, they have had Daoud for a whole night! What have they done to him?

"D'Ucello has men watching the cardinal's mansion," Sophia said. "Riccardo and I slipped out through the tunnel that leads under the street to the potterymaker's shop, but we cannot get back in that way."

"Getting there is the easiest part of it," said Tilia. "Cassio will hire a covered cart for us. The hard part will be deciding what to do once we have arrived." She smiled and patted her breasts, accentuated by the gossamer fabric of her sleeping gown. "I must put some clothes on."

"While you dress, can I see Rachel?" Sophia asked. She noticed three ironbound chests, ornamented with circular enameled medallions, standing in a row against the wall beside Tilia's bed. Each was secured with a padlock. They must hold the gold Tilia's customers brought to her.

"I will take you to Rachel," said Tilia. "She is as well and happy as when you saw her last. But do not tell her what has happened to David."

"There is no point in frightening her," Sophia agreed. "But when we leave Orvieto, I want to take her with us."

"Whether you believe it or not, I am looking after her welfare," Tilia said. "Just yesterday, John the Tartar offered me five thousand florins to let him take her to Perugia with him when he follows the pope there. He flew into a rage when I refused him. So, you see, I have even braved the fury of the Tartars for Rachel's sake. Perhaps you will begin to judge me a little more kindly."

Turning to leave the room, Sophia froze momentarily. It had not occurred to her that Tilia would know that she had once hated her. The woman *was* penetrating. She felt a little more confident that Tilia would have the wisdom to help her in this calamity.

Tilia, holding a candle, opened Rachel's door for Sophia. More glittering gold had been added to the girl's bedroom since Sophia had last visited her, and when the candle flame illuminated it, the room seemed to blaze. Sophia blinked at the gold curtains before the windows and the heavy cloth-of-gold draperies surrounding the bed.

All this, she thought, was to impress that horrible Tartar who came here to lie with Rachel. How lucky Sophia had been to be able to share her bed with a man she loved.

But thoughts of happiness with Daoud—memories—were like a knife in her heart, now that he had been taken from her.

Tilia pulled the drape aside, and there was Rachel, curled up nude on top of yellow silk sheets. Her skinny arms and legs made her look even younger than she was. Sophia felt heartsick as Rachel's eyes opened wide at the sudden light. She sat up in bed, dragging the sheet across her body, then drew back against the wall. She looked terrified. Sophia wondered what sort of awakenings Rachel was used to in this place, and a sudden return of her rage at Tilia made her tremble.

Well and happy, is she?

But she dared not be angry with Tilia now. Tilia was the only person who could help her.

Rachel's black eyes fell on Sophia, and the fear went out of her face. It was replaced by a glad smile that hurt Sophia's heart all the more.

I abandoned her to this, and yet she is happy to see me.

"I will leave you two to talk," Tilia said.

Sophia sat on the gold sheets and took Rachel's hand when Tilia was gone. For a moment she forgot her own grief and fear, as an urge to comfort Rachel pushed to the fore.

"All of us are going to be leaving Orvieto soon, and when we do we will take you with us," she said. Rachel's dark eyes glowed.

Sophia went on. "Wherever we go, you will not have to stay with Tilia anymore and do—what Tilia expects of you. We will find a home for you."

She was not sure how she was going to keep such a promise, but she decided that Daoud would have to kill her before she would let him put Rachel in another brothel.

Again the knife in her breast as she remembered she might never see Daoud again.

Rachel shrugged. "I may be better off doing this than I would be as some man's wife." She looked down at her hands, and Sophia saw that her fingers were long and slender and quite beautiful. "John Chagan has made me very rich, you know."

Sophia thought of the three locked chests in Tilia's room. She would have to make sure that Rachel, when she left this place of shame, got all the gold that was rightfully hers. And how outrageous, that Tilia had been filling Rachel's head with lies about how lucky she was.

"Tilia and the others here have to believe that this is the right life for them. But there is not a woman here who would not trade whatever riches she has earned for a real home, with a husband and children.''

Rachel was silent a moment. Her face was all straight lines, Sophia saw, yet delicate and feminine at the same time.

As a woman, she will be much more beautiful than I.

"Even you?" Rachel said suddenly.

Sophia was surprised. "We are not talking about me. I am not—a courtesan.''

"What are you?" Rachel asked softly, shyly.

What word is there to describe me?

She had thought often about other women and how different their lives were from hers. Sometimes, to survive, she had to give her body to men when she did not want to. She had been in danger of death. She had known love and wealth and power. She had lived this way since her parents and the boy she had loved were killed, and she could not imagine living any other way.

"I am just a person who does whatever she needs to," said Sophia. How could she sit here and talk like this, when Daoud might be dying? A chill went over her, as if she were in the grip of a fever, and she almost cried aloud.

"Something is wrong," Rachel said. "Why are you here so early in the morning?" That look of terror was coming back into her face.

The door opened, and Tilia was there, dressed in a long green silk tunic and a yellow satin surcoat. Light was beginning to show through Rachel's windows. Sophia held Rachel's hand for a moment and then let go of it and stood up to leave.

"Take me with you," Rachel said, seizing Sophia's wrist.

"Not now," said Sophia quickly. "We will all be together when we leave Orvieto.''

Rachel's eyes overflowed with tears. "I do not want to stay here. I want to go with you now.''

"What have you been saying to her?" Tilia said angrily.

"Nothing," said Sophia. She turned to Rachel. "See, Madama will be angry with me. She thinks I have been frightening you. Now show her that you are calm and are willing to stay here.''

Rachel's thin shoulders slumped. "As you wish, Signora.''

In the midst of her fear for Daoud, a pang of guilt shot through Sophia. She had upset Rachel and then spoken gruffly to her. She rushed to her and hugged the thin body against hers.

She kissed Rachel quickly and followed Tilia out.

* * *

Sophia followed Tilia through the door of Ugolini's cabinet after Tilia thrust it open without even knocking. Ugolini's eyes bulged at the sight of Tilia, and he threw down his pen.

He was still in a panic, Sophia saw, heartsick. Even if they could come up with a plan to rescue Daoud, would he be willing to do anything?

"Now, of all times, you should not be here," he cried at Tilia.

Without a word Tilia marched across the Syrian carpet, her broad hips swinging under her green gown. She went around Ugolini's desk and held out her arms to him. With a slightly embarrassed glance at Sophia, he stood up—he was the same height as Tilia— and let her take him into her arms. He leaned his head on her shoulder for a moment, then handed her into his chair.

They really are lovers, thought Sophia, seeing the little cardinal's sudden wistful smile. The sight of that smile gave her new hope. Perhaps Tilia could restore his courage. Only Ugolini had the power and authority to do anything about Daoud's imprisonment. Tilia had to bring him back to himself.

"Did you not want me to know, Adelberto, what happened to David?" she demanded, looking down at the parchment he had been writing on. "What is this?"

"I am calculating my horoscope for this day. The stars are telling me I have overreached myself and have only myself to blame for my downfall."

"For your downfall? Dear God, Adelberto, have you given up hope already?"

His words dimmed Sophia's hopes. He believed in his stars.

Ugolini, dressed in a white gown tied at the waist with a cord, walked to the half-open windows and pulled the violet drapes across them, darkening the room. A breeze made the drapes billow inward and blew out the flame of the candle on his desk, plunging the room into a deeper darkness. Unbidden, Sophia picked up a wax taper from Ugolini's worktable, igniting it from the fat, hour-marked candle in the corner away from the window, and went lighting candles in the candelabra around the room. Talking in the dark would only drive their spirits lower.

If only Lorenzo were here. He would have a plan by now, and be doing something about it.

Ugolini held out his hands to Tilia. "I am doomed, and I do not want you dragged down with me." He turned to Sophia, whiskers bristling over his grimace. "You should have left her out of this."

If I had left her out of it, there would be no hope at all, Sophia thought, sitting on the small chair facing Ugolini's worktable. She looked with appeal at Tilia, who nodded reassuringly.

"Tilia needs just as much as any of us to know what is happening," said Sophia. "And you need to talk to her." Ugolini's hands were trembling, she saw. She, too, was afraid, both for herself and Daoud. Fear was a black hollow eating away at her insides.

Oh, Daoud, what are they doing to you?

He might come out of the Palazzo del Podesta blind, or with arms or legs cut off, or mad, she thought. When she saw him again, she might wish him dead—and herself along with him.

She wiped the cold sweat from her brow with the hem of her silk cloak. In the heavy, hot air, the scent of Tilia's rose-petal sachet filled the room.

"Only a miracle can save us," said Ugolini, pacing and waving his hands. "I have been praying to God that He take the soul of David of Trebizond before he breaks under torture and dooms us all."

Sophia reeled with the pain his words brought her. She wanted to claw Ugolini's eyes out. She sprang up from her chair, fists clenched.

"May God take *your* soul!" she screamed at him. "And send you straight to hell!"

Ugolini turned and stared at her as if she had struck him.

"Be still, Sophia," said Tilia quietly. "That will not help."

Panting heavily, Sophia sat down again. They needed Ugolini so badly, and he was so *useless*. She wanted to weep with frustration.

"Of course God will damn me," Ugolini cried, throwing his arms into the air as he paced the room, his white gown rippling. "Why should He spare me or any of us, when we have been working against His Church?"

It is not my Church, thought Sophia resentfully. *It is the schismatic Latin Church he speaks of.* Remembering that she was probably the only person of her faith in Orvieto, she felt terribly alone.

Almost as alone as Daoud must feel.

"It seems that you no longer know who you are," said Tilia sourly to Ugolini.

"Eh? What do you mean?" He turned quickly and peered at her.

She talks to him as if she were his nursemaid, Sophia thought. *And that is what he needs.*

"You are one of twenty-two men who *rule* the Church," said Tilia firmly. "You will elect the next pope, and very soon, by all signs. You are not a citizen of Orvieto, subject to this podesta."

She spat the word. "You are one of the most powerful men in Italy."

"I am the creature of the Sultan of Egypt, and soon the whole world will know it," Ugolini moaned. "Oh, God, how I wish you had never come to me with his bribes."

So it was Tilia who had recruited Ugolini for this work. There were depths to this woman. If anyone could have an effect on Ugolini now, she could. But Sophia wondered if even Tilia could reach the cardinal in his present state.

"Are you sorry you met me, Adelberto?" said Tilia softly.

"No, no!" said Ugolini hastily.

He rushed over to where she sat at his table and put his hands on her shoulders.

"Without you," he said earnestly, "my life would have been flat and empty."

Love, thought Sophia. *He loves her. That might make the difference.*

"And I helped you become wealthier than you ever dreamed possible. I helped you buy the red hat."

"True," said Ugolini. "But Fortune raises men high only so they may fall farther when she casts them down."

Tilia brought her large hand down hard on Ugolini's marble-topped table. "Enough of this talk of the stars and Fortune. Look here, Adelberto, for this little *cimice,* this bedbug of a man, d'Ucello, to walk into the house of Cardinal Ugolini and arrest one of his guests—it is insufferable! You must not permit it."

Sophia did not dare to breathe as she watched Ugolini's face for a sign of returning strength.

"No doubt you are right," said Ugolini, nodding slowly like a boy being taught his lessons.

"You must bring pressure to bear on this man," Tilia went on. "With most of the cardinals following the pope to Perugia, you are now even more important in Orvieto."

Thank God for Tilia. At this moment Sophia was willing to forgive Tilia even the corrupting of Rachel.

Ugolini said, "Yes, but if last night I could not stop him from taking David, what can I do now?" He spread his empty hands.

Another gust of wind lifted the purple drapes and sent scraps of parchment from Ugolini's table to the carpet. Sophia saw circles and triangles and whole constellations flying across the room.

They would have to enlist the aid of someone who had influence over the podesta, Sophia thought, someone who was friendly enough to Ugolini to be willing to speak on his behalf. With the pope gone, the most powerful person in the city was—

As soon as the thought came to her, she spoke. "The Contessa di Monaldeschi. Cardinal, you must go to her and ask her help."

Her heart rose to her throat, choking her. Tilia and Ugolini stared at her. Would they listen? Would they spurn her idea?

"Why should *she* help me?" said Ugolini.

"She admires you," said Sophia. "She told me so the night of the reception she gave for the Tartars. Now that the pope has left Orvieto, she probably feels neglected."

Wide-eyed, Ugolini shook his head. "But David is accused of involvement in the attack on her palace. Just yesterday I saw her cackling like a strega while her men chopped off Marco di Filippeschi's head and murdered half his family. They even impaled a baby on a spear, and she shouted with glee."

"That has nothing to do with us," said Sophia, though the image revolted her. "She has no reason to connect David with the Filippeschi."

Tilia nodded vigorously, shaking her body and the chair she was sitting in. "Sophia has an excellent idea, Adelberto. If the Contessa di Monaldeschi pleads for David, if *she*, the injured party, is convinced of his innocence, the podesta must yield."

Sophia felt more confident as she saw that Tilia was on her side. She pressed the attack.

"Again and again d'Ucello has shown that he does whatever the Monaldeschi expect of him," she urged.

"He used to do whatever *either* family expected of him," said Ugolini. "Until so many Filippeschi perished that they ceased to matter."

Ugolini went to the window. A blast of hot, damp wind roared into the room, and he raised his hand protectively in front of his face.

"It will storm soon," said Tilia. "It cannot be soon enough to suit me. A storm will break this terrible heat. As soon as the storm passes, you must go to her."

Ugolini nodded slowly. "If I fail to convince her, I will be no worse off than I am now."

"You will convince her," said Tilia. "You might as well start to put on your red robes."

Real hope sailed across the sea of terror to Sophia now, and it was a galley, a galley with sails painted a cardinal's red. She felt it bearing her up over her dread for Daoud and for herself.

"I will go to the contessa with you," said Sophia. If he gave way to panic again, she could stop him from doing too much damage.

"And I will return to my house," said Tilia, standing up.

"No," said Ugolini. "It was dangerous enough for you to come here. We know this mansion is being watched. Stay here until nightfall."

Tilia smiled, went to him, and held his small, pointed face between her hands. "I will stay. And if you succeed in persuading the contessa to have David freed, we will have something to celebrate, you and I."

To celebrate! What a wonderful thought. Sophia had begun to feel she would never celebrate anything again.

But moving Ugolini to act was only the first step, she reminded herself. The contessa might prove to be against them, and Daoud might still be doomed.

Sophia watched, eaten up by anxiety, as the Contessa di Monaldeschi advanced slowly into her smaller audience chamber, leaning on her grandnephew, a plump boy in red velvet.

"I hope you have not come to scold me, Cardinal Ugolini," the contessa rasped.

Could this old woman really have laughed to see a baby impaled on a spear, Sophia wondered as she and Ugolini bowed.

"Dear Contessa, scold you?" Ugolini said with a chuckle. "Whatever for?" Sophia was delighted to see how completely he had, to all outward appearances, cast off the terror that gripped him a short time before.

Like all of us, when terror strikes, he needs to feel he can do something.

"Ah, Cardinal. Surely you know." When she reached Ugolini, the tall, bony old woman clutched at the boy's arm with both clawlike hands and began, with an effort that made her compress her withered lips, to lower herself to the floor. It hurt Sophia just to watch her struggle to genuflect before the cardinal.

The contessa had aged a great deal, Sophia thought, since she first saw her, over a year ago. She was thinner, more bent, moved with much greater difficulty. Ugolini reached out to try to stop her from kneeling.

"Please, Dona Elvira!" he cried. "Do not trouble yourself so."

"No, I am a good daughter of the Church," said the contessa. "And through you I pay homage to God."

The old woman's maroon satin gown crackled as she bent her knees. Even kneeling, she was almost as tall as Ugolini. Gold bracelets rattled around her skinny arms, and heavy medallions dangled from gold chains around her neck. A net of gold threads held the coiled braids of her white hair in place.

Once she was on her knees, her grandnephew pulled off his red cap and bowed to Ugolini with a sweeping gesture. His hair was a mass of tight black curls. Had he, too, watched the massacre of the Filippeschi, Sophia wondered. And what had that done to the boy?

"Please let me kiss your ring," the contessa said. She seized his hand and planted a loud, smacking kiss on his sapphire cardinal's ring.

"It is I who should pay homage to you, Dona Elvira," said Ugolini.

Sophia immediately stepped forward to help the contessa struggle to her feet. The boy took the old lady from the other side. Sophia caught a glimpse of him looking at her with bright, amused eyes. Eyes that were too old for the face of an eleven-year-old boy.

When she got close to the contessa, Sophia smelled an odor that made her think of a damp cellar. Together Sophia and the Monaldeschi heir walked with the old lady to a broad-armed chair, where she settled herself, gasping. Two manservants set smaller chairs for the cardinal and Sophia facing the contessa.

The contessa's grandnephew leaned elegantly against the back of the old lady's chair, the fingers of his chubby hands interlinked. Sophia glanced at him and caught his glittering eyes roving over her body. He saw her looking at him, and smiled faintly and without embarrassment.

Contessa Elvira raised a trembling hand. "Cardinal Piacenza had been most unkind. I had a letter from him this morning condemning me in the rudest terms for our triumph over the Filippeschi canaglia yesterday in the Piazza San Giovenale. He accused me of sacrilege, because I shed the blood of Marco during a Mass. When else could I have taken him and his foul brood unawares? God gave me the opportunity."

"Nothing happens save by the will of God," Ugolini murmured.

"Esattamente! Yet Cardinal Piacenza has the audacity to tell me that I am in a grave state of sin and that I have led Vittorio here into sin as well."

Glancing again at Vittorio, Sophia noticed the sword, short enough for a boy but long enough to kill, that hung from his jeweled belt.

Ugolini shook his head. "No one has the right to say that another is in sin. Only God sees the soul. *Judge not, lest ye be judged.*"

Sophia found it hard to believe that this was the same man whose panic she had struggled to overcome a few hours earlier. He was suddenly the perfect clergyman, attentive, sympathetic, sententious.

"Yes, and for what should I be judged?" The contessa lifted both hands now. "For exacting justice?"

"If you have any doubts, dear Madama," Ugolini said, "I will be happy to give you absolution."

That was a nice touch, thought Sophia. If she confessed to him, that would certainly put her under his influence.

But even as they talked, across town the podesta's men might be tearing Daoud's body to pieces. Sophia felt her stomach knot. She shook her head as vigorously as she dared, to drive away the hideous images without attracting attention to herself.

Hurry! Dear God, make them hurry!

"I *have* no doubts," said the old lady firmly. "Besides, I have my own chaplain. I would not wish another person on earth to know me as well as he does. But I do thank you for your kind thought, Cardinal. I am glad to see that not all the princes of the church think alike in this matter."

"I am sure Cardinal Piacenza is quite alone," said Ugolini.

The contessa shrugged. "I do not know about that. Since His Holiness left, no one has called on me. I have been feeling quite abandoned."

Now Sophia began to feel a stronger hope than ever. The old lady liked to be flattered by princes of the Church. Perhaps she could be won over after all.

"Surely your guest, Cardinal de Verceuil, attends you often," Ugolini ventured.

The contessa sniffed. "That Frenchman. He is no more civilized than his Tartars. I would rather he left me alone. The French are all rather barbaric. Of course, that fine young Simon de Gobignon— he is most attractive." She grinned with a lasciviousness that startled Sophia. "This palace has not been the same since he went back to France."

"Back to France?" Ugolini stared. "I thought he, too, was going to Perugia."

Sophia felt a ball of ice suddenly encase her heart. She had told Ugolini, as she told Daoud, that Simon was going to Perugia. She prayed Ugolini would not suspect that she had been lying.

"Oh, no," said the contessa. "France. He told me himself when he took leave of me. And when he returns, I think Ghibellini everywhere in Italy will have reason to tremble. Because the might of France will follow him. I am only sorry he will not come in time to save Orvieto from the Sienese. One of my sergentes just reported that the Sienese army is but a day or two away from here.''

And Lorenzo with it, thought Sophia. *If only he would hurry.*

"What will you do, Contessa?" Ugolini asked. "As a Guelfo family, do the Monaldeschi intend to leave Orvieto before the Sienese arrive?"

He was straying from the subject, thought Sophia impatiently.

Never mind the damned Sienese army. They cannot do us any good.

The old lady tossed her head, her hooked nose jutting defiantly. She laid her hand on Vittorio's.

"We will stand fast. This family has lived in this city since the days of the Etruscans. I expect our militia to put up a good fight. After our honor has been satisfied, we will ask, with dignity, for terms."

"Very brave," said Ugolini.

The militia of Orvieto, thought Sophia, was under the command of the podesta. If d'Ucello was involved in fighting the Sienese, what might that mean for Daoud?

Dona Elvira looked at the cardinal slyly. "Are you also staying in Orvieto, Your Eminence?"

"For the moment," said Ugolini.

Sophia was surprised that Ugolini did not say more, but the conversation seemed to be going the way he wanted it to.

"You may be able to help us, Your Eminence."

Sophia felt more elated than ever. If she wanted help from Ugolini, then surely she would be willing to help him.

"Nothing would please me more, Contessa."

"You are from the south, from Manfred's kingdom. You might have some influence with these Ghibellini. Perhaps a word from you would help to keep our house and our property intact."

Ugolini threw out his arms. "Dear Contessa, anything. Of course, as a loyal supporter of the pope I do not ordinarily have dealings with Ghibellini."

"Of course not," the contessa agreed. Vittorio smiled. He had a small, chiseled mouth, such as Sophia had seen on the men in ancient Roman sculptures.

"But whatever little I might be able to do, I am entirely at your service," Ugolini said.

"I have always considered you my very good friend, Your Eminence. Even though you opposed the alliance of Christians and Tartars and they were my houseguests."

That startled Sophia. The contessa made it sound as if the Tartars had left her home.

"*Were* your houseguests, Madama?" Ugolini asked. So, he had noticed it too.

She sighed. "Yes, they and that boorish French cardinal left for Perugia this morning, not long before you came. They chose a bad day to leave. This morning's storm is not the end of the rain. Another storm is coming. Every joint in my body aches."

"These storms clear the air," said Ugolini.

The contessa held up a sticklike finger. "Exactly as the storm yesterday in the Piazza San Giovenale did."

Now she was bringing up her grievance, Sophia thought. Evidently she had offended a number of cardinals with the massacre of the Filippeschi.

A servant brought a small table of some shiny black wood and set it in their midst. Its legs were carved in the form of twisting, wingless dragons. Perhaps it was a gift to the contessa from the Tartars. Sophia had seen such furnishings in Constantinople and knew they came from the distant East, where the Tartars ruled.

Another servant brought a tray with small sweet cakes filled with a paste made of crushed white raisins. A third poured the pale yellow wine of Orvieto into silver goblets for them. Sophia sipped her wine, but her stomach churned with fear for Daoud, a fear held rigidly in check. She could not drink much, and she could not eat at all.

Every so often she glanced at Vittorio di Monaldeschi, and each time she did, she found his eyes fixed on her.

Ugolini wiped his mouth after finishing off a cake. "As Fortune's wheel turns, all of us need friends at one time or another."

"How true," said the old lady.

"I come before you today to presume upon our friendship to ask you a favor, Madama," said Ugolini.

"We need each other, as you have said, Your Eminence."

Sophia prayed that the contessa would agree to help.

Ugolini told how the podesta's men had arrested Daoud the previous night. Sophia watched the contessa's face for some sign of sympathy, but the old lady remained as expressionless as a bird.

"I am shocked that the podesta would arrest your houseguest," she said. "But what can I do? After all, Signore d'Ucello holds the office because he has our confidence."

Which means that he stands aside while you murder your enemies.

Ugolini spread his hands. "Precisely because he has your confidence, dear Madonna, I know he will listen to you. We have had no word of what has become of our guest and friend."

"I want *everyone* punished who had anything to do with the attack on my palace," said the contessa, clenching her bony fist.

And what if the contessa were to discover that the man they were talking about had incited that attack and used it as cover for his own attempt to murder the Tartar ambassadors, Sophia thought. She would want him torn to bits in the piazza. New waves of terror washed over her.

And she would want those who helped him punished along with him. Sophia glanced at Ugolini and saw that he was sweating.

Dear God, do not let him falter now.

"Of course, Contessa," he said. "That is why I have come to you. Because you, and not the podesta, are the one truly injured. But the arrest of David is a terrible mistake. I place before you my belief in this man's absolute innocence. I am prepared to swear to it. He was not even here in Orvieto when that dastardly attack occurred. He was in Perugia. There are countless witnesses. I know this man. He is a *good* man, a merchant, not a warrior."

"I remember him," said the contessa. "A very good-looking blond man. I heard his conversation with the Tartars and I began to wonder myself about the wisdom of allying ourselves with them."

"It is probably because David did testify against the Tartars that the podesta thinks he might be connected with the attack on your palace," said Ugolini. "But such a man as David would have nothing to do with such mascalzoni as the Filippeschi. I, too, have opposed the alliance, and yet you and I are friends. It is one thing to disagree in a civilized way. It is another to turn to behave like a scoundrel. David has the same horror of murder that we all do."

Remembering what she had heard about the killings in the cathedral plaza, Sophia wondered if the contessa had any horror of murder at all.

"I am sure that is true," said the contessa. "But the podesta must have good reason for detaining this David."

Despair overwhelmed Sophia. The tears that had been falling in her soul sprang to her eyelids and began to run down her cheeks. She should not show her feelings like this, she thought. But what did it matter, when Daoud was dying and no one would lift a hand to save him?

"Why are you crying, child?" said the contessa. Sophia heard sympathy in her voice.

"Forgive me, Contessa," she said, sobbing. "This is very rude of me."

"Does this man mean so much to you?" asked the old lady, her rasping voice softened.

In her anguish, Sophia was still clear-headed enough to see that she might use that anguish. She threw herself down on the terrazzo floor and clasped the contessa around the knees.

"Sophia!" She could hear Ugolini's chair scrape as he stood up. The boy took a step toward her.

"It is all right," said the contessa. "You love this man, do you not?" She patted Sophia's hair.

"Yes," Sophia wept. "And I swear to you, he is innocent."

He is, too, because he believes that everything he is doing is right.

"Your Eminence?" said the contessa. "You approve of your niece and this man from Trebizond?"

"Oh, certainly," said Ugolini waving his hands. "He is a fine man."

"Hmm," said the old lady. "That night at my reception I thought you and the young Count de Gobignon were attracted to each other."

Sophia felt a strange stab of guilt.

"Oh, he is too far above me, Contessa," she said. "A count. David is a merchant. We are right for each other."

It is true that David and I are much more suited than Simon and I.

"It makes me feel young for a moment to see a beautiful woman in love." The contessa stroked Sophia's cheek with dry, rough fingers.

Sophia opened her eyes wide and looked the contessa full in the face. "Please help us, Contessa, for the sake of love."

The contessa sighed and smiled. "I will send for d'Ucello. I will request that he stop questioning your friend." She looked across at Ugolini. "You must give me your word, Your Eminence, that this David will not leave Orvieto until all doubts about him are settled."

"Oh, thank you, thank you!" Sophia kissed the shiny knuckles, wetting the blue-veined hand with her tears.

"Sophia, stand up," said Ugolini, touching her shoulder. "This is embarrassing."

Vittorio helped her to her feet, holding her waist more tightly than was necessary.

Embarrassing? If not for my outburst, there would be no hope of freeing Daoud.

But I must live in terror awhile longer. Until I know he is well. That they have not done anything to him. Oh, God, let him come back to me healthy and whole.

LIII

RACHEL SAT ON A DIVAN BY THE WINDOW IN HER ROOM. SHE HAD drawn the curtains back and pushed the shutters open so that she could see out and feel the cool breeze. She held a small leather-bound book in her hand, *Geography of the World*, by Yucaf ibn Faruzi, a Spanish Jew. It was one of the small store of books Angelo had owned, written in Hebrew, that she had kept with her to help her pass the long hours she spent alone. Besides enjoying reading, she felt she was somehow pleasing Angelo, who had taught her to read Hebrew.

She was reading about Egypt when the second storm of the morning struck Orvieto and the window no longer admitted enough light to read by. A few water droplets blew in through the open window to fall on the open pages. She carefully blotted them up with the hem of her satin robe, but she was afraid more rain would damage the vellum pages. So she shut the book, and watched the lightning flash and listened to the thunder.

Tilia's house was built halfway down an incline, so Sophia could see water foaming in the ditch that ran through the center of the street. So heavy was the rain that waves were flowing down the cobblestones. Where a raindrop struck the water, the splash was like a little crown.

A dark shadow appeared at the high end of the street, a hooded figure. Another followed, and another. They rose higher and higher, until she could see that they were riding horses. What were men doing out in a storm like this? Were they coming here?

They were. The first men reined up their horses outside Tilia's front door, dismounted, and moved to the shelter of the overhanging houses across the street. More men on horses, some on mules, and many more on foot, gathered outside the house. All wore hoods or broad-brimmed hats to keep the rain from their heads. Rachel's heart began to thud in her chest when she saw there were too many for her to count. She saw the gleam of helmets under some of the hoods, the wet glitter of mail when an arm or leg emerged from a cloak. A train of mules carrying heavy packs came down the street and stopped.

Rachel began to tremble. These men had not come for pleasure. There were too many of them, and their dress and manner was full of menace. She was glad that the heavy rain forced them to keep their heads down; otherwise, one of them might have looked up here and seen her. She drew back a little from the window.

A line of covered carts drawn by pairs of mules pulled up behind the crowd of armed men. The cart in the lead was bright yellow and red, and its paint glistened wetly.

Did anyone else in the house know this crowd was out there? Perhaps no one else was looking out a window. She ran to the door of her room, just as she heard a pounding from below.

Then there were shouts, bangs, and crashes, the shrill shattering of glass and porcelain, the heavy thumps of bodies falling. Rachel opened her door. Other doors swung open along the shadowy third-floor corridor. Someone stepped out with a candle. Frightened women's faces were white in the candlelight. She saw Antonia, Angela, Gloria.

She did not see Tilia. She must still be with Sophia, wherever they had gone this morning.

Oh, if only Sophia had taken me with her as I begged her to. I knew something terrible was going to happen.

"What is it?" the women cried to one another. "Who is down there? Wounds of Jesus!"

Cassio emerged from Francesca's room, tying the drawstring of his hose. He was a big man, his bare chest matted with black hair, and the sight of him comforted Rachel until she looked into his face as he hurried past her and saw that it was tight and pale with fear. And he was carrying a naked shortsword.

But Cassio's appearance emboldened the women, and they left their rooms to crowd toward the top of the stairs that led to the lower floors. Rachel joined them.

"I saw a lot of men outside," Rachel told the others, her heart battering against her breastbone. "Armed men, with horses and mules and wagons."

Antonia, a round-faced woman, hair dyed red with henna, pulled her robe around her. "Another party setting out for Perugia, I suppose. They probably stopped by for a little farewell fun."

"Then why are they fighting downstairs?" Francesca said, anxiety sharpening her voice.

Thunder shook the house, drowning out the clamor of the brawling two stories below. Then Rachel heard the clang of steel and Cassio's voice crying out angrily.

The carpeted stairs at the end of the corridor shook under heavy feet. Women's screams, mingled with the cries of men, arose on the lower floors. She pushed her way to the head of the stairs and looked down.

A group of men were coming up. They had thrown back the hoods of their brown cloaks, and their pointed helmets reflected the candlelight. Rachel backed away as she saw that the half-dozen men with helmets were brandishing long broad-bladed daggers.

The women around her started screaming and darting back into their rooms. Rachel bolted for her own room.

"Rei-cho!" The man's shrill cry shot an arrow of terror through her. That was John's voice.

She turned in the doorway of her room and saw the Tartar standing at the head of the stairs, his soft black cap hiding most of his white hair. Beside him was a stocky, middle-aged woman, and flanking them were the swarthy men with their daggers. John and the other men were all smiling, as if, as Antonia had said, they had come only for a bit of pleasure. But the tumult downstairs, shaking the house more than the thunder, belied that.

John spoke to the woman and she called to Rachel. "Signore John must go to Perugia." Her Italian was strangely accented. "He wishes you to come with him. He will give you many costly gifts."

Rachel took a step backward into her room. "No. I do not want to go."

Not now. Not when Sophia had just come to tell her they were going to take her south with them. South to Manfred's kingdom, where Jews were treated like everyone else. Where she might yet find a place for herself and forget that she had sold her body.

John and the woman advanced down the corridor, their guards with them. Some of the swarthy men pushed open the doors of the rooms they passed and looked in. The doors could not be barred from the inside. Tilia had always insisted on that, so no client could lock himself in with a woman and harm her. The men with the daggers grinned at one another and talked in a strange language.

"No, I don't want to go!" Rachel screamed. She darted into her room and slammed the door. Frantically, she looked around for something to hold it shut.

The door started to open, and she threw herself against it. It closed for a moment. Then she was hurled away from it as it swung inward, John behind it. She screamed in fear.

The Tartar, who was not much taller than Rachel, strode into the room. He walked with what appeared to be a swagger because he was slightly bowlegged. He was talking rapidly in his language, advancing on Rachel and smiling. He held out his arms. The stout woman stood in the doorway, watching without expression.

Rachel backed away from them, her body rigid.

"You must come with him now. He is in a great hurry. An army of the pope's enemies is less that a day from Orvieto, and they want to take Signore John and Signore Philip prisoner."

"Then let him escape," Rachel cried. "I do not want to go with him." She was standing before her bed now. The woman spoke to John and he answered quickly, still smiling.

"He says you are precious to him and he cannot leave you," she said tonelessly.

She had to get away now, or be John's prisoner for the rest of her life.

Panting more from fury than from exertion, Rachel made a sudden jump to her right, and when John stepped in that direction to grab her, she darted to the left and ran out the door. John's translator made no effort to stop her.

That would not have fooled him, except that he was not expecting me to do anything, she thought as she ran down the corridor.

She held one thought in her mind—she must get out of this building. She heard screams and sounds of struggle from the rooms of the other women. She saw Francesca fighting with a helmeted man, and her eyes met Francesca's over the man's brown-cloaked shoulder. Only one of the dagger-wielding men was in the corridor now, and she had surprised him. He shouted at her and ran after her.

Gathering up the skirt of her robe, she raced down the stairs, taking the last four in a leap. The dark man with the dagger was right behind her, and behind him she could hear John's shout. There was anger in the Tartar's voice now. That terrified her even more.

He did not think I would get away from him this easily.

The dark man grabbed her flying robe, and she felt the silk tear. She had nothing on underneath the robe. She would not let that stop her from running. She must not let anything stop her.

She heard the man behind her calling as she ran down the stairs to the first floor. She was in the corridor now, and she saw that it was swarming with men in helmets and mail, struggling with Tilia's women. Some of the men had their breeches down.

She saw tall, beautiful Maiga striking out with her fists at the helmeted men. But they were wrestling with her and forcing her onto her back. Agonized pity for Maiga blazed up within her, but she ran on.

One of Tilia's black African servants was lying on the floor across the corridor. His eyes were open and he was not moving. Again she felt a surge of pity.

But then terror gripped her.

They are killing people here! My God, what are they doing, what are they doing?

Instead of going on down the stairs from the first floor gallery to the ground floor, she leapt over the body of the black man and ran into the crowd of men and women struggling in the hall.

I am small and I am quick, she thought, and that gave her the courage to keep running. The men in the hall were not interested in her, and she slithered past them while John and his bodyguard stumbled along behind.

The bodyguard's voice sounded far away. Other men were shouting at him.

"Catch her yourself, you damned Armenian ape!" These men were speaking in Italian. "We've already got ours."

Rachel reached the stairs at the other end of the corridor. They led down to the same place as did the main stairs, the reception room on the ground floor. But her pursuers would not know that. Sure enough, they were following her through this first-floor corridor. She glanced back and saw that the crowd of Italian men had gotten in their way, so that half the corridor was between them.

Run, Rachel!

Frantically she ran down to the first floor. There, horror greeted her. More of Tilia's black men—she could not count—were sprawled around the reception hall.

She saw blood spattered over the frescoes. She saw a black arm lying by itself. One body had no head. She heard a scream of horror and knew it was her own voice. Why were they doing this? What devils drove them? There was blood all over the floor. Puddles of it. She had to dart around them, over them.

Terror streaked through her as a tall man blocked her path. His hood was thrown back and his cloak was open, and a jeweled cross glittered on his chest—like the one Tilia wore, only three times bigger. Their eyes met; his were staring and full of rage. His nose was big, and his mouth was small and cruel. He pointed a long finger at her, a fortune in jeweled rings glittering on his gloved hand.

"You! The one we came for! Stop!"

She stood paralyzed as a recollection of the dread face before her flashed into her mind. Dinners for John and Philip—Tilia had given elegant dinners, three or four of them—with musicians and the companionship of her ladies, Rachel included.

And this was how they repaid her courtesy.

This man had been a guest at those dinners. He was a man of very high rank, a cardinal in the Christian church. He was French, she remembered. His Italian words were heavily accented.

What will they do to me if I don't obey him? Will they burn me for being a Jew?

And there was the other Tartar, Philip, standing beside the French churchman. He looked like John—round head, brown skin, slitted eyes—except that his beard and mustache were black. He was carrying a bow in one hand and had a quiver full of arrows slung over one shoulder. Rachel froze, like a rabbit trapped by two wolves.

The tall Frenchman reached for Rachel—but another figure appeared between them, one of Tilia's black men. He blocked the tall man with the cross, giving Rachel a chance to jump for the door.

Out of the corner of her eye Rachel saw Philip, strong white teeth gleaming in a brown face, raise his bow. She heard the thrum of the string, and then a piercing scream. Anguish for the black man welled up in her.

Her torn robe was flapping as she ran out the door. She almost fell as someone seized the back of her robe and yanked on it. She twisted out of the robe and ran on, naked.

She heard John's shrill voice. He had reached the ground floor.

She was out of the house. In an instant her bare body was rain-wet from head to toe.

A group of big men holding horses stood across the street, under the overhang of the house opposite Tilia's. They were wearing swords and purple surcoats over mail shirts. They looked at her gloomily and made no move to stop her.

She had no idea where to go, but downhill was the easiest direction. Maybe hide in an alley. Knock on a door and beg for help. Try to get across town to Sophia.

Anywhere, if only she could get away from John.

Many times she had nightmares of running from something that was trying to kill her. Sometimes a monster or a demon. Sometimes from crowds of roaring people carrying torches. Always in those dreams she could not make her legs move. It was like trying to run through water. Always she tried to scream for help and no sound would come from her throat but a whisper.

Now she was able to run full speed away from that house where death and destruction were running riot. And running as fast as she could was not enough! It would not get her away fast enough from John and his armed men and that horrible cardinal. She was able to scream at the top of her lungs, but to no avail. Nobody would come to rescue her. Nobody would help her.

She had also had nightmares about running through the street naked, with hundreds of people watching. In those dreams she had been horribly embarrassed. Now she was really doing it, and she did not care about her nakedness.

She darted past the carts and the horses and mules and their drivers that filled the street from side to side. She was running naked and barefoot over the cobblestones.

She ran past the red and yellow cart at the head of the line of wagons and saw sitting beside the driver a man with a full white beard. He was looking down at her. For a moment she thought he was a rabbi. Then she saw his shaven scalp and brown robe. One of those Christian begging monks. He opened his mouth to say something to her, but she was past him already.

She heard hoofbeats behind her, and gooseflesh broke out all over her naked body.

Dear God, is he chasing me on horseback?

But she could dart into a quintana, the space between two houses. It would be too narrow for a man on horseback to follow her. She saw an opening on her left and made for it, begging God to help her run faster.

She felt something whip around her body, tearing her skin. She was jerked off her feet. She fell on her back on the wet cobblestones. She lay helpless, stunned and gasping for air. A rope was cutting into her chest just below her breasts, pinning her arms above the elbows to her sides. The rope burned her. Her back felt scraped and bruised. She saw a horse's legs beside her. John was grinning down at her, holding the other end of the rope. The rain pouring down in her face stung her eyes.

Now that she knew she was caught and helpless, her terror was transmuted into rage. What right had he to treat her this way?

"May God strike you dead!" she spat. He might not know the words, but she was sure he could hear the hatred in her voice.

He tugged on the rope to make her climb to her feet. She felt she would rather lie there and make him drag her, if he wanted her so badly, but she realized that would only hurt her worse.

She took a grip on the rope to haul herself up. The cold rain beat down, plastering her hair to her head. She wanted to wipe her face, but her arms were pinioned. Her back felt as if it were on fire.

She looked at Tilia's house and saw that a man's body was swinging, sodden and limp, above the door.

Her stomach turning at the sight, she recognized Cassio's features in the swollen, blackened face. They had hanged him from Tilia's crenellated balcony. And she had always thought he was such a big, tough man. She felt a stab of pity for him, even though he had never been especially nice to her.

Her heart grew heavier and colder in her chest as the horror sank in. These men had destroyed Tilia's house, killed the men and raped the women with the gleeful cruelty of small boys stoning a bird's nest.

Another jerk on the rope started her walking back up the street. She kept her eyes down to avoid the sight of Cassio's body.

As they passed the yellow cart, a voice called out to the Tartar, and he answered briefly in what seemed to be his own language. Again the voice, and there was command in the tone. John reined his horse to a stop.

Apprehension filled her. What new indignity would she have to suffer?

Very slowly, the brown-robed Christian priest climbed down from the cart. He pulled his hood up against the rain. Rachel put one hand between her legs and tried to cover her breasts with her forearm, lest he be offended. Fear and the cold rain beating down on her naked flesh made her shiver violently. She could not hope for kindness from this white-bearded man. After all, as a priest he must condemn her as a harlot. And if he found out she was a Jew, he would despise her all the more.

The priest reached up into the cart and took down a long walking staff and a gray blanket. Leaning on the staff, he approached her slowly. Looking at her very sadly, unconcerned about the rain soaking his robe, he draped the blanket over her head and shoulders. She gripped the edges of the blanket and pulled it across her. As long as John's rope stayed slack, the blanket would cover her, although it was already cold and heavy with rainwater.

The kindness in the seamed, bearded face warmed Rachel, and she dropped to her knees before him.

"Help me, Father," she begged. "Do not let him take me away from here."

"Get up, child." Leaning heavily on the staff with one hand, he used the other to help her to her feet, and she saw how stiffly he moved and heard him give a little groan of pain.

"You are hurt, Father."

"Just a few old broken bones," he said. "It has been months, and they are mending well enough."

He reached under the blanket that covered her, and she shrank away from his hand.

"Forgive me," he said. "I mean no harm." Without looking at her, and hardly touching her, he managed to loosen the rope around her chest so that it fell to the ground. She stepped out of the loop, and it slid away from her. She looked up and saw John coil the rope and tie it to his saddle. His face was reddened and his mouth compressed with anger.

"It is useless to try to outrun a Tartar on horseback," said the priest. "They are like centaurs. What is your name, child?"

As she told him, Rachel felt a glimmering of hope. The priest had spoken to John in his own language, and the Tartar seemed to have some respect for him. At least he was no longer trying to drag her away.

"I am Friar Mathieu d'Alcon," said the white-bearded priest. "What does this man want with you?"

Rachel felt a blush burn her face.

"He has lain with me, and he paid money to me and Madama Tilia," Rachel said, barely able to choke out the admission of her shame. "Now he is leaving Orvieto, and he wants to take me with him."

Friar Mathieu sighed and shook his head. "And so young. Jesus, be merciful." He turned to John and spoke to him in a soft, reasonable voice. Rachel sensed that the priest was chiding the Tartar gently. John's answer was a series of short phrases, shrill with anger. He finished by slicing the air with his hand in a gesture of flat refusal. Rachel's heart grew heavy with despair.

"He will not listen to me," said the friar. "He thinks he has a right to take you. His customs are not ours."

"But you are a priest. Does he not have to do what you tell him?"

"Sometimes he does what I tell him to, because he *is* a Christian, and I have been his companion and confessor for some years. But he is more Tartar than Christian, and Tartars keep many women."

Rachel's limbs turned to ice. "Does he think he owns me?"

Colder than the rain pouring down on her was the terror of being torn from the few friends she had, to be used for pleasure by a man who could not even speak to her. She put her hands to her face and started to sob heavily.

A burst of loud laughter from John made her look up. At first she thought he was laughing at her tears, but he was pointing at

Cassio's dangling body. Still chuckling, he said something to Friar Mathieu.

"He says that man used to be the stud bull hereabouts. Now he is dead beef."

Rachel shook her head. "He has no pity for Cassio—nor for me." Filled with revulsion, she thought she would rather die than spend the rest of her life with that brute.

Friar Mathieu looked off into the distance. "That is how it is with the Tartars."

Rachel shuddered. To John, Cassio was just a bundle of rags to be laughed at, and she was a plaything to be dragged through the world.

"Please help me get away," she begged Friar Mathieu. "I think I will kill myself if I have to stay with him."

Friar Mathieu closed his eyes in pain. "Do not talk that way, my child. Every person's life belongs to God."

Another voice boomed down at them from above, speaking a language Rachel had heard before but did not know. The sour-faced man with the big nose peered at them out of a cavernous hood. The French cardinal. He towered over them on a great black horse. Rachel shuddered at the sight of him.

"Pardonnez-moi, votr'Eminence," said Friar Mathieu calmly. He went on, in what must have been French, to say something which she supposed from his gestures was about John and her.

The cardinal's reply seemed as loud as thunder. He pointed at Rachel, and she cringed away. What was he saying, that she belonged to John?

Feeling hopeless, Rachel stood weeping silently while the priest and the cardinal argued what was to become of her in a language she did not understand.

Has God abandoned me because I have sinned?

She looked at Tilia's house, at the horrid sight of the hanged man above the door, cries of women barely audible over the rumble of thunder and the pounding of rain on the pavement. She saw men carrying boxes and bundles of cloth out the front door and realized that they were ransacking the place.

Cold horror swept her as she realized she was going to lose everything. Everything she had earned by her shame was in a chest in Tilia's room.

Friar Mathieu cried out something in French. In the midst of her misery, Rachel was shocked to see a beggar-priest publicly chastising a cardinal.

The cardinal stared at the friar, seemingly also shocked. He blinked as lightning flashed overhead.

Rachel said, "Good Father—"

The cardinal found his voice and roared back at the friar, jabbing a bejeweled finger at Rachel and turning on her a glare of utter contempt. His look hurt Rachel as much as if he had hit her in the face with dung. She pulled the soaking blanket tighter around herself. She saw that, staunch as the friar might be, all the power was on the other side.

"Father," she said, "if nothing can stop them from taking me, at least let me get the things I own from the house. My clothes and books." She did not mention the bags of gold ducats in Tilia's chest, though John might know of them. "Let me take them with me and travel with you.."

Friar Mathieu nodded and spoke again angrily to the cardinal.

The cardinal yanked on the reins of his horse, turning the black head around, up the street. He flung his answer over his shoulder.

Friar Mathieu turned a sad face toward Rachel. "He says you and I and John can go back into the house and get what belongs to you. And you can travel in my cart. But I am not to interfere if the Tartar desires you." He shook his head. "I promise you, child, as long as you are with me, John will not touch you. I was a knight before I was a priest. They can make me stand by and witness murder and robbery. But not rape."

Rachel looked up to see John grinning at her with proprietary pride. Like Rachel, he had not understood a word of the argument between the friar and the cardinal, but he understood well enough that Rachel was still his prisoner.

She felt a little better for having an ally in Friar Mathieu. But she promised herself that whatever John might think, he would never take her back to his country. She really would kill herself first.

The storm had passed over Orvieto by the time the cart carrying Rachel was bumping along the road to Perugia. As she sat on a bench beside the old priest, looking out through the open front end of the cart, Rachel saw patches of blue sky above the hills to the northeast.

John had gone with Friar Mathieu and helped him find her chest in Tilia's room and the key to the padlock, hidden under Tilia's mattress. He had ordered two of his Armenian guards to carry the chest out for Rachel and load it in the back of the cart, along with another chest of her books and clothing. He himself had smilingly handed her the key. As if he expected her to be grateful, she thought.

So she was still a wealthy woman, Rachel thought bitterly, even though she was also a prisoner.

With Friar Mathieu sitting on the bench up front beside the driver, she had gone to the back of the cart and opened both chests to make sure everything was there, even hefting the bags of gold. Then she had dried herself off and put on a bright blue linen tunic.

On the outside she was more comfortable now; within, desolate. Even though Tilia had sold her to the Tartar, Tilia's house had been home to her for nearly a year. She had come to know the men whom today she had seen murdered, and the women who had been forcibly taken by the Tartars' bodyguards. They and Sophia, David, and Lorenzo were the only friends she had known since Angelo was killed. Now she would never see them again.

She had not felt so wretched since the night of Angelo's death.

To comfort herself, she took out the Hebrew prayer book Angelo had given her. To have light to read by, she would have to go to the front of the cart and sit beside Friar Mathieu. The sight of her prayer book might turn the old priest against her. She remembered Angelo telling her how priests at Paris had burned a thousand or more volumes of the Talmud. Tears had come to his eyes at the thought of so many holy books, lovingly copied by hand, destroyed.

But Friar Mathieu had been kind to her even when she admitted that she had lain with the Tartar for money. He did not seem like the kind of man who would despise her for being a Jew.

Right now she desperately needed to be able to trust someone, and she decided that she could trust Friar Mathieu.

Balancing herself against the swaying of the cart, she climbed on the bench beside the old priest.

Her book was a collection of writings and prayers, including passages from the Torah. Some rabbi, or perhaps more than one, with quill pens and parchments, had taken years and years to copy it out. She had marked the Psalms with a ribbon and turned to them now.

For lowly people You save, but haughty eyes You bring low . . .

For the first time since she had seen those hooded riders approaching Tilia's house, she felt some measure of peace.

After a moment she realized Friar Mathieu was reading over her shoulder. Fear chilled her.

"One rarely finds a *man* learned enough to read Hebrew," said Friar Mathieu gently. "In a woman as young as yourself it is positively miraculous."

She smiled timidly in answer to the kindliness in his eyes. "My husband was a seller of books. He taught me to read the language of our ancestors.''

''Your husband?'' His eyes, their blue irises pale with age, opened wider. ''You have been married?'' He shook his head. ''People never cease to surprise me. I would like to know you better, child. Will you tell me about your life?''

His gentle tone gave her heart. Not since Sophia had talked to her on the road from Rome to Orvieto had anybody been interested in who she was. Talking to this good priest about her past, she could forget for a while the terror of present and future. She would tell him everything.

LIV

DAOUD SUDDENLY REALIZED THAT DROPLETS OF MOISTURE HAD appeared on the grayish-yellow wall near his face. How long the water had been forming he did not, could not, know. Long enough for some of the droplets to coalesce and run down the wall, where they joined a line of dampness where the floor met the wall.

He wondered where the water was coming from. It might be raining outside, above this dungeon. It would take, he thought, a very great rainstorm for the water to seep through down here.

He lay on his stomach on the rack table, his stretched arms and legs feeling like blocks of wood. He had no idea how much time had passed since d'Ucello left him with the threat that when he returned he would burn Daoud's manhood away with Greek Fire. Most of that time he had been awake, but had been dreaming of the paradise of the Hashishiyya.

Erculio had slept on a pile of rags in a corner of the dungeon, leaving it to the guards to make sure that d'Ucello's order was carried out and Daoud remained awake. The guards were, as Erculio must have know they would be, halfhearted about carrying out their mandate. They poked and struck him with sticks at intervals, but they did not try to injure him. Daoud was even able to sleep for brief periods between their proddings. They let most of the candles in the dungeon go out, leaving the great stone chamber in semidarkness.

Erculio managed to talk to him when the two guards were dozing. He held up what looked like a large pearl.

"There is a swift-acting poison sealed inside this glass ball. When he comes to burn your prickle off, I will slip it into your mouth. When you feel the fire, break the ball with your teeth and swallow. It will look as though the pain killed you. If you can manage it, swallow the glass, too, so they do not find it in your mouth after you're dead."

So calm did Daoud's Sufi training keep him that he was able to wonder where Erculio had got such a thing, and how the poison was sealed inside the ball, and what kind of poison it was. He could even think calmly about what it would feel like when the poison was killing him.

Erculio was taking a huge chance, he realized. D'Ucello might well discover that poison had killed Daoud; the podesta was a very clever and knowledgeable man. And if he did discover the poison, he would, of course, reason that Erculio had done it. In the midst of his calm, Daoud felt admiration for the little bent man's courage.

Inevitably with the passing of so many hours, the pain of the cuts and bruises and burns he had already suffered, and the ache of lying in the same position with his limbs stretched beyond endurance, would at times break through the mental wall he had built up against it. Remembering the words of Sheikh Saadi—*If pain comes despite your training, invite it into your soul's tent as you would a welcome guest*—he allowed the pain to wash over him. And when the first acute shock of it had passed, he was able to restore the wall.

From time to time he would think of what was soon going to happen to him. And it would be like a spear of ice driven into his heart. Again, he let himself feel the terror, the anguish, the agonized wondering, *When will he come?* and then, when his mind was numbed by the horror of it, cast it out again.

If he had not had the training of those two great and very different masters, Sheikh Saadi and Fayum al-Burz, he would have been mad with terror by now. Each time the door to the dungeon opened, the spear of ice pierced him again. Would it be now that he would lose his manhood in pain beyond imagining, pain so great that he would gladly die at once?

When no one was nearby, Erculio came close, cursed at him loudly, punched him, and whispered, "He is gone much longer than he said he would be. It is late afternoon. I told you he does not want to do this."

But he will do it, Daoud thought.

Sometime later—Daoud could not tell how long—the door swung open and d'Ucello strode in. Daoud let the cold fear flood into him. He even let himself whimper a bit. The tide of maddening terror reached its height and then receded, and he was in command of himself again.

The two guards snapped to attention, and Erculio scurried over to him. The podesta's face was set, and when he came close to Daoud, there was pain in his eyes.

"Has he spoken?" he said to Erculio.

"Not a word, Signore, and I have made him suffer greatly."

I shall be leaving this world just moments from now. I will fix my thoughts on God.

"I gave you more time than I intended to," d'Ucello said to Daoud. "There was a small battaglia at a bordello on the east side of town. A place you are familiar with. The house run by that fat old whore, Tilia Caballo. Where, according to her testimony, you were when the French cavaliere was murdered outside Cardinal Ugolini's. Your putana friend has been despoiled, I fear, and many of her menservants killed and her women hurt."

Rachel.

He desperately wanted to know whether Rachel had been hurt, and he dared not speak of her to d'Ucello. Anguish for Rachel cracked his armor against fear. He saw what was going to happen to him, felt the liquid fire, saw his death. Cold sweat broke out on his body.

He tried to turn his mind back to Tilia's house.

And Tilia, what of Tilia?

It surprised him that his anxiety for Tilia was so strong. She had come to be his friend without his ever realizing it.

He thought of Francesca, who had comforted him so during his first months in Orvieto. Of the women who had helped him initiate Sordello. All of them no doubt raped, and perhaps hurt in other ways besides.

The savages! This would never have happened in El Kahira.

It was safe enough to ask, "Who did it?"

"The ambassadors from Tartary and their guards, as they were leaving Orvieto to follow the pope to Perugia. The French Cardinal de Verceuil was there and, far from trying to prevent the wickedness, urged them on. It seems you dislike the Tartars with good reason."

The podesta paused. He still hoped, Daoud realized, to provoke or invite him into letting something slip.

If it was the Tartars, they must have come for Rachel.

D'Ucello picked up the flask of Greek Fire from the table, where it had stood these many hours, where Daoud could plainly see it. He had, most of the time, avoided looking at it.

"Were any of the women taken away?" Daoud asked. That, too, should be a safe question. Every moment he and d'Ucello talked, d'Ucello hoping he might yet learn something, was another moment of wholeness and life.

But I must not deceive myself. These are only moments. I affirm that God is One. God be merciful. God receive me. I die as Your warrior.

"Yes," said d'Ucello, eyeing him thoughtfully. "Did you have reason to think someone would be carried off?"

It hurt Daoud's neck to turn and try to look into d'Ucello's face. Daoud let his head fall to the table on which he lay.

"I visited there often. I made friends with some of the women."

D'Ucello snorted. "From now on you will have no need to go to bordellos."

To gain another moment, Daoud said, "I marvel that you possess Greek Fire. The making of it is a great secret, and it is too dangerous to transport far. If a bit of it gets loose on a ship, that ship is seen no more."

D'Ucello squinted at him. "If you were truly only a trader from Trebizond, you would be too terrified to wonder where I got this stuff."

"Allow me at the last a bit of dignity," Daoud pleaded, looking up at d'Ucello. He saw guilt in d'Ucello's shifting eyes.

"A member of the Knights Templar back from the Holy Land let me copy the formula," said d'Ucello. "Out of curiosity, I had an alchemist make it for me."

"Curiosity is a worthier motive than torture," said Daoud, hoping he was undermining d'Ucello's resolution and making the podesta feel ashamed.

But the dark eyes flashed angrily. "That is enough. Turn him on his back, Erculio. You should have done that already."

I pushed him too far, Daoud thought despairingly.

"Yes, Signore." Erculio beckoned the guards. "Here, you two. Help me."

When his arms and legs were untied, Daoud groaned at the sudden release of the tension in stiffened muscles. A savage pain tore through the numbness in his limbs.

"Be still, whoreson!" Erculio snarled, clamping a hand over Daoud's mouth. Daoud felt the glass ball pressed against his lips, and opened his mouth to receive it.

The ball was not large, about half the size of a pigeon's egg, but it felt huge in his mouth. Thinking about the swift death it held within it, Daoud wondered if it would be easy or hard to break the glass.

They were tying his hands again, and he had the ball under his tongue. If he tried to speak now, d'Ucello would know he had something in his mouth. No more delaying by talking to the podesta.

"Strip off his loincloth," said d'Ucello, and Erculio tore it away. Holding the flask in one hand, d'Ucello leaned forward, peering at Daoud's groin. Daoud could feel his penis and scrotum shrinking.

What fools we men are to be so proud of our members, and think them such sources of power. How truly vulnerable is that little bit of flesh.

One moment he was able to think, the next he was adrift on a sea of terror. His naked body shook violently as d'Ucello scrutinized him. He struggled to keep his Sufi training in mind. Only that could help him now to die bravely.

"He is circumcised," said d'Ucello, his black eyebrows twisting in a frown.

Oh, God! Cloud his mind.

"What do we know of that place he comes from?" said Erculio. "Trebizond? Maybe all the men in Trebizond are circumcised."

"Only Jews are circumcised," said d'Ucello. "And Saracens." He brought his face closer to Daoud's. "Speak, man. Why is your foreskin cut off?"

"How could he be a Saracen or a Jew?" said Erculio. "He looks like a Frank."

"Shut up," said d'Ucello impatiently. "I want to hear his answer."

Daoud lay motionless, praying that God would let d'Ucello kill him and be done with it.

"Are you part of some Jewish plot?" d'Ucello demanded.

Daoud almost smiled at that, but he only looked up at the blackened ceiling beam and said nothing.

"Answer me!" d'Ucello growled. He shook the flask at Daoud. Daoud closed his eyes. Now the fire would come.

He heard a hammering at the wooden door on the other side of the dungeon. One of the guards went to open it at d'Ucello's command.

Another delay! Now he was almost frantic for it to end. He was tempted to bite down on the little glass ball. Why must he wait and wait for that terrible flame to burn away his life?

"Signore!" Daoud turned his head and saw the clerk called Vincenzo in the doorway of the dungeon. Beside him was a man in orange and green, the colors of the Monaldeschi family. Daoud remembered the thick black brows and the stern face, the grizzled hair. He had seen this man the night of the contessa's reception for the Tartars.

"The Contessa di Monaldeschi's steward brings a message from her," Vincenzo said.

With a sigh d'Ucello set the flask of Greek Fire on the table beside Daoud. In the sigh Daoud heard, not impatience, but relief. D'Ucello was glad to put off doing this unspeakable thing, but it meant only that Daoud would have to endure a longer wait.

Because he does not want to torture me, I suffer the more.

D'Ucello was still hoping the waiting would break him. And it might. In spite of all his training, in spite of the Soma that kept him calm and held the pain away, Daoud felt himself at the very edge of his endurance. He just might break.

The podesta, the clerk, and the contessa's steward muttered together by the door of the dungeon. Turning his head, Daoud could watch them.

D'Ucello was jabbing his hands furiously toward the steward. He was having trouble keeping his voice down.

"This is intolerable!" he cried.

The steward took a step backward, but he kept his face set. He spoke in a voice too low for Daoud to hear.

"Fires of hell!" D'Ucello shook both clenched fists over his head.

He turned and pointed at Daoud. "Keep that one there on the rack till I return, Erculio."

"Where is my Signore going?"

D'Ucello opened his mouth. His face grew redder in the torchlight, and he closed it again.

"I will not be gone very long," he said. "I have to *persuade* someone of something."

"Shall I torment this fellow while you are gone?"

"Do as you please. At least see that he gets no rest."

He strode across the room to glare down at Daoud. "You will keep your manhood for another hour or so. By God's grace you have more time to think. About what will happen to you and how you can save yourself. Do not think you have escaped. I will be back.''

He lifted his hand. A bolt of panic shot through Daoud as he thought that if d'Ucello hit him hard enough he might break the ball of poison in his mouth. He held himself rigid.

D'Ucello lowered his hand.

"Damn you!" he snarled, and turned away.

Now Daoud wished d'Ucello *had* broken the glass ball. He would have to lie for hours longer now, waiting for pain and death. The thought of those hours was in itself more agonizing than all the tortures he had so far suffered. But God had chosen to let him live a little longer, and he must accept these moments of life.

"According to Vincenzo," Erculio whispered, "the contessa ordered the podesta to stop torturing you. Your allies must have gotten to her."

The guards and the clerk had left, but Daoud heard their excited voices beyond the partly open door. Erculio now had a chance to take out the poison ball. The inside of Daoud's mouth ached from holding the delicate orb, and he sighed with relief.

"There is more," Erculio said. "An army of Sienese Ghibellini passed through Montefiascone this morning. We have known that the Sienese were marching against Orvieto, but we were not aware they were almost upon us. The contessa and the podesta must discuss the defense as well as your fate."

Lorenzo was with that army, Daoud thought. Lorenzo might be able to rescue him if he got here in time.

"I fear it will be no better for you than before," Erculio went on. "D'Ucello knows how to make the contessa see things his way. He will probably persuade her that you must be tortured. And since he suspects you of being a Ghibellino agent, he will want you dead before the Ghibellini army comes."

"As God wills," Daoud croaked. A numbness had come over him as if he were already dead. This was older and simpler and more effective than the techniques of Sufi and Hashishiyya. This deadness was his body's final answer to a night and a day of unbearable pain and fear.

LV

THE WOMAN'S SHOULDERS SHOOK, AND SHE ROCKED BACK AND forth. She could not speak. Tilia sat on Sophia's bed holding the sobbing woman in her arms.

Tilia, calling her Francesca, tried to calm her. Sophia at first had thought Francesca was a madwoman. Her tunic was torn and rain-wet, her long black hair not bound up and covered but in wild disarray.

"You are safe now, piccione," Tilia kept saying. "Calm down and tell us what happened." Tilia herself was pale, her wide mouth drawn tight.

Seeing even Tilia's face grim, Sophia felt a chill of apprehension and an even greater anxiety to know what this was all about.

"I know I should not come here, Madama. Forgive me. But I did not know what else to do. I walked so far to get here, and I kept getting lost, and I was afraid to ask anyone where Cardinal Ugolini's mansion was."

"How did you know I was here, Francesca?" Tilia asked.

"Cassio told me just before—before—" Francesca was convulsed with sobs.

Tilia turned to Sophia. "I have never seen her like this."

"Your house is destroyed," said Francesca, choking and gasping and wiping her nose on her sleeve.

"Destroyed!" Tilia and Sophia stared at each other. A shock of fear swept through Sophia. Already terrified for Daoud, she was now swept by dread for Rachel and pity for Tilia.

Any more of this, and I will lose my wits.

"And they hanged Cassio."

"Oh, my God!" Tilia screamed.

Another jolt of terror. Sophia thought of that day in Constantinople when the Franks had run riot, burning whole districts and murdering townspeople. Was this another such day?

"And they—and they killed Hector and Claudio and Apollonio and the other menservants."

125

"Who did this?" Tilia was on her feet, standing over Francesca, shouting. "Who? Who?"

Was the whole world turning against them, Sophia wondered. Was it the podesta's men? The Monaldeschi?

Francesca put her hands over her face and wept softly for a moment, then continued. "The Tartars and that French cardinal who always came with them. They came with armed men, dozens of them. They were after Rachel."

Rachel!

The horror of it all was like a spear driven through Sophia's breast. She sat down on her bed as the room went black around her.

"Oh, no," she heard herself saying. "Oh, not Rachel!" Fear stopped her heart. She slumped on the bed, her hand pressed to her chest.

"When Cassio tried to stop them, they went mad," said Francesca. "The men-at-arms killed every man in the house, and they raped all the women. Some of us over and over again. And they tore the house apart and stole everything they could carry. What they could not take, they smashed. And all the while they kept laughing, Madama. They kept laughing."

Sophia felt bile burning in her throat. If she had to hear any more horrors, she was going to vomit.

Tilia sat looking stunned, shaking her head from side to side.

"What happened to Rachel?" Sophia managed to choke out.

"She tried to run away. She got out of the house. The white-haired Tartar, the one who beds with her, chased her. He must have caught her, because I heard the cardinal shouting that they had found the one they came for and they must get on the road or they would be fighting the Sienese."

Rachel wanted to come here with me this morning, Sophia thought. *If only I had brought her here, we could have saved her.* She sobbed aloud. Her stomach hurt.

"May God rot all of them with leprosy," said Tilia. She hugged Francesca hard, and then stood up.

"I must go to my house."

Going back to Tilia's would not help Rachel, Sophia thought. They had probably lost her forever. Despair dragged her down. *Rachel, Rachel!* What were they doing to her?

"First David is arrested. Now this," she said, tears running steadily down her cheeks.

I had trusted Daoud to foresee danger and guide us through it, Sophia thought. *And now Daoud—*

She still did not know whether Daoud was safe, or even still alive. Would the contessa be able to stop whatever was being done to Daoud? That had been quite enough to be terrified about.

Francesca's tear-reddened eyes widened. "David has been arrested?" Something in her tone told Sophia there had been something between Francesca and David.

Of course, she told herself. *Did you think the man slept alone until you gave yourself to him?*

She and Francesca shared some of the same grief. Sophia wanted to console her.

"Cardinal Ugolini has persuaded the Contessa di Monaldeschi to intercede for David," Sophia told her, "and the cardinal has gone to the Palazzo del Podesta, hoping to bring David back here again."

"It may be hours before David is released," said Tilia, raising a cautioning hand. "*If* the podesta does agree. Or he may persuade the contessa that he was right to arrest David."

These were the very thoughts that had been tormenting Sophia. She needed to do something.

"If you want to go to your house, Tilia, I will go with you." It occurred to her immediately after she spoke that the streets might be dangerous for both of them. But she could not stand the agony of sitting here, waiting for the possibility of still worse news.

"Sophia, you and the cardinal must not be linked to Tilia Caballo's bordello," said Tilia.

"I will keep myself hidden," said Sophia.

Sophia made Francesca comfortable in her own bed, then went down with Tilia to the great hall of Ugolini's mansion and sent for Riccardo.

Hand in hand, Sophia holding a lighted candle, the two women made their way through the tunnel that led to the potterymaker's shop.

Riccardo met them with another hired cart, like the one that had taken them from Tilia's to the cardinal's this morning. This was a covered cart full of big urns of olive oil. The air, much cooler than before the storm, felt refreshing on Sophia's face. Getting into the cart, Sophia looked up and saw big black clouds rolling across the sky, their rounded edges outlined by the red light of the setting sun.

The cart, pulled by an old draft horse, bumped over cobblestones and splashed through puddles. Tilia and Sophia sat on a bench behind Riccardo, under the cart's canvas cover, so they could not be seen from the street. All around them Sophia heard church bells ringing for the Angelus. She could close her eyes for a moment and imagine she was hearing the bells of the three hundred churches of

Constantinople. She longed to be in the Polis again, among civilized people.

That is why I am here, is it not? To keep the barbarians here, and away from there.

She saw torchlight ahead. This was Tilia's street, farther up a hill that slowed down the elderly horse.

From this distance the house looked undamaged, but what was that hanging above the door?

"Merciful God!" Sophia whispered.

She saw the body of a man suspended from a rope tied to the balcony above the doorway.

"Oh, God," said Tilia. "Oh, poor, poor Cassio." She dabbed at her eyes with the sleeve of her gown.

Now, by the torchlight, Sophia could see several men, dressed in the yellow and blue of the commune, gathered in front of the house. The podesta's watchmen.

The street was full of common folk, who had to back up to give the cart room to move forward. As it approached the front door, one of the podesta's men raised a hand to stop it.

"I will be right back," Tilia said, squeezing Sophia's arm. She clambered out of the cart with Riccardo's help. Riccardo tied the cart to a hitching post on the side of the street.

Tying her scarf across her face, Sophia watched from inside the cart. The man who had stopped the horse barred Tilia again as she started toward her house. He was a slender, middle-aged man with a prominent arch to his nose and heavy-lidded eyes. Riccardo moved toward him, but Tilia put her hand on the servant's arm. Tilia would not want the cardinal's man brawling with an officer of the watch.

"I am Tilia Caballo, and this is my house," she said in a commanding voice. "How long have you been here?"

What a brave woman Tilia was, Sophia thought. Could she herself face an officer of the watch and speak to him sternly like that?

"Since the hour of None, Madama. The podesta was here, but he had to leave."

"And what are you doing? Just standing about? Have you left that poor man's body to hang there since mid-afternoon, where women and children could see it? Take him down at once. Are you not Christians? How can you treat the dead with such disrespect?"

In the midst of her own horror, Sophia took comfort from Tilia's display of strength, and wondered how the stout little woman felt inside.

Sophia had hated her at times, and still thought Tilia had done a horrible wrong to Rachel. But what she felt for her now was mostly admiration.

After all, all of them were equally guilty of what had happened to Rachel. The blame should not fall on Tilia alone.

The beak-nosed officer called orders to others nearby. But his expression as he turned back to Tilia was surly.

"There might be some question about whether *he* was a Christian, Madama. This is, after all, a house of ill repute."

"Ill *repute!*" Tilia blustered. "This is—this was—the handsomest house of pleasure in Orvieto. And our patrons occupied the very highest levels in the Church. You would be wise to have a care how you speak of my house."

Sophia felt herself smiling. Amazing, when there was so much to weep over.

"Would I?" The officer thrust his nose at Tilia. "Perhaps you can tell me why such a splendid bordello with such fine customers needed a torture chamber in the cellar? Or why you had to keep piccioni on the roof?"

Sophia's body went cold. If they found out those were carrier pigeons and where they went, the trouble here might be deep indeed.

"So that is what you have been doing!" Tilia stormed. "Looting my home! And how much did you steal after the Tartars left? And no doubt harassing my ladies, as if they had not been through enough already. And leaving my Cassio to swing from a rope. My God, there has been murder, kidnapping, rape, and theft done here, and you prattle of piccioni. What have you done about catching the *bestioni* who did this?"

Now the officer did look intimidated. "Madama, we are not certain who did these things—"

"Not certain!" Tilia shook her fist at him. "Everyone in Orvieto knows who did this. It was the French cardinal, Paulus de Verceuil, and the Tartar ambassadors to the pope. Why are you here, standing about like fools, when you could be pursuing them and bringing them to justice?"

The French, thought Sophia. If Simon had been here, would he have allowed this to happen? She felt a twinge of guilt, remembering that she had betrayed Daoud by not telling him where Simon was going.

"What you tell us is but hearsay, Madama."

"Hearsay! Every lady in that house is a witness."

"In any case, those you accuse are beyond our reach."

''Because you *let* them get beyond your reach,'' Tilia retorted. ''Oh, you feckless man! Let me by.''

And then Sophia was alone in the cart and frightened, because she knew she was surrounded by the podesta's men and by towns-people who might well be hostile. For reassurance she smoothed the scarf over her nose and mouth and patted the small dagger that hung at her belt, concealed under her outer tunic.

She heard a creaking noise above her and looked out to see the podesta's men hauling Cassio's body up to the balcony. Tilia, she thought, was taking charge. Left to themselves, the watchmen would probably have just cut the rope and let the poor man's corpse fall to the ground.

Sophia thought of Rachel, helpless, carried off by the Tartar, and Daoud, equally helpless, in the Palazzo del Podesta. She had no idea what was happening to either of them, and horrors filled her mind. Her hands twisted together, her fingers crushing one another, and she started to cry again.

Tilia was crying, too, when she came back and Riccardo helped her climb into the carriage. She could not speak for a time, and Sophia sat with her arm around Tilia's quaking shoulders. It was for this, thought Sophia, she had come. The only way she could help Tilia was to be with her and to comfort her. And in doing so she comforted herself.

After a while Tilia gave a great sigh. ''I held Cassio in my arms for a time. I washed his poor face, which I could barely recognize. What hurts most is that all those people, those men and those women, were loyal to me, and I was not there when they suffered this awful thing.'' She wiped her eyes with the sleeve of her green silk dress and looked sadly at Sophia.

Feeling Tilia's pain for her people, Sophia liked her all the more.

''The Tartars' men probably would have killed you if you had been there.''

''To be sure. I would have provoked them to it as Cassio did. I would not have let them take Rachel without a fight.'' She gripped the cross resting on her bosom, and Sophia remembered Daoud saying it held a poisoned blade. ''Well, my poor men will have good burials. I have been very generous to the little church of San Severo in the valley south of here, and now the pastor can repay my kindness by burying the seven who died here. They may not have been good Christians, or Christians at all, but at least in a churchyard they will lie in peace. The women who are hurt badly will go to the Hospital of Santa Clara. And I must hire guards to protect the house. My ladies do not want to stay there. I do not blame them, but there is no other roof to shelter them just now, and with guards they will be safe enough. Anyway, those murderers are gone. I will come back and stay with them when I have done everything there is to do."

Sophia smiled at Tilia in admiration. She was hurt, but fought the pain by getting on with what needed to be done.

If only there were more I could do. For Rachel. For Daoud.

Tilia kept shaking her head. "They took everything of value. Thank Fortune, most of my money is on deposit with the Lombards. But the chests I kept in my room are gone, and there were bags of gold coins in them. One chest was Rachel's."

Sophia's heart sank further at that news. Now Rachel had not even gold to make up for all that had been done to her.

"The dirty ladroni," Tilia went on. "That Tartar and the other one, and the cardinal—all of them had such merry times in my house. How could they do this to me?"

"The Tartars are simply doing as Tartars do," said Sophia. "They take what they want, and they kill anyone who tries to stop them. As for the cardinal, he is a Frank, and if you had seen what the Franks did to my city, you would not be surprised at this." She felt helpless. How could what she was saying possibly comfort Tilia?

Tilia struck the heel of her hand against her forehead. "How stupid I was! When John the Tartar said he wanted to take Rachel to Perugia with him, I should have known he would not accept my refusal. I should have been prepared for this."

Sophia, remembering how Rachel had begged to leave Tilia's house with her that morning, spoke sharply before she could stop herself.

"As it was, you kept Rachel safe for him until he was ready to take her."

Tilia gasped. "That is very unfair."

Now Sophia was deeply angry with herself. She had already decided that what had happened to Rachel should not be blamed on Tilia. And she was trying—or should be trying—to comfort her. Her cruel Greek tongue had got the better of her.

Sophia was about to apologize when a shout from outside stopped her.

"The mistress of the whores' house is in this cart. I saw her get into it."

"Now she sees how God punishes fornicators."

"We should never have let her move into our street."

"Let her get her house and all of her filth out of here."

Sophia shrank back into the cart, her heart quaking. She had seen mobs tear people to pieces.

She said, "Tilia, that crowd frightens me, and the podesta's men may not be much protection. Let us get out of here, please."

"I will show you what I think of that crowd," said Tilia. She pushed her way to the front of the cart and stood beside Riccardo with her hands on her hips. Sophia could see people gathered, white faces in the moonlight, red faces in the torchlight.

"Ignoranti!" Tilia shouted. "Fannulloni! My house is the best on your street. The rest is one big, foul quintana. Where were you idlers when my men were murdered and my women were raped by a gang of foreigners? Home pissing in your pants, eh? Brave Orvietans you are. Get out of my way."

Sophia heard a muttering from the crowd, but no one tried to answer Tilia. Sophia shook her head.

If I live to be a hundred, I don't think I could ever face down a mob like that.

Tilia turned to Riccardo, whose broad shoulders beside her had lent force to her words. "Drive on."

The cart rolled forward, and the people fell back, squeezing against the housefronts to let it by. Sophia, devastated, sagged back against a great earthenware olive oil jar. She was too worn out even to cry anymore.

LVI

Now, at last, this is the end, thought Daoud as the door of the chamber of torment rasped open. He had been preparing himself for death, praying, commending himself to God. Now he hoped that without much more pain, God would take him.

Erculio, who had been sitting with his back to the wall, pushed himself to his feet and scuttled forward.

D'Ucello entered, followed by two guards in yellow and blue.

"Welcome back, Signore," Erculio cried. "Shall we now roast this stubborn fellow's ballocks?"

Erculio, Daoud sensed, enjoyed feigning the gleeful torturer precisely because it was a way of tormenting d'Ucello himself.

D'Ucello walked over to where Daoud lay naked on the rack and glowered silently down at him, his lips pressed together under his thin mustache. The podesta glanced at the silver flask on the table, but made no move to pick it up. He seemed to be studying Daoud, searching for something as he looked into his eyes.

He blinked and turned away. "Untie him."

"What are we going to do to him now, Signore?" said Erculio, still all eagerness. He needed to know, Daoud thought, when it would be time for the poison ball.

"Untie him and sit him up slowly," said d'Ucello.

"Oh, Signore!" Erculio exclaimed. "May we not play with him some more?"

D'Ucello's mouth twisted. "Enough of your infernal questions, pervertito! Do as I say."

The impact of this surprise was like a rock smashing into Daoud's Face of Steel. What was happening? Was he not to have his manhood burned away? Was he not to die?

This, too, could be a trick. Realizing that the threat of Greek Fire had not broken Daoud, d'Ucello might be making one last and very effective attempt to destroy his resolve by making it seem his fortunes had suddenly reversed themselves.

Daoud tried to bring the upwelling of hope under control, to resume the Face of Steel. But something in his bones was already sure that he was saved, and spasms of trembling ran through his body. His face felt as if it were falling to pieces, the Mask of Clay broken like a useless pot.

Bustling around the table, Erculio undid the knots at his wrists and ankles. In his surprise, Daoud relaxed his defenses against pain, and agony stabbed him like spears in every muscle of his body.

"We have not the means to treat your wounds here in this chamber," said d'Ucello. "But lower your legs over the side of the table and sit there for a moment. Then, if you can stand and walk, we will take you upstairs and my own physician, Fra Bernardino, will attend you."

Can it be? Am I to go free?

Joy burst up in him like a fountain in the desert. The candlelight seemed to flicker, and he nearly fainted. The sudden rush of emotion was unbearable.

Unless this was indeed a ruse, which seemed less and less likely with each passing moment, his suffering was over. The contessa had prevailed! But why? Why had she intervened to save him? Daoud remembered his vision of Sophia hurrying through the night to Tilia's house. Had Sophia done something that brought the contessa into it?

As he sat on the edge of the table, Daoud brought his eyes up to fix them on d'Ucello's. The dark eyes of the podesta, with the deep black rings under them, stared back. There was a look of defiance in d'Ucello's eyes, as if Daoud were the accuser and d'Ucello the one being interrogated.

Daoud's throat was tight and dry, and it ached when he tried to speak, but he forced words out.

"What are you going to do with me? Are you setting me free?"

The podesta nodded, his lips tight. "It seems that way."

"Why?"

"Be good enough to wait for an explanation until we are in private."

Daoud tried to read d'Ucello's round, swarthy face, but he could not tell whether the podesta was relieved or angry.

When Daoud did try to stand and put his weight on the burned and beaten soles of his feet, he had to clench his teeth to keep himself from screaming. His legs, which had borne the brunt of Erculio's attentions, felt lifeless, and his knees buckled. He toppled forward, and d'Ucello caught him. The podesta staggered under Daoud's weight. He snapped his fingers at a guard, who hurried over to help hold Daoud up.

As Daoud, gasping, leaned against him, d'Ucello unclasped his cloak and wrapped it around Daoud to cover his nakedness.

Such solicitude, Daoud thought wryly. *I think I have suddenly become terribly valuable to him.*

This could not be just the contessa's influence, he thought. He did not mean that much to her.

The Sienese.

That must be it. Erculio had said d'Ucello believed Daoud was a Ghibellino agent, and therefore he would want to kill Daoud before the Ghibellino army from Siena got here. But not, Daoud thought, if d'Ucello intended to surrender.

Erculio pressed something into his hand, a small leather pouch—the tawidh.

Daoud painfully bent his head toward Erculio and read gladness in the beady eyes.

"May you find work that suits you better, Messer Erculio," said Daoud. *God give you joy*, he thought.

"What he does suits him all too well, the little monster," said d'Ucello.

The podesta's men brought a litter, and two big guards, complaining about Daoud's size, slowly climbed the basement steps, stopped to rest for a time at the top and then carried Daoud up the marble staircase leading from the ground floor to the first floor of the Palazzo del Podesta. They were staggering by the time they lifted Daoud onto a bed in a small room. D'Ucello ordered the guards to send Fra Bernardino to him.

Two walls of the room were lined with books and boxes of scrolls. So many books must be worth a fortune, Daoud thought. The other walls were painted a pleasant lemon color, the ceiling a deep blue. A concave mirror, set at an angle in the wall beside the glazed mullioned window, could direct daylight toward the writing table. The translucent window glass appeared nearly black; it must be night outside. The floor was of hardwood planks, very clean and highly polished. Moving very slowly and painfully, Daoud stretched himself out on the yellow satin bedcarpet and drew d'Ucello's cloak over him like a blanket.

This was a great deal more comfortable than the table on which he had lain for what seemed like endless days and nights. He could hardly believe the vast change that had taken place.

Maybe I have gone mad and this is all like a hashish dream.

D'Ucello sat at a plain oak table piled with parchments, rolled and unrolled. The candelabra on the table supplied the light for the room. A slender blue vase with graceful twin handles stood on one corner of the table.

Though this was not a room that would find favor in the world of Islam, Daoud recognized that d'Ucello, in his own Venetian way, had a highly refined sense of beauty.

The podesta unlocked a tall box of dark wood, inlaid with ivory, that stood on his desk. Lifting the lid, he held the flask of Greek Fire over it.

"We are both lucky I did not use this," he said. He took a folded white cloth from the box and wrapped the flask. Then, carefully, he set the flask upright in the box, closed the lid, and locked it.

Daoud let out a slow sigh of relief as he saw d'Ucello push the box to one side. It was becoming easier and easier to believe that he was saved.

In spite of the pain that stabbed at a thousand places on his body, Daoud was able to smile. "I know why it is lucky for me. Why for you?"

"Cardinal Ugolini and his niece went to the Contessa di Monaldeschi and insisted that you were innocent, that you were the cardinal's guest. They begged her to command me to release you at once. The contessa is very simple in her way, and she likes to do favors for churchmen. So she sent a message to me that I must stop your torture and come to her at once."

Daoud could not think. He felt so light-headed that it might have been easy now for d'Ucello to extract admissions from him. He had been in pain and had not eaten or slept in over a day. He must pay careful attention to what he was saying. It would never do to be careless with d'Ucello.

D'Ucello smiled at Daoud, a humorless grimace that stretched his thin mustache.

"I am not going to ask your forgiveness," d'Ucello said. "I was doing what I thought right."

Daoud said nothing. He felt d'Ucello was being frank with him, but he could not find it in his heart to forgive a man who had caused him so much pain and nearly killed him. Still, searching his heart, as Sheikh Saadi would have recommended, he found that he felt no hatred for d'Ucello. Just the wariness he would have felt toward a very large crocodile.

"I have stopped torturing you not because the contessa told me to," d'Ucello went on. "I probably could have changed her mind. But then she and I spoke of something else. A Ghibellino army from Siena is about to assault Orvieto. The contessa insisted that the militia, which I command, defend Orvieto to the last drop of our blood." He smiled, again without mirth.

As I suspected, Daoud thought triumphantly. *He wants me to intercede for him with the Ghibellini of Siena.*

And another happy thought came to him: *At last Lorenzo returns.*

"How many men have the Sienese?" Daoud asked.

"According to reports I have from the peasants who live north of here, they number over four thousand men. I am amazed that even so prosperous a city as Siena could hire such a large army."

You would be even more amazed to know where they got the money, thought Daoud.

D'Ucello went on. "So, we are hopelessly outnumbered. Of course, this rock of Orvieto is the most defensible position in Italy. Even with only our few hundred we could hold the Sienese off for some weeks, perhaps even months. But not indefinitely. The Holy Father knew that, which is why he left. The city will be taken and sacked. The people will suffer greatly. If I am not killed in the fighting, I will surely be hanged. And after I and all the defenders are dead, the contessa will consider the honor of the city satisfied and will make peace with the Sienese."

"Well, you will have done what you thought right," said Daoud, after the podesta had finished listing all these evil consequences. D'Ucello's eyebrows twitched and his lips quirked, showing that he caught the irony.

Daoud would enjoy this conversation more, he thought, if his feet did not throb, if his legs did not ache, if his torn back did not burn as if he were lying on hot coals, if his head were not swimming.

"I may hold this post at the contessa's pleasure, but she does not have the right to tell me to die needlessly. And, as podesta, my first concern is the welfare of Orvieto. If I can come to terms with the Ghibellini, the city will be spared destruction."

Daoud held up a hand. The pain of the gesture was excruciating.

"Are you not a loyal Guelfo? Are you not faithful to the papal cause? How can you speak of coming to terms with the Ghibellini?" What a pleasure it was to goad d'Ucello.

The podesta squinted at Daoud, as if to see how serious his question was.

"This is a Guelfo city, and normally I would take that side. But I have no personal feelings one way or the other. What I do care about is the responsibility I have accepted, of governing this city. I carry out that responsibility best by preserving it from ruin."

And at the same time saving your own life, thought Daoud. *And biting your thumb at the Contessa di Monaldeschi who has been treating you like a servant. Oh, there are many reasons why you want to surrender to the Sienese.*

But Daoud was in terrible pain, and so tired that fatigue itself was now as much a torment as anything he had suffered earlier. He longed to cut this conversation short.

"What has all this to do with me?"

"To display my good faith to the Ghibellini, I have decided to free you."

"Why should the Ghibellini care, one way or the other, what happens to me?" said Daoud. Slowly he rolled over on his side, to make it easier to look at d'Ucello. Pain flared in his arms and legs, in his back and chest. His hands barely had the strength to pull the blue cloak with him.

"You still deny that you are of that party?" d'Ucello asked.

"I am David of Trebizond."

D'Ucello rose to answer a knock at the door. Daoud lifted himself on one elbow to see who it was. In the shadowed corridor a white-robed friar, taller than d'Ucello, was peering in, trying to see Daoud.

"We are not quite ready for you, Fra Bernardino," said d'Ucello, half-closing the door.

"Wait, Signore," the Dominican said, putting out a pale hand. "Cardinal Ugolini has come here with men-at-arms and is demanding that you release this man David to him at once."

Ugolini, here? Daoud felt a lightness in his heart. Freedom was that much closer.

"Make sure the cardinal is comfortable and is offered refreshments, Fra Bernardino," said d'Ucello, "and tell him he will not have to wait long."

Better and better.

When the door was shut, d'Ucello walked over to the bed and stared into Daoud's eyes. "If I let you go, will you speak on my behalf to the Ghibellini?"

Daoud smiled. "In my capacity as a trader?"

D'Ucello clenched his fists. "Damn you! You are too stubborn."

"So"—Daoud kept the smile fixed on his face—"you have arrested and tortured me for a night and a day. You very nearly did to me something so horrible, even now it hurts me to think about it. And you would have done it, too, if the contessa's summons had not delayed you. Now, because you have stopped doing these things to me, you expect me to be overflowing with gratitude and glad to help you make peace with the Ghibellini."

D'Ucello smiled back. "For my sparing you from torture, from mutilation, from death, you should be grateful, yes."

If he were another kind of man, he would have destroyed me with Greek Fire and let this city be ruined while he fought the Sienese. In spite of what he did to me, this is a wise man, and he deserves to live and to rule here.

But Daoud could not resist another thrust. "What I should do, if, as you think, I have influence with the Sienese, is have them do to you what you have done to me. And not spare you at the end." He felt himself getting angry as he thought of all he had been through, even though he knew anger was foolish. "I know where you keep your flask of Greek Fire."

D'Ucello's black eyes held Daoud's. "Yes. You could do that. But I think I have come to know something about you during these hours you have suffered at my hands."

"Yes?"

"I do not know what you are, but I know that you are much more than you seem to be. And you are not the sort who takes revenge on a man for doing his duty."

Daoud did not care to haggle anymore. "Allow any messenger of mine freedom to come and go through the city gates."

"Agreed."

The podesta was right, he thought. He would not seek revenge after d'Ucello surrendered to the Sienese any more than he would kill a prisoner of war. Men like Qutuz did that sort of thing, to satisfy their vanity. Men like Baibars did not. He thanked God for making him more like Baibars.

And he thanked God for bringing him alive and whole out of the valley of death.

Her first sight of Daoud was a cruel blow to Sophia's heart. His blond hair, dark with dirt and sweat, spread in lank locks on the pillow. His bloodshot eyes looked at her out of blackened lids. His lips were cracked. His face looked hollow, as if he had grown thinner just in the day d'Ucello had held him.

She ran to him across the tiled floor of Ugolini's reception hall.

He was alive, but how badly hurt was he? She prayed that when she lifted the blanket that covered him she would see that his body was sound.

He raised his hands to her as she bent over the litter. She saw that the fingernails were blackened and bloody, and her own fists clenched as she felt what they must have done to his hands. She slid her arms around his shoulders and pressed her face against his. Perhaps the men-at-arms and servants should not see the cardinal's niece embracing the trader from Trebizond, but at that moment nothing mattered to her but to hold his living body in her arms.

She heard him gasp. She was hurting him. What a fool she was!

"Forgive my clumsiness, David. I am so sorry."

He gently squeezed her hand as she drew away from him. "Your arms feel like an angel's wings."

Ugolini called his steward, Agostino, and rattled off a list of necessaries for treating Daoud's wounds—water, a pot and a brazier, clean cloths, medicine jars from the cardinal's cabinet.

Sophia walked beside the litter as Ugolini's men carried Daoud to his room on the third floor. Her hand rested lightly on his shoulder. Her feelings alternated between agony, as she imagined what he had gone through, and singing elation that he was back with her. With joy she felt movement and life in the hard muscle under her fingertips.

"Tilia and I did what we could for you," she said when the men had deposited him on his bed.

"I know," said Daoud. "Ugolini told me about your visit to the contessa. Had she not sent for d'Ucello when she did—as you persuaded her to do—I would be dead now."

She sat on the edge of his bed and put her hands over her face and wept for joy. It had all meant something, her rushing to Tilia before dawn, her going with Ugolini to the contessa, her falling to her knees before the old woman.

As the men-at-arms left, Ugolini came in with Agostino and two servants bearing a brazier and a tripod, pots of water, cloths, and jars of ointments and powders from Ugolini's shelves. Two other servants brought a table into Daoud's room, and Ugolini had the medications arranged on it.

"He also let me go because the Ghibellini from Siena are about to besiege the city," said Daoud. "He wants my help in surrendering to them."

"A pity the Sienese could not have gotten here in time to catch the Tartars and de Verceuil," said Sophia when the servants had left.

Ugolini looked up from the powders he was mixing for poultices and frowned. "Catch them? Why?"

Sophia stared at Ugolini. Then the news had somehow missed him. She felt sorry for him. Even though Tilia was very much alive, this was going to be a terrible shock.

Daoud said, "In the dungeon I heard something had happened at Tilia's house."

Ugolini's eyes grew huge. "Tilia! My God, what was it?"

"Tilia is well, Cardinal," Sophia said quickly. "Luckily for her, she was here when it happened." She wondered how much Daoud knew about what had happened, and how he felt about it. Her heart still ached for poor Rachel. Where was the child now, right at this moment? Somewhere on the road to Perugia. Being abused, perhaps, by that beast of a Tartar.

"When *what* happened?" Ugolini cried. "In the name of Christ and the Virgin, speak out!"

Sophia told the cardinal and Daoud how she and Tilia had gone to Tilia's house, and of the death and destruction they had found there. It hurt her to see the anguish in their eyes. Especially Daoud's. He *must* feel a terrible guilt about having sent Rachel there in the first place. Now he had to suffer that, along with pain d'Ucello had inflicted on him.

"The Tartars and de Verceuil!" Ugolini shouted, shaking clenched fists. "May God send a flood to drown them on the road to Orvieto! May all the devils in hell roast them!" He paced the floor furiously, his red robes rustling. "I must go to Tilia at once," he cried.

"No," said Daoud. "Too many people would see you."

"But she has no one to protect her."

"She has hired guards," said Sophia. "And those who ruined her house are gone."

Daoud's head fell back against the pillow, and his eyelids closed. His face looked masklike to Sophia, almost as if he were dead. She realized, with sudden anxiety, that he might be suffering terribly, without complaint. That would be like him. And she and Ugolini stood here talking. She must see to Daoud's hurts at once. He might have injuries within, injuries from which he could not recover.

"Send some of your trusted men-at-arms to protect Tilia," said Daoud without opening his eyes, his voice faint. "Riccardo and some others. Do not go yourself."

"Of course," said Ugolini, looking abashed. "Even though you have been tortured, your head is sounder than mine. But, you understand, *I* am tortured by the thought of what has happened to Tilia."

"I, too," said Daoud. "And to her people. And to Rachel."

"Tomorrow you can tell me what happened to you," said Ugolini at the door. "I will let you rest now." He drew a breath, hesitated, bit his lip. Sophia wished he would go.

Daoud raised his head and opened his eyes. "You want to ask something. What is it?"

"Did you—did d'Ucello—learn anything?"

"God willed that he learn nothing from me," said Daoud, sinking back again.

"*Your* will had something to do with that," said Sophia.

He held out against them. What a magnificent man.

But what price had he paid for his strength?

"God's will is my will," Daoud whispered.

"God be with you, then," said Ugolini, and left, pulling the door shut behind him.

Daoud's eyes opened. The sight of his eyes woke a warmth in her breast as if a small sun had risen inside her.

"Do you want to sleep?" she asked him.

"Yes, with you beside me."

Joy blazed up inside her at those words. She had been so afraid that torture would somehow destroy his caring for her.

"Oh, yes," she said. "Nothing would make me happier."

"But first I need you to wash and dress my wounds."

Daoud gritted his teeth and winced as first she lifted off the purple cloak that covered him, then inch by inch drew the yellow tunic up from his body and over his head. He groaned aloud when, with her propping up his heavy body, he raised his arms.

"O Kriste!" she whispered. She wept anew as her eyes traveled over the golden body she loved and saw huge, broken blisters and patches of red skin; swollen black bruises the size of hen's eggs; long, deep lacerations filled with crusted blood; the many little black scabs of puncture wounds.

"When Lorenzo and the Ghibellini get here, we will have d'Ucello and his torturers torn to pieces," she raged. She went to the table, folded a linen cloth, and dipped it in the water.

"I do not hate d'Ucello," said Daoud as she began, very carefully, to clean his wounds. "He has his work and I have mine. As for his torturer—Erculio is his name—d'Ucello does not know it, but his torturer is one of us."

Sophia's hand, moving the cloth lightly over a long, shallow cut that ran across the smooth, almost hairless skin of his chest, paused. Was he delirious?

"One of *us*? The torturer?"

Daoud looked amused. "I do not know where Erculio comes from, but he is a good servant of the God of Islam and of the sultan, who placed him there for my protection."

"For your protection? You mean he would have killed you."

Her body turned to ice as she faced the reality of how close she had come to losing him.

"Yes," said Daoud. "I thought I would never see you again." He reached out his arms, grimacing with pain. She put down the cloth and let him hold her. Her heart swelled up in her throat and tears burned her eyes.

And suddenly, as if a curtain were lifted, she saw that life with this man would always be this way. Whenever she was with him, there would always be a yesterday in which some miracle of good fortune kept him alive. There would always be a tomorrow in which he must face death yet again.

Her head rested on his chest for a moment; then she wiped her face and went back to cleaning and covering his wounds. Never mind her pain. Whatever he was feeling must be much worse.

He told her how to make poultices for his burns using wet cloths and powdered medicinal herbs Ugolini had prepared. It was like what she had done for his arrow wound, only now there were many more hurts to treat. Silently, in Greek, she cursed d'Ucello and cursed the torturer. She did not care whether Daoud forgave them. She would never forgive what they had done to her man.

When he was in the cellar of the Palazzo del Podesta being tortured, had he grieved at the thought of losing her, as she had sorrowed for him?

She worked her way down his body from head to foot, tying the poultices in place with strips of cloth. Thank God, they had done nothing to his manly part. That was often the first place a torturer went for. When would they make love again, she wondered. That depended on how long it took him to recover. Perhaps weeks, perhaps even months.

When she was finished with his front, he turned over with her help. Again she could not hold back her tears. Pain, not bodily, but real just the same, struck her at the sight of his tormented flesh. For a moment her eyes were covered with darkness. The skin of his back and buttocks had been whipped away in large red slashes. She shook her head violently, spoke a few more curses in her mind, and went to work. Daoud, who had endured most of her healing efforts in silence, cried out when she put a wet cloth on a torn spot.

"What more can you tell me about Rachel?" he asked. She suspected he wanted to take his mind off the pain.

She repeated everything Tilia's women had reported, ending that looking out the windows they had seen Rachel riding off in a cart with the old Franciscan who interpreted for the Tartars.

"I am glad to hear that old priest still lives," said Daoud, sighing. "Ah, Sophia, Rachel is a slave to that Tartar only because she had the ill luck to cross my path. I have brought destruction to many, many people."

Slowly, painfully, he turned on his back again, with Sophia helping. Lovingly she stroked the few patches of his skin that were not torn or burned or bruised.

When he was settled, he looked up at her and smiled in what she thought was a strange way. She did not see the cause of his smile at first, until he looked down at himself, and she followed his eyes. She saw that his key of life had begun to raise itself.

"Daoud! After all you have been through?"

"I want you, Sophia, *because* of what I have been through. Because of what I nearly lost. I will tell you more tomorrow about what, God be thanked, did not happen. For now"—he reached out a hand to her—"come to me."

She understood. He must feel like a man who had come back from the dead. Life was more precious to him than ever—and love. Tired and pain-racked though he was, he wanted this moment of being with her again, which must seem to him like a gift from God. And, indeed, perhaps that was exactly what it was.

He lay back on the bed, his tortured body naked except for the cloth wrappings tied over the worst of his wounds. His beautiful circumcised phallos pulsed as it grew larger. She wanted to be naked with him, and she threw off her outer tunic, unbelted her red silk gown, and pulled it over her head. Her shift followed. Then she stepped out of the purple felt slippers and stood before him, her arms held away from her body, to let him see her.

She felt the warmth of her own desire for him spread through her.

He said, "You are a spring that gushes out of barren rock. I thirst for you."

Carefully she climbed on the bed, straddling him. Slowly, so as not to hurt him, she lowered herself over him, guiding him into her with gentle fingers. A long sigh escaped him. She moved for both of them.

The instant after he groaned and reached his peak of love and pleasure, he fell asleep, still lying on his back. He had just enough strength to couple with me, she thought.

She rose from him and blew out the candles on the bedside table. The night was cool, and she closed the casement windows of his room.

There was space between Daoud and the wall for her to lie beside him. She stretched out there and stayed awake only long enough to kiss his bare shoulder.

Forcing himself to wake up seemed as much torture for Daoud as anything Erculio had done to him. He could only lie there and struggle against the agony he felt in every part of his body. His head ached. His tongue felt like a lump of dried camel dung. His throbbing muscles and bones begged him to sink back into unconsciousness. How long had he slept? Only an hour or two, he was sure.

The yellow glow of a lighted candle filled the room. Lorenzo was standing near the bed holding the candle, glowering at Daoud from under thick, dark brows as if he were angry at him.

Lorenzo.

Daoud wanted to laugh and leap out of bed and throw his arms around Lorenzo. He managed only to sit up, too quickly. Fires shot from his joints into his neck to coalesce in a burst of agony in the back of his head. He did not want to cry out in front of Lorenzo, but a groan forced itself through his cracked lips.

Sophia, wearing her red silk gown and standing by the bed—

How did she get out of bed and dressed before Lorenzo got in here?—took Daoud's shoulders gently and lowered him back to the bed.

Lorenzo set the candle on the table beside Daoud and sat beside him.

"What the devil did those bastards do to you?"

Daoud saw the rage in the penetrating dark eyes, and it delighted him, because Lorenzo was furious for his sake.

"Nothing that I will not recover from. More quickly, now that I see your infidel face. Have you come here to parley with the podesta?"

"Yes, Duke Rinaldo has sent his son, Lapo, and me to meet with d'Ucello here at Ugolini's."

Lorenzo had accomplished everything Daoud asked of him, and more. His timely arrival had saved Daoud's life. To think that Daoud had once wanted to be rid of him. Except for Sophia, he had never in his life felt so happy to see anyone as this grizzled Sicilian.

Sophia said, "I have tended your wounds enough for tonight, David. I leave you in Lorenzo's care." She smiled at Lorenzo and put her hand briefly on his shoulder.

As she went to the door, Lorenzo scooped something from the floor, jumped up, and handed it to her. "I believe this is yours, Madonna." He held out her red leather belt.

Sophia swept it from his hand. "Thank you, messere," she said coolly.

"Good night, Sophia," said Daoud with a smile. "You have brought me great comfort tonight."

"Good night, David," she said, and shot him a burning look that he hoped Lorenzo did not see.

After the door closed behind her, Lorenzo chuckled softly as he sat down again. "Tending your wounds with her gown off, was she? And no light in the room till I brought this candle in? You and she are not as discreet as you were before I left."

We could never fool Lorenzo, thought Daoud ruefully.

"The pope is gone, the Tartars are gone, the French are gone," said Daoud. "There is no one left in Orvieto that we need deceive. Find some soft cloths on the table to bind my feet." Creating the barrier between his mind and the pain, Daoud swung his legs over the edge of the bed. Lorenzo stared at him, his mouth falling open.

"What in the name of hell are you doing? You cannot get up! What wounds are under those bandages?"

"I do not mind the pain," said Daoud. "I want to meet this duke's son. Where is your army camped?"

Lorenzo's grin stretched his thick black mustache. "In the valley to the north. You should see it. After I climbed up to the main gate of Orvieto I looked down and saw the hundreds of campfires twinkling. It was as if the world had turned over, and I was looking down into the starry sky.''

Daoud wished he could go to the city walls to see what Lorenzo had described. But he had barely strength enough to walk from his room to Ugolini's cabinet.

Four men—Daoud, Lorenzo, Ugolini, and Lapo di Stefano—sat around Ugolini's worktable discussing the fate of Orvieto. The servants had moved the table to the center of the cabinet and had replaced the cardinal's usual clutter of philosophical instruments with platters of meat, loaves of bread baked fresh in the cardinal's kitchen, and trays of steaming pastries. Daoud had no appetite and was in too much pain to eat.

''When does your King Manfred intend to come up from the south?'' Lapo asked Daoud. He twisted the carcass of a roasted pigeon between thick, juice-stained fingers. His nose had been broken in some accident or fight; air whistled in and out of the flattened nostrils. Daoud judged him to be about twenty, the same age as Simon de Gobignon.

As far as Lapo knew, Daoud was an agent of the king of southern Italy and Sicily. It might have shocked him to discover that he was dealing with a Muslim from Egypt.

Daoud had to evade Lapo's question. He had no idea what plans Manfred had, if any. He could only hope that when he met with Manfred at Lucera he would be able to persuade him to invade the Papal States.

''King Manfred would come from the south much more quickly,'' Daoud said, ''if he could count on being recognized by the cities of the north as king of a united Italy.''

''That must be between my father and him,'' said Lapo, and his breath wheezed through his nostrils as he bit into the pigeon's breast. ''After all, no such title exists. There has never been a king of Italy.''

And yet there easily could be, thought Daoud, seeing the shape of the peninsula in his mind. And if that single ruler were a man like Manfred, what a strong barrier Italy could be between the Abode of Islam and the barbaric kingdoms of Christian Europe.

But in fact, thought Daoud, for all that Lapo di Stefano wore the Ghibellino symbol, the black, two-headed Hohenstaufen eagle, on the breast of his red silk surcoat, he and his father might still prefer that Manfred stay where he was. As long as Manfred remained cut off the from the northern cities like Siena by the band of the Papal States running across the center of Italy, the Ghibellini of the north could do as they pleased.

"When the French invade," said Daoud, "a united Italy can keep them out. If the cities of the north are divided, the French will take them over one by one."

"How do you know the French will invade?" Lapo asked. "We have heard that King Louis has no desire to wage war in Italy."

Daoud was beginning to feel a strong dislike for this coarse young nobleman who seemed both very sure of himself and very ignorant. He was about to reply when a man-at-arms entered and whispered to Ugolini.

"D'Ucello is here," Ugolini said.

"Have him wait below until we send for him," said Daoud quickly. He turned back to Lapo.

"I do not wish d'Ucello harmed."

Lapo stared coldly at Daoud. "Who are you to give orders?"

Lorenzo answered before Daoud could speak. "Let me remind you, Signore, that it was David of Trebizond whose gold made possible your capture of Orvieto."

There was too much conflict building up here, Daoud thought. "No, Lorenzo. Siena had the will, the fighting spirit. That was what made this victory possible. I contributed only money."

He turned to Lapo. "I do not give orders, I make recommendations based on my knowledge of this town. I recommend that d'Ucello continue as podesta. If you leave enough men under his command, he will keep the feuding families under control. Orvieto will prosper and pay you tribute that will make this expedition worth your while."

"The army of Siena has marched against Orvieto because Orvieto is a Guelfo stronghold," said Lapo. "We intend to replace the governments of all the cities near Siena with rulers favorable to us."

Daoud thought he understood Lapo, gauging him as a man who had little experience of war but who enjoyed bloodletting. He was probably disappointed that the city might surrender without a battle, without an excuse for looting and massacre. He might be hoping, as a substitute, to find someone who could be put to death publicly in some hideous way to demonstrate his power over the city.

"Of course you have come here to impose your will on Orvieto," he said quietly. "But be grateful that you do not have to fight your way up the mountain. If d'Ucello were to choose to resist, your army would be months taking Orvieto. Let us be glad the podesta was sensible and surrendered. Orvieto is a beautiful city. Its people will be eager to show their gratitude to a conqueror gracious to them. The ease with which you win their hearts will in turn impress your own Sienese people with your statesmanship. Of course, Orvieto was richer when the pope and most of the cardinals were here. A pity you could not have marched your army here sooner.''

It would have been easier on me too.

Lapo's thick eyebrows went up. ''I heard that you were tortured by this podesta. And I can see you have been badly hurt. You want no revenge?''

Daoud fixed Lapo with a hard look and slowly shook his head. ''Revenge does not interest me.''

''Just what does interest you, Messer Trader?'' The heir of Siena glowered at Daoud from under his heavy eyebrows. ''I do not trust a man who does not care about revenge.''

Revenge? Was not his presence at the heart of Christendom a kind of revenge for nearly two hundred years of Christian invasions of Muslim lands? Did it not make revenge all the sweeter that God's chosen instrument was a descendant of those very crusaders who had been sent against Islam? This dense young nobleman could not conceive of the fantastic forms revenge could take.

''I act in the interests of King Manfred,'' Daoud said. ''It is in his interest that Orvieto be part of the chain of Ghibellino cities in the north that limit the power of the pope. It is not in his interest—or yours—that Siena waste lives and money capturing Orvieto. The town can be taken without a struggle if you come to terms with d'Ucello. And I recommend that you leave him in place as podesta of Orvieto.''

Lapo shook his head. ''How can I trust a man who would betray his own city?''

Daoud felt his small remaining store of strength ebbing fast. He must finish this quickly.

''You will leave your own force here to keep him in line, of course. You will take prominent Orvietans back to Siena with you as hostages. But you should understand that d'Ucello is not betraying his city. He is willing to surrender because he knows that is best for Orvieto. Give him a free hand and strengthen his militia, and he will govern the town well for you.''

Lorenzo said dryly, ''This paragon of podestas waits in Cardinal Ugolini's reception hall to offer you the keys to the city of Orvieto. Shall we invite him to join us, Your Signory?''

Lapo di Stefano shrugged and waved a greasy hand. ''Send for the fellow. I will make my decision after I have seen him." He picked up another roasted pigeon and sank his teeth into it.

And life or death for hundreds of people depended on how this ape happened to choose in the next few moments, Daoud thought, as Lorenzo went to the door and called a servant. Why did God put such men in positions of power?

Soon there was a knock at the door, and Lorenzo went to it and admitted d'Ucello. The podesta's face was hidden by the dark brown hood of his cloak.

For all this man knows, I plan to have him killed, Daoud thought, admiring d'Ucello's courage in coming here.

"You come recommended to us as a man who can keep order in this city," said Lapo as d'Ucello took a seat.

"And we can think of no higher recommendation, since it comes from a man you have just been torturing," said Lorenzo.

"This man has the strength of the old Romans," said d'Ucello, nodding toward Daoud. "He knows when to put a personal grievance aside for the greater good."

Lapo said, "If we were willing to let you remain as podesta of this city, in return for your oath of allegiance to the Duke of Siena, how many men would you need to keep the city under control?"

"With two hundred men I could match the Mondaldeschi forces," said d'Ucello. "The Filippeschi have been crushed, and so badly that they may go over to the Ghibellino party." His dark eyes lit up. He was relishing the prospect of giving orders, Daoud thought, to the old houses that had treated him like a servant.

Can it be that my legacy to Orvieto may be an improved government? I certainly did not come here for that purpose.

But Daoud felt himself weakening. His overtaxed body would soon betray him into sleep if he did not go to bed of his own accord.

"If you have no further need of me—" he said. Lorenzo helped him stand, and leaning on him, he limped to the door.

"I owe you more than I can say," d'Ucello called after him.

"Pray to God that I do not decide to repay my debt to *you,*" Daoud answered. He did not look back, but he could imagine d'Ucello's small, grim smile.

LVII

Simon and King Louis stood side by side on the yellow, sandy west bank of the Rhone River opposite Avignon. They had just crossed over the Pont d'Avignon, a long, narrow bridge of twenty-two arches. Avignon was a compact city, encircled by butter-colored walls fortified with red cone-roofed towers. A prosperous city as well, Simon thought as he regarded the many church spires rising above the walls. Even during his brief glimpse of the city upon his arrival late the night before, he had seen many great houses.

He looked at the tall, gaunt king, whose round eyes stared thoughtfully off into the cloudy sky.

It was lucky for Simon—if it were proper to think of a man's death as lucky—that the funeral of Count Raymond of Provence, father of Louis's Queen Marguerite, had brought the king here, so close to Italy. Otherwise Simon might still be traveling northward with the pope's letter. When he landed at Aigues-Mortes he had found the whole port abuzz with the news of Count Raymond's death and of the coming of the French royal family to bury him in state and settle the future of the county of Provence.

A traveler from a foreign land looking at Louis would never imagine that he was a king, Simon thought. A plain brown felt cap covered Louis's thinning gray hair, draping down one side of his head. His robe and a cloak of thin, cheap wool, dyed black, were not warm enough for this chill September morning. Perhaps, Simon thought, the penitential shirt of woven horsehair he wore next to his skin warmed Louis even as it discomforted him. He carried no weapon at his dull leather belt, only the parchment scroll, the pope's letter, which Simon had given him the night before. Louis's shoes were of the same sort of leather as his belt, and the points of their toes were far too short to be fashionable.

Simon felt overdressed beside the king, and resolved that from now on he would try to dress more plainly.

With his long fingers, King Louis tapped the scroll tucked into

150

his belt. "He afflicts me sorely, this Jacques Pantaleone, this Pope Urban."

"The pope afflicts you, Sire?" Simon was surprised to see the king unhappy about the pope's message to him. He had expected Louis to be overjoyed at getting permission to deal with the Tartars.

A sudden worry struck him. What if the king and the pope could not agree? All his work would have been for nothing—over a year of his life, all the fighting and dying—to say nothing of the personal expense of paying forty Venetian crossbowmen for over a year and maintaining six knights—

Now five, a grief-laden thought reminded him.

Yes, and what about Alain? Was his death to be for nothing?

Worst of all, the accomplishment he had hoped would put him on the road to redeeming his family's honor would be no accomplishment at all. The year wasted, lives wasted, the shadow of treason still lying upon his name and title.

What joy he had felt only a little earlier this morning, knowing he would accompany King Louis on his morning walk after Mass. Now his eager anticipation seemed like so much foolishness.

But, of all the men in the world, this is the one I would never want to disappoint.

Whatever Louis decided *must* be right. But, dear God, let him not decide to cast away the alliance.

Louis said, "Urban grants the thing I want most in the world, but only if I agree to that which I desire least. And I do not want to give in to him."

Oh, God! The sky seemed to darken.

"What does he ask you to do, Sire?"

Louis sighed, a deep, tremulous expulsion of breath. "He asks that the might of France should be diverted into a squabble among petty princes in Italy, when Jerusalem is at stake!"

It seems more than a squabble when you are in the thick of it, thought Simon, remembering the night the Filippeschi had attacked the Monaldeschi palace.

"I cannot wait any longer to begin preparing for a crusade," Louis said. "I want to return to Outremer in six years, in 1270. That may seem to you a long time away, but for such a great undertaking as this it is barely enough. It took me four years to get ready for the last crusade, to gather the men and supplies, and it will be harder this time."

"Why 1270, Sire?" said Simon.

Louis's head drooped and his eyes fell. "To win my freedom I promised Baibars, the Mameluke leader who is now Sultan of Cairo, that I would not wage war on Islam for twenty years.''

"An oath to an unbeliever—'' said Simon.

"My royal word!'' said Louis fiercely. "And besides that, France needed twenty years to recover from the loss of thousands of men, men *I* lost, to raise up a new generation of knights like yourself to take the cross again.''

Many times during his boyhood years of living with the royal family, Simon had observed that the queen, or the king's brothers or his sons would burst out in exasperation over Louis's insistence on adherence to some principle, regardless of inconvenience or discomfort. In Simon's eyes this had always meant that the king was a better Christian than the other members of his family. Now, seeing all his work and his hopes possibly ruined by the king's refusal to come to the pope's aid against the Ghibellini, Simon was disturbed to feel a similar anger at Louis arise within him.

Simon stared at the man he loved so well, and saw that even though the king was talking of war, his thin, pale face was raised to heaven in an exalted, almost angelic look.

"But only the pope can proclaim a crusade,'' Louis said. "Unless he does so, I cannot raise an army. And if we attack the Saracens in Egypt while the Tartars strike through Syria, we will be invincible. But without the pope's permission I cannot make a pact with the Tartars. In this letter he gives that permission, but he makes it conditional on my involving France in his struggle with Manfred von Hohenstaufen.''

Simon was in despair. Louis would refuse, and the alliance would go a-glimmering.

Louis put a hand on Simon's shoulder. "Be patient awhile, Simon. My queen and my brother, Count Charles, will join us at breakfast. We will talk together of all this.''

The weight of Louis's hand sent a warmth all through him. But how could the king expect him to be patient when he had so much to lose?

"Count Charles meets with you this morning?'' Simon asked. He had known that Charles d'Anjou was in Avignon, but thought it his duty to carry the pope's letter straight to the king, without first taking the time to seek out his mentor, the king's brother.

"Yes,'' sighed Louis, "we meet for another petty squabble. My queen was the only heir of her father, the Count of Provence, and now the county is ours to dispose of. Marguerite wants to keep it in my immediate family, giving it to our son Tristan. But Charles wants it for himself. He already holds Anjou, Aquitaine, and Arles.

Add Provence to that, and he would have a domain stretching from the Pyrenees to Italy. Whatever I decide, I will offend either my brother or my wife.'' He shook his head. ''That is why it makes me so happy to talk to you, Simon. Young men understand what is really important so much better than their elders.''

''Sire, I would do anything you asked of me.'' On a sudden impulse, Simon fell to his knees on the sand and seized Louis's bony hand and kissed it.

Louis gripped his arms and raised him. Simon felt surprising strength in Louis's hands.

''Do not kneel to me, Simon,'' said the king, and Simon saw that his eyes were brimming with tears. ''But it would mean so much to me if you, of all men, would take the cross.''

If I, of all men—

Simon understood. Louis was thinking of Amalric de Gobignon, whose treachery fourteen years earlier had been the final blow to Louis's crusade into Egypt. The king's life had been shadowed ever since, Simon knew, by the memory of an entire army lost in the sands by the Nile and by his failure to win Jerusalem.

And no matter that I am not really the son of Amalric. If I inherited his title, his lands, and his power, I must inherit his shame too. And atone for it.

Louis was still holding Simon's arms. The light blue eyes froze him with their stare.

''I have sworn to liberate Jerusalem. I will do it, or I will die. If I cannot have the help of the Tartars, I will still go. If every knight and man-at-arms in Christendom refused to go with me—if I had to go alone—I would still go.''

God help me, you will never have to go alone as long as I live. If you go on crusade, I will go too.

But there must be a Tartar alliance. There must!

''Let us walk back over to the city and to breakfast, Simon,'' said Louis. ''Marguerite and Charles will be waiting for us.''

As they walked to the bridge of Avignon, preceded and followed at a discreet distance by the king's guards in blue and silver tunics, Simon felt himself torn. He wanted to please King Louis, and he wanted to redeem the name of his house. But must he live out his whole life expiating the crimes of Amalric de Gobignon, who was not even his real father?

Roland and Nicolette laid a heavy burden on me when they brought me into the world, he thought bitterly.

Again he thought of Sophia. If he could persuade her to come and dwell with him at Gobignon, he could forget the shame of Amalric and live simply and in peace, a happy man.

Since high matters of state were to be discussed here, over breakfast in the private dining room of the palace of the bishop of Avignon, the servants had been dismissed. King Louis, Queen Marguerite, Prince Tristan, Count Charles, and Simon were alone together. The large round table was piled high—a whole roast duck, a dozen boiled eels, blocks of hard cheese, a pyramid of hard-boiled eggs, bowls of pickled fruits, stacked loaves of fine white bread, trays of cheese pastries, and flagons of wine.

Simon sliced the eels and put oval white slices on each person's trencher, while Prince Tristan carved and distributed the duck. As they did so, King Louis read aloud the pope's letter granting him permission to conduct a crusade jointly with the Tartars in return for French help against the Ghibellini.

"Your next crusade will make me a widow." Queen Marguerite said, her round face white and her fists clenched on the table. "As your last did to so many other women."

Tristan, a sturdy, ruddy-faced youth a few years younger than Simon, went around the table pouring red Rhone valley wine into everyone's cup but his father's. Louis poured his own wine from another pitcher, and Simon saw that it was a pale pink. It must be more water than wine.

Louis's long, thin fingers, carrying a slice of eel to his mouth as Marguerite spoke, stopped in midair, and he slowly put the meat back on his trencher. But he said nothing.

"Do not speak so, madame," said Charles as he used a long thumbnail darkened by the dirt under it to break and peel the shell from a hard-boiled egg. "It brings ill luck." Simon heard the venomous undertone in his voice.

Even though this was the first time they had seen each other since Charles sent Simon to Italy to guard the Tartars, the Count of Anjou had hardly spoken to Simon this morning. Hurt, Simon wondered how he had offended Charles.

Marguerite, tall and stout, her head wrapped in a linen coif held in place with a net of pearls, stood with a sudden, graceless lunge that knocked her chair over. Tristan, blushing, went to pick it up, and she caught his hand.

"What need of ill luck when I have a husband bent on destroying himself, and he has a brother who is only too happy to help him do it?" She turned away from the table, pulling Tristan after her. "I take with me this boy, lest he spoil your pleasant dreams of crusading by reminding you of how and where he was born." With long, angry strides she was at the door. Tristan stepped in front of his mother to open the door for her.

"Good morning to you, madame," said Louis softly, still looking down at the slices of boiled eel that lay before him. The door slammed behind the queen and her son.

"What did she mean by that?" Charles said, sounding quite unconcerned by the queen's outburst.

"Do you not remember, brother?" said Louis. "Marguerite gave birth to Tristan alone in Egypt, while you and I were prisoners of the Mamelukes. She has never forgotten how terrified she was."

To mask his embarrassment, Simon took a big swallow of the red wine. It was thick and tart, and burned in his chest as it went down. He never enjoyed wine this early in the day. He wished he could drink heavily watered wine, as King Louis did, but he feared people like Uncle Charles would think him a weakling.

Charles popped the entire hard-boiled egg into his mouth, and spoke around it. "It is best that the queen has left us. I do not understand why she dislikes me so."

"I do not understand why you and she dislike each other," said Louis sadly.

"We will talk of that another time." Charles picked up the scroll of the pope's letter and shook it at Louis. "You must let me go to the aid of the Holy Father."

Charles's fingernails were quite long, Simon knew, because he never bothered to trim them. His hair and stubble of beard were thick and pure black, while Louis's face was smooth and his hair, what was left of it, was a silvery gray. Charles was broad-shouldered and sat erect; Louis was slender of frame and slightly stooped. It was hard to believe that two such different-looking men were brothers. But they did both have what were said to be the Capet family features—they were very tall, with long faces, large noses, and round, staring eyes, Louis's blue and Charles's brown. They both dressed plainly, but Charles dressed like a fighting man, in leather jerkin and high boots that he stretched out before him as he sat sideways to the table.

Simon used his dagger to cut himself a chunk of white bread—baked before dawn in the bishop of Avignon's ovens—from one of the loaves in the center of the table. He hoped it would soak up the wine that still smoldered in his stomach.

Louis said, "All my life, people have been trying to get me to make war on the Hohenstaufen family. Our mother, may she rest in peace. One pope after another. Now you. All call the Hohenstaufen mortal enemies of Christendom. I am still not persuaded."

Charles laughed scornfully. "Brother! Who do you think incited the Sienese to take Orvieto? And in this letter His Holiness says Manfred is preparing to march north against him."

Simon wondered if Sophia was still in Orvieto. Ever since he had heard the news that a Ghibellino army had captured the city on the rock, apparently without a battle, worries about Sophia's safety had gnawed at him. He wished desperately that he could be wherever she was, to protect her. And how he longed just to see her, to hold her in his arms, to kiss her beautiful golden face, to taste her lips, the color of sweet red grapes.

Louis said, "Manfred is only trying to protect his crown, which the pope wants you to take from him."

Simon prayed that Charles would persuade Louis, but he had little hope of it. He had many times seen the king, his mind made up, gently obstinate, never raising his voice, never losing his patience, withstanding the arguments of his whole family and court.

Then Simon, listening to the argument, became aware of something he had not noticed earlier. Neither of the royal brothers had mentioned the pope's poor health. Probably because neither of them had seen for himself how sick Pope Urban was.

He waited for a pause, then spoke. "Sire, Uncle Charles, the Holy Father seemed to me to be very gravely ill by the time I left him. He told me that he expects to die soon. If he does die now, will not this permission for the alliance with the Tartars die with him?" Simon pointed to the letter.

"Yes, it will," said Louis frowning, "We will have to start all over again with the next pope."

"Manfred could try to influence the election of the pope," said Simon urgently. "Or he could try to control the next pope by taking him captive."

Louis rubbed his high forehead. "It has been done before, more than once."

Charles's large, hairy hand clamped down on Louis's forearm. "Simon has hit upon the key to all this, brother. Think how powerful the Ghibellini are in Italy now. They control Florence, Siena, Pisa, Lucca, and now Orvieto. With all those Ghibellino cities to the north of the Papal States and Manfred to the south, is it not obvious what Manfred is planning?"

Charles struck Louis's arm again and again with the flat of his hand to emphasize his point. No one else would dare touch the king like that, thought Simon.

"Obvious to you, perhaps," said Louis wryly. "I see only a man trying to protect himself."

"The instant Pope Urban dies, Manfred and his allies will attack. He will surround and seize the entire College of Cardinals. He will force them to elect the pope of his choice. We will lose the Papacy."

"We do not *own* the Papacy."

Charles leaned back, laughing without mirth. "Well, Manfred will own the Papacy if we do not stop him. And then you can forget about your Tartar alliance. You can probably forget about crusading altogether. A pope controlled by the Hohenstaufen would probably forbid you to crusade, under pain of excommunication. Do not forget, it was Manfred's father, Emperor Frederic, who made a treaty with the Sultan of Cairo."

Simon watched Louis closely to see what effect Charles's words were having. It was obvious that they were sinking in. A troubled frown drew Louis's pale brows together and tightened his mouth. Simon's heart began to beat faster as his hopes rose.

Charles went on. "If I go now, I go at the pope's invitation. And if Urban dies—"

Louis made a reverent sign of the cross. "If it be God's will, Charles."

"Yes, yes, if it be God's will that this pope dies, I will already be in Italy," Charles said. "I can be in Rome, athwart Manfred's path, and he will not be able to intimidate the College of Cardinals when they elect the next pope. You must let me go into Italy to protect our interests. Or else give up your dream of Jerusalem."

A long moment of silence passed, Louis staring into Charles's eyes.

Louis held up a finger. "I will not declare war on Manfred. If you go, this is entirely your doing, and that of the pope."

We've won! The king has given in! Simon, wild with joy inside, forced himself to sit silent.

Charles did not look as pleased as Simon felt. "But, if you don't declare war, where will I get the knights and men?"

Louis held up a second finger. "You will get them yourself. I will not provide them. You will have to hire them. And if Manfred beats your army, I will not send more men to rescue you."

Charles shrugged. "Well, I have the best tax collectors in Europe."

Louis raised a third finger. "You will forget about Provence."

Charles looked outraged. "Forget about—" he sputtered.

Louis raised a finger. "Charles, I will not let you have both Sicily and Provence. You want too much."

Charles sighed. "Very well. Let Provence go to Tristan. You have put me in a position where I will desperately need the taxes Provence would yield. But I will make do somehow."

"I am sure you will," said Louis. "If you have to sell all the clothes from all the backs in the lands you now rule."

Louis thought a moment, and then turned to Simon, who, glowing inwardly, leapt to his feet.

"Yes, Sire!"

Louis looked startled at Simon's vehemence. "I will write two letters for you to take to Perugia. One for the reigning pope, who, I pray, will still be Pope Urban. In that I will give my permission for the Count of Anjou to accept the crown the pope has offered him and to make war on Manfred."

He stopped, sighed, and shook his head.

Turning to his brother, he said, "I do this with great sorrow and misgiving, Charles, but I fear I have no choice."

The Count of Anjou said nothing, but Simon saw his chest rapidly rising and falling with excitement.

"Should God take Pope Urban, Simon, you will hold the letter, sealed, until a new pope is elected and then give it to him. The other letter, in the event Pope Urban dies, will be for Cardinal de Verceuil. You mentioned that Manfred might try to influence the election of the next pope. Fourteen out of twenty-one cardinals are French, and if they vote together, they can elect a pope. I shall recommend a candidate they can unite behind. Again, I do not like to do this, because a king should not interfere in the election of a pope. Should Pope Urban live to read the first letter, you will not give the second letter to Cardinal de Verceuil, but will burn it, still sealed, and see that not a trace remains."

Charles shrugged. "The Hohenstaufen did it again and again."

"They *tried* to do it," said Louis, "and that is one reason that they and the popes are such enemies. But I do it for the same reason I allow you to go to Italy, Charles. To prevent a greater calamity and to accomplish a greater good."

"And who will your choice for pope be, brother?"

Louis stood up. "I do not want to compromise myself even more by letting that be known. I will write the name in my letter, and the letter will be sealed."

He stood up. "If you defeat Manfred, may God have mercy on you, Charles. You will be a king in your own right, and you will know what it is to have to make decisions like this."

Simon felt sure that making royal decisions would never be the agony for Charles that it was for Louis.

Charles stood up, too, then dropped to his knee and pressed his forehead against his brother's pale hand. "God bless you, Louis. I promise you, this is one decision you will always be happy to have made."

I will always be happy he made it, Simon thought.

Later, as they walked together through the gray stone halls of the bishop of Avignon's palace, Charles struck Simon on the shoulder. The blow threw Simon off stride, reminding him how strong Charles was.

"You did it, boy, you tipped the balance for me when you pointed out what might happen if the pope dies," Charles said with a grin. "I was quite angry with you until then."

"I had a feeling you were, uncle," he said.

Charles's nail-studded boots clicked on the stone floor of the corridor. "Have you forgotten that if it were not for me, you would still be growing cobwebs at Gobignon?"

"No, uncle, I have not forgotten."

"Then why did you take the pope's letter to my brother without telling me about it?"

Simon felt a dull heat in his face. Somewhere in the back of his mind he had always known that Uncle Charles would want to be told first about any messages passing between the pope and the king. But, feeling it would be wrong, Simon had pretended to himself that he knew no such thing.

"It was my duty to take it promptly to the king," said Simon, looking straight ahead.

Charles suddenly stopped walking. "Simon," he said, forcing Simon to stop, turn, and look at him.

"Simon, do not let your idea of duty make you forget your loyalty to me. I helped raise you as a boy. I gave you this opportunity to bring honor to your house. I will be offering you even greater opportunities."

"I have not forgotten, uncle," Simon said again.

"I do not suppose you know how to unseal and reseal a royal document?"

Simon felt his blood heat with anger.

"No, uncle." He did not feel strong enough to denounce Charles, but he tried to put disapproval into his voice. "I have never heard of anyone doing such a thing."

"Pas mal. Too bad." Charles's round eyes were heavy-lidded

with contempt. "Well, I must leave at once to begin squeezing the money for this campaign out of my subjects. Especially since I have given up my claim to Provence. I cannot wait around to see who my brother thinks should be pope. I am sure he will make a good choice."

"I am sure he will," said Simon frostily.

I pray God it is not de Verceuil himself.

Again the heavy blow on his shoulder, both comradely and threatening. "Well, then. In the future when you have important news, make sure I am the first one to hear it."

Simon felt hotter still. Uncle Charles was supposedly helping him win back his honor, and yet was proposing that he betray the king's trust. He had admired Uncle Charles all his life because he seemed to be everything a great baron should—commanding, strong, warlike, victorious, loyal to the king, the Church, and the pope. But he had always had the uneasy feeling that Charles d'Anjou was not a *good* man in the sense that King Louis was. And he had always kept in the back of his mind his mother's warning, *He uses people.* He had felt that unease strongly over a year ago, the day Charles asked him to lead the Tartars' military escort. Now he knew there was good reason for that uneasiness.

"Yes, uncle." Simon had no intention of obeying, but since Charles had no right to ask such a thing, there was no harm in misleading him. After a year in Italy and all he had been through, Simon found he feared his Uncle Charles less than he had. And trusted him less.

And now, he thought, it would be back to Italy. Back to see his efforts bear fruit, as the alliance of Christians and Tartars became a reality. Perhaps he would escort the Tartars to France, to King Louis, so they could draw up their war plans together.

But, best of all, he would seek out Sophia in Perugia. He would propose marriage to her again. Now she would believe him, now that she'd had time to think about everything he had said to her. Sophia. Seeing her in his mind, he felt as if he walked among the angels.

LVIII

Manfred von Hohenstaufen sat at a table at the far end of the colonnaded audience chamber, his pale blond hair gleaming in the candlelight.

"Come forward," he called to Daoud and Lorenzo. He beckoned to them, the wide sleeve of his green tunic falling away from his arm.

Their booted feet echoed on the long floor of polished pink marble. Daoud's stomach felt hollow. He *must* persuade Manfred to carry the war into the north at once.

A dark green velvet cloth, hanging to the floor, covered the table at which the king of southern Italy and Sicily sat. The tabletop was strewn with pens and open rolls of parchment. Two chamberlains in dark brown tunics hovered at Manfred's back. He wrote quickly on one parchment after another, and handed them to his two assistants. Even though it was a sunny morning outside, this chamber had few windows, and Manfred, to see his work, needed candelabra at each end of the table.

When Daoud and Lorenzo reached his table, he waved in dismissal to the chamberlains, and they bowed and left, carrying armloads of scrolls. Seeing Manfred at work, Daoud felt a powerfully protective impulse toward him. Manfred was not *his* king, but he had become a worthy ally, and Daoud was prepared to fight Manfred's enemies. To die, if need be, fighting them.

"An old friend of yours wants to greet you, David," said Manfred, his bright smile flashing.

Daoud saw no one. In a candlelit alcove behind Manfred hung a painting of a red-bearded man in mail armor partly covered by a black and gold surcoat. It was not painted on the wall, but seemed to be on a separate piece of wood with a gilded border, which was hung on the wall. The man looked a bit like Manfred, and Daoud suspected it must be his father, the famous Emperor Frederic. There was an idolatrous look about the painting and the way it was displayed that made Daoud uneasy. It reminded him a bit of the saint's image Sophia had kept in her room at Orvieto.

"David of Trebizond!" came a cry from beside Manfred. Manfred reached down and helped a bent, monkeylike figure scramble up to stand on the table.

"God blesses our meeting, Daoud ibn Abdallah—this time," said the dwarf Erculio.

He grinned at Daoud through his spiky black mustache. At the sight of him Daoud winced at the memory of all the pain this little man had inflicted on him. He still felt some of that pain, especially in his feet, despite the tawidh's hastening of the healing process. But Daoud also felt a sudden warmth that reminded him of the first time he had seen the little man, here at Lucera. Deformed in body and soul, required to do unspeakable things, Erculio had still found a way to serve God.

"If my lord Daoud wishes to kill me, I am at his service," said Erculio in Arabic. "I have finished the work our sultan sent me to do in Italy."

Daoud found himself smiling in spite of himself. "You would have saved me from a mutilation worse than death, Erculio. I cannot hate you for that. You did your work well."

Erculio looked like a spider when he bowed, his head touching the tabletop, his elbows bent upward. "I am my lord's slave."

He was the more admirable, Daoud thought, because despite being so deformed, he had found important work to do in the world.

"How is your former master, d'Ucello, faring with the Sienese in Orvieto?" he asked Erculio.

Erculio spread his hands wide. "Alas! The podesta is dead."

"Dead?" It was hard to believe. Daoud heard Lorenzo's startled grunt beside him.

"The Contessa di Monaldeschi never forgave him for surrendering to the Sienese without a fight," Erculio said. "Vittorio, the Monaldeschi heir, stabbed him to death in his office and then escaped into the hills. He is probably seeking asylum with the Church leaders in Perugia."

"I would rather have heard that d'Ucello killed Vittorio," said Lorenzo. "Then there would be some sense in the world."

Daoud felt a pang of sorrow, and was surprised at himself. After all, had not d'Ucello arrested him and subjected him to a day and a night of horrible torment, with the threat of worse hanging over him? But he remembered the podesta as a man of rare ability, who would have ruled Orvieto well, given a chance. His death was a waste.

Manfred said, "Erculio has told me of your arrest and your sufferings at the hands of the podesta of Orvieto. I want to hear more about that. But let us speak now of Perugia. What is Ugolini doing?"

"Lorenzo and I escorted Cardinal Ugolini to Perugia and left him there," Daoud said. "He planned to block the election of a new pope by keeping the Italian cardinals united behind himself." He paused a moment. Now should he bring up his conviction that Manfred must march northward before a new pope was elected?

But while he hesitated, Manfred spoke. "What of Sophia Karaiannides?" Manfred looked sharply at Daoud, the sapphire eyes intent. "Why did you not bring her back here with you?"

Jealous anger stabbed Daoud. Sophia had spoken little of Manfred, but Daoud had long ago realized that she and Manfred must have been lovers. He had decided not to think about that. Now Manfred was wondering what had happened between Sophia and Daoud, and perhaps wanted Sophia back; Daoud could read it in Manfred's tone and the look in his eyes.

Daoud tried to see Manfred as Sophia might have. Intensely—one might almost say blindingly—handsome, strong, graceful, his brilliant mind attractively decked out with elegance and wit, learned but carrying his learning lightly, skilled in all the courtly arts and graces. What woman could resist such a man?

But Manfred must have tired of her, as such men did, who had access to any woman they wanted. Perhaps his queen, or some new love of his, had insisted that Sophia be sent away. And once she was gone, he had realized what he had lost.

Too late now, Manfred.

But, he reminded himself, he must not let Sophia come between himself and Manfred.

Daoud put out his hands, palms up. "Sophia is with Cardinal Ugolini. The cardinal's courage fails him at times. We thought it best for one of us to stay and give him strength. And Sophia can help him run his household and entertain the men of influence he must see."

Manfred nodded, a small smile twitching his blond mustache. "Yes, she would be good at that."

Daoud thought of Simon de Gobignon and felt a flash of hatred for him. But he must report about him, too.

"She has captured the heart of a young French nobleman, the Count de Gobignon, who commands the Tartars' military escort. When Charles d'Anjou invades Italy, de Gobignon will surely be one of his captains."

"*When* Charles d'Anjou invades Italy? And a moment ago you said *when* a pope of the French party is elected."

Daoud was about to reply, but Manfred raised a hand for silence. He rose from his high-back chair. With a glance, as if for reassurance, at the portrait of the red-bearded man hanging behind him, he strode out in front of the table with his hands clasped behind his back. Daoud and Lorenzo made way for him. He walked the length of the marble floor to the door at the end of the hall. The dwarf Erculio sank down cross-legged on the tabletop, his long arms clasped around his knees, watching Manfred sombrely.

Daoud prayed, *Oh, God, help him to judge wisely.*

"King Louis has always held Charles back," Manfred said, turning suddenly to face Daoud and Lorenzo. "Louis does not believe that the pope should set Christian rulers against one another."

And help me to advise him well.

Daoud gathered his thoughts. The success of his mission in Italy depended on persuading Manfred to choose the right course. His heart beat harder. He tried to speak with all the assurance he could muster.

"Sire, there are enough French cardinals to elect the next pope. They are bound to choose a man who will give King Louis what he wants—the alliance between Christians and Tartars. And that same pope will surely offer your crown to Charles d'Anjou as Urban did. If Louis has the alliance he wants above all else, he will not stand in Charles's way."

Manfred sighed and turned away. "So, you think war is certain."

Accept it! Daoud cried out to Manfred in his heart. *Hesitate no longer.*

"Yes, once a pope is elected, " Daoud said. "But you can act before that happens. Use the time Ugolini is gaining for you. March north now, Sire, while your enemies are without a head. Join forces with your Ghibellino allies in northern Italy—Siena, Florence, Pisa, and the rest. Surround the College of Cardinals and you can force them to elect a pope of your choice. Or scatter them. Three-fourths of them are needed for the election of a pope. You might be able to stop the election altogether."

Manfred's back remained turned. Daoud looked at Lorenzo. He could not read Lorenzo's expression; the Sicilian's mouth was hidden beneath his grizzled mustache. But Lorenzo shook his head slightly, as if to say that Daoud was not having the effect he wanted. At that, Daoud felt himself waver toward despair. He commanded himself to stand firm.

Manfred walked back to the table. He stood before Daoud, his hands still clasped behind him. His face wore a haunted look. The cheerful self-confidence Daoud had always seen before was gone.

"The north is a quagmire this time of year."

"For your enemies as well as for you," Daoud said. "And they do not—yet—have anything like the strength you can muster. You can call up your vassals here in a few weeks' time. When Charles gets a summons from the new pope, he will then have to gather his troops in France and cross the Alps into Italy. By the time he is ready, you could have all of Italy under your control. And there would be no pope to give legitimacy to his invasion."

Manfred snorted and turned away. Daoud, Erculio, and Lorenzo watched him pace.

He came back and said, "No. I do not trust those you call my allies in the north. They opposed the pope, but neither do they want to be ruled by me. If I were to try to make myself king of Italy, they would turn against me."

Probably true, Daoud thought, remembering the reluctance of Lapo di Stefano, the heir of Siena, to recognize Manfred's kingship over all of Italy.

Baibars would be in the north like lightning, though. He would welcome the bad weather, because it would impede his foes while he himself would simply not *let* his own troops slow down because of it. And if any of his allies even thought of betraying him, he would kill them. But that was Baibars. This king, Daoud remembered, had at first not wanted to help him with his mission in Orvieto because it might provoke a war.

Manfred, he saw, kept raising objections because he really wanted to be left alone to enjoy what he had. He showed no interest whatever in conquering all of Italy. He was the enlightened ruler of a civilized, prosperous land, and he probably would not go to war until the enemy was on his border.

Though Daoud felt for Manfred and his wish to be at peace, he knew that no ruler could refuse the duty of war. Peace could be achieved only by conquering the enemies of peace. Every great ruler of Islam from the Prophet to Salah ad-Din and Baibars had been a warrior on horseback.

Daoud's heart felt like a lump of lead. He saw so clearly that with one stroke they could end the danger of a union between Tartars and Christians and save Manfred's kingdom.

He sighed inwardly. He had tried his best and failed.

He had no choice but to accept that. But acceptance was not

surrender. You surrendered only to the will of God. You accepted things as they were, but struggled to make them better.

The potter does not sigh for better clay, but works with what God puts in his hand, Sheikh Saadi said.

Manfred turned away from Daoud, walked around the table with another glance at the portrait, and sat down. He frowned at a parchment that lay before him, as if wishing to end the conversation.

Daoud said, "Then, Sire, let us at least prepare to defend ourselves as best we can." He untied a small leather bag from his belt and went over to the desk. Manfred looked up, his blond eyebrows lifted.

Daoud said, "Allow the sultan of the lands of Islam, who feels himself a brother to you, to come to your aid with this gift." He upended the leather bag over the table, and a flood of tiny lights spilled out. Erculio gasped and drew back from the small pile of precious stones.

Manfred stared in wonder. "This is enough to pay and equip enough knights and men-at-arms to double the size of my army. Your sultan gives with a great heart." He looked at Daoud with more warmth that Daoud had ever seen in those cold blue eyes. "Or is it in fact you who give?"

"My lord the sultan commanded me to use this wealth carefully, and to help you if your enemies should attack."

Manfred said, "These, then, remain of the jewels I sent you with to Orvieto? Twelve? You are a remarkably good steward, Daoud. I should put you in charge of my treasury."

Daoud inclined his head respectfully. "I hope you will put me where I can serve you better, Sire."

"And where is that?"

"Sire, my work here is far from done. Give me a unit of your army to command. Let them be, if you permit, fighting men of my own faith."

And I may yet kill the Tartars and rescue Rachel.

Manfred's face fairly glowed. He picked up one of the jewels from his table, a large precious topaz of a warm golden color. He took Daoud's hand, laid the rare stone on his palm, and closed his fingers over it.

"This is yours. Use it to recruit and supply a troop of your own in my service. They should count themselves blessed by God to have a Mameluke to train and lead them."

"It is I who am blessed," Daoud said.

He looked at the stone in his hand. It was a shade lighter than the color of Sophia's eyes.

He bowed again to Manfred. At last he could fight as he preferred to, leading troops in open battle. As a Mameluke.

Smiling to himself, he stroked his chin.

And at last I can let my beard grow.

A letter from Emir Daoud ibn Abdallah to El Malik Baibars al-Bunduqdari, from Lucera, 19th day of Rabia, A.H. 663

Next to the Byzantine Empire this kingdom of southern Italy and Sicily is the most civilized of Christian nations. That is to say, a Muslim might almost be comfortable here. In fact, many are.

The chief interests of King Manfred's courtiers are falconry, poetry, dalliance with beautiful women, and philosophical disputation. My lord will note that I do not mention warfare.

King Manfred seems to hope that some intervention by God or fate or chance will make it unnecessary for him to take the field against Charles d'Anjou.

Christian warriors generally prefer to wait for their enemies to come to them, reasoning that a small force of defenders can defeat a large force of attackers. That is why there are castles everywhere in Europe, even in the cities of Europe. Their wars against us, that they call crusades, are an exception, and perhaps, too, they have learned something from the failure of those invasions.

But this is also an exceptional moment. The Guelfi and the French are not ready to fight, and Manfred could win everything if he were to act now.

I tried to persuade him to invade northern Italy and bring the Papacy under his control, but he would have none of it. So we must await Charles, and defeat him when he comes. After that Italy will lie open to Manfred. Then for his own future safety he will have to place the pope under his influence.

But how I long for a day like that when I rode behind my lord Baibars to destroy the Tartars on the field at the Well of Goliath.

It appears to me now that God intends the destiny of the Dar al-Islam to hinge on one great battle. If Manfred defeats Charles d'Anjou in Italy, the Franks will withdraw to lick their wounds. The French losses will deprive Louis of the troops he needs for his crusade against us. But, if Manfred falls, then the pope and the Franks, made greedy by victory, will be eager to join forces with the Tartars and extend their empire into our sacred lands of Islam. I will do my best to see that the Franks do not defeat Manfred, and if I fail I hope not to live to see what comes after.

All is in the hands of God, the All-Powerful, the Compassionate.

LIX

COLD AND STEADY, THE RAIN DRUMMED ON SIMON'S WIDE-brimmed leather hat. His wool cloak had been soaking up water all day, and lay heavy as an iron plate on his body. It was not yet sunset, he knew, but the rain so darkened the streets of Perugia that he despaired of finding his destination.

He rode along the wide main street hunched over against the chill rain, Sordello and Thierry on either side, their two spare horses and their baggage mule trailing behind. People hurried past without looking up.

"There it is!" Sordello shouted through the rain.

Simon's first thought on seeing the Baglioni palace was, *If only we had been in a place like that when the Filippeschi attacked*.

Rain and darkness made it hard for him to see it in detail, but lighted torches and candles glowing inside the windows limned its general shape. The square central tower loomed high above the surrounding city, its stone face ruddy in the glow from the upper windows of four cylindrical corner turrets. The palace was surrounded by a high outer wall, and Simon supposed there was an expanse of bare ground between the wall and the main building. To him, the palace looked more like a great French country château than a noble Italian family's town house.

Streamers of purple cloth, betokening mourning, were draped from one turret of the gatehouse to the other, the rain-soaked ends flapping across the arch of the gateway.

The tall wooden gate, sheltered from the rain by a pointed arch, was adorned with painted carvings of the lion, symbol of the Guelfi, and the griffin, symbol of the city of Perugia. Simon and Sordello pounded on the gate, and men-at-arms admitted them. Simon unstrapped a flat leather case from his saddle and then left Thierry to unload and stable the animals. He and Sordello hurried through the rain to the front door of the palace.

Simon identified himself to the steward, who conducted him, with much solicitude about the bad weather, to the sala maggiore of the palace. In the great hall, Simon was glad to see a fire of logs burning on a stone hearth under a chimney opening. He headed for it, throwing his sopping cloak and leather hat to the stone floor. Let the servants pick them up. Riding all day in the rain had made him irritable.

"Simon!" Friar Mathieu was shuffling toward him, leaning heavily on a walking stick. The old Franciscan's painfully slow movements alarmed him. Simon put his arms about him, but gently.

"Are you feeling worse, Father?"

"The weather is reminding my bones that they were cracked not long ago. I have a fire on the hearth in my room upstairs. Come up with me and you can get out of those wet clothes."

Simon sent Sordello to the kitchen and, still carrying the leather case, followed Friar Mathieu up a long flight of stone steps.

Wrapped in a blanket, seated on a bench before the fire in Friar Mathieu's chamber with a cup of hot spiced wine in his hand, he began to feel more comfortable, and he told the old priest about his journey back to Italy from Avignon.

"King Louis dismissed me on the twentieth of September. I paid fifty livres for a fast galley to Livorno. Then we rode our horses almost to death through the hills to get here. It took us less than two weeks. Very good time, but not good enough."

Simon paused. He remembered the old pope so vividly, writing letters furiously and dispatching them hither and yon, feeling surrounded by enemies on all sides and knowing he was going to die. He had so wanted to bring the Holy Father good news. Now Pope Urban was no more, and Simon was deeply disappointed.

But surely he is happier out of all this turmoil. He is with God and at peace now.

"And what news do you bring?" said Friar Mathieu.

Simon leaned toward him enthusiastically. "The pope's last wish has been granted! King Louis has agreed to let his brother Charles make war on King Manfred."

Instead of looking delighted as Simon had expected, Friar Mathieu surprised him by sighing and staring into the fire.

"Are you not pleased?" Simon prodded him.

"Pleased about a war?" Friar Mathieu's eyes were sad under his snow-white brows.

Simon felt as if his chair had been pulled out from under him and he had been dumped on the floor. His whole being had been focused on bringing good news to Perugia.

"But Father Mathieu, this means that the alliance of Tartars and Christians is approved. By Pope Urban, anyway."

Now that Pope Urban was dead, did that mean anything? He hesitated, confused.

Friar Mathieu sighed again. "I want the Tartars to embrace Christianity. I want the holy places liberated. But this warfare in Italy seems to me a false turning in the road. However—neither you nor I can stop the march of events. What is it you are carrying?"

Simon unbuckled the fastenings of the leather case and took out a package wrapped in silk. "Two letters written by King Louis. One was for Pope Urban. The other is for de Verceuil if Pope Urban should die."

"You will have trouble delivering either one."

"The one for Pope Urban I will keep as the king ordered me, until a new pope is elected. But the other one—why? Where is de Verceuil?"

"Locked away with the other cardinals in the Cathedral of Perugia, trying to make himself pope."

The thought of Paulus de Verceuil as supreme head of the Church made Simon's lip curl. "Pope? Not him!"

"He has the support of about half the French cardinals," Friar Mathieu said, shaking his white beard. "The cardinals are supposed to be in absolute seclusion, with no messages going in or out, but the servants who bring them their meals report things in both directions. The other cardinals lean to Gerard de Tracey, cardinal-bishop of Soissons. A former inquisitor." Friar Mathieu made a sour face.

"What of the Italians?"

"Amazingly, despite the rumors about his heresy and sorcery, Ugolini has four Italian cardinals voting for him. The servants say he has promised large sums of money to those four. The other three Italian votes are going to Piacenza. That must include Ugolini's vote, since the rules forbid a cardinal to vote for himself. Voting for old Piacenza is just a gesture, of course. He probably has less than a year of life left to him. But until one or two Italians can be persuaded to vote for a French candidate, no Frenchman can get the necessary two thirds."

"Are there not fourteen French cardinals to seven Italians?" Simon asked.

"Yes, but right now there are only twenty cardinals in conclave altogether. One of the French cardinals is in England on a diplomatic mission, sent by Pope Urban before his death. So, even united, the thirteen French would be one short of two thirds. And they are far from united. It could take years to elect a new pope."

Years! Simon was horrified. What a disaster! Without a pope, the question of the alliance would languish. The Tartar ambassadors might yet be assassinated, or just die. Hulagu Khan might die. Even King Louis, God forbid, might die, and the next king would probably not be interested in crusading.

Simon, for his part, had pinned his hopes for the restoration of his family honor on the success of the Tartar alliance. A new pope must be elected, and soon.

He carefully took the two scrolls out of their silk wrappings. Both were tied with red ribbons and sealed with blobs of red wax which King Louis had stamped with his personal seal, a shield bearing fleurs-de-lis. Simon held up the one addressed "His Eminence, Cardinal Paulus de Verceuil."

"We must try to get this letter to de Verceuil at once. It names King Louis's choice for the next pope. It could end the deadlock."

Father Mathieu stroked his white beard thoughtfully. "Exactly the sort of letter the rule against messages was instituted to keep out. A king attempting to influence a papal election." The old Franciscan took the scroll in one hand and tapped it against the palm of the other. "But I think for the good of the Church and for the success of our own mission we had better get this letter to de Verceuil at once. King Louis's choice cannot be worse than de Verceuil, de Tracey, or Ugolini."

"Yes!" said Simon eagerly. "But how do we get the letter to him?"

The old Franciscan pushed himself to his feet. It hurt Simon to see how slow and painful his movements were. Damn that devil in black who had tried to kill the Tartars!

The Tartars! He had thought they were well guarded enough, and that it was safe to leave them while he carried Urban's letter and the king's reply. But if the question of the alliance were to drag on, the foes of the alliance would try again to strike at them. Fear clutched at his heart.

"Are the Tartars here in this palace?" he called after Friar Mathieu, who was hobbling out of the room holding King Louis's scroll.

"Oh, yes. The Baglioni family have given them a whole quarter of the palace. They are well enough, though they hate being trapped indoors by the weather and by the need to keep them under guard. John Chagan has with him a young Jewish girl named Rachel, whom he kidnapped from a brothel in Orvieto. The girl was an orphan, and she has been terribly abused. She is virtually their prisoner."

Simon's mouth twisted. "And we want to ally ourselves with

such men. How can such things go on in the same city with the Sacred College?"

Friar Mathieu shook his head grimly. "Nothing I have said has made any difference. De Verceuil insists that the Tartars must have whatever they want, even though it will damn their souls. They are Christians, after all. If John dies with this girl on his conscience, he will go straight to hell."

Simon sighed. "Little de Verceuil cares about that."

"Quite so," said Friar Mathieu. "Well, we must get the king's letter to him."

He hailed a passing servant. "Tell the cook I want Cardinal de Verceuil's supper sent up to me before it is brought around to him at the cathedral. Tell him to be sure there is bread with the cardinal's meal. The cardinal wants plenty of bread. And"—he turned to Simon—"what is your equerry's name?"

"Thierry d'Hauteville." What on earth was Friar Mathieu planning? Simon prayed that, whatever it was, it would work and get the letter through.

"Find Thierry d'Hauteville and have him bring the tray up to me."

Thierry had borrowed a fresh tunic and hose from one of the Baglioni family servants. His dark hair, which usually hung in neat waves, was wild and tangled from being rubbed dry.

He carried Verceuil's dinner, a mixture of pieces of lobster and venison, with bread and fruit, on a circular wooden tray with a dome-shaped iron cover. Friar Mathieu took a knife and sliced lengthwise through the hard crust of a long loaf of bread. Using his fingers, he hollowed out the bread, giving chunks of it to Simon and Thierry and eating the rest of it himself.

"The Lord hates waste," he said with a chuckle. "This is white bread, too, such as only the nobility enjoy."

As Simon watched, holding his breath, Friar Mathieu laid King Louis's scroll lengthwise in the bread and closed it up carefully. The line of the slicing was barely visible. To secure the package, he took a loose thread from one of his blankets, tied it around the loaf, and covered the thread with a bunch of grapes.

"Now, Thierry. Normally one of the cardinal's servants takes his meals to him, but tonight you will. We want as few people as possible to know about this letter. If Cardinal Ugolini found out about it, he would make such a scandal of it that he might even end up being elected pope!"

"Might not Ugolini see de Verceuil reading the letter?" Simon asked.

"No," said Friar Mathieu. "Each cardinal eats and sleeps in a curtained-off cell built along the sides of the cathedral's nave. De Verceuil and King Louis will be quite alone together."

The following afternoon the sky was heavily overcast, but the rain had stopped. From the northwest tower of the Palazzo Baglioni, Simon could see that Perugia was a much bigger city than Orvieto. Like most Italian cities, it was built on a hilltop. But while Orvieto was flat on top of its great rock, Perugia stood on sloping ground, and the town had several levels.

"Simon!"

Simon turned to see Friar Mathieu's white head emerge from the trapdoor opening to the tower roof. As he hurried over to give the old man a hand up, his heartbeat speeded up. The wait for news must be at an end. When he saw Friar Mathieu smiling, he started grinning himself.

"The letter did it," the priest said cheerfully. "We have a pope, and it is neither de Verceuil nor de Tracey nor Ugolini."

Simon felt like shouting for joy.

"Who, then?"

"Why, the person named in the letter you brought, of course," said Friar Mathieu teasingly.

"Spare me this riddling, Father," Simon begged. "Not now. This means too much to me."

"All right, all right." Friar Mathieu patted Simon on the shoulder. "This morning at Tierce I joined the crowd at the cathedral to see the color of the smoke of the burning ballots from the chimney of the bishop's palace. If the king's letter had its effect, the smoke should be white, but it was not."

Simon's heart sank. Had he misunderstood Friar Mathieu?

"Black smoke, then? But you said they did elect a pope."

"No smoke at all. The people were puzzled, and so was I, and we all waited to see if anything would happen. I was about to give up and leave when the doors of the cathedral opened, and there stood little Cardinal Ugolini, with most of the Sacred College behind him. He looked as if he had been eating rotten figs. When I saw that, I knew the news must be good. As cardinal camerlengo, he announced, 'We *believe* we have a pope.' Well, you can imagine, that took everyone aback. He explained that the one elected was not present, and his name could not be announced until he had come to Perugia and had officially accepted. Then the cardinals came down the steps one by one. Most of them looked happy to be out of the cathedral after a week of imprisonment, but de Verceuil and de Tracey looked as ill as Ugolini. De Verceuil has come back to the palace now, so you had better walk carefully."

Simon remembered that Friar Mathieu had said the cardinals had elected the man named in King Louis's letter. But apparently the man was *not* yet elected. Simon felt uneasy. The chosen one was not even in Perugia. Too much could go wrong. He searched his brain. Friar Mathieu had said something last night about one of the cardinals being absent. Which one?

"Who is the man they elected" Simon cried. The way Friar Mathieu was telling this was maddening.

Smiling, Friar Mathieu said, "That is why I did not come to you at once. A priest in de Verceuil's entourage is an old friend of mine, and I waited until I could get the rest of the story from him."

"Could the letter I brought make such a difference?" Simon exclaimed.

"Well, de Verceuil sent Thierry away before looking inside that loaf of bread. His servant and his secretary, who were living with him, stood outside his cell and heard groans and cries of rage from within. De Verceuil threw his dinner on the floor and stamped out of his cell. While the servant cleaned the cell, de Verceuil visited and spoke secretly with each of the other French cardinals in turn.

"This morning, when it came time for them to vote, de Verceuil rose and said, 'Ego eligo Guy le Gros'—I elect Guy le Gros. Then each of the other French cardinals said the same thing after him."

Le Gros! Simon thought. *Le Gros is the cardinal who is not here.*

So, that was who King Louis wanted. Simon remembered meeting him at Pope Urban's council a year ago, a stout, genial man with a long black beard. De Verceuil had mocked him because he had once been married and had daughters. De Verceuil would have to eat that mockery now.

What did this mean for the alliance? Le Gros must be favorable. Why else would King Louis have chosen him?

"But why no smoke?" Simon asked.

"When a cardinal acclaims a candidate orally after a deadlock, and the others follow suit, it is called election by quasi-inspiratio. Because it is as if the cardinals have been divinely inspired. No ballots are needed, so there is nothing to burn. In this case they were inspired by King Louis, with some help from you and me.

"When two Italian cardinals—Piacenza, who knew he was too old to be pope for long, and Marchetti, who was always opposed to Ugolini—joined the cry for le Gros, it was all over. Ugolini collapsed in tears, but he was revived enough to make the arrangements to send to England for le Gros to come in haste. Everybody was sworn to silence, and Ugolini went out to make the public announcement. Of course, despite the secrecy, all Perugia knows it will be le Gros."

"But the alliance?" Simon asked anxiously.

Friar Mathieu reached out and took his hand. "We will have to wait until le Gros is officially crowned. But we can count on one of his first acts being a call for an alliance between the princes of Christendom and the khans of Tartary. And right after that will follow a declaration that Manfred von Hohenstaufen is deposed and Charles d'Anjou is the rightful king of southern Italy and Sicily."

A feeling of triumph swept Simon.

"Once the alliance is secured," he said, "I can really believe that I have the right to be the Count de Gobignon."

"Oh?" said Friar Mathieu. "Is that the assurance you need?" He spoke in a dubious tone that made Simon uneasy. "Well, then, I hope for your sake le Gros gets here from England all the sooner. Even though I do not look forward to the war he will unleash."

I care nothing about this war between Charles d'Anjou and Manfred von Hohenstaufen, Simon thought. His work would be done when he delivered the Tartars, with the pope's blessing, to King Louis.

And at the same time, he thought, he might bring Sophia to France. In his present happy mood, the thought of her was like a sunrise. If there was to be war in Italy, if Charles d'Anjou was to invade her homeland of Sicily, she might be all the more grateful to him for offering her a marriage that would take her away from all that.

He must arrange a rendezvous with her at once.

Luckily, Simon thought, the rain that plagued Umbria this time of year had let up for three days, and the roads leading out of Perugia into the countryside were fairly dry. He would have braved a flood or a blizzard to see Sophia again, but it pleased him that there were blue breaks in the gray dome of cloud overhead. After meeting on a road northwest of Perugia, Simon and Sophia had ridden to a woodland lake that reflected the blue in a darker tone on its rippling surface.

Simon felt himself breathing rapidly with excitement as he surveyed the lake shore. It seemed almost miraculous that Sophia was standing beside him.

They were at the bottom of a bowl of land. Big rocks that looked as if they might have rolled down the surrounding hillsides lay on the shore of the small lake. The floor of the wood was thick with brown leaves. This forest, Simon thought, probably belonged to some local nobleman. Most of the countryside around here was farmland.

Even though denuded by autumn, the masses of trees on the opposite shore looked impenetrable, ramparts of gray spikes frequently interrupted by the dark green of pines. The place had all the privacy he had hoped for. He prayed that this time alone together would not end in disaster as their last meeting outside Orvieto had.

Holding Sophia's arm and guiding her down to the edge of the lake gave Simon a warm, pleasant feeling. A tremor ran through his hands when he grasped her slender waist and lifted her—how light she felt!—to perch on a big black boulder.

She laughed gaily, and her laughter was like church bells at Easter.

He scooped up leaves and piled them at the base of the rock. When he had a pile big enough for two people to sit on, he spread his cloak over it. He held out his hand, and she slid from the boulder to the leaves.

He went foraging in the wood and quickly gathered an armload of broken branches and a few heavy sticks. He made a ring of stones near the water's edge and piled the branches within it, putting leaves and small twigs that would catch fire easily under the larger pieces of wood. He added some dried moss and took flint and steel out of a pouch at his belt, struck sparks several times, and got the moss to smoke. He blew on the glowing spots till a bright orange flame appeared. In a moment the pile of branches was afire.

Sophia crawled to the fire and held her hands out to its warmth. Simon sat beside her, so close their shoulders touched. He felt a pang of disappointment when she moved just a bit away from him.

"How comfortable you've made us!" she said, sounding a little surprised. She was very much a city woman, Simon thought. She seemed to know little about the country, and he had noticed that she never looked entirely relaxed on horseback.

"Are you surprised that I know how to make a fire in the woods?" He felt inordinate pride at being able to show off this small skill to her.

"I did think you relied on servants to do that sort of thing for you."

"A knight may not always have equerries or servants to help him. I know dozens of useful things that might surprise you. I can even cook and sew for myself."

"Marvelous! The woman you marry will be fortunate indeed."

As soon as she said it, the light went out of her eyes and she looked quickly away. An uneasy silence fell over them. Her obvious dismay threw him into despair. Again he remembered their struggles and her tears—and his own—that morning in the pine forest outside Orivieto.

After a pause, with an obviousness that sunk him into an even deeper gloom, she changed the subject. "Uncle told me all about what they did when the pope died. He was with the Holy Father right to the end. Just before he died, Pope Urban said, 'Beware the Tartars, Adelberto.' I would have thought Uncle made that up, but he says all the pope's attendant priests and servants heard it. Uncle says it proves Pope Urban had changed his mind at the end about that alliance you are all so worried about."

"Maybe the pope was warning your uncle that the Tartars are angry at him for all the trouble he has caused them," said Simon, forcing himself to comment on something that, at the moment, did not interest him.

He refused to worry about whether Pope Urban had a deathbed change of heart. How beautiful her eyes were, such a warm brown color! He had everything planned out for both of them. She had only to agree. He would present her first to King Louis. How could the king disapprove his marriage to a cardinal's niece? And with the king's support, no one else could object. Besides, Nicolette and Roland would love her; he was sure of it.

She went on. "Anyway, Uncle said that the pope's chest filled up with black bile, and that was what killed him. The pope's priest-physician felt for a heartbeat, and when there was none, Uncle took a silver hammer and tapped the pope on the forehead with it."

"Really!" Simon had no idea they did that. The strange scene interested him in spite of his longing for Sophia.

"To make sure he was dead. And then Uncle called his name—his baptismal name, not his name as pope—'Jacques, are you dead?' He did this three times. And when the pope did not answer, he said, 'Pope Urban is truly dead.' And he took the Fisherman's Ring off the Pope's finger and cut it to bits with silver shears. And with the hammer he broke the pope's seal. So they must make a new ring for the new pope."

"When Cardinal le Gros is made pope, he will confirm the alliance of Christians and Tartars," said Simon, eager to put a finish to the topic and bring the conversation back to the two of them.

Sophia, her hands folded in her lap, lovely hands with long slender fingers, looked sadly toward the lake. "I suppose that pleases you."

"Why not be happy for me? My work is nearly done."

And, he wanted to add but dared not, *we can be married.*

She turned to look at him, her eyes troubled. "Uncle says the new pope will call Charles d'Anjou to invade Italy and make war on King Manfred. Will you be with the invaders?"

Count Charles will surely expect me to join him, Simon thought. Well, he would simply tell Uncle Charles that he had no wish to spend any more time in Italy.

"When the alliance with the Tartars is settled, I mean to go home."

He was about to tell her again that he wanted her to come with him, but she spoke first. "You know this Count Charles well, do you not? How soon do you think he will march into Italy?"

Simon wanted to talk about their future, not about Charles d'Anjou's plans for war with Manfred. But he tried to answer her question.

"He is pressing his people for money now. Then he must gather his army. And it can take months to move an army from the south of France to southern Italy. With winter coming on, he will probably wait until next year to cross the Alps. My guess is he'll be here in Italy next summer."

She was about to speak again, probably to ask another question about Count Charles. He quickly broke in.

"What I told you last time—that I am a bastard and that the last Count de Gobignon was not my real father—does that make you less willing to marry me?"

Her face squeezed together, as if a sharp pain had struck her. "You are not going to start talking about marriage again, Simon?"

Her words were like a knife wound in his chest. While he searched for words, his eyes explored the steep brown hills that surrounded this secluded lake. Their tops were veiled in mist, like his past.

"I have never stopped thinking about marrying you. Sophia, you are the one person in the world who can make me happy." He reached over into her lap and took her hand. It felt cool and smooth.

"I could never, never make you happy," she said. "You know nothing about me."

Why was she always saying that? What was there to know about a woman who had lived a quiet life in Sicily, was widowed at an early age, and had come to live with her cardinal uncle?

"I know enough." His eyes felt on fire with longing. "And you know enough about me to see that the differences between our families do not matter. You know what I am. And we care more about each other than we do about your uncle opposing what my king wants.''

''Oh, Simon!'' Now there were tears running down her cheeks, but she did not try to pull her hand away. It pained him to see how this was hurting her, though he did not understand why it should.

She said, ''You are telling tales to yourself if you imagine we could ever marry. You should not even think of it. Whatever your mother did, you are still the Count de Gobignon. You are almost a member of the French royal family.''

''I am sure Cardinal Ugolini does not agree that your family is so obscure,'' Simon said. ''It is time I talked to him about this. Then you will believe I mean it.''

She struck her hands against his chest. ''No, no! You must not do that. Do you not realize how upset he is about this war, and how he feels toward the French? If he even knew that I had been alone with you today, he would force me to go back to Siracusa at once.''

The feel of her hands on him, even to hit him in reproof, excited him.

''I would not let that happen,'' he said gravely.

He heard wild geese flying southward calling in the distance. Their cries made this place seem terribly lonely. Even though the little lake was only a short ride from Perugia, he had seen no sign of a human being anywhere.

The fire was burning low. He went to gather more wood.

Sophia frowned at him when he came back. ''What did you mean, you would not allow my uncle to send me away?''

He leaned closer, seizing both of her hands in his. The pleasure of holding her hands rippled through him like a fluttering of angels' wings. In his exalted state he was moved to utter extravagant words.

''I mean that if you were to leave Perugia, I would ride after you. I would fight any men your uncle had set to guard you. I would take you back to Gobignon with me, and there with you inside my castle I would defy the world.''

''Oh, Simon!''

His words sounded foolish to him after he spoke them aloud. Yet men, he knew, had done such things—Lancelot—Tristan—if the old songs were to be believed. How better to prove his love than to commit crimes and risk disgrace for her?

She was crying again. She put her hands over her face. Why, he wondered, when he declared his love for her and told her he wanted to marry her, did it make her so unhappy? If she did not care for him, she should be indifferent or angry. Why, instead, did she cry so hard?

It must be that she wants me but cannot believe it is possible.

The sight of her slender body shaking with sobs tore at his heart. He could not hold himself back; even if she fought him again, he must put his arms around her. He reached out to hold her. She fell against him. She felt wonderful in his arms, solid enough to assure him that this was no dream, yet light enough to allow him to feel that he could do anything he wanted with her.

He remembered how angry she had been in the pine forest outside Orvieto when he had tried to make love to her. Though he might be eaten up with longing for her, he must just hold her and be glad she allowed him to do that.

She raised her tear-streaked face and kissed him lightly on the lips.

The soft pressure of her lips on his made his arms ache to hold her tighter. But he fought the feeling down.

"Why do you cry so hard when I speak to you of love?" he whispered.

"Because no one has ever loved me as you do," she said. She rested her head against his chest, and he stroked her hair. His eyes lingered over the curves of her breasts. He wanted to drop his hand from her hair to her breast. He felt the yearning to touch her breast as a pain in the palm of his hand.

"But you have been married," he said. "Did not your husband love you?"

He felt her head shaking. His heart was beating so hard he was sure she must hear it.

"We were little more than children."

"I am not a child, and neither are you. Believe me when I say I want to marry you."

"Oh, Simon, I do believe you!" she cried, and she broke out in a fresh storm of sobs.

Now he could not help himself; he had to hold her tight. She leaned against him, and they slipped back until they were both lying down, he on his back and she on top of him. His hand felt the small of her back. How narrow her waist was!

He felt her move against him in a new way.

Her arms slid around him, her hands on his neck. Her lips were on his again, but this time pressing hard, ferocious, devouring. He felt her teeth and tongue, her breath hot in his mouth.

She was suddenly a different woman, not the shy cardinal's niece. She was demanding, brimming over with a need to match his. Their hands hurried over each other's bodies, touching through their clothes and then under their clothes. Simon had no time to be surprised at the change that had come over her.

She was undoing the laces down the front of her gown, then taking his hands and holding them against her naked breasts. He nearly fainted with the wonder of it.

And while he held her breasts, unable to take his hands away, her hands moved downward, fumbling at his clothing and at her own, her body sliding against him, her hand seizing his manhood, her legs opening to receive him.

He groaned and squeezed his eyes shut, and she cried out with delight as he entered her. She pushed herself upward, pressing her hands against his shoulders, arching her back. His hands moved in gentle circles over her breasts, her hard nipples pressing into his palms. Her hips thrust against him furiously. He felt waves of pleasure rising to a crest in his loins. His eyes came open and he saw, under the olive skin of her face and neck and bosom, a deep crimson flush.

Her joyous scream echoed cross the lake.

"You shall come with me to Gobignon," he whispered in her ear. They lay wrapped in his cloak, legs entangled, clothing in disarray, the wind rattling the bare branches overhead. He heard his palfrey and her horse in the brush nearby stamping and snorting restlessly. The horses must be hungry.

"You shall marry me," he said.

She lay motionless, her head under his, resting on his arm. "I will not. I cannot." Her tone was leaden, despairing.

After what had just happened, how could she still refuse him? Was she ashamed? Did she feel she had sinned?

"We are as good as married now."

"Oh, Simon." She sounded as if she were talking to a hopelessly innocent boy.

"There will be a new pope, and the alliance will be sealed, and my work will be done," he said. "I agreed to do this, and I will see it through. But I do not have to be a part of the war between Count Charles and the king of Sicily, and neither do you. All I want is to go home and to take you with me. With you beside me, my home will be all of the world that I want."

Her arms were tight around him, but she was silent. It did not matter if she did not answer him. After what had just happened between them, he felt as if he knew her mind as fully as he knew her body. She loved him and would marry him. He was sure of it.

Overhead, wild geese called.

LX

WHY DID I EVER MAKE LOVE TO HIM?

Sophia had asked herself the same question countless times since that day by the wooded lake. For two months she had managed to keep away from Simon. Now he was here, in Ugolini's mansion.

She stood before the door of Ugolini's audience room. The servant who had come to fetch her was about to open it. Sophia's hands felt coated with frost. Terrified of being with Simon again, she hated herself for what she had done. To Daoud, to Simon. And to herself.

The servant opened the door. She stepped through quickly and he closed it behind her.

And there was Simon de Gobignon, tall and handsome as ever, looking down at her reproachfully. Tension made her heart beat so hard that she wanted to put her hand on her chest to still it. Instead, she held her hand out so that Simon could bend down from his towering height and kiss it. She was so upset by his unexpected arrival that she did not comprehend his murmured greeting.

Behind Simon's back Ugolini, sitting at a large writing desk, rolled his eyes and stretched his mouth in a grimace at her. Simon was still bent over her hand, so she was able to shake her head slightly in answer to his unspoken question. Simon must have come here as a last resort, because after yielding to him in secret she had tried to shut him out of her life. She could hardly convey that to Ugolini now, even if she wanted to.

"The Count de Gobignon has come to call on you, my dear," said Ugolini, his smooth voice betraying none of his anxiety. "I have given my permission, provided it is also your wish."

"Your Signory pays me too much honor," she said softly to Simon. Her mind spun. How could she talk to Simon, when she did not understand herself well enough to know what lies to tell him?

She wondered what Ugolini would think of her if he knew all of what had happened between her and Simon when they met that day. Would he be shocked? Contemptuous? Would he tell Daoud? All he knew of her meeting with Simon in October was that Simon had again proposed marriage to her, and she had rejected him.

She said, "I find it hard to believe that Your Signory even remembers me. I do not believe we have seen each other since the reception for the Tartar ambassadors at the Palazzo Monaldeschi last year. Is that not so?"

An appreciative smile replaced the somber expression on Simon's face. His eyes twinkled at her. Doubtless he thought they were conspirators together.

The poor, poor boy.

But she could not see that look warming his sharp-pointed features without feeling it again—that surge of desire that had driven her to give herself to him two months ago.

What is happening to me?

"Many months have passed and much has happened, Madonna," he said, "but—forgive me if I am too forward—I have found it impossible to forget you. Now that we are together in a new city, I hoped to renew your acquaintance."

"This endless moving about will be the death of me," said Ugolini unhappily. "Papa le Gros no sooner arrives from England and is officially elected than he tells us he will be crowned in Viterbo and make that the new papal seat. I have hardly had time to unpack here in Perugia."

"Your furnishings seem in good order to me, Your Eminence," said Simon with a smile, looking around the large room with its row of large windows, its thick carpeting, and its heavy black chairs and tables. A large shield carved in stone over the fireplace behind Ugolini was painted with five red bands on a white background.

"These are not mine," said Ugolini, waving a hand dismissively. "Not my idea of comfortable surroundings at all. No, I simply bought this house and its furnishings from a Genoese merchant who was using it only part of the year. I would be ashamed to tell you how much I paid for it—you would think me a fool. A typical Genoese, he took advantage of my need. And now I must sell all, probably to the same merchant and probably at a loss."

"That is another reason why I wanted to see you, Madonna Sophia," said Simon. "I feared that you, like your good uncle, might find all this uprooting tiresome and might return to Sicily, and I would be hard put to find you again."

With an inward shudder, Sophia realized the strength of Simon's resolve to possess her. Only the truth would kill that determination, and she would never dare to tell him that. Besides, there was a part of her that, mad as it was, delighted in seeing how powerfully he was drawn to her.

"I am thinking of going home myself," said Ugolini. "What need for me to go with the new pope on this tedious search for ever-safer safety?"

"If you returned to Sicily," said Simon to Sophia, "it might be ages before I see you again."

His words frightened her. Was he about to ask Ugolini for her hand, and how would the cardinal deal with that?

"Forgive me if I raise an unpleasant subject," said Ugolini, "but if your Count Charles d'Anjou accepts the pope's offer of the crown of southern Italy and Sicily, it may be a long time before any French nobleman will be welcome in my homeland."

There was no "if" about what Charles d'Anjou would do, Sophia thought. That was just Ugolini's courtesy.

"I know, Your Eminence," said Simon, looking grim. "I hope you will still think of me as your friend, despite events. Just as we have been friends while we disagreed over this matter of the Tartar alliance."

Ugolini clapped his hands suddenly. "Well, it is a happy occasion when my niece has such a distinguished visitor. Count, this house has a second-story loggia overlooking the atrium. It is private enough to shield you from prying eyes, yet not so private as to place you lovely young people in peril of temptation. Sophia will show you the way."

Bowing and thanking Ugolini, Simon followed Sophia out of the room.

She turned to Simon as soon as the door of Ugolini's audience chamber had closed behind them and said, "I need my cloak for the cold. Wait here, and I will go to my room and get it." Without giving him a chance to answer, she hurried down the corridor, desperately trying to make sense of her thoughts and feelings.

Their lovemaking had been a terrible mistake. And yet, there had been times in those two months when the recollection of the two of them, wrapped in his cloak, lying on a bed of leaves, the depth of his passion for her and the wildness of her answering feelings, crept up on her unexpectedly and sent thrills of pleasure coursing through her.

As she rummaged in her chest for a warm cloak, her eyes met those of her icon of Saint Simon Stylites, and she felt shame wash over her.

How can I think that I truly love Daoud, when I gave myself so freely to his enemy?

But had that not been what Daoud had expected her to do all along? He had always been jealous, had always made it obvious that he hated the idea of her letting Simon court her. And yet, from the time he first encountered Simon, he had made it equally obvious that he expected Sophia to do whatever was necessary to make Simon fall in love with her. And from the moment Simon had kissed her in the Contessa di Monaldeschi's atrium, he had loved her, and never stopped loving her.

But to make him love her, she had pretended to be an innocent young Sicilian woman who could be overwhelmed by her love for a French nobleman. Sadly enough, she felt more joy and peace of mind as that Sicilian girl than she ever had known as a woman of Byzantium. And the confusion about who she really was had become much worse after she decided to keep secret from Daoud Simon's destination when he left Orvieto.

She felt a pounding pain inside her skull, and she pressed her hands against her bound-up hair. She shut her eyes so tight that she forced tears from them, and a little groan escaped her.

She was sure of one thing: If she had much more to do with Simon de Gobignon, the confusion she felt would probably drive her mad.

She fumbled through her chest and found a rose-colored winter cloak lined with red squirrel fur. She threw it over her shoulders and clasped it around her neck, the fur collar gently brushing her chin.

Simon was waiting where she had left him. He had allowed his bright blue cloak to fall closed around his lanky frame, so that he looked like a pillar. She wrapped her own cloak around herself, and side by side they walked to the stairs at the end of the corridor.

They said nothing to each other until they were out on the loggia under a gray sky. A chill wind stung Sophia's cheeks. She looked down at the rows of fruit trees in the atrium below. Their bare branches reached up at her like long, slender fingers.

"I cannot understand you," he said. "Why have you been so cruel to me?"

That sounded like typical courtly lover's talk, but she knew he meant the words literally. She looked at his face and saw the whiteness, the strain around his mouth, the slight tremor of his lips. He looked like a mortally wounded man.

"I, cruel to you? Did I not beg you to stay away from my uncle?

Look what you have done today. He will send me to Siracusa for certain.''

But she felt something break inside her at the sight of his pain. She had done this to him. She had hoped to give him something by letting him possess her one time, to make up for all that she could never give him. Instead, with the gift of her body she had bound him to her more tightly than ever. And then, haunted by her own feelings and the memory of what they had done together, she had simply tried to have nothing further to do with him. And now her effort to break with him was hurting both of them far more than if she had refused him that day.

''You drove me to this,'' he said, his eyes wide with anger. ''You did not answer my letters or acknowledge my poems. When I tried to speak to you in the street and in church, you avoided me. I sent you gifts, and you sent them back.''

She really would have to get out of Perugia. Back to Daoud. This would tear her to pieces.

But what about Rachel?

If she left Perugia, that would be as good as abandoning Rachel. She had sworn to herself never to do that.

Simon guards the Tartars. He must know what has happened to Rachel. Perhaps he can help her.

She stopped walking and leaned against the stone railing of the loggia. The leafless branches in the atrium below them rattled in the wind.

''There are many reasons that I did not want to see you. I do not know whether you would understand all of them. But one is that I have heard something very ugly about those Tartars of yours.'' She had decided not to admit that she knew Rachel. That would take too much explaining and too many more lies, and the lies would be like hidden holes in a leaf-strewn path, to trip her up.

''One of the Tartars, those men you guard so carefully, kidnapped a young girl from Orvieto and is holding her a prisoner now, here in Perugia at the Baglioni palace. It makes me unhappy to know that you are the protector of men who would do such things.''

Down below, two of Ugolini's servants brought out baskets of newly washed tablecloths and bedlinens and began spreading them on the branches of the trees to dry. Sophia spoke in a lower voice, giving details of the attack on Tilia's house by de Vercuil and the Tartars as if it were something she knew about only through hearsay, while Simon looked more and more unhappy.

He frowned at her. "I know of this girl. It is John Chagan who keeps her. But what is she to you? She is not even a Christian. I am surprised that a woman of good family like you should worry about a prostitute."

How easy for a count to look down on a girl like Rachel. She felt her back stiffen with anger.

How he would despise me if he knew what I was.

But what am I?

"Does it lower me in your eyes that I worry about such a girl?"

He waved his hands placatingly. "No, no. Such charitable feelings do you credit. I *would* like to help her, and I know Friar Mathieu has already tried. I just wondered how *you* came to know and care about this girl's case." He looked earnestly into her eyes. His eyes were a blue as clear and bright as that lake where they had lain together.

"The story is talked about by all the servants and common folk of the town. I feel very sorry for her. She is just a child. I find myself imagining how she feels—kidnapped, helpless, raped by this barbarian, a prisoner. Have you not seen her yourself?"

Simon nodded reluctantly, looking away. "Yes, glimpses. She stays in her room."

"She is forced to stay in her room." Sophia sensed that Simon knew more than he admitted about what the Tartar had done to Rachel and was ashamed to be connected with it.

"What has this to do with you and me?" he demanded.

"You are close to the Tartars. You might be able to help her."

Simon glowered. "If I had been there that day in Orvieto, you may be sure they would not have raided that brothel."

He might be on the enemy side, she thought, but he was not a savage like the Franks of her childhood. He was a genuinely good man, and that was what made the hopeless dream of marrying him so painful.

She put her hand on his arm and squeezed. "Will you try to get the Tartar to release the girl? Cardinal Ugolini will take her in."

When she laid her hand on the hard, wiry muscle in his arm, she did not want to let go.

I still want him! My God, what is the matter with me?

"De Verceuil would oppose me if I tried to take the girl away from John. Incredible, is it not? A cardinal involved in kidnapping a young girl for the pleasure of a barbarian?"

Sophia, taught by her Greek Orthodox priests that the Roman Church was a fountainhead of wickedness, did not think the cardinal's actions all that incredible. Besides, was she not in league with another cardinal who was helping the Muslims?

"There *must* be a way to help Rachel," she said.

He brought his face close to hers. "Sophia, I will speak to Friar Mathieu. But, as I said, he has already tried to persuade John to let the girl go free. With no success. And I am sure there is nothing more Friar Mathieu can do before tomorrow, when I leave Perugia."

She loved that serious, intent look. It was as if light were coming from his eyes.

But what he had just said took her by surprise.

"Leave Perugia? Where are you going?"

He shook his head. "No one is supposed to know."

"Simon!" She put anger into her voice, knowing he was vulnerable. If she could get some information of use to Daoud from him, she would have an excuse for having let Simon make love to her. And with Daoud far away in Manfred's kingdom, there was no chance this time that he could hurt Simon.

He touched her cheek with the tips of his long fingers, and she could feel him struggling with himself.

"Swear you will tell no one."

"Of course."

He really thinks I can be depended upon to keep an oath.

"All right. I had a message from Count Charles—he who gave me this task of guarding the Tartars. He calls me to meet him at Ostia. That is why I came here today, even though I knew you would not want me to. Knowing I would be leaving here and might not see you for months made me desperate."

Charles d'Anjou at Ostia—the seaport of Rome!

As she realized what Simon's words meant, terror raced through Sophia. She was going to fall from the loggia and break into a thousand pieces, like an icicle.

Anjou was going to take Rome and cut Italy in half. Instead of trying to cross the Alps and then fight his way through the Ghibellino cities of northern Italy, Charles must have come by sea. Now he would be able to strike directly at the heart of Manfred's kingdom.

What will Daoud do? What will happen to Manfred? If only we had Tilia here, with her carrier pigeons.

Despite her fur-lined cloak, a chill seized her.

She had feared for Daoud, that he might have to fight a great French army. And though she had long since ceased to love Manfred, she had feared for him and his kingdom. But the thought of the many obstacles between France and southern Italy had comforted her. Now, knowing that Charles d'Anjou was so close to Manfred's kingdom, she felt herself actually trembling.

He put his hand on hers. "You're frightened."

Staring down at the bare trees, she whispered, "Yes. for my people."

His hand gripped hers tightly. He bent down so that he was speaking softly into her ear.

"I know you cannot forget your people, but you could escape this war. My service is done, now that the new pope has confirmed the alliance with the Tartars. I do not have to stay in Italy."

She was glad he did not want to fight for Charles. The thought of him and Daoud meeting on a battlefield was horrible. But surely this brother of King Louis would make every effort to draw Simon into the war.

"Count Charles will want you to fight."

"If you will marry me and come to Gobignon, nothing else will matter to me. We will live content in my castle in the heart of my domain. We will shut out the world and its wars."

She turned to look at him, and the longing on his face was painful to see.

She felt the tears coming, hot, blurring her vision.

"Simon, I cannot!"

His grip on her hand was painful. "Again and again you say that to me. And you never tell me *why*. Are you secretly a nun? Have you taken vows? Does your husband still live? I demand that you tell me! Stop tormenting me like this." His usually pale face was suddenly scarlet with rage.

His anger dried up her tears.

I know how I can put an end to this.

"I will, Simon. But I am not ready to speak of it today."

"Then *when*?"

"Go now and meet your Count Charles at Ostia. By the time you come back to the papal court we will probably have moved to Viterbo. And when I see you again, I will tell you why I cannot marry you."

The shadow cleared from his face. "Do you promise with all your heart? And if I can persuade you that your reason is not good enough, then will you marry me?"

For a moment she hesitated. Even though her life depended on deceiving him, she could not bear to make such a promise. But then she saw that she could honestly agree to what he asked.

"If you still want me to marry you—yes."

*I can say that because if you ever come to know my true reason
for not marrying you, you will hate me more than you have ever
hated anyone in your life.*

He left her soon afterward. She went back to her room and cried
for most of the afternoon. Every so often she looked up to see the
icon of the desert saint staring at her. She saw the same reproach
in Simon Stylites's eyes that she had seen in Simon de Gobignon's.

LXI

THOUGH THE DAY WAS COLD AND DAMP, THE SKY AN UGLY, UN-
welcoming gray, Simon's first view of Rome brought tears to his
eyes. He came out of a small grove of cypresses on the east bank
of the Tiber to see gray walls, punctuated by square towers, spread
wide before him. Beyond the walls, out of a haze of dust and wood
smoke, above masses of peaked roofs, crenellated palace towers
rose lordly, vying for ascendancy with the bell towers of churches.
Marble buildings adorned with white columns crowned the hills.

The swift-moving brown river on his left bent around the walls
and disappeared beyond them.

Even though he did not want to be part of Charles d'Anjou's
invasion of Italy, the thrill of seeing Rome for the first time made
up for his distress.

Rome was by no means as beautiful a sight as Orvieto, but it
awed him to think that this city had ruled the world when Jesus
walked the earth. What must it have been like to be a Roman
legionary, returning to this place from a victory in some far-off
land? This dirt track would have been a well-paved road then.
Looking off to his right, he saw fragments of wall bounding the
edge of a field, and a broken, fluted column rising among olive
trees, quiet reminders that the city had once extended into these
fields and beyond.

Simon was mounted on a borrowed warhorse, a mare whose
shiny coat reminded him of Sophia's hair—a brown so dark it might
be taken for black. After many hours of riding, the mare's rocking
pace had chafed the insides of his mail-clad legs.

He rode a few yards behind Count Charles d'Anjou and the three knights Charles had appointed marshals of his army. When he looked back over his shoulder, he saw a column of mailed knights riding three abreast strung out along the Tiber for nearly half a mile, and beyond them, almost obscured by clouds of yellow dust, clinking files of men-at-arms, crossbows and spears over their shoulders.

Unimpressed by the sight of Rome, Anjou and his commanders carried on an argument.

"You are a hard taskmaster, Monseigneur," said Gautier du Mont, whose bronze hair was cropped in the shape of a bowl, slightly tilted so that the back was lower than the front. "To make your knights ride half a day in full armor when they have not seen a denier from your coffers since we sailed from Marseilles—you demand too much." The points of du Mont's mustache hung below his chin. Simon had heard he was little better than a routier, a highwayman, who had begun his knightly career by robbing travelers who passed his castle in the Pyrenees.

What Simon had seen thus far of Charles's army made the enterprise look decidedly unsavory. Before reaching Ostia, Simon had expected that the men Charles commanded would be vassals, men who had received land from him and were bound by ancient oaths. He quickly realized that all of these men were adventurers with little or no holdings of their own, in this enterprise with Charles for whatever they could gain. Charles could command them only as long as they could hope to grow rich in his service.

Simon supposed this was the best Charles could do, since King Louis had refused to help him raise knights and men and insisted that he hire them himself. Knights willing to go to war for hire could not be expected to be the better sort. Not only did Simon not want to make war on the Italians, he wanted even less to be associated with men like the ones Charles had recruited.

Unlike his three marshals, who were all bareheaded, Charles wore a helmet. A steel replica of his count's coronet ringed its pointed top. Beside him rode an equerry with his personal standard, the black silhouette of a lion rearing up on its hind legs against a flame-red background. Charles turned so that his big Capetian nose was outlined against the iron-gray sky.

"You complain, du Mont, because I ordered our knights to wear full armor?" said Charles. "I did it for their own protection. I expect to meet resistance."

Only eight hundred knights and two thousand men-at-arms, Simon thought. *Hardly enough to take Rome, if the Romans do decide to fight. Nowhere near enough to beat Manfred.*

He had been shocked when he arrived at Ostia last night and found out how small Charles's invasion force was. Being a part of this war was going to be downright dangerous.

"Time enough for us to don armor when the resistance appears," said Alistair FitzTrinian, a knight from England whose face was a mass of smallpox scars. Simon had so far been unable to look at the man without having to freeze the muscles of his face to keep from wincing.

Count Charles sighed, and held out his arm in the direction of Rome. "Look there, gentlemen," he said in a patient tone, as if instructing schoolchildren. "The Romans are not waiting for us to put on our armor."

Simon followed his pointing finger and saw a gray mass spreading out into the field near one of the city's gates, flowing around cottages and groves of trees. It appeared to be a great crowd of several thousand citizens. Fully alert now, Simon heard a dull roar, like the hum of a swarm of bees, that sounded decidedly hostile. He felt a twinge of fear.

"Get your helmets on, the three of you," Charles snapped. "Set an example for the rest, or may the devil carry you away!"

The three commanders slowly and sullenly pulled on their helmets, which had been hanging down their backs from straps under their chins. The manner of the three marshals toward Count Charles shocked Simon. If these were the leaders, what In God's name could the rank and file be like?

Any one of my Venetian archers or the Tartars' Armenian guards would be worth a dozen of these.

As the army of Anjou, with Charles and Simon and the three marshals in the lead, advanced slowly, Simon noticed that six or so men, several hundred paces in front of the shouting citizens, were walking to meet them.

In a short time the small delegation stood before Count Charles, blocking his path.

Charles raised his arm, and the knights behind him shouted the order to halt down the line. How would Count Charles deal with the representatives of an unfriendly populace, Simon wondered. This should be interesting. He might learn something.

The count turned to Dietrich von Regensburg, his third commander. "I want a troop of the Burgundian pikemen up here now. Surround these fellows." Von Regensburg, a knight with hard blue eyes, a flattened nose, and a huge jaw, saluted and swung his dun horse around to ride back to the long line of men-at-arms following Charles and his knights.

Anjou's order made Simon uneasy. Why try to frighten these Romans? Would it not be better if he could enter the city with their approval?

Then he beckoned Simon to bring his horse up beside him. "No doubt you speak Italian better than any of us. Translate for me." He glowered down his long nose at the Romans who had approached him. "I am Count Charles d'Anjou. I have come here as protector of the city of Rome, at the request of His Holiness, the pope."

Simon repeated this.

"Rome needs protection only from you!" one of the men shouted.

"There is no pope," another called out. "The old one is dead and the new one has not been crowned."

Simon could hardly believe his ears. He had heard that Roman citizens were unruly; that was why the pope had moved away from Rome. But the way these men addressed the Count of Anjou, the brother of the king of France—it was unthinkable. It was madness. The count might not understand their words, but the disrespectful tone was unmistakable.

Hesitantly, he translated. Charles stared at the six Romans, his swarthy face expressionless.

Charles's great black and white warhorse shifted his legs restlessly, and Charles stilled him with a jerk of the reins. Even the horse sensed the Romans' anger.

"Silencio!" ordered a Roman somewhat taller than the others, with a shock of iron-gray hair and an angular jaw. He wore a mantle of deep maroon velvet trimmed with white fur, and a longsword hung from his jeweled belt. He bowed courteously to Count Charles and Simon.

"Your Signory, I am Leone Pedulla, secretary of the Senate of Rome. We come, with all respect, to pray you to turn back. The city of Rome rules herself. We are most distressed to see a foreign army, a French army, approaching our walls. If you wish to visit us and confer with our leading citizens, leave this army behind. Come to us as a guest, bringing a few of your barons with you. We will then offer you our hospitality. We ask you to leave us in peace."

Simon wished himself far away as he translated for Anjou. These Romans did not know Count Charles.

As Simon was conveying Leone Pedulla's speech, a line of big, bearded foot soldiers carrying spears taller than a man, wearing leather cuirasses and wide-brimmed helmets of polished steel, marched forward, boots crunching on the stubble of the harvested field. At von Regensburg's command, the pikemen formed a ring around the Roman delegation. The Romans' eyes darted anxiously from side to side.

Charles said, "Simon, tell this impertinent fellow who calls himself secretary of the Senate just this: I order him to clear away that rabble blocking the city gates."

Simon repeated the count's command in Italian. His heart began to beat more rapidly as he sensed an evil moment coming closer and closer.

"The people standing before the walls are citizens of Rome, Your Signory, acting legally to protect the city from what seems to us a foreign invader," Pedulla answered. "I cannot tell them to go away."

Simon wished he could soften this when he translated it. Charles's mouth drew down in a harsh, inverted V.

"Very well." He turned to von Regensburg and pointed. "I would prefer to hang them, but it would take too long. Use your spears on them."

Dear, merciful God, do not let this happen! Simon prayed.

"No!" Pedulla cried, his voice shrill with horror as the German knight shouted a command and the Burgundians leveled their spears. It was the gray-haired Roman's last word. His hand had not quite reached the hilt of his sword when a bearlike foot soldier lunged at him, driving a spear through his embroidered tunic into his chest. The pikeman thrust the steel point in low enough to miss the breastbone but high enough to pierce the heart. Pedulla did not even have time enough to finish his scream.

"Clemenza, per favore!" cried another Roman who a moment ago had been shouting defiance. A spear point caught him in the throat.

Simon wished he could turn his eyes away, but he did not want Charles and his marshals to think him squeamish. His heart thundered and his stomach churned, and he feared that his body would betray him. The other pikemen moved in quickly, taking long steps as if performing spear drill, holding their pikes near the points for close work. A moment later they stepped back from a heap of sprawled, dead bodies.

God! How little time it takes to kill a man!

Now Simon did look away. The blood, the staring, dead faces, the twisted arms and legs, were too pitiful a sight to bear.

Simon remembered de Verceuil's ordering the archers to shoot into the crowd at Orvieto. This was worse. These men had been discourteous, perhaps, but they were officials of the city, on an embassy. And Count Charles had ordered them killed as calmly as he might order his army to break camp.

This was the man whose wishes had governed Simon's life for over a year. Simon felt his bond to Charles as a terrible chain and he longed to be free.

This is a taste of what will happen to Sophia's people if Charles conquers Manfred. If only she will let me take her to Gobignon, so she will not have to see such things.

Count Charles raised a hand encased in a gleaming mail glove. "Forward."

"One moment, Monseigneur," said Gautier du Mont, his sharp voice cutting through the sounds of the army resuming its march.

Charles turned to him impatiently. "What now, du Mont?"

"Monseigneur, we have just killed the emissaries of the Romans. I fear we will now have to fight that mob. Look. They are coming at us."

Simon looked over toward the city. The mass that had emerged from the city, a long line of people stretching eastward from the Tiber to a distant forest, was moving through the fields and olive groves. To Simon's eye they appeared to vastly outnumber Charles's army. Simon could see swords gleaming and spears waving. They formed no ranks and files as a professional army would, but they came on inexorably like the waves of the sea, and their shouts were angry.

Simon felt cold fear sweep away the sick pity he had felt for the executed Roman delegation. That huge mob was a formidable sight.

"Of course we will fight them, du Mont," Charles answered, his voice rising. "One charge and we will scatter them to the winds."

True, thought Simon. Crowds of villeins or peasants were no match for disciplined fighting men. But just how disciplined was the force behind Charles?

"I think, Monseigneur," said du Mont, "that before we do any fighting, it is appropriate to discuss the terms of our payment."

Oh, by God's white beard! Simon swore to himself. They were about to be attacked by five or more times their number, and these bastards were arguing about money. They ought to be stripped of their knighthoods.

"I have told you my gold shipment was late getting from Marseilles to Ostia," said Charles in a placating tone. "You will be paid. Tonight, tomorrow, or the next day it will catch up to us."

"Then tonight, tomorrow, or the next day, Monseigneur," said the pock-marked FitzTrinian, "you can command us to charge that rabble."

The Roman mob was close enough now for Simon to make out what they were shouting.

"Muorire alla Francia!" *Death to the French!*

The cry sent a bolt of fear through Simon. They would have to do something at once.

Were Charles's lieutenants actually going to sit on their motionless horses and haggle with him until these infuriated Romans fell upon them? Not just Charles's venture was at stake, but their own lives. Could they be stupid—or greedy—enough to let themselves be overwhelmed while they argued about money?

Yes, they could be. That stupid and that greedy.

Simon's fear transmuted itself to anger. These men were a disgrace to chivalry. Worse, as marshals of an army commanded by King Louis's brother, they dishonored France. He almost wanted to draw his sword against them, his disgust was so great.

"You speak of dishonor when you are refusing to attack an enemy in the field at the order of your seigneur?" Charles shouted.

"We are not refusing, Monseigneur—" Alistair FitzTrinian began.

Simon had heard enough. If Charles's hired commanders would not command, he would.

"Follow me, Thierry." Simon swung his horse around to ride toward the rear of the column. His face was hot with anger.

Simon felt little sympathy for Charles; he had chosen these men. But Simon de Gobignon, at least, was not going to let himself be set upon and murdered by a crowd of commoners, even if those commoners had ample justification. Nor was he going to allow French arms—if these blackguards Charles d'Anjou had hired could be said to represent French arms—to be disgraced. He had learned somewhat about leading fighting men in the last year. He could do what was needful, since no one else seemed about to.

He galloped past the files of mounted knights who crowded the road beside the Tiber. Beyond them were the foot soldiers. If those Burgundians who executed the Roman delegation were any example, the men-at-arms might be more reliable than the knights. Simon searched the column for the sort of men he needed.

He saw, just past the end of the line of mounted men, two score or more of archers in blue tunics with longbows slung over their backs. He was not experienced with the use of the longbow in battle, but what he had heard about its long range suggested that it might be very useful just now.

"Suivez-moi!" he shouted. The archers stared at him and drew themselves up straighter, but looked puzzled. Of course, Simon thought. The longbow was a weapon favored by the English. He beckoned with his hand, and the Englishmen ran to him. Good.

"My lord, I speak un peu Français," said one of them, whose crested helmet marked him as a sergeant. "If you give your orders to me, very slowly—"

"Good," said Simon, pleased with the man's readiness to cooperate. He explained what he wanted.

"Suivez-moi," Simon called again to the longbowmen, and their sergeant repeated, "Follow me," in English. He trotted off, keeping the dark brown mare to a pace that would allow running men to follow him.

When they came to Charles and his three mutinous lieutenants, still arguing, the Roman mob had advanced close enough for Simon to be able to make out individuals. They were almost all men, as far as he could see, with a shouting, fist-shaking woman here and there, and mostly dressed in the plain browns and grays, whites and blacks, of common folk. Men with swords and spears made up the forefront. A few men on horseback with lances and banners rode on the flanks of the mob. Someone was carrying a red and white banner, a design of keys and towers.

For a moment Simon hesitated. He did not want to kill these people.

But there was no way of stopping the Romans, and no one else was able or willing to act. If he did nothing, Charles's army would be destroyed and Simon would probably be killed along with everyone else.

He remembered something Roland, his true father, had told him many years ago: *No one who wants to live through a battle can afford to feel sorry for the men he is trying to kill. Make sure you kill them first, and then you can mourn for them afterward.*

Putting his sympathy for the Romans out of his mind, Simon began to give orders to his archers. He deployed them in a line stretching from the Tiber to a thick grove of trees to the east. Through their sergeant he told them to shoot at the front and center of the oncoming Romans. He noticed that the voices of Count Charles and his antagonists had fallen silent.

They are watching me, he thought, and hoped no one would try to stop him.

When the Englishmen had their arrows nocked and their bows drawn and aimed, Simon shouted, "Tirez!"

They understood that well enough.

The arrows flew in flat curves across the narrowing distance between Count Charles's army and the Roman citizens. Simon saw men falling and others tripping over them.

"Encore!" Simon cried, but then looking back at his little troop of archers saw to his surprise that the Englishmen had already loaded and fired a second time. He had not known that the longbow could be fired again and again so quickly, much more quickly than the crossbow. Screams of panic and pain arose from the mob before him.

I am killing poor people who are trying to defend their city.

A pang of shame swept through him, and he hesitated before giving the next order. But he remembered Roland's advice. The longer it took to drive these Romans back inside their gates, the more blood would be shed, and the more likely that lives would be lost on his side.

"Fire into the midst of the crowd," he told the English sergeant.

The arrows arced high into the overcast sky and fell like dark streaks of rain. The Romans were milling about, some trying to help the wounded, some running away, some shouting orders or pleas, trying to control the confusion.

Simon rode out in front of the bowmen.

"Advance and keep firing," he called to the sergeant. "Keep it up, keep pushing them back."

He heard an arrow whistle past him. So the Romans also had some archers among them. He was too excited to feel any fear.

The longbowmen marched out into the field, stopping at intervals to load and fire, then advancing again. They hardly had to aim. Anywhere the arrows fell in the mob, packed closer together in retreat, they would wound or kill. Simon heard shouts and screams of terror from across the field. The Romans were falling over one another, trying to get away. None of the poor devils was wearing armor.

Where were the professional defenders of the city, Simon wondered.

The great crowd was falling back toward the city's gates. Like the debris left by a wave receding from shore, bodies, dark clumps, lay thick in the stubble of the harvested fields. Simon saw a man throw his arms around the trunk of an olive tree and slowly slide to the ground. He saw the red and white banner fall, then someone pick it up and run with it. Three men lay draped over low stone walls, arms and legs twitching.

The farmers' fields between Count Charles's army and the walls of Rome were littered with the dead, the dying, and the struggling wounded. Simon wanted to call back the archers. He felt as if he had loosed a great rock from the top of a hill and it was rolling downward, unstoppable, destroying everything in its path.

The Romans were running desperately, and the pity he had forced himself not to feel while he was fighting them rose up to overwhelm him. His heart lodged in his throat like a rock, and tears crept out of the corners of his eyes.

In God's name, what have I done?

"Magnificent, Simon! You did admirably."

Charles d'Anjou had ridden up beside him and was grinning out at the carnage in the fields of stubble. His dark eyes were alight with pleasure. He struck Simon on his mailed back, one of those hard blows he was fond of.

"What presence of mind! What initiative!" He lowered his voice. "You could not have done better if we had planned it ahead of time. You saved me a fortune in gold."

He spurred his black and white charger closer to Simon's mare and leaned over to kiss him emphatically on the cheek, his stubble scratching Simon's face.

"I don't understand," said Simon.

Charles drew back and looked at him with narrowed eyes. "You don't? Well, you did the right thing. We'll talk about it later."

He turned and shouted at his three commanders. "You see, idiots! One French knight with his head on his shoulders can do what all of you and all your knights could not."

"We were not attempting to do anything," du Mont said sourly, pushing his helmet back off his bowl-shaped hair.

"Those were the bowmen I brought from Lincoln you used, Monseigneur de Gobignon," said FitzTrinian. "You did not have my permission."

In his present mood, Simon wished the pockmarked knight would make an issue of it.

"Do not make yourself more ridiculous than you already are, Sire Alistair," said Charles.

"We still have not settled this question of pay," said Dietrich of Regensburg.

"Go pick the purses of those dead men out there," said Charles with a scornful laugh.

Again Simon was sickened by Charles's manner. He had expected that the count would punish his rebellious commanders. Hanging would be an excellent idea. Flog them out of the army, at least. Instead, he continued to argue with them, even banter with them, as if they were all a pack of merchants in a money changer's shop.

To get away from the wretched business, Simon kicked his dark brown mare into motion and, followed by Thierry, rode out toward the city. He wished desperately that he were back in Perugia with Sophia.

He had seen enough killing in Orvieto, especially the night of the attack on the Palazzo Monaldeschi, to harden him. Still, it made his heart feel heavy as stone in his chest to see so many lives cut short. And by his command.

What pain it must be to die. To have your life stopped, forever.

He recalled the arrow that had whizzed past him. He could easily have been killed.

He rode toward the walls of Rome until they towered over him. The crowd of citizens who had come out to stop Count Charles were gone—those able to flee. There were only the dead and dying scattered in the stubble field around him. Simon tried to avoid looking at the wounded. If it had been one or two men, as it had been that day at Orvieto when de Vercueil ordered the crossbowmen to fire into the crowd, he would have tried to help them. But there were too many here.

His contingent of English archers marched past him on their way back to the main army, their work done. They gave him a cheer, and he, in spite of his heavy heart, did as a good leader should and smiled and waved.

"Good work, my friends! Well done."

He looked ahead again, and saw that the nearest gate, the one through which most of the retreating citizens had run, hung open. He pulled his horse to a stop.

I am not going to be the first of these invaders to enter Rome. I have no right to be here.

Five horsemen appeared suddenly in the gateway. More resistance?

These men were richly dressed, their scarlet capes billowing as they rode toward him. Their hands were empty of weapons.

The rider in the lead was a man with a glossy black beard and a sharply hooked nose. He reminded Simon a little of the Contessa di Monaldeschi.

"I am Duke Gaetano Orsini," said the bearded man. "These gentlemen represent the families of Colonna, Frangipani, Papareschi, and Caetani. We have come to greet Count Charles, and to welcome him to Rome." These men, Simon thought, must come from some of the families whose fortified towers loomed over the city.

Their sudden appearance made Simon angry. It was all happening backward. They should have come out first and made peace with Count Charles, and then there would have been no need for all this butchery.

Simon identified himself. "I will take you to Count Charles." The Roman nobles doffed their velvet caps to Simon, and he touched the brim of his helmet.

As their horses trotted across the field, Simon observed Orsini's gaze traveling coldly over the bodies of the fallen Romans. Some of them, still alive, called out to him pleadingly. He ignored them.

Simon could not resist saying, "If you had come out to welcome Count Charles before these others did, much bloodshed might have been prevented."

Orsini shrugged. "Necessary bloodshed. The mob that threatened Count Charles was incited by the Ghibellino faction in Rome. They tried to get the city militia to join them, but we held the professionals back. Indeed, we have heard you killed one of the leaders of the popolo minuto, the lower orders, Leone Pedulla. That was well done. His loss will be a blessing to this city, as will the loss of these other troublemakers."

Simon felt as disgusted with this man as he had with Charles's marshals. Unable to keep order in their own city, the nobility of Rome approved the slaughter of their people by foreign invaders. It was despicable. Count Charles would have to deal with them, but he himself would speak no more to these poltroons who called themselves gentlemen.

They rode in silence toward the advancing Angevin army of Count Charles. The count's black and red lion banner fluttered over his steel coronet. He was riding toward Rome again with his commanders behind him as if all their differences were settled.

Charles and his leaders reined up before the new delegation from Rome. The Count of Anjou greeted these representatives of the great families of Rome with courtesy, dismounting and embracing Gaetano Orsini. He assured each Roman nobleman, Simon interpreting, how happy he was to see him.

"I believe it would be best if my men and I were to camp outside the city walls for tonight," he said, looking down his large nose at Orsini.

"I was just about to suggest that," said Orsini. "The city is quite crowded."

"Perhaps less crowded now." Charles laughed, with a nod at

the fields where wailing men and women were walking, trying to find their dead and bear them away for burial. "At any rate, I will enter the city tomorrow."

"All will be prepared for Your Signory. The loyal supporters of the Parte Guelfo are eager to greet you. You will be made an honorary patrician. There will be banners, cheering crowds, music. The militia will parade for you. It will be a true Roman triumph." Orsini was all smiles and flourishes.

Charles smiled. "A triumph. Yes, and I assume that a triumph will include tribute?"

Orsini's smile faded. "Tribute?"

Charles nodded slowly. "To be exact, I will require three thousand florins to be delivered to me tomorrow morning before I enter the city, to compensate my men, whose pay is in arrears. I will have further requirements, but I will not press you for all at once. Three thousand florins will be enough for tomorrow."

Simon saw von Regensburg and FitzTrinian grinning at each other.

Orsini's mouth worked several times after Simon translated Charles's demand for three thousand florins. "But, Your Signory, we welcome you as our protector, not as one who comes to—to take from us."

Charles laughed and threw his arms wide. "Protectors cost money, my dear Orsini. I am sure the great city of Rome can scrape together three thousand florins by tomorrow. It will not be necessary for me to send my army into the city to help you find the money, will it?"

"Not at all necessary, Your Signory," said Orsini, bowing, his face flushed to the roots of his black beard.

These Guelfo nobles apparently had thought that the count of Anjou had come to Rome purely out of some high-minded desire to serve the pope and the Church, Simon thought. They were starting to learn what Simon himself had gradually come to realize: that Count Charles did nothing that did not first and foremost benefit himself.

As for himself, Simon's deepest wish was to get away from all this slaughter and pillage and dishonor, and the sooner the better.

"Rome is an old whore who lies down for every strong man who comes along," said Count Charles. "All we needed was to show our resolution when that mob came at us, and Rome fell over backward."

The two men sat across from each other at a small camp table in

Charles's tent, sharing wine and succulent roast pork killed and cooked by Anjou's equerries. Simon stared into the flames of a six-branched candlestick standing on Charles's armor chest at the side of the tent, and thought that he would far rather be exploring the wonders of Rome he had heard so much about—the Colosseum, the Lateran Palace, the Forum, the catacombs.

Simon remembered his mother's warning of years ago: *Charles d'Anjou uses people.* How often, with Charles, had he suspected, feared, that she was right? But those boyhood years in Charles's household, Simon's weapons training under Charles, his feeling that King Louis was a sort of father to him and Count Charles a sort of uncle, all made him want to trust Charles. But it was becoming impossible to do that, especially since Avignon, when Charles asked him to betray the king's confidence. Even now, though he wished they could get back on their old footing, he found himself wondering whether that old footing had been an illusion. Perhaps all along Charles had been kind to him only the better to use him.

He was terribly afraid that he knew what Charles wanted to talk to him about tonight. He had seen the sorry quality of Charles's army, and he had been impelled, almost against his will, to take the lead when the Roman mob was attacking. If Simon were in Charles's position, he knew what he would want.

"You did just the right thing today, Simon," Charles said. "Those three cutthroats would never have let themselves be overrun, nor would I. But I hadn't paid them in a while, no fault of mine, and they saw that as an excuse to try to extract a promise from me of an additional monthly five florins per knight and increases for the common soldiers as well. They thought the sight of that mob would force me to yield to them."

So their refusal to act was a pretense, Simon thought. But he began to feel disgusted with himself. Of all of them, he was the only one who had been duped.

Charles went on. "They were testing my courage. They did not know me well. They know me better now. I would have stood my ground until they were forced to turn and defend themselves. But you settled things by taking those archers out into the field and driving the rabble off. And a good thing you did, because the situation *was* risky. They might have waited too long to attack, and we might have lost lives unnecessarily. It was a dangerous game they were playing."

And a dangerous game you were playing, Simon thought. He leaned forward, resting his elbows on the table. Charles had used him, just as Mother had warned, and he felt angry enough to speak frankly.

"It was mutiny. In my opinion you should have hanged those men. They are little better than routiers. But all you did was haggle with them."

Sipping from his goblet, Charles lounged back on his cot and laughed. "Ah, Simon, I forget sometimes that you have never been in a war. This is the way it always is. Especially at the beginning. These men—du Mont, FitzTrinian, von Regensburg, and their followers—are hirelings, and when one goes shopping for an army, one buys, not the best there is, but only the best that is on the market."

Simon wanted to lean back as Charles had done, but there was no back to the stool he sat on. Charles's furnishings were as meager as everything else about his army.

"I fear for you, uncle, I really do. Not only are your knights undisciplined, but you are so few in number." He instantly regretted saying that. It would give Charles an opening to ask him for help.

Charles smiled complacently. "And you think Manfred von Hohenstaufen, with his host of Saracens and Sicilians, will march up here and chew me up, is that it?"

"Well—perhaps."

Charles swirled his wine cup and drank from it. "A bigger army would have cost me far more to ship and far more to pay, feed, and quarter while I am here. I needed this much of an army to establish myself in Rome. I do not need more until I actually make war on Manfred, and that may be as much as a year from now. Tomorrow I will enter Rome in triumph, and I will have myself declared chief senator of Rome. Eventually Guy le Gros—Pope Clement, he is calling himself—will crown me king of southern Italy and Sicily. As my renown spreads, fighting men will come flocking from all over to join my cause. And they will have to come in on my terms. Then I will be ready to march south."

The whole reason Charles had first sent Simon to Italy—to engineer the conquest of the Saracens by Christians and Tartars—was that no longer important to him? Charles had said nothing about the Tartars since Simon arrived in Ostia last night.

"The new Holy Father has already proclaimed his approval of the Tartar alliance," Simon ventured.

"Excellent," said Charles, nodding. He stood up and poured more wine for himself and Simon.

Sitting down again on his camp bed, he went on. "Your guardianship of the Tartars, too, has been superb, Simon. You proved that I judged wisely in picking you for that task. I am delighted.''

Feeling pleased with himself, Simon took a long drink of the heavy red Roman wine. ''Then, since the pope has publicly given his approval, shall I escort the Tartars to your brother the king, so they can plan the crusade?''

''The crusade?'' Charles lay back on his cot, propped up on one elbow, and stared into his wine cup and said nothing further.

''Would it not be safest to conduct them to the king at once?'' Simon pressed him. ''Our enemies may still try to kill them, even though the alliance is proclaimed.''

Charles shook his head. ''The last attempt to kill them was many months ago.''

True, Simon thought. The stalker in black seemed to have given up or disappeared.

''Yes, but that Sienese attack on Orvieto—''

Charles interrupted. ''De Verceuil got the Tartars out of Orvieto safely. And that attack was aimed at the pope, not the Tartars. After all, who has been trying to kill the Tartars, and why? Manfred's agents, because they knew that if the pope approved the Tartar alliance, my brother would then give me permission to march against Manfred.''

Simon remembered King Louis saying he wanted to be ready to launch his crusade by 1270, now only five years away.

''But preparations for a crusade take many years,'' Simon said. ''Should not the Tartars go to the king now, so they can begin to plan?''

''I do not think they should visit my brother just yet,'' said Charles. ''His mind so easily fills up with dreams of recapturing Jerusalem.'' Simon caught a faint note of mockery in Charles's voice. ''The presence of the Tartars at his court might distract him from his more immediate responsibilities.''

''Then what will we do with the Tartars?'' Simon asked, nettled.

''Let them remain with le Gros's court in Viterbo. It honors the pope to have those strange men from the unknown East at his coronation. Then, when he comes here to present me with the crown, let them come, too, as my guests. Indeed, they can stay with me after that. They will be safer with me than they would be anywhere else in Italy. And it might interest them to see how Christians make war.''

They would be safer still in France.

He could have taken Sophia and the Tartars to France together, leaving the Tartars safe and well guarded with King Louis, and then going on with Sophia to Gobignon. And getting away from Charles and his war.

"How many more months will I have to stay in Viterbo guarding the Tartars?" he said with some irritation.

Charles put down his wine goblet suddenly and stood up. He seemed to fill the tent. The candles on the chest lit his face from below, casting ghastly shadows over his olive complexion.

"Simon, I feel I can speak more frankly to you than I ever have. It is nearly two years since I asked you to undertake the guarding of the Tartars. The way you acted today showed me that you've learned a great deal in that time. You have seen the world. You have seen combat. You have learned to lead."

He praises me because I was so quick to mow down a hundred or so commoners, thought Simon.

"Thank you, uncle," he said tonelessly.

"I did not summon you from Viterbo just so you could accompany me from Ostia to Rome, Simon. You saw what my routiers— as you called them—are like. And when I am inside the city I will be in much greater danger from that Roman canaille than I was in the field today. I need a good leader with me whom I can trust. I want you to stay here in Rome with me."

Simon's chest ached as if chains were wrapped around it.

"How long?"

"At least two months. By then Sire Adam Fourre, my chief vassal from Anjou, will be here with seventy knights and three hundred men. A small force, but one I can depend on. I will feel more in control of these brigands then."

"But who will guard the Tartars while I am here?" he asked, desperately trying to think of an excuse that would get him back to Sophia.

Charles shrugged. "De Verceuil can look after them."

For over a year now he had been guarding the Tartars with his life, at Charles's request. Now Charles hardly seemed concerned about them. It was bewildering.

And when will I see Sophia again? he cried inwardly.

He could simply refuse to stay in Italy a moment longer. He could just get up right now and leave, go to Viterbo and find Sophia.

No, he could not do that. He had come to Italy to *redeem* the name of the house of Gobignon, not besmirch it further. What a scandal if the king's brother were to charge that Simon de Gobignon turned his back on him when he was in peril. What would the king and the nobles say of him then in France? He must see this through, at least until Charles was securely established in Rome.

But pray God Charles did not ask him to stay with him beyond that.

"You do not need to go back to the Tartars at all," Charles said. "It seems to me that phase of things is settled. I think it would be more important for you to go home, this summer, to Gobignon."

Simon's heart leapt with amazement and joy as the words sank in. "Yes! Yes—I want to—very much," he blurted out. "I want that more than anything else."

If I can take Sophia with me.

Charles came around the table and laid a heavy hand on Simon's shoulder. Simon, still seated, had to twist his neck to look up at him.

"Do you remember when we first spoke of your guarding the Tartars I promised even greater opportunities for glory? I said that you would ride in triumph through fallen cities."

"Yes," said Simon after hesitating a moment. He knew where Charles was leading this, and felt a hollow of dread growing in his stomach.

Charles bent down, bringing his face close to Simon's, his hand still pressing on Simon's shoulder. The Count of Anjou's eyes glowed green in the candlelight, and Simon felt paralyzed by his gaze, as if Charles were a basilisk.

"Simon de Gobignon," Charles said solemnly. "I invite you to join me in the conquest of Sicily, and to share with me in the spoils. I ask you to bring the army of Gobignon to this war."

God's blood, protect me!

"I cannot make my vassals come here," Simon ventured. His voice sounded weak in his ears.

Charles's face came closer still.

"*Make* them come? They will beg you to *let* them come. This will be the greatest war since you were a child."

Simon gathered his thoughts. "Their obligations to me are limited. Many owe me only thirty days' service. Some are not required to serve outside Gobignon boundaries, need only fight if we are invaded."

"Your father brought four hundred knights and two thousand men-at-arms with him on the crusade my brother and I led into Egypt."

Yes, and lost them all.

"But that was a crusade, and the ordinary obligations did not apply," Simon said.

"This will be a crusade. The pope is going to declare Manfred an infidel, an enemy of the Church, and proclaim a crusade against him. But this will not be like crusading in Outremer, where there is nothing to be gained but sand and palm trees and—spiritual benefits.'' Again Simon heard that hint of mockery in Charles's voice. "Southern Italy and Sicily are the wealthiest lands in Europe. Riches for everybody! Just go back and tell your seigneurs and knights about that. They will plead with you to lead them hither.'' He smiled sarcastically. "I know what a dedicated farmer you are. So get the harvest in—and then bring your army south for the real harvest. The prospect of wintering in Italy instead of in the north should delight them.''

In all his life, Simon thought, he had never wanted anything less than to lead the knights and men of Gobignon to Charles's war. He thought of Gobignon, so far away in the northeast corner of France. What business did his people have in Italy? Inevitably, many Gobignon men would die, and how would Simon face their families?

But, sadly, he realized Charles was right in his prediction. Simon could think of dozens of young barons and knights in the Gobignon domain who would ride singing to a war waged for glory and riches.

He chose his words carefully, not wanting to offend Charles. "This question of the crown of Sicily—it does not touch Gobignon in any way that I can see. It would not be right for me to lead my people to war over it.''

Surprisingly, Charles smiled. "I understand, Simon.'' He patted Simon's back. He straightened up and strode back to the other side of the table and sat again.

"You do see my point, uncle?'' Simon said nervously.

Charles nodded, still smiling. "Why, indeed, should the Count de Gobignon come to the aid of the Count d'Anjou? I am glad to see a bit of shrewdness in you. It means you are growing up. But I will answer you in one word. Apulia.''

Simon hunched forward. "Apulia?''

"The southeast of Italy. The richest of Manfred's provinces. Where he has always chosen to live, and his father Frederic before him. Simon, Count de Gobignon, Duke of Apulia. How does that sound? In one short war you would double your land holdings and triple your wealth. Now do you see how this war touches you?''

What Simon realized, with a clarity that chilled him, as if he had suddenly seen in Uncle Charles the mark of some dread disease, was that he and Charles d'Anjou were utterly different kinds of men. As Count of Anjou and Seigneur of Arles, Charles already ruled a domain bigger than Gobignon, and he thought it the most natural thing in the world to want more.

Why do I not want more? Should I? Is something wrong with me?
It was all too much for Simon to think through now, while Charles

was pressing so. He had to get away from him. It occurred to him that he could agree now to join forces with Charles, then go back to Gobignon and renege on his promise. Charles would be far too busy fighting in Italy to try to force him to bring troops from Gobignon.

No, that probably would not work. It would be stupid to think he could outwit a man as experienced in statecraft as the Count of Anjou. Once Simon promised, Charles would no doubt find a way to force him to make good.

"Uncle Charles, I cannot decide in one evening the future of thousands of people whose lives and souls I am responsible for."

Charles shook his head. His face was darkening; he was getting angry.

"You sound like my brother, talking about the difficulty of making royal decisions. God's bowels, boy! Deciding what's best for our subjects is what we were born to do. Where is the Gobignon in you? Your father, Count Amalric, for all he went wrong at the end of his life, would have known how to seize a moment like this. How do you think that splendid domain you've inherited was built up? Empires must grow, or they wither and die. It is a law of life."

Simon was never more glad he was not Amalric's son.

"I must go back and look at the old agreements and treaties, Uncle Charles. I must see what kind of service each baron and each knight owes me, and for how long and under what conditions I can call on them. Let me see what my rights are as seigneur. Then I will be able to tell you how many knights and men I can bring to you."

"Suit yourself, but I will wager few of them will hold you to the letter of their obligations. As I said, when they see the chances for gain, they will want to come. If need be, pay them. Your treasury is fat. You have had no wars to pay for for many years. Whatever you spend, you will make back a hundredfold when we take Manfred's kingdom."

He did not notice that I did not actually promise to bring any men back with me.

To seem to promise and yet not to promise—Simon felt rather proud of himself for finding a way out. He felt like a fox who had thrown a pack of slavering hounds off the scent. He had freed himself from the trap Anjou had built for him. Perhaps the count was right. Perhaps this time in Italy *had* done him some good, made him a cleverer man. He drank deeply of the red Roman wine and secretly toasted himself.

He would honor Charles's request to remain at his side in Rome for a time, fighting for him if need be. Then to Viterbo.

Over a year ago he had agreed to care for the Tartars, and he would be judged, and would judge himself, on how well he had done that. He did not like leaving it to de Verceuil. Even if Papa le Gros, as the Italians called him, were all in favor of the alliance, the Tartars still had many points to settle before the war—the final war—on the Saracens became a reality.

"Before I return to Gobignon," Simon said, "I must go to Viterbo and make sure that the Tartars are well guarded."

"Suit yourself." Charles waved a large hand in acquiescence.

To Viterbo and Sophia.

He felt again the ecstasy of that day by the lake, the closeness, the union of their flesh. How beautiful it had been! Even here, in Charles d'Anjou's tent outside the walls of Rome, he felt a hot stirring in his body at the remembrance of their afternoon of love.

How could she not want that again? She must. He was sure of it. She wanted, as he did, a lifetime of love. That was why she wept whenever he tried to convince her that he meant to marry her.

She had promised him faithfully that the next time they met she would tell him what the obstacle was to their marrying. Whatever the reason was, he would sweep it aside and carry her off to Gobignon with him.

Friar Mathieu could marry them before they even left Viterbo. Then if Grandmère or his sisters had any objections, they would have to swallow them. They could be together in his castle this summer, when the rivers were flowing fast, when the trees were heavy with fruit and the fields were green and the forest was full of fleet deer and clever foxes. How she would love it!

Sophia. A thousand visions of her cascaded through his mind, of her dark red lips smiling, her eyes glowing like precious stones, her proud carriage. And he remembered the feel of her limbs tangled with his, her passion the proof, despite her fears, of the depth of her love for him.

It would be maddening to stay away from her for the two months Charles had asked of him, but after that they would have the whole of their lives together.

LXII

SOPHIA HEARD A MURMUR FROM THE RIDERS AHEAD, AND LOOKED up. It was warmer here in the south, and she had opened the curtains of her sedan chair. Following the path around the side of a hill, the two men carrying her had brought Lucera into view.

It seemed not to have changed at all in the year and a half since she had left with Daoud and Lorenzo. The octagonal walls and square towers of Manfred's citadel, warmed by the setting sun, rose above the small city standing in the center of a plain surrounded by hills.

Her skin tingled at the thought of seeing Daoud again. But her heart, which should have been light with happiness, ached, tormented for months by a decision she could not make.

A cry from the men-at-arms leading the way startled her. Her eyes followed a pointing arm and saw, high on the rocky slope of a nearby hill, a mounted warrior.

He glittered in the sunset. He was too far away for her to see the details of his costume, but gold flashed on his breastplate, on his hands and arms, and on the white turban that shaded his face. One of Manfred's Saracens probably, sent out from Lucera to bid them welcome.

She saw that their path descended gradually into a valley. The Saracen's horse was scrambling down a steep slope to meet them. The warrior leaned back in this saddle to balance himself, riding easily down to the valley floor.

As she drew nearer to him, her heart started to hammer in her chest. The lower half of his face was covered by a short blond beard. The face was still in shadow, but the nose was long and straight.

Most of all, it was his carriage that told her who he was. He held himself so perfectly erect that he almost seemed made of some substance lighter and finer than ordinary flesh. And yet there was not a trace of stiffness in his posture. Like a young tree. Some vessel seemed to open within her and spread a gentle, joyous balm throughout her body.

Ahead of her, Ugolini, alerted by his guards, had thrown back the curtains of his sedan chair and was leaning out. He was bareheaded, his white side-whiskers fluttering in the breeze. He must be beside himself with excitement, Sophia thought, at the prospect of reunion with Tilia.

The horseman touched his right hand to his white turban in salute to Ugolini, and rode on past.

How splendidly he was caparisoned, from the white plume in his turban to his jeweled, carved stirrups. The breastplate over his long red riding robe was of polished steel, inlaid with gold in Arabic spirals. Jewels sparkled on the hilt and sheath of his sword.

He was close enough for her to see his face clearly. His new beard gave him a commanding, princely look. Seeing him like this, she understood better what the word *Mameluke* meant. She felt as if a new sun had arisen before her. How unbelievably lucky she was to be loved by such a man.

But, like an enemy in ambush, the pain of her indecision struck her in the heart.

The more fool I am to have betrayed him.

He drew up beside her and rode around her sedan chair so that the head of his glistening black horse was toward Lucera. In a sudden movement he leaned down from the saddle. An irresistible arm encircled her waist and pulled her up out of the sedan chair. For a moment she felt alarmed and amazed, as if she were flying through the air. Then, before she could scream, she found herself comfortably seated across the great horse, her shoulder resting on his breastplate, his arms around her.

Her only fear was that she might faint at his touch.

And like that they rode into Lucera. Together for all the world to see.

What exquisite irony! She gazed around the bedchamber Daoud had led her to, hardly able to believe her eyes. The big bed with its golden curtains was the same, and so was the window with its pointed arch. This was the very room, the very bed, in which Manfred and she had made love for the last time.

Manfred must have deliberately chosen to give this room to them.

Daoud's weapons hung on the wall, and his armor was mounted on wooden stands. Chests of clothing and other possessions were lined up along the wall. Soon the servants would be bringing her things in too.

This room—another thing she could not tell him about. She despised herself. But it might well offend him if he knew of Manfred's little joke, and enmity between Daoud and Manfred at this moment could be disastrous.

Manfred needs Daoud. Why is he so foolish as to risk angering him?

Daoud and she stood staring at each other. They had said little so far. She felt overwhelmed, and she supposed he did too. She felt her longing for him as a strange not-quite-pain in the pit of her stomach.

He took her shoulders in his hands. How good to feel his strong fingers holding her.

"How long has this been your room?" she asked.

"For about a month. Rather grand, is it not? The king says it is suitable to my rank. I have my own command, a division of his mounted Muslim warriors. I call them the Sons of the Falcon."

Suitable to my rank.

She wondered how much Daoud knew about herself and Manfred.

"What troubles you?" he asked.

So many things.

"Manfred," she said, choosing the worry easiest to speak of.

He stroked her cheek gently. "No need to torment yourself. I understand how it must have been."

But would you understand about Simon?

She said, "But can Manfred accept what you and I are to each other?"

He shrugged. "You see that we are together in his palace. You saw that I rode with you before me on my horse through the streets of Lucera and into Manfred's castle."

"I see that Manfred must know about us. Are you sure he does not want me back? It can be fatal to cross a king."

"When we got the message that Ugolini and you were coming here instead of going to Viterbo, I talked with Manfred, not as subject and king, but as man and man. He was most gracious, as Manfred usually is."

"What did he tell you?"

"That indeed he still cares for you. Too much, it seems."

"Too much?"

Daoud's teeth flashed in his blond beard. "His queen, the mother of his four children, Helene of Cyprus, usually looks the other way when Manfred beds beautiful young women. But she saw in you too serious a rival. He had to send you off with me, or the queen would have had you poisoned.''

Sophia's eyes strayed to the bed in horror. She remembered now that before she left here, Manfred had hinted at something like that.

"Poisoned! And I am safe now?"

Again the white grin in the blond beard. During the six months they had been apart, she had begun to think that her love for him might have seduced memory and enhanced his good looks beyond reality. But now in the flesh he surpassed even the image her memory had cherished.

"You are safe as long as you stay away from Manfred and he from you. There will be a feast tonight, in honor of Cardinal Ugolini. You will see how carefully the king will avoid you.''

Daoud pulled her close to enfold her in his arms. He had taken off his surcoat and breastplate, and with her head against his chest she could feel his heart beating strong and fast under his silk robe.

"And you?" she said. "Do you hate the thought that Manfred and I were lovers?"

In that very bed.

"It is far in the past," Daoud said. "Before you met me." He held her away from him and looked at her with laughter in his blue eyes. "Even the Prophet married a widow.''

His gentle acceptance, his easy assumption that all was over between herself and Manfred, tore at her heart. If she even mentioned Simon, it would be different. That was not in the past. That was after she had met Daoud, after they became lovers. For the thousand-thousandth time she cursed herself for letting it happen.

God, I am a whore! As bad as the worst painted prostitute plying her trade under the arches by the Hippodrome.

No, worse than that, in a way. A prostitute had a clear reason for doing what she did with men. The more Sophia thought about the time she let Simon possess her, the less she understood it. And even a prostitute knew her occupation and her place in the world. From the night that Alexis cast her adrift, Sophia had, in a way, been lost.

But there came to her a glimmering of hope. Daoud had a place here with Manfred, and she had a place beside Daoud. Could it be that at last she had a home?

Then she should do nothing to endanger it. She should say nothing about Simon.

"Come to bed," he whispered, still holding her and taking a step in that direction.

The feel of his arms around her and his body pressing against her sent ripples of need for him through her. But now, with thoughts of Manfred and—much worse—of Simon, confusing her, she felt frightened, unready. She needed more time.

"I have had no proper bath in days, Daoud. I feel the grime of the road all over me."

"Of course." He smiled. "And now you can have a proper bath. Let me see to it."

In the year and a half since she left this place, Sophia had all but forgotten the bathing rooms in the lowest level of Castello Lucera. She had not used them as much as she had wished to, when she lived here before. In her strange position as a foreigner and one of Manfred's loves, she had not felt comfortable bathing with the other women who lived in the castle.

But tonight, as she and Daoud undressed in the green-tiled anteroom, they had it all to themselves. Daoud must stand high indeed with Manfred to have arranged that, she thought.

In the light of the oil lamp hanging overhead, his naked body was a golden color, and free, as far as she could tell, from the marks of insult the podesta's torturer had inflicted upon it last summer.

She was not naked. She wore a linen gown that opened down the front. Her continued worrying over whether or not to tell him about Simon made her want to stay covered as long as she could.

But with a smile he pulled her gown apart and slipped it off her shoulders and down her back to the floor.

A glance down his body told her that he wanted her now. The sight thrilled her, but she still felt uneasy and not able to give herself wholeheartedly to him and to the act of love.

"Let us attend to the grime," she said with a small smile.

In the next room, its walls tiled in white, she lay in a round sunken tub filled with hot water piped in from the castle kitchen. It was large enough for Daoud to stand over her in it. He took over the task of washing her with scented soap imported from Spain.

At first she simply lay back and enjoyed her renewed acquaintance with the amenities of Manfred's kingdom, so much more like Constantinople than life in the Papal States had been. But as the hot water relaxed her and as Daoud's hands, slippery with soap, slid over her skin, she felt the rising warmth of desire. Nothing mattered but this moment. She wriggled her legs and hips against him in small, almost unwilled movements.

"The grime first," he said with a soft laugh, and continued methodically to soap her until she was mad with wanting him.

He picked her up in his arms and carried her into the next room, its tiles the red-orange of sunset, which was taken up by a great pool of very hot water. Usually this chamber would be occupied by anywhere from six to a dozen men or women. But tonight Sophia and Daoud were quite alone.

Still carrying her, he descended the steps into the hot pool. Ribbons of steam rose around them. He lowered her into the water. When she stood neck-deep in it, the heat was almost unbearable, as if she were about to be boiled to death. But then the heat soaked into her until her very bones felt liquefied. Her whole being melted until she was not a person who felt desire, she *was* desire itself.

With her arms around his neck she pulled his head down and kissed him, flicks of her tongue tip luring his tongue into her mouth.

He pressed her back against the warm tile wall, and she knotted her legs around his waist as he took her standing up.

Moments later her ecstatic cries were echoing through the bathing rooms.

They forgot about time.

Her voice rang again and again in the vaulted chamber. They made love in the hot water and then lying on linen cloths on the masseur's slab beside the pool. They nearly fell asleep in each other's arms.

Laughing at their bodies' foolishness, they plunged into the last pool, cold water in a blue-tiled room, then hurried through a door to the place where they had started and dressed again.

When they were back in their room, Daoud's voice was drowsy as he lay beside her on the gold-curtained bed.

"You must have bypassed Rome when you came down, with the Count of Anjou and Simon de Gobignon both there," he said.

At the mention of Simon's name Sophia's pleasant sleepiness fled, and she felt an ache in the pit of her stomach. Should she tell Daoud or not? She still could not decide. The uncertainty itself had become almost as great an agony as the fear of what would happen if she told him. She rolled over with her back to him, so that he could not see her face.

"Yes," she said. "We went east into the Abruzzi and through L'Aquilia and Sulmona. Terribly mountainous country. It took us much longer, but it was safer."

But if I do not tell him, every time he takes me in his arms I will know that I am lying to him. I will always be aware that I am keeping something back from him that he would want to know. I betrayed him with Simon, and each time I have the chance to tell him and do not, I am betraying him again.

"Before Charles took Rome, Lorenzo and Tilia and I passed near the city, but skirted around it. It would not do to have someone from that inn recognize us."

"How well I remember that night." It was then that she had first seen how resourceful and how ruthless Daoud could be.

"Lorenzo and I could talk about it now without getting angry," Daoud said. "He told me he tried to help the old Jew, Rachel's husband, because a man does not forget the faith and the people he was born to."

"And you wondered about yourself?" said Sophia.

"Exactly." The palm of his hand felt wonderfully hard against the flesh of her buttocks. "And, strangely, I found myself thinking of Simon de Gobignon."

She felt her body stiffen and tried to make herself relax. "What could have made you think of him?" She had never told Daoud about Simon's shadowed childhood. She wondered if he had heard of it from someone else.

"I asked myself, what if the Turks had not overrun Ascalon and killed my parents and carried me off? And the answer came that I would have been very like Simon de Gobignon. He grew up, you see, having all the things I lost."

"What things?"

"A family, a home, the Christian faith, freedom, knighthood, his country. Even his name."

This talk about Simon was making her desperately uneasy. She wondered if she could tell Daoud to go to sleep and forget it all.

"And I saw at last why I hated him so much," Daoud went on. "I hated him in part, of course, because of you. I had already started to love you, and the thought of him possessing you made me furious. And yet it was my duty to send you to bed with him. Fortunately, that never had to happen. But there was an even deeper reason for my hating him."

"What was that?" she asked.

"Envy. Envy that I could not admit to myself."

"Not admit to yourself? Why?"

His hand on her was motionless. She sensed that it was an effort for him to put his thought into words.

"Because I was afraid to. That is always why we do not admit a truth to ourselves. My Sufi sheikh often said, *The things you most fear, those you must turn and stare at until you are no longer afraid.* I was afraid I might betray my faith."

"You mean renounce Islam?" A chill went through her. What a

disaster for all of them that could have been. She could well understand how the thought of that might frighten him.

"Yes. I had to put that possibility out of my mind. So I hated Simon de Gobignon without knowing why. Because I did not understand my hatred, I hated him all the more."

If only we could stop talking about Simon.

But the man she loved was telling her something very important about himself. She had to set her own discomfort aside. She had to listen.

"And now you do not hate him?" She turned over in the bed. She wanted to see his face.

There was a peacefulness in his eyes such as she had never seen before. Always, they had seemed to burn, white-hot. Now they were clear and fathomless, like the sky.

"I do not hate him. I realized, as I rode along with Lorenzo, that if your new faith is strong and your new people are good, you can remember without danger what you loved of the old. I will always love the sound of the Christian priests chanting in the cool dark of a church. I will always feel especially at home in a Christian castle. But the voice I hear in the depths of my soul today is the true voice of God, and that, Simon de Gobignon will never hear. Unless God's all-powerful hand reaches out for him as it did for me."

Awed, Sophia said, "I have never heard anyone speak as you do. With so much wisdom. Except, once or twice, a priest."

He closed his eyes. "I speak as I am inspired to speak. In Islam there are no priests that stand between God and man. There are the more learned and the less learned, but each man and each woman can hear God."

Daoud had bared his soul to her. She wanted to do the same. Love was not merely the coupling of naked bodies, but the union of naked minds. How could she ever be happy with him while lying to him?

But she did not love Simon. What had happened between them had been a moment of being overwhelmed by feeling. It had been done, not by her, but by Sophia Orfali.

She had felt sorry for Simon and wanted to comfort him. She had been moved by the purity of his love for her, and her body, which had not known Daoud for months, ran away with her. It was a shameful thing, but not an important thing, because it did not change her love for Daoud.

It would be important to Daoud, though. He would feel that she had betrayed him. He would want revenge. He would hate Simon.

Most important, the peace with his own childhood, reached after painful struggle, might be destroyed. The beautiful state of mind he had shown her might be lost.

For the sake of his peace, she must keep silent.

She hated the decision. It meant that a part of her would always be locked away from Daoud, and he would never know it.

Very well, then. Let *that*, and not his wrath at the revelation, be her punishment for having let herself go that day with Simon by the lake. That would be the mutilation she would always bear. Perfect union with Daoud would be a promised land she would never enter. By suffering that, she would silently make restitution to Daoud for the wrong she had done him.

All the while she had been thinking, he had been gazing at her. Just as she reached her final decision, his eyes closed and his breathing deepened. She reached out and touched the sparse blond hairs in the center of his chest, lightly so as not to wake him.

I lost everything too. He and I are so alike.

Mother and Father. Alexis, whom she had loved in the simple way that Simon loved her. All lost in one night of fire and steel. And after that, the life she led had been so little like that of other women. A life so strange and venturesome she did not know what to think of herself. And yet a life she had loved much of the time.

If Simon reminded Daoud of what he had lost, almost any woman she met did the same for Sophia.

Why, she wondered, had a man's seed never quickened within her? She was twenty-four years old, and she had never been with child. Not once since girlhood had her monthly flow of blood failed.

I am barren, she thought sadly, as she had countless times before. *Barren and alone.* Just as well. Even one baby would have been an impossible burden in the years since she fled to Michael.

But now, if Daoud were to get her with child, what joy that would be. At this moment, it seemed, she had nothing to do except be a companion to Daoud. There had never been a better time in her life for having a child. And even if she could never be wholly one with Daoud, she could be one with their child.

There were remedies for barrenness, she thought, and sometimes they worked. Wise old women knew them. She might seek out such a woman. Tilia must know a great deal about preventing conception, perhaps she knew something about how to make it happen.

There would be no more work of the sort she had done for Michael and then for Manfred. She was known in the north. She could not go back there. And once Manfred defeated the French and drove them out of Italy, he would want *men* to help him govern. A woman had no place in governing, unless she were married to a man of power or had inherited a title of her own.

A child, after all this was over, might be all she would have left. Daoud could be killed fighting the French. Her heart stopped beating for a moment, and then began pounding in fear.

She put that thought out of her mind quickly. She must believe that he would not be killed. And there was good reason to believe so, with all he had survived already.

No, it was more likely she would lose him when the war was over and he went back to his people. He loved his faith, loved the land that had first enslaved him, then made him a warrior. And she could never go back to Cairo with him. What she had heard about a woman's lot among the Muslims sounded like a living death. He had never said so, but he probably had a wife in Egypt. Several wives perhaps, as Muslims were said to do.

Live as just *one* of his wives? Her stomach burned at the idea. Unthinkable!

Could she persuade Daoud to come with her to Constantinople? Daoud could serve the Basileus brilliantly, as a strategos, a general, or as a mediator between Byzantines and Saracens. A man of his experience would be invaluable. Ah, but to achieve to the utmost of his ability, though, Daoud would have to join the Orthodox Church. And that, after the words he had just spoken, she could never imagine him doing.

Well, but she *could* imagine it. Why spoil the beautiful dream of herself and Daoud together amid the glories of the Polis? For the moment she could indulge her fancy and tell herself anything was possible.

Allowing her mind to drift among these visions, she fell asleep.

LXIII

"ECCO! THE RESIDENCE OF CARDINAL PAULUS DE VERCEUIL," SAID Sordello with a flourish of his hand. The narrow Viterbo street on which Simon, Sordello, and Thierry had been riding opened out suddenly, and they were facing a huge cylinder built of small stones, blackened with age. Simon felt his mouth fall open in wonder, and he quickly snapped it shut. He would not let anything de Verceuil might do seem to impress him.

They rode across a drawbridge over a moat full of water that smelled of rotting things, its surface coated with a green slime.

"It looks a bit like Castel Sant'Angelo in Rome," Simon remarked.

"It was a pagan temple in ancient times," said Sordello.

After passing through the gatehouse, they found themselves in a stone-paved semicircular courtyard. The palace was built against the rear half of the old Roman inner wall and towered above it.

"No more lodging with some noble family or other," said Sordello proudly. "Now our party has a residence of its own."

I would rather have almost anyone but de Verceuil as my host.

Simon hoped he need stay here for only a short time. Just long enough to find Sophia, overcome her reservations about marrying him, and be off to Gobignon. His heart beat harder as he thought of seeing her again after those lonely, miserable months in Rome.

Thierry took their horses to be stabled, while Sordello ushered Simon through a cavernous hall lit by a few small windows near the ceiling. Two men-at-arms Simon recognized as part of his troop of Venetian crossbowmen snapped to attention just inside the door, and after a frantic scramble through his memory Simon managed to greet them by name.

To Sordello Simon said, "I thank you for meeting Thierry and me at the city gate and guiding us here." They crossed the entrance hall. "After a long ride, one does not want to have to find one's way around a strange city."

Sordello smiled smugly in acknowledgment. "Little enough for me to do, Your Signory, for one who has done so much for me. Come, I'll show you to the room His Eminence has set aside for you."

He led Simon up a great flight of marble stairs from ground level to the first floor of the mansion.

"I am capitano of the crossbow troop again," Sordello said suddenly, halfway up the stairs.

"Who decided that?" said Simon irritably. "I appointed Peppino capitano after Teodoro was killed."

Sordello's bloodshot eyes caught Simon's. "Peppino was most courteous about yielding to me when I rejoined the Tartar ambassadors' guards. After all, I am senior to him." They came to the top of the marble stairs, and he held out a hand to indicate stone steps leading to the second floor.

Damn! Simon had removed Sordello from his position for nearly killing the Armenian prince, and it was pure insubordination for the fellow to bully his way back into it in Simon's absence and without his consent. It was typical of Sordello's infuriating combination of guile and gall.

Simon reproached himself for not leaving clear orders on who was to lead the crossbow troop when he left Sordello with them and was off to join Count Charles in Rome. But his head and heart had been full of Sophia then. Discipline demanded that he depose Sordello and reinstate Peppino.

Yes, he thought, if he were intending to stay here, he would do exactly that. But if he did it and then left again, it would probably only provoke a duel to the death between Peppino and Sordello. Let things be. A few weeks from now, at most, he could forget the whole damned lot of them, Tartars and all.

But Sordello's reemergence as leader of the crossbowmen raised another question: Would it offend the Armenians?

They came now to wooden steps leading into the shadowy upper reaches of de Verceuil's castle. Simon looked dubiously at them.

"Trust me, Your Signory, as in any palace, the best apartments are on the top floor."

Trust you? When God invites Lucifer to move back into heaven.

And it was equally unlikely that de Verceuil would provide anything truly grand for Simon. He shrugged and let Sordello climb the wooden steps ahead of him.

"What about the Armenian prince, Hethum? Does he still want your blood?"

Sordello laughed and looked back over his shoulder. "All settled, Your Signory. I know Viterbo, as I know most of these Umbrian hill towns, and I entertained all the Armenians for a night and a day, at my expense. The best taverns, the best whorehouses. Hethum and I are friends now."

One did not entertain so lavishly on the fifteen florins a month Sordello would receive as capitano of the archers. Doubtless he had found other ways to line his pockets.

The mention of whorehouses reminded Simon of the plight of the girl Rachel. He must find out if Friar Mathieu had done anything to help her.

On the musty-smelling fourth floor of the cardinal's palace, Sordello led Simon through five connected rooms. Two of them were bare of furniture, but Simon saw rumpled beds and traveling chests in the other three. In the last one a black-robed priest sat at a desk by a window, writing. He frowned at Simon and Sordello as if to reprove them for disturbing him.

"These are the good apartments?" Simon said when Sordello ushered him into a bare chamber with a small bed in one corner and a smaller trundle bed beside it. The window was large, but covered by wooden shutters. Simon pushed them open to let in more light.

Sordello shrugged. "This is truly the best available, Your Signory. The cardinal has many people in his employ, and many guests. I would not leave those shutters open too long if I were you. Even though it is only April, the flies and mosquitos are numerous already. A wet winter always brings them out."

Not worth the trouble to complain about the room. I won't be here that long.

"Tell Friar Mathieu I am here, Sordello, and tell Thierry to have a hot bath sent up to me."

"Yes, Your Signory. But unless you are willing to wait till midnight, I suggest you go down to the kitchen for your bath. The cardinal's servants are obedient to him and care not a fig for anyone else, and your equerry will find none willing to carry a tub of hot water up four flights of stairs."

This was too much. "Now damn your lazy buttocks, Sordello! I am paying you out of my own purse, and you have had no work to do since I left you in Perugia. You see that a hot bath reaches me by Vespers, or forget you were ever in my service."

Sordello's weather-beaten cheeks flushed, but he bowed and left.

Simon leaned on the sill of his window, looking out over the tiled rooftops of Viterbo. All the buildings he could see were built of a dark gray stone, giving the place an ancient look even though, for all he knew, many houses might be quite recently built. This palace Cardinal de Verceuil had bought for himself seemed to occupy one of the highest points. Just as Perugia had been bigger than Orvieto, so Viterbo was bigger than Perugia. Guards in the black and gold of the local militia paced the high city wall from one massive tower to another. About twenty years ago this city had withstood a siege by King Manfred's father, Emperor Frederic. That was one of the reasons, Simon had heard, that Cardinal le Gros, now Pope Clement, had chosen it.

He heard a rhythmic thumping behind him, then a knock at his door. He opened it to see Friar Mathieu, bent and thinner, his white beard sparser-looking, leaning on a walking stick. They hugged each other, Simon holding the old Franciscan gingerly.

"The safest place on this floor to talk is the loggia," said Friar

Mathieu. "We can share our news there." He bowed to the priest in the next room and greeted him by name and was answered with a grunt.

"One of de Verceuil's large staff," said Friar Mathieu when they were out of the priest's chamber. "It is no accident that his room is next to yours."

"I am surprised de Verceuil lets you live here, Father."

"His Eminence would rather have me far away, but Pope Clement insists I stay close to the Tartars. And there was a letter from King Louis saying the same. After all, people who speak the Tartars' language are scarce this side of the Danube. And His Eminence may dislike me, but the king and the pope both trust me. More, perhaps, than they trust him. So the cardinal put me in a cubbyhole near John and Philip, where I am quite content."

They came to the stairs, where a doorway led out to the loggia. The floor was of red tile, and the walls and columns painted a pale green. Benches and potted trees just beginning to bud were set along the loggia. They were facing west, overlooking the courtyard. They sat on a bench, their faces shaded by the overhanging roof, their knees and feet in the sunlight. Simon enjoyed the late afternoon warmth on his legs, tired from a week's riding. He looked forward to his bath.

"I am sure Pope Clement himself will be eager to see you," said Friar Mathieu. "I hear he has been deluging Count Charles with letters demanding to know when he will march against Manfred."

"Count Charles does not have a big enough army yet to attack Manfred," said Simon, thinking how glad he was to be away from the dour, driven count. "And it seems that Manfred would rather wait for him to make the first move. Anjou says he will not be able to recruit more knights and men until the pope officially gives him the crown of southern Italy and Sicily."

"His Holiness wants Charles to come to Viterbo to be crowned. He refuses to set foot in Rome."

"Charles is determined to be crowned by the pope in Rome. He keeps mentioning that Charlemagne was crowned in Rome."

Friar Mathieu smiled. "So, the fate of Italy is in the hands of three men who are each unwilling to make a move." Sunlight turned his beard to silver. "And what are your plans? Have you returned to us for good, or will you go back to Count Charles?"

At the thought of the prospect before him, Simon felt a warmth within rivaling the afternoon sun. "Tell me, Father—where can I find Cardinal Ugolini's niece, Sophia?"

Friar Mathieu's eyes seemed to sink deeper into the hollows under his white brows. "Ugolini and Sophia are not here in Viterbo."

Simon felt as if a wintry chill had fallen on the loggia. "What? Where have they gone?"

"They never came here. None of us, not even the pope, realized Ugolini was gone until the day of the papal coronation, when he still had not appeared. It was a scandal. After all, Ugolini was cardinal camerlengo under Urban. Papa le Gros—Clement—was furious. The rumor is that Ugolini has fled to Manfred. The pope intends to strip him of his rank for leaving the Papal States without permission."

The pain of loss made Simon cry out, "But Sophia! What of Sophia?"

Friar Mathieu shook his head sadly. "She must be with Ugolini. They are probably both in Manfred's kingdom."

Simon fell back against the plaster wall, gasping. "But—a message—there must have been a message for me. She must have left some word."

"With whom?" Friar Mathieu spread his hands. "She knows I am your friend, but I heard nothing from her."

In all the time since he left Perugia, Simon's vision of Sophia, his dreams of their life together, had sustained him. He thought constantly of her during those dreary weeks while Count Charles was parading around Rome, giving orders to sullen Italians, exercising his troops, arguing with his captains, and hanging those who made difficulties.

On a loggia much like this one, at Ugolini's Perugia mansion, Sophia had made the promise that had given him hope. All he needed, he was sure, was to know what stood between them, and he would be able to overcome it.

And now, as suddenly as if Sophia had been on a ship and a wave had swept her overboard, she was gone.

He felt himself getting angry at Friar Mathieu. He could not believe what the old priest was telling him.

"She promised me!" he blurted out.

"Promised you what?" said Friar Mathieu softly.

"That she would tell me why she could not marry me."

There was a long silence, while Simon stared at the rooftops of Viterbo, silhouetted against a golden sky.

"You wanted to marry her?" Friar Mathieu asked in a soft voice.

"I *want* to marry her," said Simon, his voice sullen.

After another long pause he added, "I was hoping you would marry us."

"Simon," said Friar Mathieu quietly, "How much do you really know about Sophia?" Simon thought he heard pity in the old man's voice.

He felt a twinge of fear, and inched away from the Franciscan. Almost against his will, his head turned toward Friar Mathieu. He felt himself forced to repeat the little that Sophia had told him about herself since they met. The thought of that afternoon by the lake came to him, stabbing him like a spear. He would not tell Friar Mathieu about that, not yet. This was not confession.

Friar Mathieu did not meet Simon's intent gaze, but looked downward, and Simon saw deep, shadowed pouches under his eyes.

"Simon—you recall the girl Rachel."

What of her? Simon wondered, annoyed at the change of subject. Then he remembered.

"It was Sophia who asked me to speak to you about Rachel."

"Just so. I had already tried everything, including prayer, to get John Chagan to free Rachel, but I could not move his heart. He prizes her almost to the point of madness. But I did continue my efforts, because you asked me to. I begged, appealed to his better nature—he does have one—and threatened the fires of hell. Nothing worked. For a time, when we learned that Hulagu Khan had died, we thought that John and Philip would have to go back to Persia. John even spoke of taking Rachel with him and making her his chief wife. Do you have any idea what an honor that would be for Rachel?"

"No," said Simon impatiently, not caring.

"Tartars take new wives and concubines, but their chief wives hold that status for life—usually. For John to say he wants to supplant his chief wife with Rachel shows the depth of his passion for the girl."

"Father, what does all this have to do with Sophia?" Simon burst out.

"I come to that now. I had long talks with Rachel to find out if she really wanted to be rescued from the Tartar. She told me about her life before she came to Orvieto, about what it was like in Tilia Caballo's brothel."

"And?"

"While we talked, Rachel let slip some things about Sophia that— I hate to hurt you, Simon, but she said things that made me think Sophia is not what she has seemed to be."

Anger vibrated in Simon's voice. "I do not want to hear any

brothel gossip. Rachel is a prostitute and a child. What could she know about a woman like Sophia?''

He had an urge to get up and leave. But he realized that behind his anger, and fanning it, lurked the fear of learning something he did not want to know.

Friar Mathieu put a gentle hand on Simon's arm. "Did you tell Sophia about Count Amalric's treason, and about who your real father is?"

"Yes."

"Because you wanted her to know you. If you love Sophia and want to marry her, you have to know all about her. There is no other way."

"But I want her to tell me, if there is anything to tell."

"Perhaps she cannot."

"Blood of Christ, why are you torturing me?"

The old priest shook his head. "Do you understand that if there were any way out of this conversation for me, I would take it?"

Simon looked at the faded old eyes and saw the pain. "Yes."

"I do not want to tell you what Rachel said. I respect her confidence. And I do not like passing on suspicions like this. Come and talk with her yourself."

"Right now? Here in this palace?" Simon shivered with an inner cold.

"Yes. De Verceuil and the Tartars have been invited to a supper at the Palazzo Papale. Rachel is alone in her room. I made sure of that a little while ago."

Feeling like a man going obediently to his own beheading, Simon said, "Let us go and talk to her, then."

In the corridor, Simon saw Sordello and Thierry.

"Your bath is ready, Monseigneur," said Thierry.

"I will bathe later," said Simon, trying not to let the whirlwind of his emotions show in his face.

"There is no way to keep the water warm, Your Signory," said Sordello.

"*Then let it freeze!*" Simon shouted. He turned away quickly and followed Friar Mathieu.

Simon at first did not see the small figure huddled in a far corner of the high, gauze-curtained bed. Rachel's room, on the floor below Simon's, was much bigger than his. The outer wall, which curved slightly because it was part of the old temple, was lined with blue-veined white marble. A large window admitted dim light through oiled parchment and curtains.

"Rachel," said Friar Mathieu softly in Italian. "Here is the Count de Gobignon, whom I told you of. He is in charge of the men who guard your—protector. He is Madonna Sophia's friend. She has asked him to try to help you."

Simon felt a twinge of guilt. Could he be Sophia's friend if he was trying to get Rachel to reveal Sophia's secrets? But Sophia had disappeared without a word to him. If she had secrets, he had to know them, even if he had to deceive this child to get at them.

But at the same time he desperately wanted to learn nothing about Sophia that would hurt him.

Rachel used a red ribbon to mark her place in the book she was reading, climbed down from her bed, and curtsied to Simon. Her skin was as white as the marble on the wall. She wore a pale blue gown. Her small breasts pushed it out in front ever so slightly. Simon could see why Sophia had kept referring to her as a child. He could not imagine how anyone, even a Tartar, could want to couple with so delicate-looking a creature.

Even with books to read and a spacious chamber, she must feel like a prisoner.

He forgot his own anguish momentarily in pity for her plight. He wanted to take the wide-eyed girl gently in his arms and hold her.

Simon and Friar Mathieu sat on small gold-painted chairs, and Rachel sat on the edge of her bed. Simon racked his brain for a way to start the conversation. It must seem to be about Rachel, but it must tell him about Sophia. He was not even sure what he was trying to find out.

Even though he had not spoken and had tried to look friendly and not threatening, he could imagine how much his presence must frighten her. A French count. To her that must almost be like being visisted by a king. And she probably feared Christians anyway. If she decided she must protect Sophia from him, he would get nothing from her.

Simon was grateful when Friar Mathieu cleared his throat and spoke.

"Count Simon is anxious about your welfare, my dear, " said the old Franciscan. "He was quite surprised to learn that Cardinal Ugolini and Madonna Sophia had not followed the pope here to Viterbo. He was wondering whether Madonna Sophia had left some word with you about where she was going."

Rachel shook her head. "I have not seen her since John took me from Madama Tilia's house." Her black hair was wound in braids around her head, exposing her small ears, made to look smaller still by the large gold hoops she wore in them. Similarly, a gold necklace with a jeweled pendant emphasized the slenderness of her neck. Her arms and hands seemed weighed down with bracelets and rings. The Tartar must be showering her with gifts.

"And Madonna Sophia gave no hint of her plans when she visited you at Madama Tilia's?"

Friar Mathieu asked it as if it were the most natural question in the world.

My God, what would Sophia be doing at Tilia Caballo's? At a brothel!

Simon felt his stomach clench. He did not want to hear Rachel's answer.

"No, Father. The last thing she told me was that everyone would be leaving Orvieto soon. And when we did, I would not have to stay with Madama Tilia anymore. I begged her to take me back with her to Cardinal Ugolini's, but she said she could not. Later that day John came for me. I never spoke with Madonna Sophia again." She looked uneasily at Simon.

Sophia had said she knew about the girl only through the gossip of servants and townspeople. Could this girl be lying about having met Sophia? But she would have no reason to do that. So it must have been Sophia who lied about never having met Rachel. He felt as if a dagger had struck him in the back.

And she had certainly never said anything about going to Tilia Caballo's. How could he learn the true connection between Sophia and Rachel without making Rachel suspicious?

"That is just it, Rachel," he said. "Things have been happening so rapidly, and I was away from the pope's court and the Tartar ambassadors for months. Sophia and I have not had time to talk to each other or to send messages. But when I last saw her, she asked me to look after you. She cares very much for you."

Rachel smiled faintly. Her lips were a pale pink. Her eyebrows were black and straight over her dark brown eyes, giving her an earnest look.

"Oh, yes, Your Signory. I know she cares for me."

"Are you also from Sicily, Rachel?" Simon asked. "Did you know Sophia's family in Sicily?"

"No, Your Signory. I am from Florence."

Florence. Florence was controlled by the Ghibellini.

"Does anyone in your family know you are here with this Tartar? Is there anyone you would like me to get a message to?"

Rachel's eyes widened and filled with tears. "They are all dead, Your Signory. And if any of them were living, I would rather be dead myself than have them know what has happened to me."

"Then Sophia is the only friend you have in the world?" Simon waited a moment, then tried a blind guess. "Perhaps Sophia has gone back to the place where you first met her."

"No, no," said Rachel. Suddenly, she looked terrified. She shrank back from Simon.

She is dreadfully frightened, Simon thought.

Friar Mathieu was right. Sophia was hiding something. Anguish stabbed Simon again.

"What is it, Rachel?" said Friar Mathieu. He shook his head at Simon.

"If you want to help me, if you love her, just leave me alone. She was kind to me as no one else has ever been. She was my friend. Stop trying to find out about her."

What was this girl hiding? What was Sophia hiding? Simon felt as if he were surrounded by enemies, all of them plunging their daggers into him.

"Does a friend send a young girl like you to a brothel?" said Friar Mathieu softly.

This brought no reply from Rachel. She put her hands to her face and sobbed.

Simon could bear no more. He stood up abruptly. He was torturing this girl. And in a way, she was torturing him.

He said, "Rachel, we will leave now. I am sorry I frightened you. In truth, I have no wish to hurt you. But, I—I am upset too. Listen to me. If you ever decide you want to get away from here, tell me. I will not let John or Cardinal de Verceuil or anyone else stop you if you want to be free."

Rachel took her hands away from her face. "Where can I go? Tell me that, Your Signory. Where can I go?" Her eyes, rimmed with red from crying, were pools of darkness in her pale face. The sight of her tears made Simon's own eyes burn.

Friar Mathieu stood up, leaning heavily on his stick. He took Simon's arm, whispered a good-bye to Rachel, and drew Simon out of the room. Silently they went back up to the top-floor loggia. Simon seethed and churned, his mind full of confusion and pain.

They sat together on a bench in the deepening twilight. The sun was down and the sky over the distant hills was copper-colored.

"How clumsy I was," Simon said. "She will tell us nothing now."

"You learned quite a bit," said Friar Mathieu, "if you think about what she told you."

"I know this much," said Simon. "I have been a fool. Sophia has been lying to me."

"Everyone in love is a fool, Simon. The more in love, the more they want to believe whatever the beloved tells them. Only a man or woman in love with God can be a fool without risk."

From the distant walls of Viterbo, the guards called the hours to one another. Their long-drawn cries echoed against the stone building fronts.

"What did you mean, think about what she told me?"

Friar Mathieu sighed. "Rachel said that Sophia told her after they left Orvieto she would not *have* to stay with Tilia Caballo anymore. Rachel was not at Caballo's of her own free will. And you may have noticed that when I suggested that Sophia sent her there, she did not deny it."

Simon felt another rush of anger at Friar Mathieu for trying to make him believe evil of Sophia. "Are you saying that Sophia forced that girl into a brothel? Father, Sophia is too much of an innocent to be a party to anything like that."

But he remembered that moment of deepest intimacy they had shared last autumn outside Perugia, the moment he had delighted in reliving thousands of times. She had surprised him with the suddenness of her passion, with the swift, sure way she had guided him into taking her and had taken pleasure from him. Of course, he had throught, she would know what to do. She had been married. But surely a chaste widow who had known only one man in her life would have shown some hesitation, some timidity, some inner struggle?

Simon felt rage building up within him. He hated these doubts. He wanted to lash out at someone.

Friar Mathieu's voice came to him again, mild but inexorable. "Rachel said she asked Sophia to take her *back* to Ugolini's. Rachel must have lived at Ugolini's when she first came to Orvieto. If you say that Sophia could not have been the one who put Rachel in Caballo's house, I accept it. But Ugolini could have. Or David of Trebizond."

"You will drive me mad. Stop going step by step like a schoolman. Of what are you accusing Sophia?"

Only his reverence for Friar Mathieu kept him from shaking the old priest.

Friar Mathieu patted Simon's knee. "I am going step by step because I myself am trying to think this out. And I want to be sure, for your sake. Rachel knew something, or had learned something. So they put her in Caballo's brothel for safekeeping."

"They?"

"Ugolini. David of Trebizond. And Sophia, at the very least, must have known the reason, or she would not agree to let Rachel go to the brothel. If Sophia knew so much, then perhaps—I say perhaps—she knew more about Ugolini and David and their dealings than she admitted to you. I keep thinking of that night at the Palazzo Monaldeschi when she drew you to the atrium, conveniently for David of Trebizond, who was goading the Tartars into publicly embarrassing themselves. Was she as uninvolved then as she led you to believe?''

Each of Friar Mathieu's sentences was another dagger blow, plunging deep into Simon, sending agony through him, the sharp point searching out his heart.

Friar Mathieu was proceeding in the same painstaking way he had probed Alain's body until he discovered what killed him. Alain, whose murderer had never been found, who had died outside Ugolini's mansion.

Alain! Oh, my God! Could she have known how he was killed? What had really been happening at Ugolini's mansion?

Simon bent double, digging his fingers into his skull. His head might burst apart if he did not hold it tightly. Could all the love he thought he had found in her be a lie? Could she be an *enemy*?

''You are destroying my life,'' he muttered, his hands over his face.

He felt the light touch of the old man's hand on his shoulder. ''When a leg wound festers, the surgeon has to cut the leg off to save the man's life.''

And the old soldiers tell me the man always dies anyway, Simon thought bitterly.

''I am doing this not just for you, Simon,'' Friar Mathieu went on. ''There was a secret war being waged in Orvieto to prevent us from allying ourselves with the Tartars. The person behind it was probably King Manfred of Sicily, who wants to keep Charles d'Anjou out of Italy. Ugolini was Manfred's agent. And Sophia may have been Ugolini's weapon against you.''

No! Impossible! I love her. I could not love her if she were on the side of evil.

Simon struck his knee with his fist. ''I must find out the truth. I must go after her.''

''After Sophia?''

''Yes. If she is in Manfred's kingdom, I will find her and get her out.''

''Whatever Sophia has done, she has already done, Simon. You cannot undo it, or simply pretend that she has done nothing at all.''

Simon lurched to his feet. Staggering in his agony, as if those knives were still striking him from all sides, he reached the railing of the loggia and gripped it. The sky had deepened to violet, and a single silvery star glowed in the west. He remembered the magic his mother had taught him of wishing on a star. He could not wish this awful pain away.

"I do not know what she has done. And I refuse to believe ill of her until I have spoken to her."

"But you cannot go into Manfred's kingdom and look for her. You are certain to be caught and imprisoned. You could very well be killed."

Simon turned. Friar Mathieu was a dim figure huddled in the deep shadows of the loggia, his beard a light patch in the darkness.

"You think Manfred is behind all this," Simon said.

"Yes. Look you, when Urban died and Clement was elected—it was the letter you carried from King Louis that broke the cardinals' stalemate—Ugolini and Sophia saw they could do no more at the papal court, and they left. Maybe they were afraid they would be discovered."

Manfred. Simon knew little about King Manfred. Up to now he had hardly any reason to dislike him, and so had no reason to join Count Charles in making war on him.

Now all was changed. It plainly had to be to Manfred that Sophia had fled. And if Sophia had betrayed him, she must be serving Manfred.

And Mathieu was right. He could not go alone into Manfred's kingdom and bring Sophia out. If she had lied and betrayed him, she not only would refuse to come with him, she doubtless would betray him again, and he would end up a prisoner.

But there was another way he could go after Sophia.

With an army at his back.

Yes, he would go to Gobignon and send out his heralds. He would summon his vassals to a council of war at the chateau. Then, after the harvest was in, he would ride forth under the purple and gold banner of the three crowns with all the power of Gobignon behind him.

He would find Sophia if he had to tear Manfred's kingdom apart to do it. Find her and get the truth. As his wife or as prisoner, she would be his!

LXIV

On a dais high above Simon, on a gilded throne under a cloth-of-gold canopy, Charles d'Anjou sat, wearing the crown studded with rubies, emeralds, and sapphires placed on his head by Cardinal Paulus de Verceuil, as legate for Pope Clement, a few hours ago. Simon stood below him in a half-circle of Roman nobles and Charles's commanders. The Tartars and Friar Mathieu were beside Simon.

Behind them, the great hall of the Palazzo Laterano, Roman residence of the pope, was packed with French seigneurs and knights and the popolo grosso of Rome. The hall was stifling, and Simon felt sweat trickling inside his tunic. Even in early May Rome was already too hot to live in. He wondered how Anjou and his army would manage to survive the summer here.

Anjou beckoned to Gautier du Mont, who swept his cap from his bowl-shaped head of hair and hurried up the dozen steps, a sword that reached to his ankle swinging at his side.

Simon felt a hollow in his stomach large enough to hold all of Rome. Soon Charles would call him up to the throne, and he would have to give him an answer. A month ago in Viterbo he had been determined to bring the Gobignon army to Italy. In the intervening days, doubts had unsettled him. Did he really dare to commit the fighting men of his domain to the war? Each time he tried to decide, his mind gave a different answer, like dice endlessly tossed. His head ached and his eyes burned from lying awake all last night after his arrival in Rome just in time for the coronation.

Over and over again he heard what Friar Mathieu had said: *Not so long ago you even doubted your right to be Count de Gobignon. And are you now ready to lead the men of Gobignon to bloodshed and—for many of them—death?*

Du Mont had finished his conversation with Charles and, with repeated bows, was descending from the dais with his face toward the throne and his hindquarters to the gathering. Now that Anjou was a king, one did not turn one's back on him. A far cry from du

Mont's behavior toward Charles of only a few months earlier, and another mark of Charles's increased stature since his arrival at the gates of Rome. Still, he had been required to compromise on his coronation. He had been crowned in Rome as he wanted, but not by the pope. Only de Verceuil, who felt himself exalted by the occasion, was perfectly happy with that arrangement.

As du Mont rejoined the crowd at the base of the throne, Simon's eye was drawn to the red silk cross sewn on his blue tunic. After the coronation, the pope's proclamation of a crusade against Manfred had been read. Charles's men must have had their crosses sewn on in anticipation.

Men like du Mont, von Regensburg, and FitzTrinian were now holy warriors, all of whose past sins were forgiven. If any of Charles's followers should die in battle, they would go straight to heaven.

Having seen those cutthroats in action, Simon thought their new state of holiness absurd. But now that Pope Clement had declared the war against Manfred a crusade, it would be so much easier to recruit an army from Gobignon.

Simon wore no cross, an outward sign of his indecision.

An equerry in red and black whispered to Friar Mathieu, who turned and spoke to the Tartars. John and Philip ceremoniously unbuckled their jeweled belts and draped them over their necks. As the bowlegged little men started up the steps, Simon heard snickers from among Charles's officers at this Tartar gesture of submission. The more fools they, he thought, to laugh at the customs of men who had conquered half the earth. Friar Mathieu followed the Tartars, holding the equerry's arm.

Innumerable conversations, echoing against the vaulted ceiling of the great Lateran hall, battered on Simon's ears. To his right he heard Cardinal de Verceuil's deep booming. Unwillingly, he turned, and saw the cardinal's wide-brimmed red hat, its heavy tassels swinging, rising above the crowd as did the voice coming from beneath it. De Verceuil was happy to dress like a cardinal today, since he was taking the place of the pope. Simon knew he would soon be trading his scarlet regalia for mail. Eager to share in the spoils of Manfred's kingdom, he was going back to France to raise an army from his fiefs and benefices scattered around the country.

Simon saw several other cardinals' hats here and there in the crowd. He wondered if any of the Italian cardinals supported Charles's adventure.

None of them disapproved openly, that was certain. Only Ugolini had protested, and his form of protest had been flight. Enough to cost him his red hat. By papal decree Adelberto Ugolini was no longer cardinal-bishop of Palermo. Simon had sought out priests and merchants traveling from southern Italy, asking them what had become of Ugolini. But news from the south was sparse these days, and news of Ugolini nonexistent.

Simon had spoken in Viterbo to a pair of Dominican friars recently come from Palermo. They had known Ugolini before he became a cardinal, but did not remember that he had any sisters, much less a niece. They had never heard of a Siracusa family called Orfali. Simon raged at his inability to learn anything at all about Sophia. It was as if she had fallen into a black pit.

John and Philip were kneeling before Charles at the top of the steps. Friar Mathieu stood beside the Tartars, interpreting for them and for King Charles. Charles was talking loudly enough for Simon to hear. Like many men, he tended to raise his voice when addressing those who did not speak his language.

"You must tell the great Abagha Khan that it is customary for rulers to send gifts to newly made kings. Tell him we look forward with delight to the wonderful things he will send us from the Orient."

More useful, in Simon's opinion, would be a detailed proposal from the late Hulagu Khan's son on how and when Christians and Tartars should launch their war on the Saracens. Stories had come from the East that Hulagu Khan's frustration over his failure to conquer the Mamelukes had hastened his death.

As he waited to climb the stairs and kneel before the new king, Simon reminded himself that he could still refuse to join Charles's war on Manfred.

He became aware of the dull pain around his heart that had been with him ever since he discovered that Sophia had vanished. Even when he forgot the suffering, it weighed down his footsteps and bowed his shoulders.

And the worst of it is that I would rather live perpetually with this misery than stop loving Sophia.

But how could he go on loving her if she had been his enemy all along?

Was there any such person as Sophia Orfali? All the time he was courting her, she could have been working against the alliance. She might even have known the man in black who had nearly killed him.

That thought struck him like a bolt of lightning. For a moment, he was blind to the sights around him, deaf to the sounds.

No! It cannot be!

If she really had been that evil, it could be only because she had been corrupted by living in Manfred's kingdom. He remembered the words of de Verceuil's sermon this morning at Count Charles's coronation.

The Hohenstaufens, that brood of vipers, have too long vexed Holy Church, persecuting pope after pope. May it please God that the bastard Manfred be the last of them. May we see the destruction of that family of blasphemers and infidels, secretly in league with the Saracens. We declare Manfred von Hohenstaufen anathema and outlaw. Blessed be the hand that strikes him down.

If it was Manfred who had turned Sophia into a tool of the infidels, then how right that Simon's hand be the one to strike Manfred down.

Now, bowing, the Tartars were carefully backing down from the royal presence. Friar Mathieu turned and teetered precariously at the top of the steps. Charles, seeming not to understand the Franciscan's infirmity, stared at him without moving from his seat. The equerry who had helped him climb made a move toward him, but Simon was already up the steps and gripping the old Franciscan's arm.

"Thank you, Simon." Friar Mathieu turned to Charles. "Sire, I hope you will forgive the sight of this old man's back. I am afraid my legs lack the power to climb downstairs backward."

"To be sure, Father, to be sure." Charles waved a hand in dismissal.

If King Louis were on that throne, Simon thought, he would probably have lifted Friar Mathieu in his own arms and carried him down. Simon so wished it were Louis, rather than Charles, he was serving. But perhaps by serving Charles he was serving Louis.

Perhaps.

Simon and Friar Mathieu descended a step at a time. Friar Mathieu was leaning on Simon, but he seemed to weigh nothing.

"Count Simon," Charles called when Simon reached the bottom. "I would speak with you next."

When Simon mounted the dais, Charles ordered his herald in red and black to call for silence.

"All honor to Simon, Count de Gobignon!" Charles called from the throne when he had the attention of the assembly. "For nearly two years he has guarded the ambassadors from Tartary. He has risked his very life in battle for them. His sagacity and bravery have brought new glory to his ancient name."

Simon felt dizzy with exaltation. He had not expected this, from the newly crowned king. His face burned. At a gesture from

Charles, he turned to face the crowd. The gathering in the great hall of the Lateran was a multicolored, murmuring blur. The dais on which he stood seemed suddenly turned into a mountaintop.

"Now," Charles went on, "Count Simon and his vassals join us as allies in battle against the godless Manfred. May the deeds he has yet to do bring even more renown to the house of Gobignon. I guarantee you, Messeigneurs, the day will come when Simon de Gobignon will be known as one of Christendom's greatest knights."

Simon's bedazzlement at Charles's tribute to him turned in an instant to anger. By publicly announcing a decision Simon had not yet made, Charles was trying to force him to commit himself to the crusade. For a moment Simon was tempted to tell Charles that he would crusade at his side when the Middle Sea froze over.

But as he stood looking down at Charles's barons and the nobles of Rome, half turned toward Charles, half turned toward the assembly, the clapping and cheering were overwhelming him. His eye was drawn by a red hat above the rest of the crowd, and he was delighted to see that de Verceuil's face seemed a deeper red than his vestments.

Simon's anger at Charles faded as the moment lifted him up in spite of himself.

He who had dwelt in the shadow of treason all his life, who had hidden himself, when in great assemblies, for fear he would be noticed and treated with scorn, now honored by this multitude in the capital of Christendom in the age-old palace of the popes!

Was it not to achieve this that he had come to Italy?

If only Sophia could see.

He did what he felt was required, and knelt before Charles, taking the new king's extended hand and kissing a huge ruby ring.

In a low voice Charles said, "I have prayed that I would have your help, Simon. Can you not tell me that my prayer has been answered?"

If he refused Charles and went back to Gobignon, he would never see Sophia again. And he would probably never again know a moment like this, when he felt so *right* as the Count de Gobignon.

But he was still offended by Charles's claiming a commitment that Simon had not given him.

"It seems you already know your prayer has been answered, Sire."

Charles frowned for a moment, then smiled and patted Simon on the shoulder. "Forgive me. I want so much for you to join me that I spoke as if it were already true. Will you make it true?"

He looked up into Charles's large, compelling eyes and nodded slowly.

"I will come after the harvest is in, Sire. I will come with my army."

Rachel slid from the bed, trying to shake it as little as possible so as not to wake John. Letting her robe of yellow silk flutter loosely about her nude body, she hurried behing the screen that hid her commode and opened the chest that held her most private belongings. She took out the device of bladder and tubing Tilia had given her long ago, and with a pitcherful of lukewarm water washed John's seed out of herself quickly. Over the year and more that she had been with John, she had never let him see her using the thing. Men such as John, she knew, took pride in their power to get a woman with child.

She was fourteen now, and her breasts were filling out. Many women had babies at fourteen. She would have to be more careful than ever. She stretched her mouth in a grimace at the thought of a baby that looked like John.

As usual, she had endured, not enjoyed, the Tartar's mating. Another change she had noticed in herself, though, was that she had begun to understand how women could feel pleasure with a man. Several times since last spring a yellow-haired man had appeared naked before her in her dreams, and had lain with her. When she woke she could not remember the man's face, but she still felt the exquisite sensations his body gave her, and she sometimes had to caress herself until a surge of pleasure relieved the yearning stirred up by her dream.

Other times, when John came to her late at night and she was very sleepy, she closed her eyes and was able to imagine that the yellow-haired man was with her, and then she actually enjoyed John's attentions, which pleased him very much.

She tied the robe's sash and went to the window. The breeze from the west was strong and salt-smelling, and she was thankful that she was here, in a villa by the sea, and not in Rome. August, they said, killed one out of every three people in Rome. She sat on the wide sill and looked out. She did not lean out too far; she was four stories up, overlooking jagged boulders piled along the shore.

Afternoon sunlight sparkled on the Tyrrhenean Sea, and a flash of sun on the helmet of a guard patrolling the beach caught her eye. One of Sordello's Venetians, she thought, judging by his bowl-shaped helmet and the crossbow he carried. The men-at-arms of the Orsini family, who had lent this villa to the French party, wore helmets shaped to the head, with crests on top.

She heard the bed creaking behind her, and the Tartar groaned.

"Pour me another cup of wine, Reicho," he called.

"You have had three cups already, Usun," she said, but obediently went to the table and poured red wine from a flagon into his silver cup.

He had taught her his original Tartar name, Usun, and he liked to hear her say it. With the help of Friar Mathieu and Ana the Bulgarian, she had learned to understand and speak his language fairly well. She knew now that "Tartar" was merely a European word for his people, that they called themselves "Mongols."

He pulled his silk trousers up and knotted the drawstring. His belly had been flat when she first met him. Now it was swollen as if *he* were having a baby, and excess flesh sagged on his shoulders and chest. His decline was partly from too much wine and partly from too little activity. She rarely saw John without a wine cup in his hand, and by evening he was often surly or in a stupor. He talked to her less, and was less often able to couple with her. If he spent many more months like this, he would sicken and die like a wild bird kept in a cage.

"I had *six* cups this morning before I came to you," he boasted. "Wine makes me strong." He drank off half his cup and set it on the marble table.

She sat beside him on the rumpled bed. "You need to get out, Usun. Go riding."

He shrugged. "Too hot." He grinned, stroking his white beard. "But next year we will ride to war."

"Next year?"

"King Charr has promised to let me and Nikpai—Philip—ride to war with him when he attacks Manfred."

In her anxiety she seized John's arm—she rarely touched him—and said, "You must insist that your guardians let you go out riding regularly. And you must stop drinking so much wine. Otherwise you will be very sick."

His black eyes were wider and moister than usual. "You worry about me, Reicho?"

She took her hand from his arm. "I don't want to see you die," she said. She did not know why she felt that way. After all, he had enslaved her, and every time he possessed her body it was virtually rape. And if he died, she might be free. But, she supposed, she had gotten to know him so well that she felt sorry for him.

She did not like to hear about this war against King Manfred. Friar Mathieu had told her gently that her lost friends, Sophia, David, and the others, were very likely all spies for Manfred. If Sophia were in King Manfred's employ, that made no difference to

Rachel. From all she had heard, Jews were better treated in Manfred's kingdom than anywhere else in Italy. The French, on the other hand, were often cruel to Jews. It would bring sorrow and suffering to many people if Charles d'Anjou conquered southern Italy and Sicily.

She wished she could be with Sophia. But Sophia was probably in Sicily, and how could Rachel, all alone, cross half of Italy to find her?

The locked box she kept under the bed, which held all the gold and jewelry Usun had given her, was far too big and heavy for her to carry. And even if she could escape and take it away with her, she could not protect herself from robbery. But it would be the worst sort of stupidity to leave without it. It was all she had from these awful years. It was less like a treasure, though, than like a block of stone to which she was chained.

If she were ever to escape, she would first have to get away from the guards, the Armenians and the Venetians, all of whom had orders to watch her and make sure she did not run away. That Sordello, the capitano of the Venetians, seemed to have his eyes on her whenever she went out of her room.

She was alone in the world. Nowhere to go. There were moments when she felt so lost and unhappy she wanted to climb out the open window of her room and throw herself down to the rocks.

"Maybe next year, when King Charr goes to war, I will not be here," Usun said suddenly.

"You must wish you could be back with your own people," she said.

If I am lonely, think how he must feel. Except for Philip, there is no one like him anywhere in this part of the world. Only a few people speak his language. Everything looks strange to him.

"We are waiting for orders from our new master, Abagha Khan," said Usun. "Another letter must come soon. It is now six months since his father died."

Rachel felt her heart fluttering with anxiety. "And when Abagha Khan's message comes, what do you think it will say?"

"He will order us either to go to the king of the Franks or to go back to Persia." He took a swallow of wine. Rachel saw that his white beard was stained pink from all the red wine he had spilled on it.

"Then you might go home again?" said Rachel. "Would you like that?" Her hands trembled, and she twined her fingers together in her lap to still them.

Usun laughed and drank. "Not home, Reicho. My home is farther away from Persia than Persia is from here. It is so far away and there are so many enemies in between that I may never see it again. But I do not care. My people have a fine domain in Persia.''

He drank, and held out his empy cup. She filled it with a shaking hand. If he went back to Persia, she might be free of him. Unless her worst fears turned out to be true.

"So, you may soon say good-bye to me." She dared not let him see how eager she was for him to be gone.

He looked up at her, and the light from outside etched the thousand tiny criss-crossed wrinkles around his eyes. "No, Reicho. If I go back, you must come with me."

Her heart turned to ice, just as if he had told her he was going to kill her. She had suspected this and had prayed it would not be so. Everything he said and did, from the day he took her from Tilia's house, showed that he meant never to let her go. She was to be his prisoner for life.

"Usun," she said, trying to keep her voice calm, "I do not want to go with you."

He stared at her, his brown face wooden.

"You are afraid," he said. "But you must not be. When you come with me, you will be a very great lady. I am a baghadur. I am as great a lord as King Charr is here. I know that people of your religion are treated badly by the Christians. Among my people all religions are equal. The Ulang-Yassa, the law of Genghis Khan, commands it." When he spoke the name "Genghis Khan" there was a reverence in his voice, like a Christian speaking of Jesus.

She was reminded of Tilia, telling her why it was better to be a harlot than a wife. She wanted to weep with frustration, as if she had been pounding her fists against a stone wall. How could a man who seemed content to have left his own homeland behind forever understand how *she* felt?

"Usun, it does not matter to me that I am lowly here and might be great there. This land is where I was born and grew up, and no matter how much I suffer here, it is my home. I do not want to live among Tartars and Persians. I would be so terribly alone. I beg you, do not try to uproot me from this land."

"You would not be alone," he said in a low, sad voice. "You would have me."

"I could never be happy with you." It was a terrible thing to say, but only the truth might make him change his mind.

He did not look at her. He drained his cup and thrust it at her as if striking a blow.

"The flagon is empty," she said.

"I will go." He stood up and pulled his tunic on over his head. He was no taller than she was, but as she sat on the bed and stared up at him, he seemed to loom over her like a giant. His black gaze was empty of feeling as stone.

"It does not matter whether you are happy. You are mine and you will come with me."

She shrank away from him, terrified. The face he showed her was the face of the man who had dragged her naked through that Orvieto street.

She threw herself full length on the bed, sobbing. Her heart felt ready to burst with anguish.

Oh, God, only You can help me. Send someone to deliver me, or I will die.

LXV

PRIDE SWELLED DAOUD'S HEART AS HE WATCHED THE COLUMN OF Muslim cavalry suddenly change direction and sweep like a long roll of thunder through the valley. A flutter of orange banners on their flanks, and the men at the far end of the line launched into an all-out gallop, while the riders at the near end slowed to a high-stepping trot. The whole line pivoted like a great scythe, enveloping the flank of an imaginary enemy.

"Very impressive," said King Manfred. "They get their orders from those colored flags?" He and Daoud stood on the rounded brow of a grassy hill, watching the Sons of the Falcon displaying their skills for their king. The valley Daoud had found for the demonstration was a natural amphitheater, a flat, circular plain at least a league in diameter surrounded by hills. Normally it was used as grazing land.

For over a year Daoud had been training these two hundred men, picked from hundreds of volunteers from Manfred's Saracen guards. With so much time, he had been able to forge and polish the Sons of the Falcon into a weapon that could be the vanguard of Manfred's army.

He hoped that what Manfred saw today would put him in a war-

like mood, a mood to ask Daoud for his advice. He prayed for the
chance to urge Manfred not to wait for Charles d'Anjou to invade
his kingdom, but to march north and attack Charles at once.

O God, open Manfred's mind.

For Manfred to delay the start of his war against Charles d'Anjou
even this long could well be disastrous. A year ago Manfred could
have moved out from southern Italy and smashed Charles, as a man
rises from his couch and crosses the room to crush a mosquito.
Sadly, like many a man who sees a mosquito across the room,
Manfred had chosen to remain on his couch.

And the mosquito was fast growing into a dragon.

Lorenzo Celino and Landgrave Erhard Barth, the grand marshal
of Manfred's army, stood on either side of Daoud and Manfred.
Scipio stood beside Celino, who rested his right hand on the dog's
big head. Half a dozen nobles and officers of Manfred's court were
gathered a short distance away from the king and his three companions. Lower down the hillside, scudieros held the party's horses.

"Those flags would be useless at night," said Barth, speaking
Italian with a heavy accent, which Daoud knew to be that of Swa-
bia, the German state from which Manfred's family came. "And
they would be hard to see on a rainy day." He was a broad-faced
man with a snub nose. All of his upper front teeth were missing,
which caused his upper lip to sink in and his lower lip to protrude,
giving him a permanent pout.

Irritated, Daoud spoke to Manfred rather than to Barth. "There
are many ways to signal. Colored lanterns at night. Horns. Drums.
These men have learned all those kinds of signals and can respond
to them quickly."

Daoud's muscles tensed as he thought that the big German and
he might have it out today. Barth, he felt sure, was one of the
advisers who was holding Manfred back.

"I like the idea of signals," said Manfred. "In every battle I
have seen, no one knows what is going on once the two sides meet.
Our knights do not know how to fight in unified groups as the Turks
and the Tartars do."

The Sons of the Falcon rode to the base of the hill from which
Manfred was reviewing. Omar, Daoud's black-bearded second in
command, spurred his horse up the slope, leapt from the saddle,
and rushed forward to kneel and kiss Manfred's hand.

"You ride splendidly," said Manfred in Arabic.

"Tell the men I am very proud of them, Omar," Daoud said.
Omar flashed bright white teeth at him.

To Manfred Daoud said, "Now, Sire, if it be your pleasure, the

Sons of the Falcon will demonstrate their skill in casting the rumh—the lance.''

Manfred nodded and waved a gauntleted hand. He was dressed in a long riding cloak of emerald velvet, with an unadorned green cap covering his light blond hair. His only jewelry was the five-pointed silver star with its ruby center, which Daoud had never seen him without.

Just as I still wear the locket Blossoming Reed gave me.

Omar bowed, and vaulted into the saddle with an agility that brought a grunt of appreciation from Manfred. Waving his saber, he rode back down the hill.

A scaffold and swinging target for the lances had been set up halfway across the valley. Recalling his own training—and Nicetas—Daoud watched his riders form a great circle in the plain below them. He heard in his mind a boy's warbling battle cry, and felt a deep pang of sadness.

''Why do you call them the Sons of the Falcon, Daoud?'' Manfred asked.

''Because I know the falcon is the favorite bird of your family, Sire,'' Daoud said. Manfred grinned and nodded.

He thought, *And because the falcon does not hesitate.*

Daoud admired Manfred. He was said to be the image of his father, and that made it easy to see why Emperor Frederic had been known as ''the Wonder of the World.''

Easy to see why Sophia loved Manfred for a time.

But as a war leader, Manfred was frustrating to work with. He seemed to have no plan for fighting Charles d'Anjou. All over southern Italy and Sicily, knights and men-at-arms were in training and on the alert, but days, months, seasons, followed one another and Manfred ordered no action.

Daoud's own goal remained the same he had set for himself a year ago in Orvieto: To spur Manfred on to make war and to help him win a victory.

And when the war gave an opportunity, Daoud would once again try to kill the Tartar ambassadors. They were now, Manfred's agents in the north reported, in Rome under Charles's protection. Perhaps he could even rescue poor Rachel.

Daoud smiled with pleasure as the riders below formed a huge circle, one man behind the other. He was able to recognize individual men he had come to know over the past months—Muslims from Manfred's army whom he had picked and trained himself—Abdulhak, Mujtaba, Nuwaihi, Tabari, Ahmad, Said, and many others. They were as eager for this war to begin as he was.

At a shouted command from Omar, who sat on his horse in the center, the circle began to rotate, the horses running faster and faster. Each man balanced a lance in his right hand, and as he rode past the swinging target ring, he hurled it. The ring was pulled from side to side with long ropes by attendants, just as when Daoud had trained as a Mameluke.

As lance after lance flew through the moving target, Manfred gave a low whistle of appreciation. Daoud had ordered the ring to be a yard wide and the distance from horseman to target fifty feet. It was easier than it looked for men who had practiced for months, but the rapidity of it made a beautiful spectacle. Daoud's eye caught a few misses, but he doubted that Manfred noticed.

"Like falcons, swift and fierce and sure," said Manfred. "But a bird is just bone and muscle and feathers, Daoud. These men are lightly armed and armored compared to Christian soldiers. These two hundred of yours could never stop a charge of Frankish knights."

Daoud tensed. This was an opening.

"True, Sire, when Frankish knights in all their mail get those huge armored war-horses going at a gallop, nothing can withstand them. But we Mamelukes have defeated the Franks over and over again by not letting them use their weight and power to advantage. They must close with their enemy. We fight from a distance, raining arrows down upon them. If the enemy pursues you, flee until he wearies himself and spreads his lines out. Then rush in and cut him to pieces. Attack the enemy when he is not expecting it."

"That might do well enough in the deserts of Outremer," said Manfred, "but European warfare is different. There are mountains and rivers and forests. We cannot spread out all over the landscape."

Daoud threw an exasperated look at Lorenzo, whose dark eyes were sympathetic, but who shook his head slightly, as if to warn Daoud to be politic in his argument with the king.

"There is one principle that you can adopt from Mameluke warfare," said Daoud, choosing not to contradict Manfred, "and that is speed."

"Our Swabian kinghts and our Saracen warriors ride as swiftly as any in Europe," Barth growled.

"Once they get moving," said Lorenzo sharply.

He isn't always politic himself, thought Daoud.

"Forgive me for speaking boldly, Sire," said Daoud, "but a whole summer has gone by since Pope Clement proclaimed a crusade against you and declared that your crown belongs to Charles d'Anjou. And there has been no fighting. Is this what you mean by European warfare? In the time it takes Europeans to get ready for one war, we Mamelukes would have fought five wars.''

As he spoke he proudly recalled what an Arab poet had written of the Mamelukes: *They charge like lightning and arrive like thunder.*

Manfred turned to watch the riders. A royal privilege, Daoud thought, to conduct an argument at one's chosen pace. He pushed down the urge to say more, forced himself to be patient, waited tensely for Manfred to reply in his own time.

He felt a movement beside him and turned to see that Lorenzo had moved closer to him. He gave Lorenzo a pleading look, trying to ask him to join the discussion. Manfred respected Lorenzo and listened to him.

Lorenzo replied with a frown and a nod. He seemed to be saying he would speak up when he judged the moment right.

When the men who had cast came around to the opposite side of the circle, fresh lances thrust upright in the ground by their servants were waiting for them. Each warrior leaned out of the saddle, seized a lance, and rode back around at top speed to throw at the target again.

After a moment, Manfred turned back to Daoud and said, ''Charles d'Anjou has been hanging about in Rome all through the spring and summer claiming to be king of Sicily. This morning I asked to see my crown, and my steward brought it to me from the vault. The pope's words had not made it disappear. Rome is not Sicily. Anjou is welcome to stay in that decaying pesthole until he takes one of those famous Roman fevers and dies.''

No doubt, thought Daoud, Manfred's gesture in calling for his crown had amused his whole court. And put heart into any who feared Charles's growing strength. Manfred was charming, no question. But meanwhile Charles d'Anjou, who by all accounts had not a bit of charm, *was* in fact growing stronger day by day. Those of Manfred's supporters who were afraid had good reason, and Daoud was one of them.

It was agony to think how the opportunity to beat Charles now was slipping away.

''So, you will wait for Charles to come to you,'' said Daoud.

Manfred smiled. ''And he, I suspect, hopes that I will come to him. Charles has to pay his army to stay in Italy. The longer he puts off attacking me, the more his treasury is depleted. My army waits at home, sustaining itself.''

Daoud said, ''Now that Charles's war is called a crusade, barons and kinghts are joining him from all over Christendom. Many of them are paying their own way. Sire, when Charles decides he is ready to move against you, his strength will be overwhelming.''

Lorenzo spoke up. ''And meanwhile the pope has placed your whole kingdom under interdict. No sacraments. No Masses. Couples cannot marry in church. Can we weigh the pain of mothers and fathers who think their babies that die unbaptized will never see God? And what about the terror of sinners unable to confess, and the dying who cannot have the last sacraments? And the grief of those who had to bury their loved ones without funerals? Sire, your people have not heard a church bell since last May. They grow more restless and unhappy every day. And it does not help your cause when they see your Muslim and Jewish subjects freely practicing *their* religions.''

''I am surprised to hear *you* pay such tribute to the power of religion, Lorenzo,'' said Manfred with that bright grin of his.

The grim lines of Lorenzo's face were accentuated by the droop of his black and white mustache. ''I have never in my life doubted the *power* of religion, Sire.''

Having used up all their lances, the Sons of the Falcon were now shooting arrows from horseback, riding toward lines of stationary targets that had been set up at the far end of the valley.

''Do you have a proposal, Daoud?'' said Manfred with a sour look. ''Let me hear it.''

Daoud felt an overwhelming sense of relief. This was the moment he had been hoping for all day.

''Sire, do not wait for Charles to come out of Rome,'' he said. ''In January, February at the latest, assemble your army and march north.''

There, he had made his cast. Would it pierce the target?

''I could go all the way to the Papal States only to find Charles lurking behind the walls of Rome. I cannot besiege Rome. That would take ten times as many men as I have.''

''No,'' said Daoud. ''His army will not let him stay in Rome. By the end of winter they will have stolen everything in Rome that can be stolen. Charles will have to promise them more spoils and lead them to battle, or they will desert him.''

Manfred nodded thoughtfully. ''In truth, greed is what drives them.''

Daoud added, ''And call on your allies in Florence and Siena and the other Ghibellino cities to stop any more of Charles's allies coming into Italy. They cannot all come by sea as he did. Many times I have heard people in your court say that Charles has cut

Italy in half. Nonsense. He has put himself between two millstones."

Manfred's eyes lit up. "Yes, I like that way of looking at it."

The Sons of the Falcon had ridden to the far end of the valley and were now roaring back, standing in the saddle and firing arrows over the tails of their horses.

"Sire," said Daoud. "Not to act is to act." He felt urgency building in him as he sensed that he was persuading Manfred.

"I remember my father saying something like that," said Manfred. "What do you think, Erhard?"

Daoud's heart sank. The beefy Swabian would undoubtedly counsel more waiting.

In thought, Landgrave Barth sucked in his upper lip and pushed out the pendulous lower one until it seemed he was trying to pull his nose into his mouth.

"Anjou will have to campaign against you soon, Sire, for the reason Herr Daoud has just given," he said slowly. "His men will not allow him to stay in Rome and endure the privation of a siege. When they learn you are coming, they will demand that he march out to meet you. He is probably planning an attack for next April or May, when the weather is best. He must expect reinforcements— but, so he does not have to pay them for long, he will not want them to come until the very moment he is ready to invade. So, if you attack him in January or February, you catch him unready." He finished with a vigorous nod of his head. "I recommend it."

Daoud felt a new and unexpected warmth toward Barth. The landgrave was not such a dull-witted old soldier after all.

The Sons of the Falcon had finished their archery exercise. In four ranks, fifty mounted men abreast, they drew up at the base of the hill and saluted Manfred, two hundred scimitars flashing in the afternoon sun.

Manfred stepped forward to the crest of the hill and raised his hands above his head. *"May God bless your arms!"* he shouted in Arabic.

The wild, high-pitched ululations of his Muslim warriors echoed against the surrounding hills as Manfred, smiling, returned to his companions.

He said, "In three months time, then. No more than four. The weather will decide. I will call in my barons one by one and tell them to prepare. We must keep this a secret for as long as possible."

Daoud, Lorenzo, and Barth all bowed in assent. Daoud felt a surge of joy. He had succeeded in persuading Manfred to strike at

Charles. Manfred's reasons for not wanting to move were sound ones, he knew. He had spent long hours considering them himself, but he was certain that if Manfred did nothing, he was surely doomed. At this moment Manfred and Charles were nearly evenly matched, Manfred a little stronger, Charles growing in strength. To a great extent it would be luck—or the will of God—that determined the outcome. Daoud could not control luck or God. But he could make the best possible plan and give his all to it.

Suddenly, he badly wanted to get back to Sophia in Lucera. Usually he enjoyed being out with the troops, overseeing their training. Today he begrudged the time. Every moment seemed precious. Three months would be gone before he and Sophia realized it. Then he would be riding with Manfred's army, perhaps never to see her again.

He must make sure she would be safe no matter what happened. Perhaps Ugolini or Tilia could help. Sophia would want to travel with the army—with him—north. She was not a woman to pine at home while men marched away. He must discourage her; it was too dangerous.

But to discourage her would probably be impossible.

Simon listened to the drumming hooves behind him on the dirt road and thought, *I will be hearing this sound all day long every day for months.* He supposed that after a while he would no longer notice it, but today, the day after his departure from Château Gobignon, his ears seemed to ache from the incessant pounding.

And the hoofbeats were a constant reminder that he was really leading the Gobignon host to war.

All summer long the conviction had been growing upon him that this was a bad war, and all the suffering it caused, all the deaths and mutilations, would be on his conscience forever. No matter that the pope had proclaimed it a holy crusade against the blasphemer Manfred. Popes could be wrong about wars.

Simon's father, Roland, had vividly described for him the horrors of the Albigensian crusade of a generation ago, when knights of northern France had fallen upon Languedoc like a pack of wolves— like Tartars, in fact—reducing it to ruins. And that crusade had been proclaimed by a pope.

In days to come the rumbling in his ears would be louder, the feeling that he was guilty of great wrongdoing harder to bear. He looked over his shoulder and saw thirty knights mounted on their palfreys, another twenty equerries and servants on smaller horses, two priests on mules, five supply wagons, two of them full of weapons and armor, one hundred foot soldiers and sixty great war-horses in strings, a page boy riding the lead horse in each string. This was the Gobignon household contingent. At today's end he would have three times that many of every category, and by the end of the week his army would have swollen to its full size of four hundred knights, fifteen hundred foot soldiers, and all the equer-ries, attendants, horses, and baggage they needed.

And, a year or more from now, how many of them would come back from this war? He thought of Alain de Pirenne, lying on a street in Orvieto. He thought of Teodoro at the Monaldeschi palace, his chest crushed by a stone, his warm blood pouring out of his mouth over Simon's hand. How many of these men would die mis-erably like that?

Thierry de Hauteville and Valery de Pirenne—Alain's younger brother—the two young men who rode behind him, caught his eye and grinned delightedly. He managed a smile in return, but feared it must look awfully weak. The bright red silk crosses sewn on their chests caught his eye. He wore one, too, on the breast of his purple and gold surcoat. His oldest sister, Isabelle, a fine seamstress, had sewn it there and embroidered the edges with gold thread.

All three of his sisters, Isabelle, Alix, and Blanche, had worked on the crusaders' banner, red cross on white silk, that rippled above Simon. Equerries took turns riding with the banner according to a roster Simon himself had written. Beside the crusading flag, an-other equerry carried the banner of the house of Gobignon, three gold crowns, two side by side and one below them, on a purple background.

His sisters' three husbands rode to war behind him today. Since he was unmarried and had no heir, one of them would be Count de Gobignon if he should fall.

And with more right to the title, perhaps, than I have, he thought unhappily. And he felt as if icy fingers stroked the back of his neck when he thought how much one of those three knights back there stood to gain by his death.

His little troop raised no dust; the road was damp and covered with puddles from yesterday's rain. Thank God it had not rained hard enough to turn the road into mud. As it was, the weather made his leavetaking gloomier than it need have been. The empty fields, littered with yellow stubble, lay flat under the vast gray bowl of a cloudy November sky. The only feature in that landscape was a darker gray, the bulk of Château Gobignon with its round towers rising on its great solitary hill. The road they traveled ran back to it as straight as if it had been drawn with a mason's rule.

I should stop this enterprise now, Simon thought. *I should turn back before it is too late.*

The longer they were on the road, the harder it would be to declare suddenly that Gobignon was *not* going to war in Italy, to tell his barons and knights to return to their homes and hang up their arms. If he did so at this moment, he would provoke great anger in these men of his own household. Today and tomorrow great barons would be joining him, mature men—his vassals—but men of weight and power in their own right. Their scorn at his change of heart would be almost unbearable.

But did he want to be another Amalric de Gobignon, leading the flower of his domain's manhood, hundreds of knights and thousands of men-at-arms, to war, with only a handful coming back? If this was a bad war, God might well punish Charles d'Anjou with defeat. And Simon would share, not in the glory as Charles had promised him, but in disaster and death.

And I am not rightfully the Count de Gobignon.

He knew, though these men did not, that he had no right to call them out to war. If Simon de Gobignon, a bastard and an impostor, led this army to its destruction, what name was there for such a crime?

The voice of Valery de Pirenne, Simon's new equerry, broke in on Simon's tormented thoughts.

"I am not sorry to be leaving home this time of year. What better place to spend the winter than sunny Italy?"

I have already caused the death of this young man's brother. Will I kill Valery too?

"It rains much in Italy in January," said Thierry, now Sire Thierry d'Hauteville, having been knighted by Simon at the beginning of November on the Feast of All Saints. His tone was lofty with experience.

"Bad weather for war," said Henri de Puys, whose experience was ten times Thierry's—or Simon's, for that matter. "But the rains should be over by the time we reach that infidel Manfred's kingdom."

"Look there," said Thierry. "More knights coming to meet us."

Simon saw a line of about a dozen men on horseback, three canvas-covered wagons and a straggling column of men on foot with spears over their shoulders. The oncoming knights and men were tiny in the distance, marching along a road that would meet Simon's route.

Oh, God, now it will be harder to turn them back.

"That will be the party from Château la Durie," Thierry said, pointing to the horizon where the four towers of a small castle were just barely visible.

A distant bell was ringing out the noon hour as Simon's troop met those from la Durie. All of the new knights wore red crosses on their tunics. Sire Antoine de la Durie was a stout man about de Puys's age with a huge mustache called an algernon, whose ends grew into his sideburns. Simon and de la Durie brought their horses together and embraced. The knight smelled like a barn.

"How was your harvest, Sire Antoine?"

Large white teeth flashed under the algernon. "Ample, Monseigneur. But not so ample, I trust, as what we shall gather in Sicily."

They all wanted this so much.

How his chief barons had cheered and roared and stamped when he announced this war to them at his Midsummer's Eve feast in the great hall at Château Gobignon! It was at that very moment, when he had seen the ferocious eagerness of his barons for war, that he had begun again to doubt.

Antoine de la Durie gestured with a callused, bare hand to three young men on horseback whose russet cloaks were patched, but whose longswords proclaimed their knighthood. They grinned shyly at Simon.

"These are the Pilchard brothers, Monseigneur. They are not Gobignon vassals, but they are Madame de la Durie's cousin's sons, and I vouch for them. They beg to go crusading under your leadership."

Under my leadership! God help them!

"You are right welcome, messires. When we stop for the night, see my clerk, Friar Amos, and have him add your names to our roll."

The young men dismounted, rushed to him, and kissed his hands.

Why did he not send them away, send all these knights away, tell them there would be no war in Italy? Because he was afraid of his own barons and knights, the men he was supposed to lead. Because he felt he had set something in motion that could not be stopped, like one of those horrendous avalanches in the Alps.

If they were to keep going, he must—without mishap—cover ten leagues a day to reach Rome by February. He must study again the maps Valery was carrying in his saddlebags, especially the one he had just received, along with a letter, from Count Charles—King Charles.

The infidel Manfred, Charles had written, had stirred up the Ghibellino cities of northern Italy. They were lying in wait for allies of Anjou, who might come down from France or the Holy Roman Empire. Simon must not waste troops fighting the Sienese or Florentine militia. So he should enter Italy by way of Provence and Liguria, then cut across eastward to Ravenna and thence down to Spoleto and Viterbo, and finally to Rome. The roundabout route would take longer, but Charles would expect Simon in Rome by the first of February. Charles intended to march against Manfred at the beginning of April.

Two months to reach Provence, march along the Ligurian coast, perhaps as far as Genoa, which was safely Guelfo, and then pick his way around the nests of northern Ghibellini to Rome. It could be done, but only if his army met with no unexpected obstacles—a Ghibellino army, for instance, or a bad winter storm.

And then, beyond Rome, what would they find?

Once they were there, at least he would not have to make the decisions that determined the fate of these men. The reponsibility—and the blame if they failed—would be Charles's.

The greatest war since you were a child, Charles had promised.

And none of the Gobignon men would ever know that they were fighting because he had fallen in love with a woman named Sophia—if that was truly her name—and she had let him taste her love and then had disappeared.

He remembered a trouvere at a feast singing of how the Greeks went to war because Helen, wife of one of their kings, ran off with Paris, prince of Troy. But that was just a story.

Sophia—her face and form arose in his memory, and there was a strange happiness mixed with the pain, as if he were glad of his suffering. He had heard songs about the sweet pain of love, but he had never before now understood them.

And even now he could not think of Sophia as an enemy. His heartbeat quickened at the thought that there was a chance, very small but still a chance, that Sophia might truly be someone he could love, and that he could free her from whatever entanglement had dragged her into Manfred's power.

By the end of the day the sound of hoofbeats around him was no longer a drumming, but a thundering. And all around and above him was a fluttering of banners. Each of the larger contingents that joined him had brought the standard of its seigneur.

The road south was climbing into forested hills. At the crest of the first hill Simon tugged on the reins to slow his palfrey, and turned to look back. In the fading light of the overcast day, Château Gobignon was a violet outcropping on the flat horizon, its towers indistinct. This would be his last sight of it, perhaps for years. And tomorrow he would cross the boundary of his domain. That was a point past which there was no return. Once the host was assembled, once they had crossed the Gobignon border, it would not matter what he told them. If he refused to lead them, they would find another leader.

He saw two more banners rising above the crest of a bare ridge to the west. Then the heads and shoulders of men, then the horses they rode. They waved and halloed. More followed them. And still more.

Simon met the newcomers by a stream that trickled through a small valley lined with birch trees. Seigneur Claudius de Marion, the leader of the large new party, lifted his square chin as he reached over and clapped Simon heartily on the shoulder.

"The valley widens out up ahead," he said. "I propose that we camp there. The forest beyond is thick and not a good place to ride through at night. And, Monseigneur, to be frank, I do not want to send my daughter home after dark."

"I will be quite safe, Father, if Monseigneur the Count wishes to press on for the night."

The young woman riding a tall gray and white stallion beside Claudius de Marion had humorous blue eyes and a wide mouth. Her upper lip protruded slightly, an irregularity Simon thought quite pretty in her. She had not inherited her father's nose, which was shaped like an axe blade; hers was small and turned up at the end. Her single yellow-gold braid, which circled round from under her blue hood and hung down between her high breasts, seemed to glow in the gathering dusk.

Simon remembered dancing in a ring that included her at last Midsummer's Eve feast. She had worn a woven wreath of white daisies in her hair.

"Barbara insisted on accompanying me to our meeting," said de Marion with an indulgent grin. "I could not persuade her to bid me farewell from our castle."

Barbara's smile was wide and frank, like her father's. "In truth, Monseigneur, I had to see all the knights and men you have gathered. I knew it would be a brave sight, such as I have never seen the like of. God grant you a glorious victory. Will you take wine?"

She held up an oval wineskin, and at Simon's nod and murmur of thanks she worked her horse over to his with a click of her tongue and a pat on the neck. She rode like one born to it, thought Simon. Which she was.

She squirted the wine into his open mouth. It was red and strong, and it lit a welcome little fire in his belly.

As they rode deeper into the valley, Simon asked himself, where had Barbara de Marion been when he had been earnestly searching for a wife? She had been a child, and his eyes had passed right over her. How different his life might have been if she had been a little older two years ago. Seigneur Claudius was one of his chief vassals and a good friend, and would doubtless have had no objection to a marriage. Simon might never have gone to Italy.

But there was room in this heart for only one love. And there was only one course his life could take now.

Somehow, with the sight of this maiden and the realization that he might have fallen in love with her once but never could now, a door closed in Simon's mind. His destiny lay in Italy. He could no more forget Sophia and return to Château Gobignon like a snail crawling into its shell than he could spit himself on his own sword.

As for these men, they were going to Italy for their own gain, not to help Simon find Sophia, nor yet to help Charles d'Anjou become King of Sicily. Or even to protect the pope from his Hohenstaufen enemies. He had not had to appeal to their feudal obligations in summoning them to war. As Count Charles had predicted, they all *wanted* to come. All they cared about was a chance for riches and land and glory after years of doing nothing but managing their domains. They marched of their own free will. He only pointed the way.

He remembered something Roland had said to him: *Once you have made your choice, put your whole heart and soul into it. Never divide yourself.*

Which, Simon thought, was exactly why, even though he would pass near Nicolette and Roland's home in Provence, he would not visit them. He knew well their feelings about crusades, and he could be quite sure of the loathing with which they would view this war. Roland had even spent a good part of his youth at the court of Emperor Frederic, Manfred's father. No, he had enough doubts of his own without letting his parents add more.

Even so, from his belt hung Roland's gift to him, the jeweled Damascus scimitar. He did not like to admit to himself that he was superstitious, but with this scimitar Roland had gotten out of Egypt alive in the face of the most terrible dangers. Somehow, Simon saw the scimitar as a talisman that might also get him through this war.

He glanced over at the beautiful Barbara de Marion and felt a rush of gratitude. Knowing that, lovely as she was, she could never make him forget Sophia, had helped him make his decision.

LXVI

"IT HAS BEEN FOUR YEARS SINCE I MOUNTED A HORSE AND DREW my bow in battle," said John Chagan with a grin. "A man grows old if he does not fight."

Rachel paused in her work of setting up their tent for the night to stare at him, wondering if he knew how unready for fighting he looked. The pouches under his eyes were as prominent as his cheekbones, and the cheekbones themselves were criss-crossed with tiny red lines.

It had been nearly a month since he had taken his pleasure with her in bed. She was glad enough of that, but she felt sorry for him, even knowing that his death in battle would free her. The way his hands trembled, he would be lucky to get an arrow nocked, much less shoot it at an enemy.

The tent flap was pushed aside, and a Venetian crossbowman backed in holding one end of Rachel's traveling chest. Another man followed at the other end.

"What have you got in here—marble blocks?" the first archer grumbled as he set the box down on the carpeted tent floor beside the bed.

"My helmet and sword and coat of mail," said Rachel with a smile. "I would not want to miss the battle."

Fear whispered to her that the armed men who traveled with the Tartars must be aware that she had valuables in that chest. If any of them ever got an opportunity, they would not hesitate to steal it from her. And stab her to death to get at it, if they had to. She hated carrying the heavy box everywhere. But even if she could have found a safe place for it in Rome, she had no way of knowing whether she could ever get back there to claim it. The chest held her prisoner as much as John did.

She had thought that while she and John traveled with Charles d'Anjou's army, she might be able to slip away. Perhaps if there was a battle, she might escape in the confusion. But she could not do it alone, not if she wanted to take the chest.

"You can take my place if you are so eager," the second Venetain laughed. "I've seen battles enough."

"Where are we?" she asked.

"Icerna. Still in papal territory."

"Where are we going?" She heard a movement as she asked the question, and looked over at John. He was pouring himself a goblet of red wine while eyeing Rachel and the Venetians distrustfully. He had learned no Italian, and perhaps he thought she was flirting with the two archers.

"We are coming to a town called Benevento. Right on the Hohenstaufen border. Supposed to be a papal city, but you never know. Border cities usually give their support to whoever is closer to them with the bigger army. The rumor is that whether the town is Guelfo or Ghibellino, King Charles will let the troops have their way with Benevento. And high time. How is a man to live on the miserable wages our would-be king doles out to us?"

"Enough of your damned complaining!" a deep voice boomed. The flap of the tent flew open, letting in a blast of chill air, and Cardinal de Verceuil strode in. Terror raced through Rachel. She quickly dropped a quilted blanket over the chest containing her treasure.

De Verceuil threw back the fur-trimmed hood of his heavy woolen cloak and, though his words had been for the Venetian archers, glared at Rachel accusingly. She felt herself trembling. He was dressed in bright red, but like a soldier, not like a man of the Church. He wore a heavy leather vest over his scarlet tunic, and calf-high black leather boots.

God help me, what is he going to do to me?

Sordello, the capitano of the Tartars' guards, followed the cardinal into the tent. His lopsided grin was as frightening as the cardinal's angry stare. His eyes narrowed, and Rachel felt her face burn as he looked her up and down.

"Out!" Sordello snapped at the two Venetian crossbowmen. After they were gone, the tent flap opened still another time, and Friar Mathieu hobbled in, leaning on his walking stick.

"We do not need you," de Verceuil growled in his French-accented Italian.

"John needs me," said Friar Mathieu. "To translate for him. And I think Rachel needs me too."

"Stupid savage should have learned Italian by now," said Sordello.

Ah, you are very brave, capitano, insulting him in a language he does not understand, thought Rachel contemptuously.

De Verceuil glowered at Friar Mathieu.

"You cannot protect her."

"Protect me from what?" Rachel's voice sounded in her own ears like a scream, and her heart was pounding against the walls of her chest.

"John can protect her," said Friar Mathieu, "if he understands what is happening."

He looked full into Rachel's face, and there was a warning in his old blue eyes. She was almost frantic with fear now. She had not been so frightened since the day John and the rest of them had invaded Tilia's house and carried her off.

What was Friar Mathieu trying to warn her about?

"What do you know of Sophia Orfali, Ugolini's so-called niece?" de Verceuil demanded in his French-accented Italian.

Friar Mathieu has betrayed me!

Rachel looked over at the old Franciscan and saw him close his eyes very slowly and deliberately and open them again. *Keep your mouth closed,* he seemed to be trying to say to her. She had to trust him. She could not believe he would say anything to turn de Verceuil against her.

"I—I know nothing," she said. "Who is this you are asking about?"

"What happens here?" John asked Friar Mathieu in the Tartar language. "Why are the high priest and this foot archer in my tent? I did not invite them. Tell them I send them away."

Friar Mathieu started to answer in the Tartar tongue. Rachel strained to hear him, but Sordello's ugly laughter overrode the friar's voice.

"I escorted Sophia Orfali to Tilia Caballo's brothel more than once, " Sordello said. "And I know she was going to visit *you* because I overheard her telling that to that devil David of Trebizond."

So it was Sordello, not Friar Mathieu, who had been talking to de Verceuil. She should have known.

Rachel heard Friar Mathieu now. "I am talking to *you*, not to John," he said in the Tartar's tongue, and she understood that Friar Mathieu meant her. Neither de Verceuil nor Sordello understood the language of the Tartars, or knew that she knew it. As long as Friar Mathieu did not address Rachel by name and kept his eyes on John, who looked confused, it would appear that he was talking to the Tartar and not to Rachel.

De Verceuil strode over to the wine bottle standing on the low table by John's bed. Without asking permission, he picked it up and drank deeply from it.

"The Tartars travel with the best wine in this whole army," he declared. "Better than the cheap swill King Charles carries with him." Sophia glanced at John and saw that he was glowering at de Verceuil.

Friar Mathieu said in the Tartar tongue, "Sordello went to the cardinal with the story that you must be some sort of agent for Manfred and therefore it is dangerous for John to keep you with him."

Why would Sordello do that now, Rachel wondered. He could have accused her anytime in the past year. She could not question Friar Mathieu, though, without giving it away that he was talking to her. Did Sordello have some plan to get the chest away from her and desert?

"They know hardly anything about you," Friar Mathieu said. "Do not be afraid. Admit nothing. Deny everything. I think Sordello knows more about Ugolini's household, and about Tilia Caballo's brothel, than is safe for him to admit. Say nothing, and I believe they will frustrate themselves."

John smiled and nodded at Friar Mathieu. "I see what you are doing," he said in Tartar.

De Verceuil was looming over her. "Speak up! What was your connection with Ugolini's niece? *Was* she Ugolini's niece?" Even though she was standing up, he looked down on her from an enormous height. His deep voice and great size terrified her.

She said, "I know nothing about any cardinal or any cardinal's niece."

De Verceuil seized her by the shoulders, his fingers digging in so hard she felt as if nails were being driven into her muscles. She was almost dizzy with panic.

"You lying little Jewess!"

Suddenly Rachel felt a violent shove, and she was thrown back against her quilt-covered chest and sat down on it hard. She looked up and saw that John was standing before de Verceuil. It was he who had pushed them apart. His arms were spread wide.

"Do not dare to touch her again!" John shouted in the Tartar tongue. He turned to Friar Mathieu and jerked his head at de Verceuil.

"Tell him!"

When Friar Mathieu had repeated John's command, the cardinal answered, "Tell Messer John that we have reason to believe that this Jewish whore is an agent of Manfred von Hohenstaufen, the enemy we are marching to destroy. She met with Sophia Orfali, Ugolini's niece, and Ugolini and his niece have both fled to Manfred. Manfred has tried before now to harm Messer John, and he could do it through this girl.''

John shrugged and glowered at de Verceuil when he heard this.

"Foolishness. Reicho does nothing but read books and comfort me. She has no friends, and no one comes to talk with her. Except you. Go away.''

De Verceuil took another swallow from the wine jar.

"Put that down!'' John shouted. De Verceuil did not need to have that translated. He put the jar down, frowning at John, offended.

"Sordello is right,'' de Verceuil said. "The man is a savage.''

"Do you want me to tell him so?'' said Friar Mathieu.

De Verceuil replied to this with a haughty stare.

"Tell him this,'' he said. "Tomorrow we march to Benevento. King Charles has sent scouts and spies into Manfred's lands, and they have learned that Manfred is moving in our direction with a large army. Larger than ours, if the reports are to be believed. We would be stronger still if your friend the pusillanimous Count de Gobignon were to be put in an appearance.''

Rachel remembered the Count de Gobignon, that tall, thin, sad-looking man who had so frightened her with his questions about Madonna Sophia.

Everyone was asking questions about Madonna Sophia. There was no doubt that Madonna Sophia and her friends had some secret. Rachel had always known that, though she did not want to know what the secret was. Whatever it was, Rachel promised herself that no one would get a hint of it from her.

"Count Simon was reported coming down the east coast of Italy,'' said Friar Mathieu. "He could have joined our army if King Charles had been able to wait for him in Rome.''

"King Charles did not choose to wait in Rome,'' said de Verceuil.

"Oh, I think he did,'' said Friar Mathieu. "I think he would have been happy to stay in Rome if his supporters, such as his marshals and yourself, had not pressed him to move southward when you heard Manfred was on the march.''

"I did not know that you ragged Franciscans were experts on military strategy,'' said de Verceuil.

"We are not. Indeed, war greatly grieves us. But we do possess common sense.''

What if there were a battle and Manfred won? Rachel thought.

Would Manfred's soldiers kill John? Would they treat her as one of the enemy? Would they rape her, steal her treasure? She had always hoped to escape to the kingdom of Sicily, and now she was in the camp of Sicily's enemies.

"Will there be a battle?" she asked timidly of no one in particular.

De Verceuil's head swung around toward her. "Do not worry about the battle, little harlot," he said in an unpleasantly syrupy voice. "Yes, I expect we will be too busy tomorrow and the next day to concern ourselves with you. After that, perhaps we will have some Ghibellino prisoners to help us find out what you have been up to. And you will furnish our weary troops with diversion."

Rachel felt as if her body had turned into a block of ice. Was he saying that he would let the troops have her? That would kill her. After something like that, she would want to be dead.

"Please—" she whispered.

"Yes, diversion," said de Verceuil, reaching down to take her face between his hard, gloved fingers. "It has been many a year now since I have seen a Jew burn. And when you go up in flames, it will mark a new beginning for this Sicilian kingdom of heretics, Jews, and Saracens. You will be the first, but not the last."

He let go of her face just in time to avoid being pushed away by John. He took a last swallow of wine and turned and strode out of the tent, followed by Sordello, who turned and gave Rachel a last leering, gap-toothed grin.

"Is that a great man among your people?" John asked Friar Mathieu, his face black with rage. "Among my people he would be sewn into a leather bag and thrown into the nearest river."

Rachel sat on her traveling box, her hand pressed between her breasts to quiet her pounding heart. She could hardly believe what she had heard, that de Verceuil wanted to burn her at the stake as an agent of Manfred's after the coming battle.

Oh, God, let Manfred win, please.

His name was Nuwaihi, and he was so young that his beard was still sparse. He came riding with his two companions out of the blue-gray hills to the north, and brought his pony to a skidding stop beside Daoud. He turned his mount and they rode on together, side by side, in Manfred's vanguard.

"I saw the army of King Charles, effendi, I and Abdul and Said," he said in Arabic, gesturing to include his comrades. "The Franks are on the road that leads from Cassino to Benevento. They are about two days ride from here. We hid behind boulders close to the road, and we counted them. There are over eight hundred mounted warriors and five thousand men on foot. They have many pack animals and wagons and merchants and priests and women following them. Just as our army does.'' His breath and that of his pony steamed in the cold air.

Daoud felt a prickling sensation rise on his neck and spread across his shoulders. Two days' ride. The armies could meet tomorrow. Tomorrow would decide everything.

Now, if only Manfred could conceive a plan for outmaneuvering Charles. If only he would take Daoud's advice. He knew Europeans preferred to fight pitched battles, and he prayed that Manfred would not choose that way.

"Did you see a purple banner with three gold crowns?'' Daoud asked.

Two weeks ago a courier from the Ghibellini in northern Italy had brought word that Simon de Gobignon's army had passed through Ravenna, on the Adriatic coast. It seemed unlikely to Daoud that de Gobignon would catch up with Charles in time to take part in the coming battle.

"No purple banner. They fly the white banner with the red cross.'' Nuwaihi turned his head to the left and spat. "And all the soldiers have red crosses on their tunics.'' He spat again. His fierceness pleased Daoud.

At one time, he thought, he would have been sorry to learn that Simon de Gobignon was not with Charles's army. He would have longed to meet Simon on the field and fight and kill him. But now he understood that he had hated Simon because Simon resembled the Christian David that he might have been. It did not matter to him that he would not meet the French count again. Instead, he could feel relieved that Charles would not have Simon's knights and men as part of his army.

Nuwaihi went on, "Their Count Charles, he who would be king, was at the head of the column. I knew him because he wears a crown on his helmet. His banner is red with a black lion rearing up on its hind legs.''

Daoud looked over his shoulder and saw Manfred not far behind him, on a white horse with a black streak running from forehead to nose. The king of southern Italy and Sicily, in a cloak the color of springtime leaves, was the center of a mounted group of his favorite courtiers. One strummed a lute, and they were singing together in Latin.

A brave spectacle. Manfred rides into battle singing Latin sonnets.

A Mameluke army on its way to war would have mullahs praying for victory and a mounted band playing martial music on kettle-drums, trumpets, and hautboys.

The young blond men around Manfred, Daoud knew, were nimble dancers, witty talkers, skilled musicians, and expert falconers. How well they could fight he had yet to see. Manfred was the oldest of them, but right now he looked as young as the others. He had on no visible armor, though Daoud knew he regularly wore a mail vest under his lime tunic.

Behind Manfred, all on glossy palfreys and wearing mail shirts, rode his Swabian knights, Lorenzo Celino and Erhard Barth in the first rank. The Swabians' grandfathers had come to Sicily to serve the Hohenstaufens, and they still spoke German among themselves. Like their king, they wore no helmets, but most of them had fur-trimmed hoods drawn tight around their heads to protect them from the February wind. Above them fluttered the yellow Hohenstaufen banner with its double-headed black eagle.

The column of knights, four abreast, stretched westward down this main road. The lines of helmets and pennoned lances disap-peared over the crest of a pass cutting through the bleak mountain range that formed the rocky spine of Italy. Snow outlined the crev-ices in the rocks that towered above the army of Sicily.

Manfred's host moved at a leisurely rate Daoud found typically European. The march west, after they had assembled at Lucera, had taken two weeks. The mounted warriors were held to the pace of the foot soldiers. Twice the army had been struck by sleet storms that changed the road into a river of mud. Rather than press on, as Baibars would have, Manfred had ordered his army to halt and seek shelter in hillside forests.

In some of the valleys the army had been able to spread out and march briskly over frozen fields and pastures. But then, along a mountainside or through a pass, the road would close down again, and the flow of troops would slow to a trickle.

Daoud turned back to Nuwaihi. "Were you close enough to the road to see the Tartars I told you of? Two small brown men with slanted eyes?"

"Yes, effendi, they were riding near the head of the Franks. Just as you told me, they had eight mounted men wearing red cloaks guarding them. And before and after them marched many men carrying crossbows."

Their people are such masters of war. How they will laugh at the idiotic way Christians fight each other.

Daoud wondered whether the enemy army were mostly Frenchmen, or as mixed a host as Manfred's troops were. Manfred's thousand knights and four thousand men-at-arms included Swabians, south Italians, Sicilians, and Muslims.

If only, instead of three scouts, we had three hundred men lying in ambush along that road, we could have broken Charles's attack and perhaps killed him and the Tartars then and there.

Daoud thanked Nuwaihi, Abdul, and Said and sent them to join the Sons of the Falcon, riding today as the rear guard. He rode back to Manfred, hoping he could persuade the king and his commanders to use wisely the great army they had assembled.

Soon Manfred, Erhard Barth, several of Manfred's German and Italian commanders, Lorenzo, and Daoud were dismounted and gathered in a field beside the line of march. Manfred's orderly had brought a map of the region and spread it out on the ground, weighting the edges with rocks.

As Manfred crouched over the map, his five-pointed silver star with its ruby center hung over a town, represented on the map by an archway and a church surrounded by a wall. The drawing was marked with the Latin name "Beneventum."

"We can be in Benevento by nightfall," said Barth. "And Anjou's army will probably arrive at the same time. There is but one road they can follow." He pointed to a brown line that ran down from a large oval, at the top of the map, drawn around a collection of buildings and marked "Roma." Between Rome and Benevento was a series of towns, each indicated by a drawing of one or two buildings surrounded by walls. Mountains were shown as rows of sharp little points.

"Benevento is a Guelfo town," said Manfred, "and deserves to have us move in on it and quarter our troops there. The town is at the end of a long valley that runs north to south. The opening at the north end of the valley is a narrow pass. Anjou's army must come through that pass. They will find it easier to get into the valley than to get out, because we will be waiting for them."

Daoud felt a surge of exasperation, and quickly pushed it back down. Anger would not help him.

"Waiting for them?" he said. "If we are making war, we do not *want* to meet them."

Manfred frowned. "If we drive them up against the north end of the valley, we will have them trapped." Manfred smashed his fist into his palm. "There will be nowhere for them to escape to."

He is getting tired of my giving advice that contradicts the way he thinks things should be done. After all, he did win battles before I came here.

But to simply meet Charles's army face-to-face, like two bulls butting heads, seemed lunacy to Daoud.

"Such a battle will be bad for both sides," he said. "We will butcher each other."

Perhaps I should have spent less time training my men and more trying to teach Manfred.

"We do outnumber them," said Manfred testily.

"And if every one of their men kills one of ours and every one of our men kills one of theirs, there should be a few of our men left at the end of the battle. Do you call that a victory?"

"Show some respect for your king!" a Neapolitan officer snapped.

"No, be still, Signore Pasca," Manfred said to the Neapolitan. "I want to hear Emir Daoud out. What can we do, except meet them and fight them?"

Daoud remembered how he had wished that instead of scouts he had set men to ambush the Franks. He studied the map.

"Let us send men into the mountains around here and here." He ran his finger over the angular shapes the mapmaker had drawn around Benevento. "Then, when Charles's army is in the valley, we will fall upon it from both sides and destroy it."

No one spoke for a moment. The younger Swabian officers were looking at him with mingled horror and disgust. Manfred stared at the map with embarrassed intensity.

Erhard Barth broke the silence. "Such an ambush would not be according to the customs of chivalry, Herr Daoud. Even if we were to win the battle in such a fashion, the victory would bring us so much infamy that it would be better had we lost."

"We are not in Outremer, thank God," said a Swabian with a long scar on his cheek.

"And we are not Saracens," said the one called Pasca. "Most of us."

"In other words, our noble commanders would refuse to fight?" said Lorenzo, glaring angrily at the other officers.

How would Baibars deal with these men, Daoud wondered. He might cut off a head or two and lavish gold and jewels and robes of honor on the rest. But Daoud had placed himself under Manfred's orders. And Manfred's army was not disciplined as Islamic armies were. European armies were made up of bands of warriors led by men who might or might not choose to take orders from their overlord.

"You cannot turn my men into Saracens," said Manfred firmly. "Even my Saracens fight like Europeans, because they have lived in Sicily for generations. You have trained two hundred men in your Mameluke methods of fighting, and I have seen that they are a brilliant unit, but you would need many years to teach your ways to thousands of knights and men. And I must give my Germans and Italians a plan that will be acceptable to them.''

Erhard Barth's mouth drew down in an apologetic grimace. "It is the way we are used to fighting, Herr Daoud."

It was infuriating. Daoud felt rage burst in him like Greek Fire. With a silent inward struggle, he brought it under control. For good or ill, his destiny was bound to Manfred's.

When the conference ended, Daoud's horse picked its way among the shrubs and rocks beside the road, retracing the line of march back to the supply caravan. Daoud felt a powerful need to spend a few moments with Sophia. She had insisted on coming with him. He had wanted her to stay out of danger. Now, tormented by misgivings about the coming battle, he feared for her even more. But nothing now could spare them from tomorrow's peril and it lifted his heart to know that she was here.

LXVII

DAOUD WOKE TO A DISCREET SCRATCHING ON THE CURTAINS OF his bed. Somewhere in the street a drum was beating, sounding farther, then nearer again, as the drummer marched up and down the streets of Benevento, waking the fighting men quartered there.

"I am awake," he rasped.

"May God look with favor on your deeds this day, my lord," came the voice of his orderly, Husain, through the heavy curtains.

Sophia's back was warm against his chest. His left arm, on which she had been sleeping, was numb. She wriggled her shoulders and then turned over to face him. He freed his arm and rubbed his face against hers, his beard brushing her cheek.

She wrapped one arm around him and twined her legs around one of his. Her free hand moved down, fondling him. His hands glided over her body, trying to memorize the feel of her. She murmured with pleasure into his ear.

She opened her eyes suddenly. "Will it be bad for you to do this with me?"

"What to do you mean, bad?"

"Deprive you of strength for the battle?"

He chuckled softly. "If you made me stop now, I would be filled with such a rage that I would slay all of Charles's army single-handed."

Her hand stopped pleasuring him. "That would be good. Then we must stop."

"No, " he said. "I would rather go into battle with a beautiful memory and a clear head. As for my strength, God will restore it moments after I spend it. He always has, I assure you."

"Then let us not wait." She pulled him over on top of her and accepted him into herself, tightening around him. A flood of breathless Greek endearments filled his ear.

He had never been with a woman who cried out as Sophia did during the act of love. Try as she might to muffle her sounds, she was certain in the final surge to lose control. He was sure Manfred's other officers quartered in this house must hear her.

Well, let them hear her, and envy him.

She let him rest upon her, happily released, until his body withdrew itself from her.

A shadow crossed his mind.

That may have been the last time for us.

They lay side by side. A faint light penetrated the bed curtains from somewhere in their room, and by that light he could see her smiling. He smiled back, but his body was growing tense. Fear of what he would face in the hours to come was building inside him.

The face he loved, the warmth of her body so close to his, made him wish he need never leave this bed. His arms and legs felt heavy, rebellious. If he commanded them to move away from her, they would not.

In truth, I would have to be mad to want to go out and butcher infidels rather than stay here with Sophia.

But he could not stay with her. Today would decide everything. He forced his reluctant limbs to push him away from her. She did not try to hold him.

Outside the heavy bed curtains, the air in the room felt cold as death.

Standing alone in the middle of the floor, he felt a sickening void of apprehension in his belly. As Sheikh Saadi had taught him, he faced his fear. He was terrified of death and defeat. Probably there had never been a warrior anywhere in the world who had not felt this way on the morning of a battle. Probably the Prophet himself, before battle, had feared for himself and for those he loved.

I cannot control today's outcome, for myself or for the men I fight beside. But I can dedicate my mind and heart and will and limbs to God. I can fight for Him to the uttermost of my strength. Passive toward God, active toward the world.

Naked, he walked to the door leading to the balcony and pushed it partway open. A draft of even chillier air made his skin prickle and fluttered the flame of the candle Husain had lit when he woke them. The sky was still black and full of stars. Dawn was a long way off.

He was on the third story of this house in Benevento and could see over the roofs of most of the surrounding houses. Men hurried through the streets swinging lanterns. The drum was still beating a rapid tattoo in the near distance, joined now by horses' hooves clattering on the cobblestones. Here and there a candle glowed behind shutters. Far away, probably in the main camp of Manfred's army, north of town, a trumpet called.

He shivered, and closed the shutter against the winter wind.

Sophia had pushed the bed curtains aside and was sitting on the edge of the bed with a blanket wrapped around her, watching him.

On the bedroom table, Husain had carefully laid out a pitcher and basin and Daoud's underclothes. Daoud took the tawidh by its thong and tied it around his neck. Next he picked up the silver locket and turned the little screw that opened it.

The magic was still working.

But when he looked into the locket, he saw the same face that was looking at him from across the room. A feeling of happy relief filled him, driving out the foreboding that had darkened his mind earlier in bed with Sophia.

He was sure now that whatever connection the locket had with Blossoming Reed was lost. Love had changed the image. He had been testing it ever since he arrived at Lucera, and it always showed him Sophia's face. He could hope that whatever spell Blossoming Reed had placed upon it, when she warned him, *your love will destroy both her and you,* was now broken. He closed the locket and set it down on the table.

He had said good-bye in his heart to Blossoming Reed sometime during these years in the land of the infidel. He had loved Blossoming Reed, but he had never known love in all its fullness and completion until Sophia. And, knowing that he had violated the one commandment Blossoming Reed had laid upon him, and carrying her threat in the back of his mind, his love for her had withered.

She was still as vivid in his mind's eye as she had been in the locket before Sophia supplanted her. But his feeling for her now was one of sad renunciation. Whether or not he survived this war, they must be forever parted.

He filled the earthenware basin with water from the wooden pitcher and began a ritual washing, first his hands, then his face, then forearms from wrists to elbows, then his feet up to the ankles.

"How can you stand the cold?" Sophia said.

Daoud shrugged. "I have to." He did not want to talk now. He wanted to empty his mind for prayer. He tied the drawstring of his braies. Then he pulled on red silk trousers, flaring below the knee and tight at the ankles, and drew a cotton shirt over his head.

He went to the balcony again to check his directions. There was Venus. That was east, then. He took a small rolled-up carpet out of his traveling chest and laid it over the rug on the bedroom floor. He oriented the prayer carpet toward the southeast and stood at the end of it.

He began the salat, bringing his hands up to the sides of his head and saying, "Allahu akbar, God is great."

He repeated his prayers, the bowing, the kneeling, the prostrations, whith great care and full attention. With his forehead pressed to the rug, he submitted himself and this day utterly to the will of God.

Finished, he looked over at Sophia. She was still sitting on the edge of the bed, watching him silently. He looked long at her, drinking her in. It weighed heavily on his heart that he had to leave her, and even more heavily that she would be terribly frightened for him until he came back.

As he feared for her.

Compassionate God, Cherisher of Worlds, protect her.

He began to dress for battle.

Husain had spread out his armor and weapons on top of his traveling chest. Daoud's breastplate was made of many rectangular pieces of steel laced together with leather thongs and overlapping each other. Two larger plates, side by side, were attached over his heart, inlaid with the spiraling gold design that marked him a member of the halkha, the sultan's personal guard. Worked into the design were verses from the Koran. On the left plate, "He succeeds who purifies the soul," and on the right, "And he fails who corrupts it." The breastplate was divided at the sides, where it could be strapped together. Baibars himself, after Daoud returned to Manfred, had arranged for a bribed Genoese sea captain to smuggle it to him. Daoud was proud of it, and the men of the Sons of the Falcon would be proud to see their leader wearing it.

He pulled on a quilted tunic of embroidered red silk, its padding stuffed with linen. Then he dropped the breastplate over his head. He heard a movement behind him, and then felt Sophia fastening the breastplate at his sides.

The storehouse of Manfred's Muslim armorers offered blades of the finest Hindustan steel, and from it Daoud had selected a saif for himself. It gleamed in the candlelight as he drew it from its sheath. He examined with pleasure the gold inlay near the hilt. There was not a nick or a scratch anywhere on the blade. He took a heavy silk scarf from the clothing on the table and tossed it in the air. He held the blade under it, edge up. The scarf fell on the blade and then dropped to the floor in two parts.

He sheathed the sword and buckled it on. He put on his bayda, his egg-shaped helmet, and wrapped the silk of his turban around and around it, and when it was properly tied, pinned it with an emerald clasp.

"Someday you must do that slowly for me, so I can learn how to wrap your turban," said Sophia. "I would like to do that for you." A pang of sorrow for her struck his heart as he realized she was speaking of their future together to convince herself that there would be one. He wished he could free her from fear.

While he dressed, she had quietly been dressing, too, in a long blue gown and a fiery orange woolen mantle.

He looked down at the weapons laid out on the chest, selected a dagger, and stuck it in his belt. Next to the dagger lay the Scorpion, the tiny crossbow, assembled, with a box of finger-length darts beside it. Surely not a weapon for a battle, he thought.

"Here." He turned to Sophia and handed her the crossbow. "I know you have a dagger, but you can use this to protect yourself too. Sometimes I coat the darts with a drug that makes a man unconscious, sometimes with deadly poison. These darts are poisoned—be very careful with them. Most people have never seen a weapon like this, so it will surprise them. And you do not have to get close to your enemy to use it."

"I do not need protection," said Sophia. "You will be out there protecting me."

"If you take it, it will put my mind at ease," said Daoud.

"For that reason only," said Sophia, dropping the tiny crossbow and the box of darts into a leather bag on top of her own traveling chest.

Daoud picked up the locket. Its hammered silver outer surface glowed softly in the candlelight.

"Please take this too," he said. "You have seen me wear it many times. After I have left you today, open it. I believe you will see a picture—an image—of me."

She lowered her head and rested her hands on his armored chest as he hung the locket on its silver chain around her neck.

He unfolded his forest-green linen cape and draped it over himself, clasping it at his throat with a gold chain.

He took her in his arms, carefully, so as not to hurt her with the steel breastplate, and pressed his lips against hers for a long time.

A knock at the door broke their kiss. "My lord, your horse is ready," said Husain's voice.

At the door of the house, Ugolini and Tilia, both of them heavily cloaked against the cold night air, were waiting for them. In the light of the single small oil lamp burning beside the doorway, they were two short, bulky shadows, Tilia much bulkier than Ugolini.

"We heard you moving about," said Tilia. "We came down to wish you victory."

"What do the stars say about today?" Daoud asked Ugolini.

"Yesterday, the twenty-first of February, the sun moved from the house of Aquarius the water-bearer to the house of Pisces, the fish." Ugolini shook his head dolefully. "The fish is the sign of Christendom."

"Adelberto, you are a poor astrologer," said Tilia heartily. "A good astrologer would find something encouraging to say. For example: It would not be good for Christendom for Charles to win. The French would dominate the Church and corrupt it. True Christianity will triumph if Manfred wins."

"Do not use the word 'if,' Madama Tilia," said Daoud with a smile.

"I know Manfred is going to win," said Ugolini. "Otherwise I would not have followed his army all the way to Benevento. I believe he will go on the the Papal States and will persuade Pope Clement to restore me to my rightful position."

"If Pope Clement *waits* for Manfred after Charles is defeated," said Tilia dryly.

That was Ugolini's explanation of why he had come north with Manfred's army. Daoud wondered what Tilia's was. Both risked being imprisoned and probably executed should Manfred lose and Charles capture them.

"Did you see Lorenzo leave?"

"Moments before you came down," said Tilia. "That big dog

of his, Scipio, is inconsolable. I can hear him keening in the stable. I think Adelberto and I will take him up to our room and comfort him."

Daoud said, "It is a rare moment when Scipio is not at Lorenzo's side. And I think, too, he can sense when his master is in danger. As we all are today. It would be kind of you to care for him."

With a tremulous attempt at laughter, Sophia said, "And who will care for me?"

Tilia laid her small hand on Sophia's arm. "We will stay with you, Sophia, if you want, until Daoud returns." She pulled Ugolini inside the door and it closed behind them, leaving Daoud and Sophia alone.

Sophia moved close in the lamplight outside the entrance of the merchant's house and looked up at him, her eyes large and solemn. "Nothing but you matters to me. Come back to me."

Daoud still wished he could convince her that she had nothing to fear. But that was foolish. She knew all too well that there was much to fear.

"I don't want you to be frightened," he said.

"I will try not to be."

"I will come back." There was so much he wanted to tell her, so much he realized now he had not said about how he loved her as he had never loved another woman in his life since—

Since his mother.

They were two people who had been utterly alone in the world, who had both lost everyone precious to them. All they truly had was each other.

Oh, God, let me come back to her. I ask this not for my happiness, but for hers.

"I know I will see you again." She smiled suddenly. "Can you find your way to me?"

He looked up at the building and then at the street. Bulking large against the stars was the huge square shape of an arch, which had been built over a thousand years ago, he was told, by a Roman general to commemorate his conquest of Jerusalem.

With this talk of stars and portents, he felt it must mean something that this victory arch should be here in Benevento. Were not these wars of Muslim and Christian that had shaped his destiny wars over Jerusalem?

He said, "I will ride through that arch, and you will be on the third floor of the house with the carving over the door of San Giorgio slaying the dragon."

She smiled, her teeth white in the lantern light. "That is the Archangel Michael overcoming Satan."

"How am I to tell one Christian idol from another?"

She pushed at him. He saw the tracks of tears glistening on her cheeks. His own eyes burned.

"Go quickly now."

He turned, fearing the sight of his tears might break her heart, as hers had broken his. He set his foot in the stirrup and vaulted into the saddle of the brown Arabian Husain was holding. He waited for Husain to mount his own horse and then started down the street. He kept his face set toward the triumphal arch. He dared not look back.

In her room, Sophia went through her chest and found her icon of Saint Simon Stylites. She kept the icon hidden when Daoud was around. He believed that praying to saints' images was idolatry, and she especially did not want him to see her praying to a saint named Simon. She knelt, clasped her hands, and prayed to the desert saint.

Oh, holy Simon, bring him back to me. You who dwelt in the desert, you who know what it is to be alone on your pillar, keep safe this man who came alone out of the desert. Protect him from the swords and spears and arrows of his enemies. He is not of our faith, I know, but I love him so, and is not Love another name for God?

She pressed both hands flat against her belly and doubled over, weeping.

Daoud had just ridden through the northern gate of the town when he heard his name called from above. He saw a pale blond head, gleaming in the first rays of sunrise, looking down at him through the battlements of a square gate tower.

"Up here, Daoud, come up!" Manfred's voice.

"This is the best vantage point we could ask for," Manfred said when Daoud arrived on the tower platform. "Unless we were to climb those mountains over there."

Lorenzo was on the tower roof with Manfred, and Landgrave Barth, and six or so of Manfred's blond young noblemen, all in splendid cloaks of peacock blue, sunset orange, and bloodred. They wore glossy silk surcoats over mail that covered them from chin to fingertips. Manfred was in mail, covered by a knee-length yellow and black surcoat. He held his bronzed helmet, decorated with three nodding ostrich plumes dyed emerald green, tucked under his arm.

"Have they come?" Daoud asked.

Manfred nodded, his face sterner than Daoud had ever seen it. "Anjou is in the valley."

Daoud looked out from the tower. Like a field of wildflowers, hundreds of their own multicolored tents, each one tall and pointed at the top, spread out over the rolling brown landscape just beyond the town wall. In front of the tents the divisions of Manfred's army were forming up in squares. The faint notes of a military band came to Daoud's ear. It was European music, which sounded jagged, harsh, and disconnected to him.

He saw the Sons of the Falcon now, over on the left, their rows straight, sitting quietly on their horses, moving little. They all wore red turbans wrapped around their helmets; he had insisted that they dress alike so as to be easily recognizable. They, too, had their band, a dozen men who played kettledrums, trumpets, hautboys, and cymbals from horseback. The band was silent now, but would play when the Sons of the Falcon rode into battle.

"Long ago the Romans called this town Maleventum, bad wind," said Manfred beside him, "because they believed that the winds from the north brought pestilence down from the swamps around Rome."

Just the sort of thing Manfred would know, Daoud thought.

"Even though the people who live here chose a more attractive name," Manfred went on, "we see that the ancients were not wrong. Look what plague the wind has blown down from Rome today."

Daoud's eyes followed Manfred's pointing arm to the narrow north end of the long valley in which Benevento lay. The road from Rome entered the valley at the north end and ran through it to the gate above which they were standing. Rows of tents filled the northern opening of the valley, and the tiny figures of horsemen and foot soldiers were forming dark lines across the light brown fields.

Last night peasants from that end of the valley had come flocking into Benevento with cartloads of possessions and stored crops. Even though they were supposedly supporters of the papal cause, the people who lived around Benevento felt safer under Manfred's protection.

But this valley was a stone coffin, Daoud thought. Hills on either side, squeezing together at the top of the valley, the town lying across the bottom end. In this box, how could he use the Sons of the Falcon well? He pummeled his brain.

One thing he could at least achieve. He remembered Nuwaihi's report that the Tartars were with Charles's army. He turned to Lorenzo.

"It falls to you to finish the Tartars. Make your way into Charles's camp while the battle is on."

Lorenzo's mouth turned down under his thick mustache. "It will take time. I can take a wagon and go around through the hills and pretend to be a peasant offering to sell wine and food to Anjou's people."

"Take some men with you."

Lorenzo shook his head. "That would arouse suspicion. If I go alone, whoever is guarding Charles's camp will see no reason to fear me."

"I went alone into the Palazzo Monaldeschi to kill them, and I could not do it."

"And I, with my poor Sicilian skills, cannot be expected to succeed where Daoud ibn Abdallah, who was trained by the Old Man of the Mountain himself, failed. Is that what you are thinking?"

Daoud smiled ruefully. "Well—"

Lorenzo frowned at him ferociously. "You have given me the task. Let me carry it out as best I can."

Daoud gripped his arm, feeling muscle like oak. "Go with God, my brother."

"May your Allah bless your struggle today, Daoud." One last, long look from the dark brown eyes, and Lorenzo turned away.

Again, as he had with Sophia, Daoud felt anguish that he had not told Lorenzo enough of his gratitude, his respect, his love.

And if Lorenzo dies an unbeliever, I will not meet him in paradise.

Manfred was standing at the battlements, staring north at his enemies, looking, it seemed to Daoud, more sad than angry.

"Sire," Daoud said, "I know what you plan for today's battle. But I beg the favor of one change. Let the Sons of the Falcon be the first of your warriors to strike at your enemies."

Manfred turned toward Daoud, and as he did the melancholy vanished from his face. He looked cheerful and spoke briskly.

"Let us review the plan. My heaviest cavalry, the Swabian knights, will hit them first. The Swabians will try to break the enemy and drive them back up the field. Our foot archers will form up before Benevento and protect it from any Frenchmen who might evade our cavalry charge. Daoud's Sons of the Falcon will ride in column up the west side of the valley, turn, cut the French knights off from *their* foot soldiers, and attack them from the rear.''

Erhard Barth nodded. ''Excellent, Sire. But, if I may, Herr Daoud has a good suggestion. We have seen the skill of his archers and lancers. Let them lead the way, forming a screen for us. Let them fill the air with arrows. The French will falter. Then the Sons of the Falcon will move out of the way.'' He spread his big, square hands apart to show how the Sons of the Falcon would part to left and right. ''And we will hit them with a wedge.''

A better plan, Daoud thought. He had underestimated Barth. And perhaps the king he served.

Manfred nodded. ''Go to your men, Daoud. You will have my orders shortly.''

Looking into the faces of the two hundred men he had picked and trained over the past year, Daoud felt a great weight on his chest. He could even read the expressions of some in the front. Mujtaba, earnest. Ahmad, fierce. Omar, determined. Nuwaihi, who had first sighted Charles's army, eager. It was frightful enough to face one's own death in battle, but to know that he was leading to their deaths men he knew and loved—the burden was great. These men were like his children, and they would follow him to destruction, and he wished before God that he did not have to think about that.

Gathered in a semicircle, the Sons of the Falcon listened silently as Daoud spoke to them from horseback . He made his voice big, so that it echoed from the walls of Benevento, behind his men.

''You are fighting not only to help King Manfred keep his throne,'' Daoud shouted. ''Not only to protect the kingdom of Sicily from conquest by these greedy foreigners.''

That was ironic, in a way, because, to be sure, the Hohenstaufens were not native Sicilians. Nor were these Muslims. But both they and the Hohenstaufens had lived in Sicily for generations, and surely that gave them more right to rule here than the French.

''You are fighting for Islam!'' he cried. Their wild cheering rang in his ears.

''You are fighting that you and your families may profess the faith and live by the faith. This right, your wise rulers of the house of Hohenstaufen have granted you. But if Charles d'Anjou rules this land, your mosques will be turned into churches, your mullahs will be hanged, your Korans will be burned, and your children's children will never hear the sweet words of the Prophet, may God commend and salute him. They will be raised as Christians and will never know they were anything else. For us this war is jihad! Holy war!''

The waves of their cheering swept over him, and their scimitars flashed in the rising sun. He had told them the truth, but there was an even greater truth he had not told them. They were fighting, not just for Islam in Sicily, but for Islam everywhere. If Manfred won this battle, it would end, for this generation at least, the threat of Christians and Tartars uniting to destroy Islam. But how to explain that in these few remaining moments? Enough that they knew that they were fighting for the faith in their own land.

Seeing their eagerness, he felt proud of them, and proud of himself. The weight of sadness he had felt when he first faced them was lifted, and his heart beat strong within him.

The cheering faded quickly, replaced by a murmuring. Men were pointing past him. A faint rumbling came to his ears.

At the north end of the valley a long line of horsemen was moving forward, bright banners fluttering above them, and creamy clouds of dust billowing up behind them.

Barth rode up to him, his eyes bright, his thick lower lip curving upward in a smile. "King Manfred has agreed to let you attack first. The Swabian knights are now ready. We will be behind you. Slow their charge, and then we will smash them." He struck a mailed fist into a mailed palm.

Exultation bubbled up within Daoud like a desert spring. Dizzy with joy, he thought Baibars must have felt like this when he alone led the Mamelukes against the Tartars at the Well of Goliath.

A certainty that the battle was as good as won spread through him.

"If we leave you any Frenchmen to smash," he said to Barth, who laughed, saluted, and rode away.

Have a care, he warned himself. *What happens today will be as God wants. I want only whatever God wants.*

He jerked on the reins of his brown Arabian to turn toward the French charge. They were still far away. The valley was long. He called Omar and Husain to him.

"Bows and arrows. Spread out in a line. When we are formed up, advance at a trot on my signal."

He unstrapped his bow from his saddle and slung it over his shoulder and across his chest.

The five flag men lined up behind Daoud. On their right rode a naqeeb holding high the green banner of the Sons of the Falcon, inscribed in dazzling white lettering with a verse from the Koran:

HAVE THEY NOT SEEN THE BIRDS OBEDIENT IN MIDAIR? NONE
UPHOLDETH THEM SAVE GOD.

Omar rode down the line relaying Daoud's orders to the officers
and flag men. When all was ready, Daoud raised his hand and
brought it down. A single line of two hundred horsemen, they
moved out at a trot. While his men could fire arrows from a galloping horse, the slower the horse was moving, the more accurate
the shooting.

He could see what was coming at him much more clearly now.
The middle and rear ranks of the crusaders were obscured by dust,
but in the front ranks a hundred or more helmeted heads bent over
the armored brows of their huge horses. The long poles of their
steel-tipped lances pointed at him.

To be hit by one of those knights galloping at that speed, with
all that weight of steel and horseflesh, would be like being hit by a
boulder from a stone caster. If the Franks got much closer, there
would be no stopping them.

Daoud unslung his bow. From the corner of his eye he saw the
flag men, whose duty it was to watch his moves and signals, lift
five red pennants high. He did not need to look to know that the
Sons of the Falcon had all dropped their horses' reins, guiding their
horses with their knees, and were drawing their bows.

His bow, like those his men carried, was double-curved, made
of multiple layers of horn and hardwood. His arrow had a thick
steel tip that could punch through mail armor like a spike driven
by a hammer. He took aim at a big Frank in the middle of the line.
The intersection of the limbs of the red cross on the Frank's white
surcoat made a perfect spot to aim at. Between two beats of his
Arabian's hooves, he loosed his arrow.

The flight of Daoud's arrow was the signal for the red flags to go
down. Two hundred arrows whistled across the rapidly narrowing
gap between crusaders and Sons of the Falcon.

Daoud saw the man he had fired at throw his arms wide. His
lance dropped as he leaned sideways from his saddle. He crashed
to the ground and disappeared under the hooves of the horses behind his. His lance fell across the paths of the oncoming crusaders
and another of the big war horses tripped over it, dumping its rider.

All along the crusaders' front, knights were spilling from their
saddles, horses were falling, lances were flying.

*Over a hundred years they have fought us, and they have never
learned to use the bow from the saddle.*

Many riders in the crusaders' front rank were still galloping toward them. And more in the rear ranks were dodging or leaping

the fallen knights and horses. Daoud whipped a second arrow from the quiver hanging at his side, nocked it, and took quick aim.

His arrow went true again. He saw the targeted man fall. And the Sons of the Falcon were pouring volleys of arrows into the Franks. Every third crusader, in the front ranks at least, must be a dead man.

Daoud heard himself yelling in triumph. If they broke this first French charge, the rest of Manfred's army could sweep the field clear of the enemy.

The charge was slowing down, but it was still coming on.

"Split ranks! Pass them on either side!" Daoud called to Omar, who relayed the order to the flag men.

Daoud heard a sound like an earthquake behind him and looked around. The elite of the German knights, Manfred's Swabians, were galloping on in an arrowhead formation. If the French knights and their horses were big, the Swabians looked even bigger. He saw the nodding green plumes of Manfred's helmet at the very point of the wedge. The surcoats of knights and horses were ablaze with red and blue, orange and yellow.

Beyond Manfred's knights Daoud saw lines of crossbowmen formed up before the walls of Benevento. Sophia was there in that little town. He wanted to keep himself between Sophia and the French.

But Omar had relayed his order to the flag men and the yellow and green flags had gone up, and, disciplined as any of his men, he rode off to the left, turning the side of his Arabian toward the onrushing crusaders.

When he reached the right flank of Charles's knights, he turned again so that he was riding past them. He fired arrow after arrow as he went, as fast as he could and still hit his mark.

He saw a tall figure in a red surcoat with a red helmet shaped like a bishop's miter. Almost certainly de Verceuil. The cardinal brandished a club with an iron ball at the end of it. Daoud loosed an arrow at him, but de Verceuil lifted a red shield bearing a painted gold cross that caught the arrow and sent it spinning away.

I wonder if he recognizes me.

Looking north, Daoud saw Anjou's foot soldiers with spears and crossbows advancing at a run, but they were far behind the last of the Frankish riders. Charles must have thrown all his knights—eight hundred of them, Manfred had said—into this first charge. He, like Manfred, must have hoped to end the battle—even the war—with a single charge.

Farther to the north, beyond the foot soldiers, a dozen or so horsemen in yellow and purple cloaks gathered under a red banner bearing a black figure. It was too far away for Daoud to see clearly, but he knew that a black lion on a red background was the standard of Charles d'Anjou.

Now Daoud and his left half of the Sons of the Falcon were beyond the French knights. He ordered the flag signals that would turn his wing to ride back the way they had come.

Dozens of Franks had died under their arrows. The charge had slowed, with confusion on the front and confusion on the sides. Daoud felt ripples of triumph course through his body. They had done the very thing Manfred said no Saracen cavalry could do.

We stopped the charge of the Frankish knights.

But looking toward Benevento, Daoud felt triumph turn to dismay. The flying wedge of Manfred's knights had pushed itself deep into the French line, but then had come to a stop. Even though the Sons of the Falcon had hurt them and halted them, the Franch had held their formation. They had not broken under the Swabian attack.

Daoud groaned in anguish. Both sides had stopped in their tracks, and where they faced each other their formations had crumbled into a hundred individual combats.

This was just what Daoud had feared and warned against. Endless butchery, futile bloodletting, a battle that would go as badly for the winner as for the loser.

There must be another way, Daoud thought desperately. *There must be a Mameluke way to win this.*

LXVIII

THIERRY REINED HIS HORSE TO A STOP AND DOFFED HIS HELMET IN salute to Simon. From the wild look in the young knight's eye Simon sensed at once that he had seen something extraordinary.

"What is it, messire?" he demanded. "Did you see Manfred's army?" Papillon, the brown and white mare Simon used as a palfrey, stood still while Simon patted her neck.

"Manfred's *and* Count Charles's," Thierry panted. "Both armies. They're already fighting, Monseigneur!"

"Merciful God!" A battle meant *the* battle. One battle must surely decide this war. Manfred would have brought together all the fighting men of southern Italy and Sicily. And Simon knew, from the series of urgent messages he had received from Charles on the road, that the count had left Rome with every man he could muster, and that there was no more help on its way to him.

Except for this army.

Simon glanced up at the sun. Halfway up the eastern sky. Some big clouds, but it was going to remain a clear, cold day. If the battle had started at dawn, it could be over by midday.

"Pass the word to advance at a trot," he told de Puys. "Foot soldiers to proceed by forced march."

Antoine de la Durie spoke up. "Monseigneur, should we not call a halt and rest and plan? We cannot plunge blindly into the midst of a battle."

"We will have to plan as we ride, messire," Simon said brusquely. "King Charles is outnumbered, and needs us *now*."

He felt a small inner glow. He was getting to be quite practiced at putting older men of lower rank in their place—the sort who formerly intimidated him.

He turned to Valery de Pirenne. "Tell Friar Volpe to join me here. And you, Thierry, come with me. You can tell the friar what you saw."

Simon pulled Papillon's head over, jumped the narrow ditch along the side of the road, and took up a position on a rocky hummock, Thierry beside him. Looking over the long column of his army never failed to make his heart beat faster. A dozen banners in front, led by the red and white crusader flag and the purple and gold of Gobignon. Mounted knights two or three abreast followed by files of foot soldiers and baggage trains and strings of chargers and spare horses. The mounted rear guard so far back it was usually out of sight.

He could see the rear guard because the army was traveling along winding mountain roads, as it had been the day before and the day before that. They were crossing the center of the Italian peninsula. They had been through the highest of the Apennines yesterday and were now descending the western slopes.

A chill anxiety enveloped his body. To have come all this way only to be too late—what a calamity that would be! He could not allow it.

Friar Volpe came galloping up on the back of his big mule. How

wise of Charles to have sent this friar to meet Simon at Ravenna.
The Dominican had spent most of his adult life wandering all over
Italy preaching, and he made an excellent guide. It was he who
brought the news that Charles was no longer in Rome and there
was no need for Simon's army to go there. A more direct route to
Anjou's army would follow the Adriatic coast, then turn southward
into the Apennines on entering the Abruzzi, the northernmost reach
of Manfred's kingdom

Friar Volpe was a fair-skinned man with a sharp nose, large lips,
and round brown eyes. His thick reddish-brown hair fell over his
forehead and ears, growing luxuriantly everywhere except for the
tonsure on top, where it was just a red stubble.

"Benevento," he said when Simon told him about the battle,
and glanced up at the sun. "We could arrive in the valley of Benevento well before noon. There is a high ridge along the east side
of the valley. Benevento is a crossroads town. The roads meet at
the south end of the valley."

"That was where I saw Manfred's camp," said Thierry.

"I have to see this valley myself," Simon said. "Could we climb
this ridge you spoke of?"

"Shepherds and their flocks go up and down the hills all year
round," said Friar Volpe. "There are many paths."

"Many paths," Simon echoed. "Excellent. Be good enough to
lead us there."

Simon ordered the army to continue along the main road to Benevento until they reached a roadside shrine to San Rocco. Farther
than that, Friar Volpe said, and they might be seen from Benevento.

Friar Volpe led Simon at a fast trot till they were out of sight of
the army. Thierry and Henri de Puys had insisted on coming along,
arguing that Simon might meet some of Manfred's outriders. They
turned onto a zigzag track that sometimes disappeared altogether
over bare rocks as it climbed to the top of a long ridge.

They came out of a stand of wind-twisted pine trees to the bald
top of the ridge. The ringing of steel on steel, the pounding of
horses' hooves, and the cries of men drifted to them from below.

"Hold the horses, Thierry," Simon ordered. He and de Puys
and Friar Volpe moved forward at a crouch. When he could see the
battlefield, Simon lay down and crawled, his mail scraping over the
rocks, the tip of his sheathed sword bumping along.

Is this what a battle looks like, then?

He was reminded of times when he had stepped on anthills in
the woods and thousands of the little creatures milled about in
confusion under his feet. Masses of men below heaved and strug-

gled. Dead horses lay by the score, large dark lumps. Smaller objects lying about the field like rocks might be dead men; it was hard to tell from this distance. Much of what he saw was partly veiled by clouds of gray dust.

He felt a breath of fear on his neck at the thought that he must take his army into that cauldron. He tried to make sense of what he was seeing. Where were the leaders?

The half of the field nearer him was hidden by the trees growing lower down on this ridge. Ignoring de Puys's whispered warnings, he crawled farther forward for a better view.

Now he saw the town of Benevento at the south end of the valley, a city of moderate size whose walls were fortified by a dozen square towers. And before it a smaller city of many-colored tents. Above the tents, a yellow banner with a black splotch in its center. That would be the Hohenstaufen eagle.

Then those tents at the other end of the valley, where the road entered from the north, must be the French camp. Simon saw many more banners, too far away to recognize, on poles in the center of that camp.

He saw no fighting at the north end of the valley. Closer to the battle, a small group of horsemen sat on a low hill, apparently observing. Above them a red and black banner hung from a long pole. That could only be Charles himself, and his chief commanders, under the banner of the black lion. Lines of foot soldiers screened them from the main fighting.

I should go down there, or send someone, to find out what Count Charles wants me to do. But there is no time.

Again Simon's gaze swept the battlefield. The innumerable small struggles, mostly in the center of the valley, told him that neither side was winning. Again the Saracen warriors with the turbans caught his eye. They were the only group of mounted men acting together. Moving in a v-shaped formation with the center back and the tips of the two wings well forward, they advanced slowly across the field. But with such confusion around them, where could they effectively attack?

Never mind that. Where can I effectively attack?

He lay on his belly, his chin resting on his intertwined fingers, his breath steaming in the air in front of him. Thierry, de Puys, and Friar Volpe were waiting behind him. And behind them, the army he had brought here. A sudden terror froze his limbs. The day was cold, but he felt colder still, staring at the swirling fury below him, listening to the shouts and screams, the thundering and clanging.

There would not be time to get orders from Count Charles. There would hardly be time to consult with the experienced men—de Marion, de la Durie, de Puys—among the barons he had brought with him. The plan, the decisions, would have to be his alone.

At what place, at what moment, should he throw the Gobignon army into the battle? If he just led them into the present confusion, his columns of knights and files of archers would at once fall apart into more knots and whirlpools of combat like those he saw below. His army could be wasted, ground up like wheat in a water mill. The turmoil in his mind was as bad as the chaos he had seen on the field.

The floor of the valley was uneven, and rolling hills hid the battle from Lorenzo's eyes, but the clash and clamor of the fighting carried to his ears as he approached the French camp. It was empty except for about ten sentries, some armed with crossbows, others with pikes, who stood at its perimeter. They were all turned to watch the battle, their backs to Lorenzo despite the creaking of his wagon and the clip-clop of his horse's hooves.

The tall tents were dusty, stained, and patched, their colors faded. Lorenzo spotted a party of horsemen in bright cloaks atop a hill outside the camp. One helmet was topped with a gilded crown.

Charles was being sensible, standing back from the battle and watching it—unlike Manfred, whom Lorenzo had seen just as he was leaving the Hohenstaufen camp, riding into the fray waving his great broadsword. Lorenzo shook his head sadly.

What my king needs is less gallantry and more ruthlessness.

Holding up a parchment covered with elaborate handwriting and a large seal of green wax with long ribbons, he pulled his cart up to the nearest guard, a stout, white-haired man with bleary eyes. Naturally, only the least able-bodied would be left to guard the camp this day. And the worst they would be expecting would be attempts at thievery by the whores and traders whose tents and wagons lay a short distance up the road from the camp.

"Here is my safe conduct from King Charles's ally, the bishop of Agnani," said Lorenzo briskly. He held his breath anxiously while the guard stared at him.

"We are in the middle of a battle, man. You can't just drive your cart in here. What do you have in it?"

The guard barely glanced at the document Lorenzo had spent a precious hour forging. Lorenzo was relieved. He was not at all sure the scroll would bear close scrutiny, although only one soldier in a thousand could read. And any clerics who might be along with

Charles would probably be on the edges of the battlefield, succoring the wounded and dying.

"I bring a gift of wine from the Bishop of Agnani to the ambassadors from Tartary."

"I will have to taste the wine," said the white-haired guard importantly.

"Of course," said Lorenzo with a grin, and as the guard climbed into the dark interior of the cart, almost fully occupied by two big wine casks standing on their bottoms. Lorenzo unhooked a tin ladle from its wooden wall and handed it to the stout man.

Stupid as well as unfit this guard was, thought Lorenzo. He could stun him with the sack of sand and stones hidden under his tunic or slit his throat with the dagger in his boot. But then he would have a body to get rid of. This particular body would be more of a problem dead than it was alive and conscious. Lorenzo turned a spigot and let some of the red wine flow into the ladle.

The guard smacked his lips and grunted. "Too good for those slant-eyed barbarians."

"Right, my friend," Lorenzo agreed. "But the bishop cultivates their friendship because he finds them interesting. These high-horse folk have no common sense."

"If you want to know what is interesting," said the guard, "what is interesting is the pretty little putana the older Tartar travels with. They say she's a Jewess. I have often wondered if she would be partial to other older men."

Rachel! That pig of a Tartar dragged that poor child here to this damned war.

"That is interesting, all right. Now, where the hell do I find these Tartars?"

The guard poured himself another ladle full of wine without bothering to ask, and drained it with more loud lip noises. Then he and Lorenzo climbed out of the cart.

"Their tent is the one with blue and yellow stripes in the center of the camp. You see it? But I do not think you will find them there."

Lorenzo had suspected that the Tartars would not stay in their tent. If they were out watching the battle with Charles's commanders, it would be well-nigh impossible to kill them in full view of so many of the enemy. But that had occurred to him before he left Manfred's camp. He had thought of another way to carry out Daoud's orders. Along with the casks, he had brought one jar of a very special wine, laced with enough belladonna to kill a whole army of Tartars. He would leave that to greet them on their return from the battle. Then he would unhitch his dappled brown and white gelding, a good riding horse, and scout around the edges of the battle to see if there was some way to get at the Tartars more directly.

A crossbowman sat on the ground at the entrance to the blue and yellow striped tent. He picked up the bow that lay on the ground beside him and jumped to his feet when Lorenzo drove up. Lorenzo remembered seeing him guarding the Tartars in Orvieto, and his heart beat heavily for a moment, but the man gave no sign of recognizing him.

Lorenzo held up his splendid parchment and explained his mission.

"They are not here," said the guard sourly.

"Well, the Bishop of Agnani is an important ally of your King Charles. Help me unload this wine." Lorenzo went around the cart and pulled the back down to make a ramp.

"It is good wine." Lorenzo continued, "and you can drink your fill after we get it into the tent. The Tartars will not miss a few cupfuls."

Grumbling despite the promised reward, the guard helped Lorenzo manhandle the cask to the back of the cart, tip it, and roll it down to the ground. Then they unloaded the other one.

The guard stood back to let Lorenzo roll the first cask by himself through the loose flap into the Tartars' tent.

"Stay away from the girl," he growled at Lorenzo's back. "His Eminence the cardinal says she's under arrest."

Lorenzo stiffened, and a chill gripped him. What danger was Rachel in now?

As Lorenzo straightened up, he heard a gasp.

The tent was lit by a single candle and the daylight that filtered dimly through its silk walls. It was held up by two center poles and an oblong framework from which the sides were hung. Around the edges were camp beds. Between the center posts was a table. Charcoal glowed in a brazier, warming the interior of the tent.

A shadowy figure rushed toward him. Lorenzo backed away, his hand reaching inside his tunic for the sandbag.

"Lorenzo!"

"Rachel." His voice was choked.

Her arms gripped him as tightly as if she were drowning. He felt warmth flood through him.

"Ah, Rachel." He had not seen her since he had taken her to Tilia Caballo's, and not a day went by that he had not cursed himself for doing so. She looked well, her face pink, but thinner than he remembered. She was, he realized suddenly, very beautiful.

"I thought your name was Giancarlo," said a dry voice. Lorenzo looked up to see the old Franciscan monk who traveled with the Tartars standing near him.

"What is going on here?" The Venetian burst into the tent. "Get your hands off that woman." He drew the shortsword he wore at his belt.

Lorenzo instantly let go of Rachel and stepped back. He bowed low, spreading his hands in a courtly gesture.

"Forgive me, messere," he said in a placating tone. "A long-lost cousin." His hand darted for his boot and seized the handle of his dagger.

"I don't believe that for a—" the Venetian began, but his guard dropped slightly, and his words were cut off when Lorenzo's blade plunged into his chest.

"Jesus have mercy!" said the old Franciscan. The Venetian dropped to his knees and fell on his face on the carpeted wooden floor of the tent.

"Try to give an alarm and you are dead too, Father," Lorenzo growled.

"No, Lorenzo, no!" Rachel cried. "Friar Mathieu is a good man."

"Perhaps that would not matter to Messer Lorenzo," said Friar Mathieu, his eyes fixed on Lorenzo with a penetrating stare. "If, as I suspect, he serves that elegant blasphemer Manfred von Hohenstaufen."

Lorenzo gave a short bark of a laugh. His heart was galloping.

Friar Mathieu knelt and whispered prayers in Latin over the dead Venetian. With his thumb he traced a cross on the man's forehead.

"You think there is no good to be found in King Manfred's camp?" Lorenzo said. "I am not surprised. You Franciscans pride yourselves on your ignorance."

Rachel's hand rested lightly on Lorenzo's arm. "Lorenzo, I beg you, do not insult Friar Mathieu. He has been my only friend since John took me from Madama Tilia's house. What are you doing here?" Her face lit up with hope. "Have you come to take me away?"

Lorenzo's mind was working rapidly. Apparently, Friar Mathieu was a decent sort, and Lorenzo had no desire to kill him. But what to do with him? Rachel might have given him the answer. This was, in fact, a God-given chance to get her away from the Tartars. And Daoud, he knew, would bless him for it.

"Where are the Tartars, Rachel?" he said.

"They put on mail and took bows and arrows and swords, and they have joined the fighting."

Lorenzo was astonished. "Charles is risking their lives in this battle? Pazzia!" And the would-be king of Sicily himself was not even fighting.

"Yes, it does seem mad, does it not?" said Friar Mathieu.

"Well, that is good," said Lorenzo. "I was afraid I might have to fight them for you, Rachel. Why did this lout say you are under arrest?"

"The cardinal accuses me of spying for King Manfred. He says you were all spying—you, Madonna Sophia, Messer David. Is that true?"

Lorenzo looked from Rachel to Friar Mathieu. There was no need to keep it from them any longer. For good or ill, all would be settled today.

"In a word, yes."

"Ah!" Friar Mathieu exclaimed. "I knew it."

Lorenzo felt himself grinning suddenly. "I could tell the cardinal that you knew nothing about us, but I do not think my testimony would help you. Perhaps it would be best if I just got you away from here."

Rachel's face was like a sunrise. "Oh, yes, yes!"

"Good. Wait one moment now."

He went out of the tent and looked around. There were no guards in sight. He rolled the second wine cask into the tent and set it beside the first. He dragged the Venetian's body into a corner, where anyone looking in would not see it.

"You have actually come here in the midst of this battle to rescue Rachel from John the Tartar?" said Friar Mathieu.

The old priest might still have a protective feeling toward the Tartars, Lorenzo thought. Best not to tell him the real reason.

"I guessed that right now there would be less of a guard on her," said Lorenzo. "And if you are as ashamed of your part in what has happened to her as I am of mine, you will help me. You really should come with me."

"Willingly," said Friar Mathieu. "I have no great confidence in your ability to protect Rachel."

"You seem to have done little enough for her yourself," said Lorenzo gruffly. Friar Mathieu appeared angry as he opened his mouth, but then he closed it again, without speaking.

A good Christian. Turning the other cheek.

Trying to see in all directions at once, Lorenzo carried blankets from the tent and threw them into the back of the cart. He took the long-necked jar of poisoned wine from under the driver's seat. Looking around for guards and seeing them all gazing southward toward the battle, he went back into the tent and put the wine on the table.

"This wine was my disguise," he said. "I am bringing a gift of wine for the Tartars from the Bishop of Agnani." Much better to tell them no more than that.

"My chest, my treasures," Rachel said. Lorenzo sprang at the box she pointed out and gripped it by both handles. He was shocked at its weight.

"My God! I do not know if I can—"

A sudden fear came over him. There was no time for this! If he were caught now, with the dead Venetian, Rachel would surely be executed, and he along with her.

He hoisted the box to the level of his hipbone, feeling as if his spine would snap. Rachel and Friar Mathieu put their hands under it, easing the load a little. Panting, the three of them wrestled the chest out of the tent, and with one heart-bursting effort Lorenzo heaved it up into the rear of the cart.

He glanced about him and saw that they were still not being watched.

He picked up the dead archer's crossbow and quiver of arrows and set them beside the driver's seat at the front of the cart, although he hoped he would not have to fight his way out of this place.

Bustling Rachel and Friar Mathieu into the cart, he had them hide under the blankets, in case any of the guards around Charles's camp should want to look inside.

It seemed to him that he held his breath all the way from the Tartars' tent to the edge of the French camp. But the elderly guard he had spoken to barely glanced at him as he drove by with a wave.

The battle seemed unchanged as his cart creaked and rattled along the narrow dirt track leading through the hills west of the valley. Save that more dead littered the rolling brown landscape. Charles still stood on his mound, not deigning to get into the fight himself.

Horsemen and foot soldiers struggled in crowds the length of the valley. The Tartars, whom he had come to kill, must be fighting down there somewhere. With luck they would die, either on the battlefield or later.

He kept his eyes moving, watching everything. Arrows or stragglers from the battle might get the three of them. They would not be safe until they reached Manfred's camp. If then.

"Oh, Lorenzo, I'm so happy!" Crying, Rachel threw her arms around his neck.

Embarrassed, he said gruffly, "Easy, child. I have to see what is going on down there." He gently pulled her arms loose.

The track had climbed high enough to give him a view of the south end of the valley. With a glow of pleasure he saw that Daoud had kept the Sons of the Falcon intact. There was their green banner with its white inscription. There were their turbans, red dots forming a line across the valley.

A warm feeling swept over him as he made out Daoud's figure in the center of the line. Never had he met a man he admired more, not even Manfred. He caught himself praying that Daoud would live through the battle and be victorious.

He had seen the Sons of the Falcon attack earlier today and check the first French charge with their volleys of arrows. Now they seemed to be riding to attack again. What was their objective?

A flash of light above the battle caught his eye. Sunlight reflected on metal. He looked across at the bare gray rocks that topped the high ridge on the other side of the valley. He could see beyond the rocks the tips of a pine forest. Again the flash of light.

Helmets.

Ten or more conical helmets appeared between the forest and the rocks. Men were crawling over the top of the ridge. The lower slopes of the ridge, on the valley side, were heavily forested. Those men would be quite hidden from anyone looking up from the valley.

Who were they? And how many? The hills over there could conceal hundreds. They could be some of Manfred's troops, sent up there to make a surprise flank attack. But Manfred had rejected just such a plan.

He remembered now a conversation between Daoud and Manfred at dawn. Not all of Charles's allies had yet arrived. The Gobignon banner, for instance, had not been seen with Charles's army.

That could be a whole fresh army of Frenchmen up there on that ridge, about to fall like an avalanche on Manfred's forces.

And Daoud's Sons of the Falcon were rapidly advancing up the valley.

Lorenzo felt himself trembling. He wanted to scream a warning.
I have to reach Daoud.

He jerked the horse to a stop and called to Rachel and Friar Mathieu.

"I have to leave you."

"Lorenzo!" Rachel's eyes were huge with terror.

He took her hands. "Listen. I love you like my own daughter.

But I have just seen something—I have to warn them. Daoud—
David—will be killed.''

"David of Trebizond?'' said Friar Mathieu. "You called him
Daoud?'' The old priest's eyes were alight with sudden understanding.

"Never mind.'' Lorenzo heard his own voice rising in panic. He
took a deep breath to steady himself, then plunged back into
the cart and seized the saddle he had tucked away in the back. He
jumped down from the cart, unhitched the gelding, and threw
the saddle over its back.

"Oh, my God, Lorenzo!'' Rachel screamed. "Take me with you.
Don't leave me here.''

"I will be back for you,'' he said as he fought to get saddle and
bridle on the horse. "I swear it. I have no time to talk. I have to do
this.'' Wanting something more than a dagger to defend himself
with, he grabbed the crossbow he had taken from the guard at the
Tartar's tent, and strapped the quiver of bolts to his waist.

The gelding expelled a breath as he threw himself on its back.

Rachel was still screaming, but he could not make out her words
over his horse's hoofbeats as he galloped away.

"Forgive me!'' he cried over his shoulder.

LXIX

DAOUD'S DARK BROWN ARABIAN STALLION SIDESTEPPED A KNOT
of fighting men. Daoud's heart beat slowly and heavily in his chest
like a funeral bell. The field was still a chaos. The battle was still
in doubt. But in individual combats more of Manfred's men than
Charles's were falling. Daoud had seen—and it had made him almost angry enough to want to break out of his formation and pursue
them—a group of Apulian crossbowmen running off the field. Bands
of Charles's knights were getting together and overwhelming smaller
bands of Manfred's.

It was the power of Christianity, Daoud thought. Charles's men
had been told by the pope himself that they were crusaders waging
a holy war and would be taken up into heaven if they died in battle.

Manfred's Christian warriors had been excommunicated, without the sacraments, for over a year, and many of them believed that if they were killed they would go to hell. Daoud could not be sure how strongly the men on either side felt about these things, but it could be enough to tilt the battle slowly in Charles's favor.

On Manfred's side, the only ones who felt they were waging a holy war were the Sons of the Falcon.

Daoud recalled Lorenzo's words to Manfred months before: *I have never in my life doubted the* power *of religion, Sire.*

Manfred himself had disappeared into one of these whirlpools of combat. Daoud had searched everywhere for Erhard Barth, who should be pulling Manfred's army together and giving orders, if Manfred would not do it himself. He could find the marshal nowhere. There were no plans. There were no leaders.

The Arabian's broad back rolled easily under him. He had kept the Sons of the Falcon in formation, ordering them to advance, hoping for a chance to strike a decisive blow. Staying out of the fighting they passed, moving around the groups of struggling men and reforming ranks, was frustrating for his men, but so far their discipline had held.

Staying together had protected them too. He estimated he had lost only about twenty men so far.

Music, familiar martial music of the kind he had often heard in El Kahira, flared up behind him, sending a thrill up his spine. The little mounted Muslim band had kept pace with the Sons of the Falcon.

He and the Sons of the Falcon had reached the midpoint of the valley. Benevento behind him and Charles's camp ahead were equally distant. In both directions the sights were the same—horsemen flailing at each other with swords and axes and maces, crossbowmen and pikemen struggling among the horses' legs. Few arrows flew now, because an archer was as likely as not to hit someone on his own side.

Daoud narrowed his eyes. He saw again at the north end of the valley the brown hill, a bit higher than any near it, the cluster of men on horseback.

Sunlight glittered on a helmet adorned with a crown.

He felt suddenly lifted up. He wanted to laugh aloud.

Lord of the worlds! You have shown me the way!

With one blow they could end the battle.

"Omar!"

His second in command rode to his side, white teeth shining in his thick black beard.

Daoud pointed up the valley. "Do you see that red and black

banner and that group of knights under it? Do you see a gold crown
shining on a helmet? That is Charles d'Anjou, he who would steal
our lord Manfred's throne.''

"I see him, Emir Daoud. May God send him to the fire whose
fuel is men and stones.''

"May we be permitted to help God send Charles d'Anjou to that
fire. There is nothing between him and us but men fighting one
another and a line of foot soldiers we can sweep away with our
arrows.''

"I see, My Lord. I see.''

"Pass the order to charge. Charge at the red and black banner.''

"Gladly, My Lord. Death to Charles d'Anjou!''

The blue flags, signal for a charge, rose and waved over the Sons
of the Falcon. Daoud felt the tension build in the men riding beside
him. He unslung his double-curved Turkish bow and held it high
for all his men to see.

The naqeeb who carried the banner rode out before them, holding up the green silk with its verse from the Koran.

"Yah l'Allah!'' Daoud shouted. He put all his strength, all his
will, into the cry.

His men took it up.

"Yah l'Allah!''

"Allahu akbar!''

He brought the bow down to his side. The blue flags dipped. The
kettledrums rumbled and thundered to a crescendo. The trumpets
blared. He drove his heels hard into the Arabian's flanks. The horse
catapulted forward instantly, throwing Daoud back against his saddle.

He leaned into the cold wind, squinting his eyes against the rush
of air, feeling it blow through his beard. He looked to the right and
to the left. The Sons of the Falcon were racing beside him, these
good men, these warriors to whom he had taught his Mameluke's
skills, these comrades he had come to love.

Now we are truly Sons of the Falcon. We dive to kill our prey.

His left hand held the reins lightly, giving the horse his head. At
this speed he had to trust the horse to find the way. They were
partners. They jumped over a dead crossbowman. They leapt a
great fallen Frankish charger. Daoud felt as if he had wings. He
laughed aloud. They dodged around a melee. He rocked to the
jolting as the horse's hooves hit the ground.

There ahead, the red and black banner planted in the soil of the
hill was much closer. Daoud could clearly make out the black ram-
pant lion. He could see the tall, broad-shouldered man wearing a

bloodred cloak and the helmet with the gilded crown. The man was staring this way, perhaps only now becoming aware of his danger.

A crossbow bolt hummed viciously past Daoud's ear. To his right a man cried out and fell from the saddle. Hamid. He felt a moment's pain.

No time for fear or sorrow. He crested a small hill and saw lines of crossbowmen on a long rise of ground that ran across the valley. They were far away, still small figures, but growing larger as Daoud galloped on. They were turning their backs, having just fired. Their first volley had hit only a few of Daoud's men, because the Sons of the Falcon were still out of their crossbows' short range. Facing Daoud now were the big rectangular shields they wore on their backs. The row of shields leaned away from him as the men bent to draw their bows.

Charles d'Anjou and the men around him were gesturing and pointing. Did they really expect these archers to save them?

Daoud pulled an arrow from his saddle quiver and nocked it.

"The instant they turn, shoot!" he shouted. He heard his order echoed as the word was passed down the line. The red flags went up. He took aim at the back of a man in the center of the crossbowmen's line.

The archers whirled, bringing their bows up. The red flags dipped. As he felt his galloping horse's hooves leave the ground, Daoud released the string. He saw the man he had targeted drop his bow and fall to the ground.

The Falcons' arrows swept the crossbowmen like a scythe. The powerful Turkish bows could shoot farther and be reloaded faster than the European weapons. The few archers not felled by their volleys ran to the sides of the valley to safety.

Charles was too far away for Daoud to read his expression, but his arms were waving frantically, as if he were trying to conjure up knights out of thin air. The men around him clutched at him, clearly telling him they must ride for their lives. One of Charles's men had pulled the red and black banner out of the ground and looked ready to gallop away with it.

Daoud slung his bow across his back and drew his long, curving saif from the scabbard. The noonday sun flashed on it as he held it high. His men roared and brandished their own swords.

The band had caught up with them, and the trumpets and hautboys screamed death to the enemy while the kettledrums rumbled.

There was nothing left to protect Charles d'Anjou now. There was not even time for the French leader to run for it. He seemed to know it. He had his sword out and he held up a white shield with a red cross.

Urging the Arabian on, shouting the name of God, Daoud raced toward triumph.

On hands and knees Simon stared horrified as the long line of red-turbaned riders charged at Charles's position.

The Saracen riders still had half the length of the valley to cross before they reached Charles's position. The French foot archers—some of them must be the same men Simon had briefly commanded before the gates of Rome—were lining up to protect their king. There was time, but very little.

"God have mercy!" exclaimed Antoine de la Durie.

Simon backed away from the hilltop, stood up, and turned. All down the side of the ridge hidden from the valley of Benevento, rows of knights sat on their great horses, hefted lances, thrust at the air with their swords. Some were still struggling into their mail shirts with the help of their equerries. Hundreds of faces looked up inquiringly at Simon. Trees hid the rest of his army, farther down the slope.

He took the polished helmet Valery held for him, its top adorned with an angry griffin spreading its wings, and set it down over the padded arming cap that held it in place.

De la Durie, de Marion, de Puys, and ten more barons gathered around him. They waited silently for him to speak.

He was shaking inwardly, and prayed that it would not show. He was afraid of death and of defeat. But, thank God, he was no longer in doubt about what to do. He knew.

"Over a hundred Saracens are about to fall upon King Charles. There is no one near to help him. We must go down there now and stop them. Straight over the side of this ridge. Mount your horses."

"But, mercy of God, Monseigneur!" cried de Puys. "That slope is long and steep. There is a forest. The men will fall. The horses will break their legs. We must find a path."

"There is no time to explore, de Puys. There are many paths down. We will find them. The horses will find them. We must go now. In a moment King Charles will be dead!"

The equerries holding the Gobignon and crusader banners rolled them up to take them through the forest.

Valery brought Simon's favorite war-horse, the pearl-gray destrier called Brillant. Simon braced himself for the effort, in full armor, of mounting the huge horse. He set his foot in the iron stirrup, hoisted himself, swung his leg, heavy with mail, over the saddle, and settled himself. He drew the Saracen blade Roland had given him.

A Saracen blade to fight Saracens.

He put fear and doubt out of his mind, drew a deep breath and roared, ''Suivez-moi!''

He spurred Brillant and slapped the charger's neck. ''Good horse! Find a way down.''

Then he had plunged over the edge and into the forest on the other side. He crouched, hiding his face behind Brillant's gray neck, as thick as a tree trunk. A branch struck his helmet with a clang, stunning him slightly, and he bent his head lower.

Twisted trees rushed at him and past him. All around him he heard men shouting, some yelling in wild abandon, some crying out in fear. He heard a terrible crash and clatter and the mingled screams of a man and a horse. Behind him came a thundering like a landslide as more and more of his knights plunged over the edge of the ridge.

He had time to think in jubilation that he had given a frightening, difficult order, and the men had obeyed. Hundreds of knights and men-at-arms were plummeting down this perilous slope because he had told them to.

If I die today, I die a leader.

But would they reach the valley in time to save Charles d'Anjou? While they rushed and fell and fought their way through this forest, that battle line of Saracens was galloping over easy, rolling ground with only Charles's archers to impede them. Just now Simon was crashing through woods so thick he could not see the battlefield.

Then there was light ahead and a meadow of brown grass. Brillant broke through the brush at the bottom of the slope.

The red-turbaned line was a little past the place where Simon had come out. They were riding those light, fast Saracen horses.

Where were the lines of crossbowmen? Gone—and now Simon saw bodies scattered on the ground where the foot archers had stood.

Charles's banner was still on the same hilltop. In moments the Saracens would be upon him.

''Faster! Faster!'' Simon shouted, slapping Brillant's neck as the huge war-horse ran at top speed to overtake the Saracen line.

Daoud charged on, his eyes fixed on the crowned figure under the red and black banner.

The pounding of hoofbeats in the air all around him was suddenly louder than he thought possible. He had been hearing the ululating, high-pitched war cries of his men, but now heard screams of pain and shouts of battle and deeper war cries, voices shouting in French.

Coming from the right flank.

He turned. He glimpsed a purple banner rushing toward him. A white and red banner along with it. The horse beside his was thrown against him by a blow that all but knocked him senseless. Caught between the two horses' flanks, his right leg felt as if it were being crushed. As pain shot up into his hip, he reeled dizzily in the saddle and clutched the reins till his left arm ached, his right holding his saif aloft so as not to stab one of his own men.

His horse fell against the one on his other side. All around him horses and riders were thrown to the ground. The Sons of the Falcon were flung about wildly, their forward momentum broken by some unimaginable force that had hurled itself upon them.

At the sight, he felt a giant hand reach into his chest and tear his heart out.

The Sons of the Falcon were buried under an avalanche of mail-clad Frankish warriors riding huge armored war-horses.

My God, my God! Why are you doing this to us?

He wanted to fling himself down from his horse and smash himself on the ground, screaming out his grief. In an instant he had been flung from joy to the very darkest pit of despair. In an instant he saw that everything was lost. His staring eyes were dry. This was all too sudden, too shocking, even for tears.

Where had these devils of Franks come from?

Down out of the hills to the east. They were still coming, hundreds of them, pouring down the forested slope and charging over the level ground of the valley. Broadswords, maces, battle axes, rose and fell. Their war shouts filled the air.

"Dieu et le Sepulcre!"

"L'Eglise et le Pape!"

"Le Roi Charles!"

He saw the green and white Falcon banner go down. He heard the band instruments give out their last ugly sounds as they and the men who played them perished under maces and axes. He saw with agony the deaths of men he had trained and ridden with—Husain, Said, Farraj, Omar—heads smashed, bodies cloven. He felt in his own body the blows that killed them.

Daoud recognized the purple banner now. Three gold crowns.

He had seen it before in Orvieto. Simon de Gobignon had come at last to this battle.

He should feel hatred for de Gobignon, but all he felt was a numb despair.

His few remaining men crowded against him, forcing him to fall back. He rode back toward Benevento, away from the triumphant army of Gobignon, crushed with sorrow. The Sons of the Falcon, the force he had taken a year to build, had been destroyed in a flicker of time, as if the earth had opened and swallowed them.

Lorenzo wept and cursed himself for being too late to warn Daoud before the French attacked. He stood on the edge of the field, holding his horse's reins in one hand and his crossbow in the other, watching the French knights sweep across the valley from east to west, trampling everyone in their path. Through his tears he saw the purple and gold banner of Gobignon fluttering against the cold blue-and-white sky.

Simon de Gobignon. If only we had killed him in Orvieto.

All about him, men rode and ran and fought. Singly and in twos and threes, horses without riders ran wildly this way and that. He wondered if Daoud was still alive. What had happened to King Manfred and the other Hohenstaufen leaders? Charles d'Anjou still occupied his hill at the north end of the valley. Almost overwhelmed at the moment help arrived, he had never moved.

There were fewer and fewer of Manfred's men in sight, and more of Charles's with their accursed red crosses.

A line of about a dozen horsemen was coming toward him at a walk. Most of them wore crosses, but they looked like neither French knights nor their Guelfo allies. Lorenzo rubbed his eyes to clear his vision of tears and took a harder look. Two men rode in the center wearing bowl-shaped steel helmets and gleaming gray mail shirts without surcoats. They held short, heavy bows in their hands. The brims of their helmets shaded their faces, but Lorenzo could tell that their skin was browner than any Frank's or Italian's.

The men flanking them on either side wore conical helmets and what seemed to be leather breastplates and carried long, curving sabers. Bows were slung over their shoulders. One man on the right end of the line was dressed in a steel cuirass.

Lorenzo realized that he was seeing the Tartars and their Armenian bodyguards. And the man with the steel breastplate was Sordello. At the sight of the old bravo, Lorenzo felt fury boiling in him. Back in Orvieto, that man had deserted Daoud and him. Despite that, Daoud had sent him money through Ugolini in Perugia and Viterbo, and Sordello had sent them snippets of information. But Lorenzo had privately vowed that the next time he saw Sordello he would squash him like a bedbug. And now he appeared again, just after Simon de Gobignon smashed Daoud's final hope of victory.

The Tartars talked and gestured to each other, surveying the battlefield. Their attention and that of their guards was on a melee that was rolling rapidly toward them. A boiling mass of horsemen, the survivors of Daoud's Sons of the Falcon battling with the vanguard of the Frankish knights, was struggling its way to the western side of the valley.

Partly hidden from the approaching Tartars by his horse, Lorenzo readied his crossbow. He hooked the bowstring to his belt and put his right foot in the stirrup in front of the bow. He kicked out sharply, straightening his right leg, and the bowstring snapped into place behind the catch. It would be a pleasure to kill Sordello, but his first duty was to kill the Tartars. And thus he would he pay the French back for Daoud's defeat. This would be much more satisfying than leaving poisoned wine in their tent. He raised the bow, loaded a bolt, and stepped out into the Tartars' path.

"You little monsters!" he shouted. The younger Tartar, Philip, brought his head up, giving Lorenzo an even better shot. Lorenzo depressed the catch, and the bolt smashed into the center of Philip's chest, right through the mail shirt. His eyes huge, Philip fell out of the saddle. His frightened horse galloped away.

Lorenzo ducked back and bent to draw his bow. A moment later something hit the side of his horse and the animal gave an agonized whinny and fell to its knees. By that time Lorenzo had his bow cocked and loaded again. He rose up from behind his dying horse.

John was just drawing his bow for a second shot.

"For Rachel!" Lorenzo called, and shot John in the same place he had hit Philip, the center of the chest. The force of the bolt knocked John backward.

John toppled from his horse and slid to the ground. He cried out some words in his Tartar language, shivered, and lay still.

Lorenzo stood a moment, breathing heavily. He felt the satisfaction of a man who has done a hard job that he had long wanted to complete. There was no satisfied blood-lust, no gloating over vengeance achieved. It was just the good feeling of an archer whose arrows had gone true.

"Kill him!" Sordello shouted.

The Armenians and Sordello thundered down upon him. Lorenzo set the crossbow stirrup on the ground and put his foot into it, but he knew he would not have time for another shot. He tensed himself for the bite of those saber blades into his unarmored body.

Then, like a curtain, the fleeing remnant of the Sons of the Falcon and the French knights in pursuit on their gigantic horses swept between Lorenzo and the Tartars' guards. Still clutching the crossbow, he ran.

A bay Arabian horse, riderless, its eyes rolling in frenzy, galloped toward him. Lorenzo threw down the crossbow and sprang into the animal's path, spreading his arms wide. The horse tried to dodge around him, but Lorenzo grabbed the reins, dug his heels, in and jerked the horse to a stop. He spoke soothingly and rubbed its head, and when it was calm enough, he scooped up his weapon and heaved himself into the saddle.

He felt a grim satisfaction at having killed the Tartars. But it was too late, and not enough. Daoud's brave attempt to finish Charles had been smashed, and the battle was all but lost.

He must get back to Rachel and Friar Mathieu. If, out of this tragedy, he could rescue Rachel, that at least would be something.

Striking right and left with his saif, Daoud hammered on lifted shields, on mailed arms, on helmets, on longswords. Few of his blows did damage, but they forced a way for himself and his horse through the ring of Frenchmen surrounding Manfred's defenders. Mustached faces, blind with fury, thrust themselves at him, and he struck at them with fist and shield and sword. He drove his horse into a narrow space between the rumps of two huge destriers, pushed them apart like Samson bringing down the temple of the Philistines, and was facing one of his own Sons of the Falcon, a dark-skinned man with blood and dirt smeared over his black beard.

"Ahmad! Make way for me."

"My Lord. I thought you were dead." Ahmad nudged his horse to one side, enough to let Daoud through, and then with his lance drove back the French knight who tried to follow him.

Past Ahmad, Daoud looked about and saw that Manfred's surviving warriors had formed a large, irregular ring, facing an ever-increasing press of crusaders. More of Manfred's followers were crowded inside the circle. He saw some men move out and join those fighting the French while others fell back and took a brief respite. Many dead men lay on the ground, and many wounded who were too badly hurt to stand. The wounded who remained on their feet were still fighting.

Daoud saw with a pang of sorrow that there among the dead lay Erhard Barth, the landgrave. At least Manfred's marshal had died fighting for his master and would not have to live with the memory of defeat.

The trampled brown earth within this ring was all that was left of the Hohenstaufen kingdom. Daoud's anger was deep and weary, at himself for failing and at the fate that had destroyed his hopes today. This morning, he thought, he had imagined himself feeling like Baibars at the Well of Goliath. Now he knew how Ket Bogha must have felt.

Why does God test us so heavily?

He looked for the green-plumed helmet he had seen from a distance, telling him Manfred was here. There it was, in the midst of a ring of knights with tattered cloaks and surcoats—Manfred's young poets and musicians. It made Daoud's heavy heart feel a little lighter to see that they had stuck by their king. He steered his horse over to Manfred.

"Emir Daoud! And still on your horse." The face under the bronzed helmet was red and shiny with sweat. Manfred's expression and voice were cheerful, but Daoud saw a deep, haunting anguish in his eyes.

"This is my fourth horse of the day, Sire." Daoud climbed down and bent his knee to press Manfred's mail-gloved hand against his forehead.

"I had heard you were killed."

"That new French army that came at noon overran us." No need to tell Manfred, if he did not know, how close they had come to winning. "Sire, we have enough horses and men to break out of here."

Manfred shook his head. "Nothing is left for me except to decide how the minnesingers will remember me after this day. To fall in battle will be far better, surely, than whatever shameful end Charles d'Anjou might be planning for me."

"But you need not fall into Anjou's hands," Daoud insisted.

"There is nowhere for me to escape to," said Manfred. "I have lost all my fighting men. All my kingdom lies open to Charles."

"Sultan Baibars would receive you as a revered guest. Or the Emperor of Constantinople."

And we could take Sophia there with us.

Manfred shook his head with a rueful smile. "I would be honored to eat your sultan's bread and salt. Or to visit that wonderful city, Constantinople. But I do not want to see the shambles Anjou makes of this land my father and I labored so many years to make beautiful. And—I have been a king, and I do not want to end my life as an exile."

But we are all exiles, Daoud thought.

Manfred continued. "I thank you for all your help, Daoud. You must get away while you still have a chance."

Tears burning his eyes, Daoud saw that the little space Manfred's men defended had shrunk even as they spoke. He thought of Sophia, waiting for him in Benevento. He thought of El Kahira, of Blossoming Reed, of going before Baibars and telling him he had failed to stop the alliance of Tartars and Christians.

He would never see any of them again.

He closed his eyes, and for a moment he sat in the Gray Mosque and heard the voice of Sheikh Saadi.

The Warrior of God is known, not by his willingness to kill, but by his willingness to die. He is a man who would give his life for his friends.

He looked again at the short, smiling man before him and said, "I will stay with you."

Manfred put out a hand. "Daoud, you owe me no blood loyalty. I do not ask you to die in my company."

"And yet, but for my advice, you might not be here today," Daoud said. "I owe you that. I cannot leave you."

"Many of my own men already have."

"Then I must stay."

Manfred looked deep into Daoud's eyes. "What about Sophia?"

Daoud sighed. "God knows how much I wish I were with Sophia right now. But she is the most resourceful woman I have ever known, and she has friends with her in Benevento. And I have always known I could never take her back to El Kahira. If I live, there is no other place I can go but El Kahira. It is torment for me to think I will never see her again, but whatever happens to me, Sophia and I would have to part. Perhaps it is best that we be parted this way."

Manfred gripped Daoud's arms hard. "Stay, then, and be welcome among my companions."

I have brought destruction and death to so many, Daoud thought. *Now is the time to atone.*

The company and the ground they defended grew steadily smaller as the sun sank toward the west side of the valley. Even knowing that every moment he fought was another infinitely precious moment of life, Daoud felt a leaden weariness that made him wish the battle might soon end.

He struck out with his nicked and blunted saif against yet another French knight, who seemed fresh and full of vigor while pain screamed in his own shoulders and his legs felt ready to give way under him. But there were no respites now. All Manfred's men still on their feet were fighting. All their horses were fled from the field or dead.

Daoud reminded himself that when this battle ended he would be dead, and he thrust upward with his saif to parry a longsword whose arc would have ended in his skull.

Manfred was swinging his sword beside him. By fighting, Daoud thought, they held off, not only their enemies, but the despair that he felt like a dark tide within him, and that he knew Manfred must feel too.

He wondered whether Lorenzo had gotten through to the Tartars and killed them. And if he had, would it make a difference?

A French knight with huge mustaches that disappeared under the sides of his helmet swung a battle ax, and the Muslim warrior standing next to Daoud was suddenly headless. A spray of blood splashed on Daoud.

He saw mounted knights pushing through the close-packed mass of shouting Frenchmen. One on his right wore a red-painted helmet and brandished a mace. On his left rode a knight whose helmet was adorned with some fantastic winged animal.

"Surrender!" the knight with the beast on his helmet shouted. "You have fought bravely. The battle is over. You will have good terms."

Daoud had just time to recognize the face under the helmet with a strange feeling of gladness, as if meeting an old friend.

Simon de Gobignon.

"Not till I have crushed the viper!" And that, coming from the red helmet that covered his face, was the deep voice of Cardinal Paulus de Verceuil. All in red, he loomed over the struggle like a tower of fire. So hard did he drive his charger through his own French knights that some of them were knocked to the ground. Daoud even saw one fall under the hooves of the cardinal's horse. Others scrambled out of the way.

The cardinal's war-horse reared up over Manfred, hooves flailing. Manfred dodged back. The hooves came down, and the charger leapt forward. Leaning out of the saddle, holding the mace in both hands, de Verceuil brought it down on Manfred's helmet.

"No!" Daoud screamed.

He heard a metallic crash. Manfred collapsed to the ground with a jangle of mail and lay still. Blood streaked his yellow and black surcoat and soaked the crushed green plume.

With a cry of rage Daoud threw himself at de Verceuil to drag him off his horse.

He was knocked aside by a great gray charger that forced its way between himself and the cardinal. Staggering back, he looked up into the face of Simon de Gobignon.

"No, Cardinal!" de Gobignon shouted. "You will not kill this man, too, before he has had the chance of honorable surrender."

Amazed, Daoud let his saif drop a bit. De Gobignon had ridden in, not to attack him, but to save him from de Verceuil.

But all he accomplished was to save de Verceuil from me.

De Gobignon, leaning down from his gray charger, pointed his curving sword at Daoud, but not in a threatening way. Daoud took a step backward, his saif lifted.

The struggle around them had stopped. The fighting men had fallen silent. The handful of Manfred's followers remaining were quietly laying down their arms. A German knight and a Saracen crouched weeping over Manfred's body.

Daoud's arms and legs felt as if he were pushing them through water, but he knew that if he began to fight again he would forget this weariness. The worst of what he felt was the terrible ache of grief in his chest, grief for Manfred, for threatened Islam, for Sophia.

"Look at him, look at his garb," said de Verceuil, "A Saracen with the face of a Frank. If he surrenders, he should be burned as an apostate."

"You must be blind indeed, Cardinal," said de Gobignon, "if you do not see who this is." He turned to Daoud with a grave face. "You are David of Trebizond."

"I am," said Daoud.

"And are you truly a Saracen? I have long thought that you were an agent of Manfred, but I never would have guessed, to look at you, that you were a follower of Mohammed."

"You were meant not to think that."

"This battle—this war—is over now. I give you my word that if you surrender you will be treated honorably. There will be no burning."

De Verceuil boomed, "Count, you cannot promise that!"

"I do promise it."

The two Christian warriors on horseback faced each other, the count in purple and the cardinal in red, looking almost as if they might fall to fighting.

"You need not argue," Daoud said. "I will not surrender."

De Gobignon stared at him. "You will be throwing your life away."

"No," said Daoud. "I am giving my life to God."

He could not help anyone now. Not Manfred, not Baibars, not

Sophia. Like Manfred, he had only one choice left to him. The manner of his death.

"Very well, Messer David," said the young count. He swung himself down from his charger. At his gesture one of his men pulled the horse away.

"Monseigneur!" a young man called from the circle of French-men that surrounded them. "Victory is already ours. Don't risk your life to fight one God-accursed Saracen."

"I am the Count de Gobignon," said Simon quietly, "because I uphold the honor of my house."

De Gobignon turned to de Verceuil, who still sat on his horse holding his bloody mace in his hand. "Kindly clear the field, Cardinal."

"I shall see that you have the last sacraments if the infidel kills you," said de Verceuil with a curl of his lip. He yanked his charger's head around, drove his spurs deep, and rode off, the circle of men on foot parting for him.

Daoud gazed at the young man before him with a feeling that was very like love. He had once hated Simon de Gobignon. Now he felt him almost a son, or a younger brother, or another self. If he had ever wanted to be someone like Simon, he did not now. He had penetrated such mysteries and known such ecstasies as de Go-bignon never would. He had heard and heeded the words of the Prophet, may God commend and salute him. He had served Baibars al-Bunduqdari and been taught by Sheikh Saadi and Imam Fayum al-Burz. He had fought for Manfred von Hohenstaufen and had loved Sophia Karaiannides. And soon he would stand face-to-face with God in paradise.

"I do not challenge your honor," he said.

The Frenchman was already moving into a combat stance, a slight crouch, an exploratory circling of the tip of his sword.

"But even so I fight for my honor," Simon said.

"It is right that you should know whom you are fighting," Daoud said, raising his saif. "I am Emir Daoud ibn Abdallah of the Bhari Mamelukes."

"Mameluke," said de Gobignon softly. "I have heard that word."

"You shall learn what it means," said Daoud. He did not want to kill de Gobignon, but he would if he had to, because the young man deserved nothing less than the best fight of which he was capable.

They moved slowly around each other. Under that purple and gold surcoat the Frenchman was wearing mail armor from his toes to his fingertips. A tight-laced hood of mail left only his face bare, and his helmet with its nasal bar covered part of his face.

In this kind of toe-to-toe fight the greater speed of a lightly armored fighter was not much advantage. The weight of the mail might slow de Gobignon down a bit, but fatigue would do the same for Daoud.

The scimitar de Gobignon wielded, that souvenir stolen from some Islamic warrior, looked to be at least as good a blade as the one Daoud was using.

The count sprang and slashed at Daoud's arm. Daoud stepped back easily and parried the blow.

He can cut my hand off and that would end the fight. And I might even survive the loss of a hand to be taken prisoner into the bargain. I must not let that happen.

With a shout Daoud drove the point of his saif straight at de Gobignon's face. Christians used swords for chopping, not stabbing. With a backhanded slash de Gobignon knocked the point aside. He punched with his mailed free hand at Daoud's chest armor.

Daoud felt the force of the blow, but he saw de Gobignon wince. A mailed fist could hurt flesh, but when it struck metal the fist would suffer.

Daoud slashed at de Gobignon's sword arm just above the elbow. *Let us see if that mail can withstand my sword.*

De Gobignon winced again, but the saif rebounded without cutting through the chain links, and Daoud felt a jolt in his gauntleted hand.

The sword is good, but so is the mail. I cannot cut it or stab through it.

De Gobignon rushed him suddenly, swinging wildly, lips drawn back from clenched teeth. Daoud danced away, a part of his mind pleased that he could move so quickly when he had to, tired as he was. De Gobignon's wild swings from side to side left his chest exposed. He was relying entirely on his armor, Daoud saw, to protect him.

Daoud jabbed de Gobignon under the armpit, so hard that he felt the flexible metal of his saif bend. Again the blade failed to penetrate the tightly woven chain mail, but de Gobignon gave a gasp of pain and cut his attack short. Daoud was gratified.

He glimpsed a familiar face in the circle of onlookers, a meaty, weather-beaten face with a broken nose. Sordello. Had he been guarding the Tartars on the field today?

De Gobignon attacked again, swinging his scimitar furiously at

Daoud's head. He ended the motion with his arm across his face.
Daoud gripped his own sword with both hands, and on de Gobignon's backswing raised it over his head and brought it down with all his strength on the Frenchman's wrist. The count's arm was moving into the blow, which gave it even more force.

The scimitar flew from de Gobignon's hand. Daoud threw his body against de Gobignon's and locked his foot behind his opponent's ankle. His long, thin frame top-heavy in his mail, de Gobignon fell over backward. Daoud stepped forward instantly. Groans and cries of horror were already going up from the Frenchmen in the ring around them.

Daoud planted his leather-booted foot on de Gobignon's chest hard enough to knock the wind out of him. He jabbed his saif straight at one of de Gobignon's few vulnerable places, his right eye, stopping the point a finger's breadth from the pupil.

Daoud and de Gobignon remained frozen that way.

And now, O God, tell me: What will I do with him?

A year ago he would have joyfully driven the point of the saif into Simon de Gobignon's brain. Even now, he reminded himself that to kill de Gobignon would relieve Islam of a most dangerous enemy. Daoud would have won the battle for Manfred today, and Manfred would still be alive were it not for de Gobignon's unexpected charge. For that alone, the young count deserved to die.

De Gobignon lay motionless, his face full of anger and defiance.

But what a waste. I will kill him, the other Franks will kill me, and both of us will be dead. All loss. No gain.

The sun hurt his eyes. It was low in the west, almost touching the hills that bounded the valley of Benevento

Even if I spare him, the Franks will not let me live. For what I have been, for what I have done to them, they will burn me, as de Verceuil said, or worse. Could I trade Simon's life for a decent death for myself?

He opened his mouth to speak.

A crushing blow to his chest jolted his body, throwing him back. He heard the clang of metal punching through his chest armor. An instant later a thunderbolt of pain struck just beneath his ribs and spread through his body. He cried out in agony.

Somewhere nearby a woman's voice screamed.

He sank to his knees, dazed.

What happened to me?

He still had his sword in his hand. In his blurred vision he saw de Gobignon, his mouth open in surprise, sitting up, crawling toward him. Warningly, he raised his saif, but the terrible pain in the middle of his body drained the strength from his hand, and the sword fell from his fingers to the ground.

God help me. I have been arrow-shot. I am going to die.

Fear worse than he had ever felt turned his body to ice. So total was its power over him that the fear became a greater enemy than death itself, and he gathered his forces to put it down. After a moment of struggle, though he still quaked inwardly, he began to take command of himself.

De Gobignon was looking down at him, and his face was full of shock and grief.

Someone else was standing over him. He saw a pair of leather leggings tucked into heavy boots, archer's dress. His head fell back, and he was looking up at Sordello. The bravo squatted down, bringing his face close to Daoud's.

"I am glad to see you still alive, Messer David," he said in a soft, grating voice. "So I can tell you that this repays you for teaching me about paradise."

The pain felt as if rats had burrowed into his chest and were eating their way out. He wanted to scream, but he managed to smile.

"Thank you, Sordello. You are sending me to the true paradise."

There was justice in it. He had forced Sordello to undergo the Hashishiyya initiation. He had always felt that an evil thing to do. Now he was repaid. Just as Sordello said.

But when I die, God will welcome me.

A hand clamped on Sordello's shoulder and jerked him away.

"You filthy, stinking, cowardly bastard! You killed the best man on this field."

Daoud could not see Sordello, but he could picture the expression that went with the injured tone.

"Your Signory! I save your life and you call me a bastard? The point of his sword right at your eyeball?"

"He was not going to kill me. I could see it in his face."

There was a wild, almost frightened note in Sordello's laughter. "Can Your Signory read men's thoughts? I warrant you, if you had till the Day of Judgment, you could not guess what this archfiend is thinking. You have no idea what he has done."

Daoud almost managed to laugh. The fool Sordello, as usual speaking and acting before he thought. One word more, and he would indeed hang himself.

"Tell the count, Sordello. Tell him what I have done."

God, I will forgive You for making me suffer so, if You will let me see Sordello's face just now.

And God granted Daoud's wish. Sordello crouched again over Daoud, his color maroon, his bloodshot eyes popping. It was wonderful, and Daoud breathed a prayer of thanks.

After a moment Sordello got control of himself enough to speak. "You know what you have done. You killed the Tartars."

He straightened up. "Your Signory, do you not know that John and Philip are dead? And it was this man's servant, Giancarlo, who shot them from ambush with a crossbow on the battlefield. I shot this David of Trebizond not only to save your life, but to avenge the Tartars."

"Killed?" De Gobignon turned away, beating his mailed fist against his leg. "God, God, God! Two years I've kept them alive and Anjou *loses* them!"

The count was silent for a long moment. His back remained turned, but his shoulders heaved. He seemed to be sobbing. Daoud glanced at Sordello, whose eyes glowed with triumphant hatred.

So, Lorenzo finished the Tartars. At last. I pray only that it is not too late.

He felt, not elation, but a quiet satisfaction. He thanked God for letting him hear this news before he died.

"Did you get Giancarlo?" de Gobignon asked in a quiet, choked voice.

"No, Your Signory. The battle came between us."

Daoud thought, *Thank you, O God, for that.*

"Go away, Sordello," said de Gobignon in that same subdued tone. "Go where I cannot see you. I will deal with you later."

"Your Signory, this man is capable of the most unbelievable treachery. He will tell you monstrous lies. In the moments of life he has left to him, God alone knows what evil he may do. I urge you, kill him at once. It is the wisest thing. Here, here is my dagger. Cut his throat. Avenge John and Philip—and yourself. Or, let me do it for you. Do not soil your hands."

He is terrified of what I might say about him.

In his dimming vision Daoud saw Sordello lunge at him, holding a long dagger. Suddenly he vanished. A moment later Daoud heard a crash.

"I told you," de Gobignon said. "Get out of my sight."

For a short time Daoud could see no one. He heard movements and murmurings around him. Then he felt a hand slide under his head and lift it up. A fresh wave of pain swept through his body, shocking him with its force. He thought he had already felt the worst. He cried aloud.

Soma. In the hour when I need it most, I had almost forgotten it.

He pictured the mind-created drug collecting in his head and coursing in a stream of glowing silver down his throat and branching out to all parts of his body. Cooling, soothing. Building a wall around the place down low on the right side of his chest where the crossbow bolt had driven into him. A silver globe formed around the pain, and he was able to think and speak. He felt that his head was lying on something soft.

Kneeling on his left side, de Gobignon said, "I am sorry I hurt you. I folded my cloak and put it under you to try to make you more comfortable."

"Thank you. I feel better now."

"Are you really a—Muslim? Can you talk, or is it too painful?"

"I can talk."

"I would be glad to know who and what you really are."

"And I will gladly tell you." Daoud began to feel death creeping through his limbs. The pain was sealed off, but he sensed the lower cavities of his body filling up with blood. The crossbow bolt should have gone right through him, but the rear half of his breastplate must have stopped it.

Fear began to rise in him again. Fear, and a desolating sorrow. Never to see Sophia again. Never to do even the simplest things, get up and walk, see, breathe. It was more than he could bear.

He fought to find his balance.

I cannot save myself from dying. But I can decide how I will use these last moments of life.

He wanted to tell this man, who had been his greatest enemy all along, how he had tricked him and how close he had come to thwarting their grand design of an alliance of Christians and Tartars to destroy Islam. It would make up, in a small way, for all today's defeats. For himself, that was all he wanted now. Very soon now, he would go up to paradise.

But Sophia and Lorenzo, Ugolini and Tilia, would have to struggle on in this world after he was gone. He must protect them.

"Tell me," Simon prompted.

"My father was the Sire Geoffrey Langmuir of Ascalon," he began. "My mother was Lady Evelyn." He told de Gobignon of his capture by the army of Egypt, his rearing as a Mameluke in a barracks on the Nile. He tried to explain what a Mameluke was, and what code he lived by. He told of his acceptance of Islam, his first battles.

As he spoke, his eyes wandered, and he saw the red sun half hidden by the wooded western hills. He felt the air growing colder, and he shivered. The chill was not in the air alone. His arms and legs were numb, as if they were freezing.

"Give me your cloak, Valery," de Gobignon said, and in a moment a red cloak was being spread over him.

"You were at Mansura, where my father fought," de Gobignon said.

"It was a great victory for Islam," said Daoud. "I saw only a little fighting. I was very young." He told how Baibars had entrusted him with more and more important tasks, even with the killing of Qutuz. And how at last, having trained and shaped him over the years, Baibars sent him against the powers of Europe.

"Cardinal Ugolini took a Muslim agent into his house? Introduced you to the Holy Father? *The pope himself?* By God's breath—"

He must be careful, and protect his onetime protector. And others. "It was King Manfred who sent me to Ugolini." Daoud managed to laugh. "Do you think poor Cardinal Ugolini would be mad enough to present me to the pope if he had known that I was a Muslim—a Mameluke?"

"I suppose not," said the count. Daoud focused his wandering eyes on the pale face with its sharp features that hovered over him. De Gobignon's mouth was open, working. He was afraid of what Daoud might answer.

"And Sophia? How much did she know about you?"

"She knew nothing. She knows nothing even now. She was more useful to us that way."

Sophia was probably still in Benevento, waiting for him. Charles's army must be moving on Benevento to occupy it. There would be murder and rape and looting there this night. If de Gobignon still believed in Sophia and loved her, he would try to protect her.

There was pain in de Gobignon's eyes. "Useful to you?"

"Yes. We let her encourage you. We let her fall in love with you." He watched de Gobignon's color grow warmer, pinker, as he absorbed what Daoud was saying. "Each time she saw you, Ugolini would question her afterward, as if worried about her virtue. You told her more than you realized. She told Ugolini more than she realized."

"Did *you* question her?" De Gobignon fixed his eyes on Daoud's.

"I spoke very little with her. I did not want her to suspect me."

Forgive me, Sophia, for denying our love. I do it to save your life.

"Where can I find Sophia?"

"Perhaps you can help her. She is in Benevento. She came with her uncle." Daoud managed a smile. "He thought Manfred was going to force the pope to reinstate him."

"Where in Benevento?"

"On a narrow street that runs south from the Roman arch. A house that has a statue of an angel conquering a dragon over the door. The only three-story building on the street. She is on the top floor. Get there before Charles's men do."

"You do care about Sophia."

"She is an innocent woman. I do not want her to be hurt on my account."

"What about the others—your servant Giancarlo, Tilia Caballo?"

"They thought I was a merchant from Trebizond serving Manfred as an agent."

"And Sordello? He seems to know more about you than he ever told me. It is he who killed you. If he deserves to be punished, tell me."

The sky had deepened from blue to indigo. Somewhere nearby a girl was sobbing. Daoud wondered if it was she who had screamed earlier, when the bolt from the crossbow first hit him. What was a girl doing on this battlefield?

Does Sordello deserve to be punished? De Gobignon tried to use him against me, and I had more powerful means to turn Sordello against de Gobignon. But then the sword turned in my hand. That is not Sordello's fault. Let de Gobignon think him innocent.

"We let him think he was spying on us. Actually, he told you only what we wanted him to tell you. You saw his rage when he realized how I tricked him."

With sudden anxiety, he remembered the locket. He reached out with a hand that had no strength and put it on de Gobignon's arm.

"I must tell you one thing. When you go looking for Sophia, do not take Sordello with you."

A man's soft voice overhead said, "Simon. We have been waiting till most of the men moved away. Tell Rachel no one will hurt her if she speaks to David. She wants to say good-bye to him."

Daoud looked up and saw the Franciscan who interpreted for the Tartars. He let his head fall to the side, to see where de Gobignon was looking. Rachel. Older, more woman than girl now. It had been well over a year since he last saw her.

"It is safe to come forward, Rachel," de Gobignon said. "We understand that whatever happened, you could not help it."

Rachel rushed across the intervening space and threw herself on her knees at Daoud's right side, reaching out with tentative hands to touch him. Daoud saw that she was afraid that even laying a hand on him would cause him pain.

"You cannot hurt me, Rachel."

She stroked his face, running her hand over his beard. "Oh, Messer David!" Her voice was husky with grief.

"My name is Daoud, Rachel. I am a Muslim. I have wronged you greatly. I beg your forgiveness. Perhaps this is how God punished me for the sin I committed against you."

"You wanted to help me. I know you did." She sobbed, and he felt the weight of her head on the chest armor that had failed him.

"Your servant Giancarlo—Rachel calls him Lorenzo—helped Rachel escape from Anjou's camp," Friar Mathieu said. "He left us. He saw Simon's army coming and wanted to warn you. We left the cart and wandered around the edge of the battle looking for refuge. We saw your banner here, Simon. You must protect this girl."

Daoud reached out to de Gobignon. "Find Sophia."

Friar Mathieu knelt next to Rachel, who moved aside to make room for him.

Daoud said, "Father, when I am too weak to talk, put your fingers under the collar of my tunic. You will find a small leather packet tied around my neck. Take it off and give it to Rachel." He moved his head slightly to see Rachel better. "It is a talisman made by the Sufis, Rachel. It is called a tawidh. If it would not offend your faith, I would like you to have it as a remembrance of me."

Rachel laid her hand on Daoud's and repeated the unfamiliar word. "Tawidh. I will treasure it always, and give it to my children."

Friar Mathieu said, "I heard what you told Simon about your past. You were baptized a Christian, Daoud. In God's eyes you are still a Christian. You must confess that you have sinned, and you must renounce Islam before you die, or you will not be saved. Your Christian mother and father are waiting for you in heaven. Come, I can give you absolution."

Daoud shook his head, smiling. How kind this man was, but how sadly misguided.

"Saved? Of course I am saved. When a warrior dies fighting in defense of the faith, God welcomes him with open arms into paradise. I do ask your blessing. You are a holy man. And I ask your forgiveness for throwing you down those stairs."

"That was you!" De Gobignon's eyes widened.

"Of course. I wish I could tell you all the things I have done, good and bad. I have had a life of many miracles."

De Gobignon's face hardened. "You killed Alain."

Daoud hoped the realization would not turn de Gobignon against him. Sophia's life might depend on the count's forgiving him.

"Have I not admitted that I waged secret war on you in Orvieto? Yes, I killed your friend. I later was sorry I had done it, but he could have exposed me. I hurt Friar Mathieu. But I could not kill— a priest. All the things that thwarted you in Orvieto—they were my doing."

"I hate you for those things. For Alain especially."

"The princes of Europe and the Tartars would put countless men, women, and children to the sword. They still may do it. That is what I came here to fight against. To save my people."

De Gobignon shook his head. "How can you feel they are your people? You were not born a Muslim."

"Nor was Muhammad. May God commend and salute him. My faith is the faith of the homeless, the uprooted, the exiled. The Prophet said, *Islam began in exile and it will end in exile.*"

Friar Mathieu's bearded face and anxious blue eyes seemed to float over Daoud. "You lie there, defeated, dying. Charles has conquered Manfred. Does this not mean that your faith has failed you?"

"Whatever God's purpose has been for me, I have accomplished it. God may destroy unworthy bearers of the truth, but the truth He will not destroy."

"Do you think yourself unworthy?"

"I hope I have not been. I have tried to be a good slave to God. That is what the word Mameluke means—slave."

I have wandered in the desert and now I am going to the watering place.

He wanted to say more, but there was no strength in his breath. The silver globe was cracking like an egg, and a black, irresistible tide of pain was pouring out.

"Take the tawidh from around my neck, Father," he whispered.

He felt fingers at his collar, and after a moment the thong slid free.

Make me to die submissive unto Thee and join me to the righteous. I bear witness that there is no god but God and I bear witness that Muhammad is His servant and Messenger. Amin!

He could not hold the pain back. He could escape it only in sleep. He could not see Friar Mathieu or Simon de Gobignon or Rachel. His eyes were closing. He would dream of Sophia.

Rachel clutched the leather capsule desperately, as if by holding it tightly enough she could keep Daoud alive. She felt her sorrow

crushing her as if it were a great stone pillar pressing down from
the sky. She touched his cheek with her fingertips, and his face felt
still as stone, and she knew the life had gone out of him.

She sat back and tied the Muslim amulet around her neck, as she
had seen it tied around his. Then she dug the fingers of both hands
into the silk of her gown, near the collar, and pulled at it until it
tore.

She put her hands over her face and let darkness sweep over her
mind as sobs shook her and her tears fell.

LXX

TERROR FILLED THE LITTLE ROOM LIKE A POOL OF ICY WATER. SOON,
Sophia thought, terror would drown them.

The worst for her was not knowing whether Daoud was alive or
dead.

*Before dawn I had him here in this bed. Now after sunset I have
no idea where he is.*

Sophia lay back on the bed, while Tilia sat on cushions laid over
Sophia's traveling chest. Ugolini sat in an armchair reading—trying
to read, Sophia suspected—a leather-bound book by the light of a
candle in a brass holder standing on the arm of the chair. Only the
yellow gleam of the candle and the reddish light of a low fire on
the hearth illuminated the room. From the shadows along the wall,
the icon of Saint Simon stared at her.

She wondered whether she should have spoken to Daoud of what
she had come to suspect. Her time of the month, regular as the
moon itself since she was a girl, was over six weeks late. It seemed
the brew of myrrh, juniper berries, and powdered rhubarb Tilia had
concocted for her, and which she had drunk faithfully every morning for six months, might have finally done its work.

She wanted Daoud to know, though she was not sure whether he
would be pleased. He had never said that he had any children. She
wanted to be sure she was truly carrying his child before she told
him. Tilia had advised her to wait until at least twelve weeks had
gone by without an issue of blood.

But now it hurt her that she had not told him. It would have been another parting gift she could have given him.

Darkness had fallen. The foreboding quiet of Benevento was broken by shouts in the distance, growing louder as they came closer.

She heard a scream from the street. A woman's voice, shrill with fear. She shut her eyes and shuddered. Another scream, this time a man's voice and full of agony.

Sophia's body grew colder. She looked at Ugolini and saw that he was trembling.

It was not just terror that was making her cold. The fire was burning too low. She got up and laid two more split logs on it.

Back on the bed, she reached into the neck of her gown and pulled on the long silver chain, drawing out the locket Daoud had given her. She twisted the screw and opened it and stared for a moment at the engraved, interlocking arabesque pattern.

Then Daoud's face superimposed itself, and the pattern disappeared. It was not a picture of him; it *was* Daoud, as if she were seeing him through an open window. It was magic, and it frightened her. She had never before encountered magic. His face was alive, though it did not move. His blue eyes seemed to look right at her. She never quite caught him blinking, but it seemed as if he might have, just a moment ago. He appeared about to speak to her. Just as the fresh logs on the fire made the room warmer, so her terror subsided at the sight of him.

"What is that?" Tilia asked.

"A keepsake Daoud gave me." She closed the hammered silver case and slid it back inside the top of her gown.

"We cannot just sit here," Tilia said. "We are like mice waiting for the cat to come and eat us."

"I don't like depending on someone else to save me any more than you, Tilia," Sophia said, "but all we can do is wait. Someone will come for us. Daoud or Lorenzo. Someone."

"We should have left long ago, when the men-at-arms ran away," said Ugolini. "Then we would have had horses." He looked reproachfully at Sophia. Sophia felt he had a right to. She had persuaded them to stay here. How could she have been so sure that the news that the battle was lost, which had thrown the men-at-arms into a panic, was merely a baseless rumor? It was her faith in Daoud, she thought, her certainty that no matter what happened on the battlefield he would come for her and take her to safety.

"Adelberto, you cannot ride very well," said Tilia. "And I can-

not ride a horse at all. You may be sure those poltroons would not
have carried us on litters. We could not have left then."

"You could ride if your life depended on it," said Sophia. "You
may still have to."

"My life depends on *never* getting on a horse," said Tilia. "I
would surely break my neck."

There were more anguished shrieks from somewhere nearby, and
they looked at each other and the pool of terror rose higher.

Sophia heard hoofbeats and men's voices, loud, in the street
outside. She went to the door that led out to the balcony and pushed
it open a crack. With a clattering of hooves on cobblestones, three
mounted men rode down the street, looking up at buildings. They
carried no torches, but their drawn swords gave off pale glints.
There was no way she could tell who they were or which side they
were on.

The man in the lead pointed with his sword at the house where
Sophia was. She leaned farther out, her heart pounding at her ribs,
to see the trio dismount and tie their horses.

She turned away from the doorway to the balcony and pointed
silently downward. Ugolini closed his book with shaking hands.
Tilia fingered her pectoral cross that Daoud had long ago told Sophia contained a poisoned blade. And Sophia loosened the mouth
of the leather bag tied to her belt that held the tiny crossbow Daoud
had given her.

Would she be able to use it? She had shot a longbow for sport a
few times in her life, with indifferent accuracy. But she had never
fired even a normal-size crossbow. Still, if the darts were poisoned,
she need not hit a man in a vital spot to stop him.

Sophia heard Scipio barking in the room below, Tilia and Ugolini's room, where they had tied him. There was, she knew, no one
in the house except the three of them. The house belonged to a
Guelfo merchant who had fled town when Manfred's army arrived.
But she did not hear anyone moving about downstairs, as they would
if they were looting the place. Instead, heavy footsteps came up the
stairs and a voice called, "Madonna Sophia! Madonna Sophia, are
you up there?"

Her heart leapt with relief. It was not yet Daoud, but it must be
someone he had sent. They were rescued.

She was about to explain the good news to the others when the
door to the room swung open. There, grinning triumphantly at her,
sword in hand, stood Sordello.

He strode across the room, the floorboards squeaking under his
boots, and stood facing her. The hound's barking boomed up from

below. Her heart sank. She had never trusted this man. Her flesh crawled whenever he looked at her.

"Thank God I have found you, Madonna."

Two men followed him in, dressed in the padded body armor and bowl-shaped helmets of crossbowmen. As he did, they carried shortswords.

"How *did* you find me, Sordello, and for whom are you fighting?"

His back was to the two men who had followed him. He frowned at her and shook his head slightly, as if trying to tell her not to say too much. But the little signal did not allay her suspicion of him, and her fear.

"Why, I am here in the service of Charles d'Anjou, rightful King of Sicily by decree of the pope," Sordello trumpeted. "And I serve His Signory, Count Simon de Gobignon." Gloved fists on his hips, he turned slowly to gaze around the room.

At his words, the pool of fear became a flood of terror that threatened to sweep her from her feet. She swayed dizzily. This meant the battle was surely lost.

Dear God, what has happened to Daoud?

With a life of their own, her trembling hands pressed against her stomach.

"And look who we have here," Sordello said. "His magical Eminence, the vanishing Cardinal Ugolini. And Tilia Caballo, Orvieto's most distinguished brothelkeeper, of whose establishment I have such happy memories. Are you two now reduced to being Manfred's camp followers?"

Tilia stared with wide-eyed hatred at Sordello. Ugolini's face was as blank as if he had been clubbed. What Tilia had said earlier about cat and mouse was apt, thought Sophia. Sordello was tormenting his prey.

But he could have learned where I am only from Daoud.

If Daoud had told him where to find her, it must be that Sordello was still secretly Daoud's man, as he had been in Orvieto. That must be what the frown and the headshake meant.

"You need not glare at me like that, Madama Tilia," Sordello said. "You are very lucky to be under my protection tonight."

"What will your protection cost us?" Tilia's voice was heavy with scorn.

Sordello spread his hands. "Why, whatever your lives are worth to you. You have had much practice putting a price on that which is precious."

"The battle—King Manfred?" Sophia pressed him.

Sordello's grin broadened, showing more stumpy, crooked teeth. "We—Anjou's men—are here in Benevento, are we not? Manfred von Hohenstaufen is dead. With my own eyes I saw him fall."

Sophia felt sick to her stomach. Blindly, she staggered to the bed and sat down heavily.

A long, high-pitched wail came from Ugolini. He threw his book to the floor and rocked back and forth with his face in his hands. Tilia rushed to him and held him.

Manfred, dead.

Sophia's cry of grief was as heart-tearing as Ugolini's, but she kept it inside herself. She had loved Manfred once, and even after that was over, she had delighted in attending his court and had marveled at the felicity of his kingdom.

Gone in a day! What a loss, what a waste!

"Manfred died in a most chivalrous manner," said Sordello, showing no sympathy for the anguish he was causing. "He fought to the end, a few faithful followers beside him, surrounded by enemies. Cardinal de Verceuil killed him. I think I will write a poem about it."

"De Verceuil!" Ugolini cried. "That pestilence in red robes! If only I had had him poisoned."

Had Daoud been one of the faithful who fought beside Manfred? Sophia's throat almost closed with fear as she asked the question. "What of—David of Trebizond?"

Again that little frown and shake of the head, aimed at her alone. "More of him later." There must be things he did not want to say in front of the two Venetians.

But she persisted. "Is he alive? Is he unhurt?"

Sordello nodded gravely, his yellowish eyes holding hers. "He was alive when I last saw him, Madonna."

She let out a long breath. The ache of fear in her stomach eased. Even if the battle were lost, Daoud would manage to live through it and get back to her. Perhaps Sordello was his messenger.

She felt safer on her feet. She pushed herself up and moved slowly toward the door leading to the balcony outside. Downstairs, Scipio started barking again.

"Capitano," said one of the archers. "Are we to stand here talking all night? There is a whole town for the taking here, and we are missing our chance."

"Hush, Juliano," said Sordello. "You see before you two very important and wealthy followers of the late King Manfred. What they can offer us by way of ransom will be far more than the trinkets you could pick up raiding some merchant's home."

"Ransom?" Tilia spat. "What right does a furfante like you have to demand ransom of me?"

"Why, Madama, is that not exactly what scoundrels do?" Sordello laughed.

He sat down in the spot Sophia had just vacated on the bed, laying his glistening sword ostentatiously across his lap. Sophia saw that he carried a long dagger in a sheath hung on his right side. He surveyed them all, grinning.

God, this is torture! If only I could find out what has happened to Daoud.

"You have three choices, Madama Tilia," Sordello said. "You may leave here. Outside this house you can take your chances with the victorious warriors of Charles d'Anjou, who have fallen upon Benevento like ravening wolves. Can you hear the screams? Or you can stay here under my protection, and it will not cost you even one denaro. And in the morning I will present you, all legally and properly, to King Charles, who will be most grateful to me for the service. He is exceedingly eager to round up all of Manfred's principal servants. Some he is beheading, some he is hanging. You, former Eminence, will probably pay at the stake for your heresy and witchcraft. As for you, Madama Tilia, if a rope stout enough to hang you cannot be found, you may spend the rest of your life shedding your excess flesh in a dungeon."

Ugolini sat hugging himself and shuddering. Tilia opened her wide mouth to speak, seemed to think better of it, closed it again. But red coals sparkled in her eyes.

That's better, Tilia. Keep the anger hidden until you can use it.

But Sophia's fear for Daoud grew again at the thought that he might be Charles's captive, awaiting execution. Why would Sordello tell her nothing?

"Has David been captured?" she ventured, turning from the doorway to the balcony.

Sordello smiled at her, just as Scipio downstairs broke into another burst of furious barks. In the candlelight, Sordello's face turned a deep orange with sudden anger.

"Find that damned dog and kill it!"

"Wait!" said Tilia. "That is Giancarlo's hound, Scipio. We put him down in our room to guard our belongings."

"Just what I thought," said Sordello. "That is why I wish him killed."

"But he is a thoroughbred boarhound," Tilia went on, "and since it appears Giancarlo has lost him, let him be part of our ransom. He is easily worth several hundred florins."

"I have always loathed that dog," said Sordello. "I would gladly kill it just to avenge myself on Giancarlo for killing the Tartars."

In the midst of her terror Sophia felt a stab of surprise. "The Tartars? Dead? Giancarlo killed them?" Did that mean Rachel was free?

"Yes," growled Sordello. "And if I find him, I will personally repay him by cutting him to bits, starting at his toes. For that and for the many other injuries he has done me. But Madama Tilia is right. The hound is doubtless worth too much money to kill. I will take it, then." He gestured to his two men. "Have these two display their possessions for you. Do not harm the dog. Or them, for that matter. I want them back here intact when you are done, so I know I am getting an honest inventory."

"I do not know whether we can satisfy you," said Tilia. "We did not bring everything we own with us. If you would help us get to Lucera, we could make you princely rich."

Sordello leaned back and crossed his legs. "But Lucera is far from here, and there may not be time for us to collect what you have there. In a few days King Charles will unleash his locusts and scorpions far and wide throughout this land—his bailiffs and judges and clerks and tax collectors and men-at-arms—to lay hold of every speck of gold and chip of precious stone. For now, please help my men collect what you have with you. I am sure you have plenty. That cross on your handsome bosom, for instance. I suspect a man might buy himself a small castle with that." He reached out, and Tilia stepped back, but into the grip of one of the archers.

Tears sprang from her eyes and trickled down her painted cheeks. "Please let me keep it just a little longer. If I must part with it, in the end I will, but it is very dear to me."

Sordello waved grandly. "For now, then. Go now with these fellows. And mind you, hold nothing back. They are Venetians. You can't hide anything valuable from a Venetian."

Indeed, thought Sophia, remembering tales of how the Venetians had looted her beloved Constantinople years ago. As she watched the shuffling Ugolini and the dauntless Tilia leave with Sordello's two men, she felt her knees trembling so hard under her gown that she could barely stand.

She would be alone with Sordello.

"Be wary of the dog," Sordello called after his archers. "But be careful not to hurt it."

"Sí, capitano." The door closed with a thump.

"And now, Sophia," said Sordello, lifting the sword from his lap and laying it carefully on the bed, "we settle accounts."

"I do not know what you mean by accounts," said Sophia, making her voice as cold and forbidding as she could. "But before anything else, the truth, if you can manage it. I have seen you serving Simon, and I have seen you serving David, and now you say you are on the side of Charles d'Anjou. Who do you truly serve?"

Sordello stretched his booted legs and crossed them, leaning back in the chair. "Myself, Andrea Sordello, of course. Men may command part of me, but only I own all of me. In the beginning I was to serve Simon, reporting secretly to Anjou. In Orvieto David was my master. He offered me—a rich reward. But then he threatened to kill me. I fled Orvieto, following Simon. After that I was mostly Simon's man. A little bit David's man. I sent him information from Perugia and Viterbo, and he sent me money. But first, last, and always, my own man."

"Why are you here, then?" Sophia let her hand rest on the door handle as if she might rush out on the balcony and call for help. She hoped Sordello would expect her to do that rather than try to use a weapon on him.

Sordello stood up, smiling. "Madonna, you are not aware how I have suffered because of you. Suffered with longing. You owe me much for that." He strolled over to the fire, picked up a big log from the pile next to the hearth, and set it on the burning wood.

Oh, may God shrivel his phallos! Sophia felt her stomach burn at the idea of this repulsive man lusting after her. She turned quickly, facing the balcony door, so that he could not see her grope in the bag at her belt for the tiny crossbow and the box of darts Daoud had given her. How quickly, she asked herself, could she take the crossbow out, get a poisoned dart from the box without scratching herself, load it, draw the bow, aim and shoot?

He could be across the room and tearing the thing out of my hands before I got all that done.

Helplessness made her tremble.

Having made sure of the location of crossbow and darts, she turned to him again, gripping the skirt of her gown to hide the shaking of her hands. "If you find me attractive, I am flattered, of course, but it is no fault of mine."

"You do not wish to escape from Benevento? You wish to be turned over to King Charles's judges?"

"I have nothing to fear from them."

He bared his broken teeth. "Do you think they will have trouble finding something to accuse you of? Not if I tell them what I know." Then he raised a finger. "It was David of Trebizond who told me where to find you. And you keep asking about him. I always suspected, when I was serving David at Cardinal Ugolini's, that there must be something between you two.''

''If there is any spark of mercy in you at all, do not play with me like this. Tell me if he is alive.''

She wanted to seize him by the arm, but she was afraid to get too close to him.

The light of the one candle in the room cast shadows like black blots on Sordello's grinning face. ''Play with you? Ah, but if there is a spark of mercy in *you*, then you will play with me. *Then* I will tell you everything you want to know. Being alone with you like this, I burn so with desire, I would do anything, good or evil, to possess you.''

Scipio's thunderous barks, bursting out suddenly, made her jump. She heard male voices cry out, alarmed, then Scipio's rumbling snarls. Then silence.

Sordello glowered at the floor. ''God's beard! I almost hope they did kill that brute.''

To distract him a little longer from herself, Sophia said, ''You had better hope Scipio does not hurt *them*.''

''What do I care if they suffer a few bites? The dog is worth more than they are.'' He looked up at her. ''Do you know anything about journeys to paradise?''

''I do not know what you are talking about.'' Was that a name for some carnal pleasure he wanted to have with her?

''Come away from that balcony door,'' Sordello said.

''The air is fresher here.'' From the street she heard swords clanging, men screaming and cursing, and hooves pounding. There was fighting nearby.

''Our French friends, quarreling over their loot,'' said Sordello. ''Do you stand by the balcony door because you fancy being rescued from *me* by *them*? They are animals, like that dog downstairs. What I feel for you is far more profound than the desire to rape some conquered woman. I am a trovatore, after all. I will prove it to you. Just let me see you unclothed. Like Mother Eve. I will not touch you. Undress yourself, and I will tell you what you want to know about the man called David.''

She wanted to spit in his face. She was desperate to know what he could tell her, but even if he did tell her about Daoud, how could she put any trust in him? If Daoud was alive he would find his way to her, or she to him. She had nothing to gain by cooperating with Sordello.

''You disgust me!'' she cried. ''I wish you were not even able to see my face, let alone the rest of me.'' And she turned away from him, her hand dipping into the leather bag.

She heard his heavy footsteps thudding on the wooden floor. And another outburst of barking from below.

"I wanted you to give yourself to me willingly," Sordello said. "But if you refuse me, I will take you. And while I am doing it, I will tell you about the man David."

Terror seized her and shook her as if she were a rag doll. The way that filthy pig said that—it must mean something bad had happened to Daoud. She felt paralyzed by fear and grief.

Then, sudden rage made her want to strike out at this man who was hurting her so. She had the box of darts open now. She must be very careful of the poisoned tips.

The door to the room crashed open.

LXXI

"SOPHIA!"

She dropped a loose dart back into the bag and turned.

Simon de Gobignon stood in the doorway, staring at her. The firelight made his dirt-streaked face glow. His surcoat was ripped, showing the mail underneath, and she saw dark stains on the purple and gold. He was splashed with blood, she thought, her stomach churning. His head was bare, his mail hood thrown back and his mail collar open. He held his helmet, adorned with the figure of a winged heraldic beast, under his arm.

At first sight of him she felt a glow of joy. Simon lived. And she was safe from Sordello. Triumphantly she glanced over at the bravo and felt even better at the sight of his scarlet color, his clenched jaw, the swollen veins throbbing in his temples.

Then suddenly it came back to her that Simon was an enemy too.
It has always been too easy for me to forget that.

She would have to face his questions, his accusations, his pain, his rage. She felt like a bird in flight suddenly struck by an arrow and plummeting to earth.

And a worse thought struck her, piercing her heart like a sword.

What was it that Sordello would have told her about Daoud? In God's name, what terrible thing had happened to him?

Simon's being here meant he, too, must have learned where she was from Daoud. Where, then, was Daoud?

She saw figures in the shadows outside the door, one white-haired and white-bearded, the other a small woman wearing a mantle over her head.

Simon took a few steps into the room, his mail clinking. She could tell by his movements that he was exhausted. She felt a surge of pity for him, at what he must have done and suffered. She reminded herself he had been fighting against Manfred and Daoud, on the side of Anjou. Still, she felt sorry for him.

"What the devil are you doing here?" Simon said, glaring at Sordello, his voice crackling with anger.

Why so much hatred, Sophia wondered.

"You wanted me to be gone, Your Signory, and it seemed most useful for me to come here. It occurred to me that important followers of the infidel Manfred might be here. And, indeed, on the floor below you will find his agents Tilia Caballo and ex-Cardinal Ugolini, being questioned by my men."

"And you were *questioning* this lady. Before God, I do not know what keeps me from running you through." His mailed hand reached across his waist to grip the hilt of his sword.

"Easy, Simon," said the white-haired man. He came into the room now, and Sophia recognized Friar Mathieu, the Tartars' Franciscan companion.

She looked past the elderly priest and saw who was with him.

"Rachel!"

In the midst of her fear and sorrow, Sophia felt an instant of miraculous happiness, as if the sun had come out at midnight.

She rushed across the room holding out her arms, and the girl flew into them.

"Rachel, what a joy to see you!"

"Oh, Sophia! Sophia!"

Rachel was crying, but not for joy. She was sobbing heart-brokenly. What had happened to her?

"How do you come to be with Count Simon?" Sophia asked, hoping that answering would calm Rachel.

But Rachel went on weeping into Sophia's shoulder, and Friar Mathieu spoke for her. "Rachel and I fell in with Count Simon, and we thought it safest to stay with him. And he chose to come here."

"It's all right now," Sophia said, patting Rachel's back as she held her in her arms. "Everything will be all right."

"No, Sophia, no." Rachel, it seemed, could not stop crying. Bewildered, Sophia looked up. Friar Mathieu and Simon were standing side by side in the center of the room. Sordello, his face working with barely controlled fury, had moved to a far corner. His sword still lay on the bed, Sophia noticed, but his hand was on the hilt of his dagger.

Simon and the Franciscan were looking, not at Rachel, but at Sophia.

"David told you I was here," Sophia said. "He must have."

In an instant, she understood why Daoud had told Simon where to find her. And why Rachel kept weeping and weeping.

"Is he dead?" she asked.

They answered her with silence.

A wave of dizziness came over her. She reeled, and Rachel was holding her up. Friar Mathieu took her arm, and they lowered her into the armchair. She knocked the candle to the floor, putting it out. Now the only light in the room was the red glow of the fire.

She felt empty inside.

I am mortally wounded, she thought. *I feel now only a shock, a numbness. The pain will come.*

The only reason Daoud would tell Simon where to find her had to be that he was dying and wanted Simon to protect her. Daoud truly must be dead.

Simon's anguished look, as if he were begging for something, confirmed it. But to be sure, she had to hear it.

"Has David been killed?"

Simon nodded slowly, his eyes huge with pain. "I was with him when he died. I even know now that he is not David but—Daoud." He hesitated, pronouncing the unfamiliar name.

I was with him when he died.

Daoud!

She wanted to scream, but she hurt so much inside that she could not even scream. She could not make a sound.

Daoud was *gone*. She had seen him, she had spoken to him, she had loved him for the last time.

But she *had* to see him again. Her cold hand fumbled at her neck, pulled the locket up from her bosom by its silver chain. She turned the screw that opened it and stared at the spirals and squares.

Nothing happened. The pattern, to her eyes a jumble of shapes representing nothing, remained inert.

Even his likeness was gone.

How had he died? She looked up at Simon to ask him.

And then she did scream.

Sordello crouched in the semidark behind Simon, his two-edged dagger, reflecting red firelight, poised horizontally to slash Simon's unprotected throat. His eyes glittered. His mouth shaped a slack-lipped smile, as if he were drunk, baring his gleaming, broken teeth.

Sordello seemed not even to notice her scream. Without a sound, unseen by the other three, who were all staring at Sophia, he raised his left arm to seize Simon and his right hand to strike with the dagger.

Sophia's hand dove into the bag at her waist. The loose dart could scratch her, and a scratch might be enough to kill her, but that did not matter. Her fingers found the dart. She wrapped her fist around it and flung herself out of the chair, straight at Simon.

Simon tried to fend her off, but she darted under his hands, twisted around him, and drove the dart into Sordello's throat. Blood spurted over her hand.

Sordello seemed neither to see her nor to feel the dart. His eyes stayed fixed on Simon's neck. He slashed at Simon. But Sophia's lunge had pushed the two men apart. Sordello's blade scratched Simon's neck just under his right ear. Then it fell from the bravo's fingers.

Sordello, the dart still hanging from his throat, staggered backward, his knees buckling. His body folded, and he lay sideways on the floor.

The four living people in the room were as still as the dead one. Then Simon touched his fingertips to his neck and winced. Sophia saw a rivulet of blood running down into his mail collar.

Friar Mathieu tore away a piece of the bedsheet and dabbed Simon's wound with it. He took Simon's hand as if he were a puppet and pressed his fingers against the rag to hold it in place. Then he knelt over Sordello's body and whispered in Latin.

Whimpering, Sophia stumbled back to the armchair where she had been sitting. A sob forced itself up from her chest into her throat. She felt Rachel's gentle hands helping her to sit down. Another sob came up, shaking her body. Another followed it, and another. She lost touch with everything around her for a time, buried in a black pit where neither sight nor sound nor even thought could penetrate. She was lost in wordless, mindless grief.

Then, gradually, she began to hear murmurings, voices.

Friar Mathieu said, "She saved your life."

Simon said, "I know. David—Daoud—told me not to take Sordello with me if I went looking for Sophia. As if he knew this might happen. How could that be?''

Rachel was sitting on the arm of the chair, gently stroking Sophia's shoulder.

Friar Mathieu said, ''Why would Sordello try to kill you? Because he was about to rape Sophia when you interrupted? Or because he was afraid you would punish him for killing—Daoud?''

Amazement jolted Sophia's body. She opened her eyes and stared at Friar Mathieu.

''*Sordello* killed Daoud?''

Simon answered her. ''I will tell you how he died. I must talk to you. I have waited more than a year, you know, to see you again.''

Sobs still shook her, but she nodded and wiped her face with the sleeve of her gown. He reached down. She took his arm, and he helped her up. She saw that he had a bloodstained strip of linen tied around his neck.

''The balcony,'' she said.

''Good.''

As she went to her chest to get her cloak, Sophia looked at the icon of the saint of the pillar and thought how much, even though it had Simon's name, the expression looked like Daoud's.

Simon held the door to the balcony for her. The night was cold and moonless. The bitter smell of burning floated on the freezing air. The shouts of frenzied soldiers and the agonized screams of men and women seemed to come from everywhere. Fires blazed in all parts of the town, their glow and smoke turning the night sky a cloudy reddish-gray. On the plain to the north, campfires twinkled. Somewhere out there Daoud lay dead.

She looked up at Simon. Darkness hid his face. The ruddy glow of burning Benevento haloed his head. In a quiet, even voice he told Sophia how he came upon Daoud fighting side by side with Manfred, and how he fought with Daoud after Manfred was killed. How he lay helpless with Daoud's sword pointed at his face.

''He did not move for a long time,'' Simon said. ''It was growing dark, but I saw the look on his face. A gentle look. He did not want to kill me. I am sure of it.''

And then without any warning had come the treacherous crossbow bolt out of the circle around them, and Daoud had fallen.

''It was Sordello. He could not understand my rage at him. He kept protesting that he had saved my life. He had not.''

Sophia thought of Sordello's attempt to seduce her. She clutched the wooden railing, choking bile rising in her throat.

"I am glad I killed him," she whispered. "I have never killed anyone before tonight. That I killed him was a gift from God."

Simon did not answer at once. .

Then he said, "Tonight, before Daoud died, he told me that you were innocently drawn into his conspiracy against the alliance. He said he took advantage of my love for you, and that you and he were never close. But now that you've heard he is dead, you are like a woman who has lost a husband or a lover."

He stopped. He needed to say no more. She knew what he was asking.

The enormous aching void inside her made it almost impossible to think. Daoud, even as he lay dying, had tried to protect her. Simon might have suspicions, but about who she was or what she had done, he knew nothing. Manfred was dead. Tilia, Ugolini and Lorenzo—wherever they might be now—would say nothing.

She could, if she chose, become the person Simon thought she was—the person who had given herself to Simon in love at the lake outside Perugia. She need only seize the chance Daoud had given her.

In all Italy there was no place for her now. Once again she belonged nowhere and to no one. And she could be a wife to this good young man. She could be the Countess de Gobignon, with a station in life, with power to accomplish things, to change the world.

"You want to know what Daoud meant to me," she said. "Did you tell him what I meant to you?" She was amazed at how level her voice sounded.

"I think he knew," Simon spoke just above a whisper. "I did not feel I had to tell him anything."

Then Daoud had died not knowing that she and Simon had for a moment been lovers. Did it matter? If Daoud had known, perhaps he would have killed Simon instead of just standing over him with his sword.

His not knowing had not hurt Daoud. But it was hurting her.

There was a part of myself I withheld from him. And that was my loss, because much as he loved me, he did not know me fully.

But if she regretted not telling Daoud the truth about that single moment, how could she ever bear to hide from Simon the truth about her whole life?

Could she pretend, forevermore, to be Sophia Orfali, the naive Sicilian girl, the cardinal's niece, with whom Simon had fallen in love? Could she pour all of herself into a mask? Could she live with Simon, enjoying the love and the wealth and power he offered her, knowing that it was all founded on a lie?

No, never. Impossible.

The pain of Daoud's death was nearly unbearable, but it was *her* pain, true pain. Ever since that night of death in Constantinople—a night much like this—she had not felt at home in the world. Now she saw her place. All she owned in the world was the person she *really* was, and what she *really* had done. If she deceived Simon, she would have to deny her very existence.

And I would have to deny the greatest happiness I have ever known, my love for Daoud.

If she lied to Simon, it would be as if Daoud had never been. It would be like killing him a second time. Her heart, screaming even now with her longing for Daoud, would scream forever in silence. Buried alive.

Simon must already suspect the truth. He might try to believe whatever she told him about herself. Still, some awareness of his self-deception would remain with him, even if he refused to think about it. It would fester inside him, slowly poisoning him.

Her eyes had adjusted to the darkness, and she could see the suffering in Simon's long, narrow face as he waited for her answer. Starlight twinkled on the jeweled handle of the sword at his belt. What she told him might make him hate her so much that he would kill her.

I have never been more willing to die.

"Simon, I promised you that when I saw you again I would tell you why I could not marry you. I hoped I never would have to tell you."

He said, "I had not wanted to fight in this war of Charles against Manfred, or to bring the men of Gobignon with me. When I found that you had fled to Manfred's kingdom, I changed my mind."

Her pain had been like a pile of rocks heaped upon her, and what he said was the final boulder crushing her. Her ribs seemed to splinter; her lungs labored for breath.

So I must bear the guilt for Simon's coming to the war. How many men died today because of me?

She could hardly feel more sorrow, but the night around her seemed to grow blacker. Perhaps it would be best if he did kill her. She would tell him everything straight out, without trying to protect herself from his anger.

"My name is Sophia Karaiannides. I worked as a spy in Constantinople for Michael Paleologos and helped him overthrow the Frankish usurper. I was Michael's concubine for a time. Then he sent me to be his private messenger to Manfred's court here in Italy. Manfred chose to make me his mistress. But that became difficult for him and dangerous for me. When Daoud came to Manfred asking for help in thwarting the Tartar alliance, Manfred sent me along to Orvieto to help him. I fell in love with Daoud.''

Simon leaned his long body against the outer wall of the house. Having to hear this all at once must be overwhelming.

"So you went from one to bed to the next as you went from one country to the next."

It hurt her to hear his words, his voice tight with pain, but she had expected this.

"Daoud and I did not come together as man and woman at first," she said. "He did not want to be close to me."

He staggered back to the edge of the balcony as if she had struck him, and she was afraid he might fall.

He whispered, "Not at first! But you did—"

"Yes, we did," she said, thinking, *Now he is going to draw that scimitar and kill me.*

But the only movement he made was a slight wave of his hand, telling her to go on.

"I must tell you, Simon, that it was I who first fell in love with Daoud. There were moments when I hated him—when he killed your friend, for instance—but as I got to know him better and better I could not help loving him. I had been loved by an emperor and a king, but I had never met a man like Daoud. He had begun as a slave, and he became warrior, philosopher, poet, even a kind of priest, all in one magnificent person. You probably have no idea what I am talking about. You knew him only as the merchant David of Trebizond."

"I knew you only as Sophia Orfali."

"You may despise me now that you have learned so much about me, but the more you knew of him, the more you would have had to admire him."

"How insignificant I must have seemed to you beside such grandeur." She could hear him breathing heavily in the darkness, sounding like a man struggling under a weight he could not bear.

"I did love you, Simon. That was why I cried when you said you wanted to marry me. The word love has many meanings. And your French troubadours may call it blasphemy, but it *is* possible for a woman to love more than one man."

"Not blasphemy. Trahison. Treachery."

"As you wish. But in that moment you and I shared by the lake near Perugia, I was altogether yours. That, too, is why I fled from you. I could not stand being torn in two."

"Why torn in two, if you find you can love more than one man?"

The hate in his voice made her want to throw herself from the balcony, but she told herself it would ease his suffering for him to feel that way.

"I said it was possible. I did not say it was easy. Especially when the two men are at war with each other."

"And did Daoud know about me? Did you tell him what you and I did that day?"

"No," she said, finding it almost impossible to force the words through her constricted throat. "I could never tell him."

"So you could not admit to this *magnificent* man, this philosopher, this priest, that you had betrayed him with me."

"No," she whispered. "He was jealous, as you are. At first he wanted me to seduce you. But as he came to love me—I saw it happening and I saw him fighting it—he came to hate the idea of letting you make love to me. He came to hate you, because of that, and because he envied you."

"Envied me?"

"Yes. He saw you as one who had all that he never had—a home, a family."

Simon stepped forward and brought his face close to hers. "Did you tell him about my parentage?"

"No, never."

"Why not?" His voice was bitter. "Was that not the sort of thing you were expected to find out? Could he not have found a way to use it? Were you not betraying your war against us—what do you Byzantines call us, Franks?—by withholding it?"

"I told you that loving you both was tearing me apart," she said helplessly.

"But you loved him more—that is clear."

"Yes. I loved him more because he knew me as I was, and loved me as I was. You loved me, and it broke my heart to see how much you loved me. But you loved the woman I was pretending to be. Now that you really know me, you hate me."

"Should I not? How can you tell me all this without shame?"

"I am not ashamed. I am sorry. More sorry than I can ever say. But what have I to be ashamed of? I am a woman of Byzantium. I was fighting for my people. Surely you know what your Franks did to Constantinople. Look and listen to what Anjou's army is doing tonight to Benevento."

"Daoud spoke that way as he lay dying," Simon said slowly.

A sob convulsed Sophia. It was a moment before she could speak again.

"I hope, at least, you understand us—Daoud and me—a little

better," said Sophia. "Kill me now, or hang me or burn me tomorrow. As I feel now, death would be a relief."

"I know how you feel," said Simon. "I, too, have lost the one I loved."

"Oh, Simon." She felt herself starting to weep again, for Simon and Daoud both.

"What do you want to do?" he asked.

"What does it matter? I am your prisoner. And Rachel. And Tilia and Ugolini. All of us."

She remembered the hope she had been harboring these past few weeks. If she died now, would another life within her die? If she lived, how would she care for that life?

He sighed. "For me this is all over. If I hurt you, what good would that do me now? It would be just one more unbearable memory to carry with me through life. One more reason to hate myself. I want to know, if you were free to do as you wish, what would you do?"

Her mind, numbed with sorrow, was a blank. With Daoud dead, the remainder of her life seemed worthless to her. Even the thought that she might be carrying Daoud's child seemed only added reason for sorrow.

"Now that all of Italy is in the hands of Manfred's enemies, I suppose I would go back to Constantinople," she said. The thought of returning home to the city she loved was a faint light in the blackness of her despair.

"For my part, I would not stop you from going," he said. The weary sadness in his voice stung her.

If he meant it—and he seemed to—she should be relieved. Overjoyed, even. But all she felt was the weight of her grief, pressing pain into the very marrow of her bones.

"What do you mean to do about Tilia Caballo and Ugolini?" she asked.

"I am sure King Charles wants them, but I do not care to be the one who dooms them by turning them over to him."

King Charles. The title sounded so strange. That was how the ones who supported him must speak of him, of course. And her heart wept a little for Manfred, whom she had not thought of in her agony over Daoud's death.

She heard the note of disdain toward Charles in Simon's voice and wondered at it.

"You will not deliver Charles's enemies to him? After coming here and helping him win his war? Have you turned against him?"

"Gradually—too gradually, I am sorry to say—I have come to

see that Charles d'Anjou was not the great man I once thought him to be. When I learned that John and Philip were killed, that killed any remaining feeling I have for Charles. So I will help you if I can. But where can you all go? All of southern Italy and Sicily will be overrun with Anjou's men. I cannot keep you, and you cannot safely leave me."

"Let us go back to the others," said Sophia. "It will be best if we talk together about this."

She could hardly believe he was serious about letting her escape Her pain-wracked mind was unable to come to grips with what was happening to her. How she needed Daoud! He would know what to do. As she entered the firelit room her eyes blurred with tears.

But she saw at once that there were more people in the room than when she had gone out on the balcony with Simon.

One of them was holding a crossbow leveled at Simon. Her heart stopped. Then she recognized him, and she let her breath out in relief. Black and white curly hair, graying mustache, broad shoulders. Lorenzo.

She heard a growling. Scipio stood there, held tightly on a leash by Tilia. Ugolini was beside her.

Rachel hurried to Sophia and took her hand. "I'm glad you are back. I was frightened for you."

"Simon wants to help us," said Sophia, taking Rachel's hand. She could not give up in despair, she thought, while she had Rachel to care for.

"You took long enough to come in off that balcony, Count," Lorenzo said.

"Put down your crossbow," Sophia said. "Count Simon has decided to be a friend to us."

"I would not regret giving our new friend just what *my* friend Daoud got today from his man Sordello," Lorenzo said.

Tilia said, "Do you—know, Sophia? About Daoud?"

Holding herself rigid against this fresh reminder of her grief, Sophia said only, "Yes."

Friar Mathieu said, "Lorenzo, the man who killed Daoud lies there on the floor. No need to talk about revenge." He pointed to a corner of the room where Sordello's body lay.

Needing a moment's relief from her pain, Sophia said, "Lorenzo, how did you ever get here?"

Still holding the crossbow pointed at Simon, Lorenzo spoke without looking at her.

"After I got Rachel and Friar Mathieu out of the French camp,

I saw this fellow's army charging down from the hills to attack Daoud and his Falcons." Lorenzo shook the crossbow.

Sophia prayed that he would put the crossbow down. What if by accident he unleashed a bolt at Simon? If Simon were to die before her eyes, that would surely be more than she could bear.

"I had to try to warn Daoud," Lorenzo said. "I left Rachel and the friar there and rode off. I never did reach Daoud." He hesitated a moment, eyeing Simon, then smiled, a hard smile without warmth or mirth.

"I got your precious Tartars, though, Count Simon."

Simon nodded, his eyes bitter. "Sordello told me it was you who killed them." He took a step toward Lorenzo, who shook the crossbow at him again.

Put it down! Sophia wanted to scream.

"Yes. That worm-eaten spy of yours told you, eh?" Lorenzo jerked his head in the direction of Sordello's body. "He was trying to guard them at the time. He did a bad job of it."

"Mère de Dieu!" was all Simon said. Anger reddened his face, but he was looking off into space, not at Lorenzo.

"After that," Lorenzo went on, "I found the wagon, but Rachel and Friar Mathieu were gone. I found another riderless horse and hitched it up, and I drove the wagon into the forest west of here. Rachel, I buried your chest. I hope I remember where.

"By then it was nightfall. I used my forged safe conduct to get me back into Benevento. Then I had to dodge the mobs of drunken Frenchmen running wild all over town. I knew where you were staying, Sophia, but it took me all night to get into this house past Count Simon's guards. I spent hours in hiding and scrambling about on rooftops."

"I thought I would die of fright," said Tilia, "when Lorenzo came through our window."

Thank God for Lorenzo! How I love him. Nothing can stop him. Nothing can kill him.

"What were you planning to do with these people when you came here, Count?" Lorenzo said. "Turn them over to your master, Anjou?"

Sophia turned to look at Simon. He stood composed, his empty hands at his sides, his face, pink in the glow from the fire, calm as a statue's.

"*Your* master—Daoud the Mameluke—asked me to come here," Simon said.

"*Please* put your crossbow down, Lorenzo," Sophia said again.

"Are you sure, Sophia? This crossbow might be the only thing that keeps us from getting dragged off to be hanged. This high-horse bastard has fifty men outside."

Greek Fire blazed in Sophia's brain.

She screamed, "Do not call him a bastard!"

"Sophia!" said Simon wonderingly. "Thank you!"

She stood trembling, but almost as soon as the words flew from her mouth, the fit of rage passed.

I must be going mad.

But she had done no harm. She seemed to have made things better.

"Forgive me, Count." Lorenzo laid the crossbow on the bed. "It was rude to call you that. But you did ruin our hope of victory today. Daoud had the battle won. He almost had his hands on your bloody Charles d'Anjou, when you charged out of the hills with your damned army. And now the king I served for twenty years and my good friend are both dead." He rubbed the back of his hand across his eyes. "That was hard, Count. Very hard."

So it was Simon's charge that turned the battle, Sophia thought. *And it was because of me that he entered this war.* Her grief grew heavier still.

"You may hold those things against me," said Simon, "and I might hold against you the deaths of John and Philip, whom I dedicated my life to protecting."

Listening to that grave, quiet voice, Sophia realized that Simon no longer seemed young to her. It was as if he had aged many years since she had seen him last.

As long as she had known him, she had thought of him as a boy. And yet, from what she was hearing, if Charles d'Anjou was now king of southern Italy and Sicily, it was to Simon that he owed the crown.

"But I know who really killed the Tartars," Simon went on. "It was Charles, Count Charles, now King Charles, who no more wants to make war on Islam than your friend Daoud did. Charles kept the Tartars with himself and away from King Louis, and he let them go out on the field while the battle was raging, no doubt hoping they would die."

Lorenzo frowned. "You mean Charles used me to get rid of the Tartars?"

Simon nodded. "He could not have known it would be you, but he made sure they would be in harm's way. Charles is very good at using people. My mother warned me about him long before I let him persuade me to come to Italy to guard the Tartars, but I did

not listen. But now, how are we going to get all of you safely out
of Benevento?''

He kept coming back to that, Sophia thought. He seemed determined to save them from Charles d'Anjou's vengeance.

"We may still have the wagon I hid out in the forest," Lorenzo
said. "And if you truly mean to help us, you might appropriate a
horse or two. There are many horses hereabouts whose owners will
never need them again."

"I can write you a genuine safe-conduct that will get you past
Charles's officials and agents," Simon said. "If you travel quickly
enough, you may get ahead of them into territory still friendly to
you. There may be no army left to oppose Charles, but it will take
him some time to get control of all the territory he has won. Where
might you go?"

Sophia took Rachel's hand again, and they sat on the bed. Remembering that she and Daoud had shared this bed last night,
Sophia felt the heaped stones of sorrow weigh heavier still.

I will never hold him again.

To distract herself from her pain, she tried to listen to what people
around her were saying.

"To Palermo first," said Lorenzo decisively. "At a time like
this, with the king gone, every family must fend for itself. I want
to get to mine at once." He turned to Rachel, and his mustache
stretched in one of the smiles Sophia had seen all too rarely. "My
wife, Fiorela, and I would be honored to have you as a member of
our family, Rachel."

Rachel gave a little gasp. "Truly?"

"Truly. I have been wanting to propose it for a long time."

Again Sophia thanked God for Lorenzo. She almost wished he
would offer to take her into his family too.

Simon stared at Lorenzo. "You are—were—an official at Manfred's
court, and your wife's name is Fiorela?"

Lorenzo frowned. "Yes, Count. What of it?"

Simon's interest puzzled Sophia. Could there be some connection between him and Lorenzo?

"We must speak more about her later." Simon flexed his mail-
clad arms. "It will not be safe for you to try to leave Benevento
until morning. I will see to it that my men guard this house from
the looters till then. They will not, of course, know who is in here
with me. Meanwhile, you all had better sleep, if you can."

Weary and broken by sorrow though she was, Sophia knew that
to try to lie down in the dark would mean nothing but hours of
suffering. She would sleep only when she fainted from exhaustion.

And she dreaded the agony she would feel when she woke again and remembered what had happened this day.

Tilia cleared her throat politely. "Your Signory, it will be hard to sleep in the same room with dead bodies."

Simon frowned. "Dead bodies?"

"Well—I hope you will not hold it against myself and the cardinal—but besides Sordello here, there are two of his henchmen in the room we have been occupying."

"Also dead?"

"Also dead. They were trying to rob us."

Now Sophia remembered that Sordello had brought two Venetians with him, and she remembered the barks and growls that had come up through the floorboards while she was alone with Sordello. What had happened down there between Ugolini and Tilia and Sordello's men? And Scipio?

Sophia looked at Tilia and noticed that she wore a small smile of satisfaction and was fingering her jeweled pectoral cross.

I need not worry about Tilia, she thought grimly.

Simon sighed. "There must be a basement in this house, a root cellar, something of the kind. Lorenzo, you and I will find a place to take the bodies."

The room grew cold with Sophia and Rachel alone in it, and Sophia put more logs on the fire, thankful that the merchant who had hurriedly vacated this place had left plenty of wood. She lay down in the big bed beside Rachel.

Hesitantly, Rachel told Sophia that she, with Friar Mathieu, had been present at Daoud's death. She showed Sophia the little leather capsule, and Sophia, remembering the many times she had seen it around Daoud's neck, broke into a fresh storm of weeping.

Rachel held it out to her. "I think perhaps you should be the one to have it."

"No. He gave it to you." Sophia wiped her eyes, drew out the locket and opened it, looked sadly at the meaningless tracery of lines on its rock-crystal surface, barely visible in the light from the low fire.

"This locket is what he gave me. It seems the magic in it died with him, but it is a precious keepsake." She remembered that she had been looking at the locket when Sordello tried to kill Simon. Why had he tried to do that? It made no sense, but because of it she had killed Sordello, and of that she was glad. She had avenged Daoud.

Desperately needing to know every detail of Daoud's death, Sophia questioned Rachel until, in the middle of a sentence, the girl fell asleep.

Sophia lay wide awake in the dark, crying silently. Lying there was hell, as she had expected it would be. After what seemed like hours, the fire on the hearth died. She got up and piled three bed carpets over Rachel.

She wrapped herself in her winter cloak and slipped out of the room. Going, she knew not where, but unable to remain still. Wanting only to distract herself from her pain with a little movement.

She went down the stairs, passing the silent second-floor room were Ugolini and Tilia lay. She heard men's voices from a room on the ground floor.

The cabinet of the merchant who owned this house was just inside the front door. There Sophia found Simon and Lorenzo seated facing each other at a long black table. Scipio, lying on the floor near the doorway, opened one eye, twitched an ear at her, and went back to sleep. With a quill Simon was writing out a document, while Lorenzo used a candle flame to melt sealing wax in a small brass pitcher on a tripod.

Simon gave her a brief, sad smile. He had taken off his mail, and wore only his quilted white under-tunic.

Lorenzo stood up, went to a sideboard, and poured a cup of wine. Silent, he handed it to Sophia. It was sweeter than she liked, but it warmed her.

She took a chair at the end of the table. The two men sat there so companionably that it was hard to believe that for more than two years they had been enemies. She recalled with a pang how Daoud had said he no longer hated Simon. If only he could be here to be part of this.

"One cannot predict these things," Lorenzo said, continuing the conversation that had begun before Sophia arrived, "and I certainly do not believe in trying to make them happen, but my son, Orlando, is at a good age for marriage. And so is Rachel."

Simon looked up from his writing. "You would let your son marry a woman who had spent over a year in a brothel?"

Lorenzo gave Simon a level look. "Yes. Do you disapprove?"

Simon shook his head. "From what I know of Rachel, not at all. But there are many who would."

Knowing Lorenzo Celino, Sophia thought warmly, she was not surprised that he did not feel as many other people would.

"Rachel is brave, intelligent, and beautiful," said Lorenzo. "What happened to her was not her fault. And now she knows infinitely more of the world than most women. If she should take an interest in Orlando, he would be lucky to have her. And then Rachel will be your cousin, Count Simon. She will surely be the only Jewish girl in all Europe who is related—if only by marriage—to a great baron of France.''

Sophia frowned at Lorenzo. Cousin? What was the man talking about?

Raising his head from his scroll, Simon saw her look and smiled. ''I have just discovered, Sophia, that Lorenzo Celino here is my uncle.''

Sophia felt somewhat irritated. Were the two of them playing a sort of joke on her?

''No, it's true, Sophia,'' said Lorenzo. ''My wife came from Languedoc years ago as a refugee from the war that was being fought there at the time. Her maiden name was Fiorela de Vency. And her older brother, Roland de Vency, went back to France and eventually married Simon's mother, making him Simon's step-father. So you see, I am Simon's uncle by marriage.''

Simon smiled broadly. ''Roland told me long ago that he had a sister Fiorela who was married to a high official of Manfred's. I would far, far rather have you for an uncle, Lorenzo, than Charles d'Anjou, whom I have often called Uncle.'' He gave Sophia a meaningful look.

She understood. Simon might like Lorenzo, but not well enough to tell him that Roland de Vency was more than a stepfather to him, and therefore Lorenzo's wife more than an aunt by marriage.

Only his mother and father and his confessor know that, he once said.

And I.

Weighed down with grief though she was, she managed to smile back.

Simon put down his quill, closed the lid on the ink pot, and blew on the parchment to dry it. He poured red wax at the bottom of the sheet, took a heavy ring off his finger, and pressed it into the blob. He handed the document to Lorenzo to read.

''You have been well educated,'' said Lorenzo. ''You write as handsomely as a monk.''

''Charles will have his men out looking for you, as one of Manfred's ministers,'' said Simon. ''I advise you not to wait for them to catch up with you in Palermo. Of course, Charles may offer you a chance to work for him. The help of men acquainted with Manfred's regime will make it much easier for him to take over.''

Lorenzo's mustache twitched as he smiled sourly. ''Work for him? I know you do not know me well, but I hope you jest. Otherwise I would have to consider myself insulted. Manfred and his father, Emperor Frederic, built a fair and civilized land here. Learning and the arts of peace flourished, unchecked by superstition. Charles will doubtless destroy all that. I propose to make it very hard for him to hold on to what he has conquered this day. Anjou will not thank you if he learns it was you who turned me loose."

"See that he does not learn it, then."

Lorenzo frowned. "You won the battle for Charles. Now you seem willing to do him all sorts of mischief." He leaned across the table and fixed Simon with his piercing, dark eyes. "Why?"

Sophia leaned forward, too, eager to hear Simon's answer.

Simon sighed and smiled. "Because today at last I saw through Charles's double-dealing with me in the matter of the Tartars." His smile was a very sad one. "And I want to help you, out of what I still feel for Sophia."

Sophia felt the tide of sorrow rise again within her. Her mouth trembled and her eyes burned. Simon was looking down at the table now, to her relief, and did not see her response to his words. He might have been looking away, she thought, to hide the tears in his own eyes.

Lorenzo stood up briskly. "I am going to try to find an empty bed or a soft carpet for a few hours sleep. Tomorrow we leave early, and we travel far."

After he and Scipio had gone, Simon said, "I loved you. At least, I loved a woman who had your face and form, but did not really exist. Against my will, I have asked myself, since I saw you again tonight, if there is any way that dream of mine could be salvaged. Have you thought about that?"

Sophia shook her head. In her heart there was room for nothing but pain.

She said, "Just as you wish you had not been the cause of Daoud's death, so I wish I had not hurt you so. But that is all I can say. Simon, a dream may be very beautiful, but it is still only a dream."

"I suppose we are lucky that we can sit here and talk about it, you and I, and that we are not trying to kill each other."

"That is not luck, that is because of who we are. Simon, one thing hurts me very much. I do not know what happened to Daoud after he died. Is there any way I could—see him?"

His eyes big and dark with sadness, he shook his head. "Even if you could, the body of a man dead many hours, of wounds, is a terrible sight. And then that would be your last memory of him. You would not want that. *He* would not want that. And if you went near the bodies of Manfred's dead, you would be in great danger. Someone might recognize you. Remember that many who served Manfred will be eager to get into Charles's good graces. You must protect yourself."

She did not care about protecting herself.

"What will happen to Daoud? What will they do to him?"

She realized she was still talking of Daoud as if he were alive. She could not bear to speak of "Daoud's body."

"The men who died fighting for Manfred will be buried on the battlefield," said Simon. "They cannot be buried in consecrated ground because those who were Christians were excommunicated under the pope's interdict. And many, like Daoud, were Saracens. I believe King Charles is planning some special honor for Manfred's body."

Manfred's body. Hearing those words, the enormity of what had been lost, beyond her own sorrow, came home to her.

And what of Daoud's spirit, she wondered. Did she believe that a part of him was still alive? Had he gone to his Muslim warrior's paradise? If she were carrying his child, would he want her to raise it as her own? She realized that she was crying again. How could her eyes produce so great a flood of tears?

She heard footsteps and felt Simon's hand resting lightly but firmly on her shoulder. She dropped her head to her arms, folded on the table, and gave herself up to sobbing.

LXXII

SIMON, CARRYING THE HEAVIEST ROCK HE COULD HOLD, WALKED in procession directly behind Charles d'Anjou. They came to the low wooden platform where the body of Manfred von Hohenstaufen lay, covered by his great yellow banner with its black double-headed eagle. Charles set his foot, in a handsome purple boot, on the banner, and leaned over the body with a large stone.

"Requiescat in pace. May you rest in peace, Manfred von Hohenstaufen."

Carefully Charles set the rock down on the banner-draped figure and stepped back with a small smile of satisfaction.

"Now you, Simon."

Simon stepped onto the platform. His arms, stiff and sore from yesterday's fighting, ached as he lifted the stone to place it. He laid it next to Charles's rock on the inert, hidden form and stepped back.

Gautier du Mont of the bowl-shaped haircut was next. He bowed to Charles and Simon and put his rock beside theirs.

"Simon, come with me," said Charles. "We have had no chance to talk since yesterday." He led Simon to a small nearby hill, where they could watch the long line of Charles's army winding single file through the gray valley of Benevento under an overcast sky. Each man, by Charles's order, carried a stone to lay on Manfred's cairn.

"If not for you, Manfred would be burying me today, Simon," said Charles, his large eyes solemn. "I am in your debt forever, for my kingdom and my life."

That should make this a bit easier for me.

"Thank you—Sire."

Du Mont and FitzTrinian, Fourre and de Marion, laid their stones as Charles and Simon watched. The Burgundian, von Regensburg, had been killed yesterday, impaled on a Saracen foot soldier's spear. Simon felt little regret at his passing.

"We are burying Manfred as our pagan ancestors were buried," said Charles, "but I hope this gesture of respect helps reconcile his former subjects to me. I fear trouble with them. It has already started. Last night, after the battle, several men died mysteriously."

"Oh?" said Simon.

"The death that shocked me most was de Verceuil's."

Simon was amazed. "The cardinal?" He could hardly believe it. He remembered de Verceuil's departure just after the cardinal had killed Manfred, as Simon and Daoud were beginning their final combat.

"Poisoned," said Charles. "I do not know if it was done by Manfred's followers or by an enemy of his in our own ranks. You had not heard?"

"No."

Even though one expected to hear, after a battle, of untimely deaths, Simon's blood ran cold with shock. De Verceuil did not seem the sort to oblige his fellow men by dying unexpectedly.

A cold wind blew across Simon's neck and whipped the bright purple woolen cloak Charles was wearing. Charles touched his hand to his gold crown, larger than the count's coronet he had worn on state occasions in the past, as if fearing that it might blow away.

"He went to the Tartars' tent looking for them before we learned they had been killed," Charles said. "Saw a jar of wine on the table. He was thirsty after the fighting, and took a long drink straight out of the jar. Those who saw him said that in an instant his skin turned hot and red. First he cried out that he was blind, then he raved about terrible visions and began laying about wildly with his mace, so that his attendants were forced to flee. Then he went into convulsions, and within the hour he was dead."

Simon remembered Lorenzo saying something about having gone to the Tartars' tent.

He was going to make doubly sure he killed them this time. Instead, he killed Manfred's killer.

"A tragedy," Simon said, sorry that, despite the duty of Christian charity, he could feel no sorrow.

"Then there was Sordello, your captain of archers who guarded the Tartars. Did you not hear about him?"

"He has not been under my command since I left the Tartars with you in Rome," said Simon. He kept trying to think about de Verceuil and prayed that his face would not give away his knowledge of how Sordello died.

"He and two of his men were found this morning in a building in town. Sordello had a small puncture in his throat, and one of the others had been stabbed in the chest with a very thin blade. One of my priest-physicians looked at the bodies and believes both of them were killed with poisoned implements. And it appeared the throat of the third had been torn out by the fangs of some enormous beast."

"Perhaps a watchdog," said Simon. "After all, when troops are turned loose on a town, one must expect that a few of the citizens will fight back."

"I am sorry to lose Sordello," said Charles. "A despicable man, but often useful."

The rocks covered Manfred's body completely now. Only the edges of the yellow banner were still showing. Those who had placed their stones stood around in groups to watch the cairn grow.

"These Sicilians will not settle down until the remaining Hohenstaufens are out of the way," said Charles. "Manfred has three sons and a daughter. I have to find them and lock them up. Too bad I cannot have them executed, but they are just children."

Children!

Simon prayed that Manfred's children escaped from Charles.

He stood facing Charles, knowing that he was as tall as the new king of southern Italy and Sicily and that he no longer felt afraid of him. Fighting in this battle, his near-death at Daoud's hands, the shock and pain of what Sophia had told him—all together, these things had changed him. He no longer doubted that he deserved to be the Count de Gobignon. It did not matter who his real father was. What mattered was that there was no one else in the world who could rule Gobignon as well as he. In the past two years he had become the Count de Gobignon in truth as well as in title. And now all he wanted was to go back to his domain.

To bring up the subject, Simon said, "Friar Mathieu is most grieved at the deaths of the Tartar ambassadors, but it means you no longer need him here. He has asked me to take him back to France with me. He has permission from his order to go. He wants to tell King Louis in person about his journey among the Tartars. And he wants to spend his remaining years in France. As for me, I am eager to see my mother and stepfather in Provence."

Now that I can face them with a clear conscience.

Charles frowned, throwing his head back and staring down his long nose at Simon. "You want to go back to France now? But our work here has only begun."

"If you wish to offer any of my vassals fiefdoms or positions in your new kingdom, they have my leave to accept. I promised them that when they came with me."

"But you cannot leave before taking possession of your own dukedom."

"Thank you, Sire. But I have decided that for myself I want nothing."

He had rehearsed that sentence in his mind a hundred times. He was delighted at the sound of it and even more delighted at the stupefied expression on Charles's face. It was not often one surprised a man like Charles d'Anjou.

"*Nothing?* But that is preposterous. You have come all this way, won this great victory—has your head been addled by chivalrous romances? This is not the world of Arthur and Lancelot."

Simon recalled Manfred's last stand on the field yesterday and thought, *Perhaps that world ended with him.*

Surely Charles, keeping himself well out of the battle and threatened only when Daoud desperately tried to reach him, had been no figure out of chivalric romance. This was a man he could not trust, could not admire, and especially could not like.

"Too true, Sire. But it is a world in which people need decent rulers. I do not need more land, and the land I already have needs me. If I divide myself between a domain in northern France and another one here in Italy, I cannot govern either well. And, frankly,

I do not want to live in the midst of a strange people as a foreign conqueror.''

Giving up this dukedom, too, gives me a better right to be Count de Gobignon.

"You overestimate the difficulty of governing," said Charles.

No, you underestimate it, thought Simon. For Charles governing was a simple matter of squeezing the people and their land for all they were worth. And killing anyone who protested, as he had those citizens outside Rome. If the people were strange to him, all the easier to oppress them.

"Perhaps what comes easily to you is difficult for me, Sire," he said.

Charles shook his head, then quickly reached up to steady the heavy crown. "I do not understand you. But that province is too valuable for me to press it on someone who does not want it. I can use it to reward others who have served me, not as well as you have, but well enough."

"I hoped you might see it that way."

"But think, since I asked you to guard the Tartars—it has been nearly three years—you have taken part in great affairs and you have added to your reputation and restored luster to your family name. You have led your Gobignon vassals to a victory that has brought them glory and riches. You have, I tell you again, won my lifelong gratitude. Why separate yourself from all that now? By what you did yesterday you wiped out the stain on your family name. Your father betrayed his king and his crusader comrades, but now you have won a victory for a crusade and saved the life of a king.''

Yes, but how different those crusades, and how different those kings.

He kept reminding himself that Manfred was an enemy of the pope and Daoud an enemy of Christendom, but the thought haunted him that through him great men and a noble kingdom had fallen. Again and again he tried to push out of his mind the idea that he had been wrong to come here and fight on the side of Anjou. But he knew it would remain with him, troubling him, for the rest of his life.

"If you want to show gratitude to me, Sire, the one favor I ask is that you not press me to stay."

Charles fumbled in a heavy purse at his belt and drew out a long silver chain. He held it out to Simon.

"Here. I want you to have this, at least."

Simon bowed gravely and held out his hand. Attached to the chain was a five-pointed star with a large, round ruby in its center.

"Beautiful. Thank you very much, Sire."

"It was Manfred's. He prized it highly, I am told. Called it his 'star of destiny.' You earned it, I think, by giving me victory yesterday. I hope it brings you a better destiny than it did him."

Uneasily, feeling that the star was property stolen from a dead man, Simon took it. He unbuckled the purse at his belt to drop it in.

"Put it on," Charles urged.

Reluctantly, Simon hung the star around his neck.

"I will treasure it," he said tonelessly.

"It is little enough. If you will only consider staying with me, you will share in spoils that will make that look like a trinket. City by city I am going to take over not just this kingdom but northern Italy too. I will unite all of Italy. The Papacy will be solidly under French control. And then Constantinople. I bought the title of Emperor of Constantinople from Baldwin II when he fled to Paris after Michael Paleologos deposed him."

The name of Michael Paleologos was like a blow to Simon's stomach. Probably it was no more than a name to Charles, but Simon could hear Sophia saying she had been that same Michael's concubine for a time. He suffered again as he had last night when he stood with her on the balcony of that house and she told him at last the truth about herself. He had felt then as if he were drowning in a lake of fire. And added to his own anguish had been the realization that her pain, the pain of the woman he had loved and still loved, had been worse than the worst of what he felt.

Charles was still going on about his accursed ambitions.

"I mean to make that title a reality. Not since Rome will so many lands around the Middle Sea have been united in one—empire."

The vision moved Simon, but not as Charles evidently hoped. It sickened him, and he felt himself in the presence of a monster. Had Charles forgotten already the heaps of corpses strewn on this battlefield at dawn, that only now were being hauled away by the wagonload?

Simon remembered the long list of the Gobignon dead that Thierry had handed him this morning on his return to camp. He thought of the horribly wounded knights and men he had visited, men who, if God was kind to them, would be dead in a day or two. His eyes still burned from all the weeping he had done this barely begun day.

And this man, who had made the rescue of the Holy Land, the

defeat of Islam, and the alliance of Christians and Tartars seem all-important to him, now spoke of sacrificing thousands and thousands more lives entrusted to him so that he could realize his dream of being another Caesar.

God grant that he does not get what he wants.

The wind from the north blew steadily down the length of the valley. The pile of rocks over Manfred's body had grown so high the men now had to throw their stones to reach the top.

"What of our plans to liberate the Holy Land, Sire? What about the alliance of Tartars and Christians? That is what I gave the last three years of my life to. Surely that is not dead because John and Philip had the ill luck to get killed on this battlefield."

Charles pulled his purple cloak tighter around him against the wind. "The timing is wrong for an attempt to retake the Holy Land. I have no intention of taking part in a crusade against the Egyptians, with or without the Tartars."

There it was. Charles had confirmed what Simon suspected about him. He felt indignation boiling within him, but he tried not to let it sound in his voice.

"Sire, why did you let the Tartars go into the battle yesterday and lose their lives?"

Charles's eyes narrowed. "I know what grief you must feel, having guarded them so carefully for so long. But they insisted. They had fought against Christians. So now they wanted to see how a battle looks from our side. They knew the risks. They had been warriors all their lives. They were my guests, and I had to let them do what they wanted."

Simon looked out at the valley. The line of men carrying rocks to Manfred's cairn stretched far into the distance, disappearing finally beyond the crests of rolling fields. The line still looked as long as ever. It wound past a long, narrow mound of freshly turned brown earth—the mass grave dug at dawn by prisoners for the dead of Manfred's army. The man called Daoud—Simon still thought of him as David—who for more than two years had fought Simon relentlessly, lay somewhere under that mound of earth. The man Sophia had loved.

Near at hand the soldiers who had added their rocks to the pile were dismantling Manfred's camp. Tents collapsed in flurries of colored cloth.

All these fighting men. And King Louis could have added twice as many to these. What could they not have accomplished if they had invaded Palestine at the same time a Tartar army struck at the Saracens from the east?

He decided to probe further. "Now there can be no planning for a crusade—until the next ambassadors come from Tartary. Is that your wish?"

Charles smiled. "Oh, eventually we will want to make war on the Saracens. After Italy is united, after the Byzantine Empire is ours once more. Toward that day, we want to maintain the bonds of friendship with the Tartars. If they send us more ambassadors, we will treat them royally and shower them with fair words."

"And send them home with nothing," Simon added.

"For now," Charles agreed. "For now, instead of planning war with Egypt, I believe it is more in my interest to do as the Hohenstaufens did when they ruled Sicily—cultivate friendly relations with the Sultan of Cairo."

Simon was silent for a moment, amazed that Anjou could be so open about his lack of principle. He felt his face grow hot and his voice quiver as his anger forced its way to the surface.

"Everything you have done and said has been for one purpose only, to make yourself king of Sicily. I guessed as much, and now I know. And that is why I do not want a dukedom in your kingdom. Because I do not want to be used by you anymore."

Charles drew himself up and fixed Simon with an angry stare. "Curb your tongue, messire! You may be the Count de Gobignon, but you owe me the respect due a king."

"You are not my king, thank God," Simon retorted. "My king, your brother, King Louis, taught me that each and every man and woman on earth is precious to God. That a king's duty is to care for his people, not use them as if they were cattle."

"A good philosophy for the next world," said Charles scornfully.

"It is the philosophy by which your brother rules in this world," said Simon fiercely. "And that is why everyone loves him. Not just his own French subjects, but all Christians."

Charles's olive skin darkened to a purple shade. "Consider this, messire—when Louis last went to war he led a whole army to destruction in Egypt. When I go to war, I lead my army to victory and the spoils of a fair and prosperous kingdom. Louis was born a king. I made myself a king. Now. Which of us is the better ruler? Answer me that."

Simon stared at Charles's engorged face and felt dizzy with triumph. Not only had he lost all fear of Charles d'Anjou, but he had broken through Charles's mask of regal authority and had provoked him to reveal his naked envy of his brother.

He answered quietly, "You might conquer this whole world, and my sovereign seigneur, King Louis, would still be a better king than you are. And a better man.''

Charles stared at Simon, his eyes huge and thick veins standing out in his temples. Simon stared back, keeping himself outwardly calm, but inwardly exulting in his new freedom.

There is nothing I need prove to this man or to anyone else. I am myself.

The last bond of loyalty between himself and Charles d'Anjou was broken.

The silence stretched on, until it seemed to Simon that this was the longest moment of his life.

Charles blinked and let out several long breaths. ''Ah, well. As God is my witness, you and my brother are two of a kind. You deserve each other.'' He shook his arms, which he had been holding rigid at his sides, and reached up and tapped the crown down more firmly on his head.

He lumps me with King Louis. He does not know the great honor he does me.

Charles said, ''I hope, for the sake of what we have been to each other, that you will be discreet about what I have said to you. If you visit my brother when you go back to France, you must not cause ill will between him and me.''

''I doubt that even if I wished to I could cause bad feeling between you,'' Simon said. ''He has known you all your life, and if he has not broken with you by now, it must be because he loves you too much.''

He turned abruptly and left Charles standing alone on his little hill.

The star swung at his neck, and he thought of going back and throwing it at Charles's feet. But, no, he decided he would keep it, and honor Manfred's memory.

The grief of these two days still darkened his world, but there was one small brightness. He might not have accomplished anything to liberate the Holy Land, but he had freed himself from Charles d'Anjou.

It hurt Simon to see Sophia's face. Her eyelids were red and puffed. Her cheeks were hollow and her lips pale. She was still beautiful, but it was a sorrowful beauty, like that of a grieving Madonna.

''I see you are wearing Manfred's star,'' Sophia said.

''Forgive me.'' He felt a flash of hatred for himself. How stupid of him! She must think he was wearing it like a captured trophy.

He said, "Charles gave it to me. I swear to you, I mean no disrespect to Manfred. Just the opposite. It must hurt you to see it. How thoughtless of me! Anjou insisted on my putting it around my neck just now. I am only going to keep it safe in memory of Manfred, not wear it. Let me take it off."

You are babbling, he told himself. *Be still.*

"No," she said, touching his hand lightly, briefly. "No one has a better right to wear it than you."

Simon said, "I want you to know this—Daoud succeeded."

"What do you mean—succeeded how?"

They stood just outside the walls of Benevento by the side of the road leading to the south. A group of Charles's men-at-arms, past whom Simon had just escorted Sophia and her friends, lounged before the gate.

"Last night I suspected it, but this morning I talked to Anjou, and now I am certain. There will never be an alliance of Christians and Tartars. Anjou never wanted it, and he will do everything in his power to prevent it. It would interfere with his own ambitions."

Her amber eyes looked into his, and he felt the pain she was holding rigidly at bay within herself.

Oh, God, those eyes! How he had dreamed of spending the rest of his life in their gaze. Now, after today, he would never look into them again.

She said, "Does it disappoint you that there will be no alliance?"

"Once it would have. After all, I gave everything I had to trying to make the alliance succeed. But I did that for King Louis and for my own honor more than because I believed the alliance was a good thing. Indeed, I often had doubts. I pray my people will never take part in such horrors as the Tartars have committed."

Sophia shook her head. "If you are right, then I only wish Daoud could have known before he died that his purpose was accomplished."

The thought came to Simon that Daoud might be aware of that, in the next world, but it seemed a childish fancy in the face of her sorrow, and he said nothing.

Even now, she thought only of Daoud.

Oh, why could not everything be different? Why could she not be the cardinal's niece, the lovely woman he had fallen in love with? Why must she be a stranger with a Greek name he had already forgotten because he had heard it only once, a plotter, a spy, an enemy?

He looked at the jagged blue mountains, mostly bare rock, that rose behind Sophia, and in despair thought of climbing up there and throwing himself off a cliff. The road she would be taking led into those mountains.

Celino, mounted on a sturdy brown mare, held Sophia's chestnut horse for her. Ugolini and Tilia Caballo, dressed in dark peasants' clothes, sat together on the driver's seat of Celino's cart, Tilia holding the reins. Where were those two going, Simon wondered. When he said good-bye to them he had not thought to ask. No place in Sicily would be safe for them. Well, they probably would not have wanted to tell him.

Rachel, sitting on a powerful-looking black mule, gave Simon a little smile and a nod when he glanced her way. He smiled back.

May you find a good man, Celino's son or another. And may the rest of your life be entirely happy.

"You are going back to Constantinople, then?" he said to Sophia. He had to drag the words out of himself.

She nodded. "I can get a ship from Palermo. Rachel has kindly offered to pay my passage. Lorenzo found the chest full of gold she got from the Tartar, right where he buried it out in the woods. So Rachel is still rich. As for me, I am quite destitute."

God's mantle! That never occurred to me. What an idiot I am.

"Would you—"

She raised a hand to silence him and shook her head. "I would not."

He shrugged and nodded. "Take this from me at least—a warning to your emperor. Charles wants Constantinople. He has a claim to the crown of Byzantium. He told me just today that he means to do to Michael what he did to Manfred."

Sophia gave him a crooked little smile. "Michael will never let him even get near Constantinople. I hope I can help with that."

"If ever I can do anything for you—"

Her smile grew wider. "Do not be too quick to promise that, Simon. If we ever meet again, we may be on opposite sides." In a softer, sadder tone she added, "Again."

He took a step closer to her. "If so, I will not be so easily deceived. Now I know the real Sophia, the one who did not love me."

Her smile fell away. "I think the real Sophia did love you, Simon. Every time you told me how you loved me, it was as if you were taking me up to a mountaintop and showing me a beautiful land I could never enter. And the worst of it was that because I could not enter, neither could you. We were both barred forever from happiness."

The look on her face made him want to burst out weeping. He held his breath and pressed his lips together hard to stifle the sob.

When he was able to speak, he said, "I think I would have loved the real Sophia if I could have known her."

She shut her eyes as if in terrible pain and pressed the palms of her hands against her stomach.

He reached out to take Sophia in his arms, but she stepped back from him, and he saw that the tears were streaming down her pale cheeks. She held out her hand.

He clasped her cold hand in both of his and said, "I will never forget you."

The sun was setting in the desert to the west of El Kahira, the Guarded One, giving a red tint to the white dust that drifted above the many roads that led to this city. Tilia Caballo sat on a silk cushion by the pool in the vast interior garden of the palace of the sultan, known as the Multicolored Palace because its walls and floors were inlaid with many different kinds of marble and its ceilings painted in azure and gold. Tilia dabbled her hand in the pool and breathed deep of the scent of jasmine. A fountain threw white water high in the air, and orange and black fish circled in the rippling pool. In the shadows nearby a peacock screamed.

She heard footsteps behind her. The merest glance over her shoulder told her who it was, and she swiftly turned and knelt, pressing her forehead and the palms of her hands against the cool blue tiles.

She saw the pointed toes of scarlet boots before her. She raised her head a bit and saw the boots themselves, gem-encrusted leather.

"Tilia." The voice made her shiver.

"El Malik Dahir," she addressed him. *Victorious King.*

"God blesses our meeting, Tilia."

She sat back, and he lowered himself to a cross-legged position facing her. In the ten years since she had last seen him, he had aged little. He had won the battle of the Well of Goliath, had made himself sultan, and had reigned over a kingdom threatened from East and West. Yet his yellow face was unlined, and there was no gray in his drooping red mustache. She looked at the white scar that ran vertically down his blind right eye; then she looked at his good left eye, and saw that it was still bright blue and clear.

"Forgive me, Tilia, for not being able to greet you when you arrived in El Kahira. I was inspecting the crusaders' defenses at Antioch—from the inside."

She laughed. Amazing that such a striking-looking man should manage again and again to move among his enemies in disguise. But he had been doing it most of his life.

"My lord travels far and fast, as always."

"You have traveled farther. You are comfortable?"

"Who could fail to be comfortable, under Baibars's tent?"

"And Cardinal Ugolini? Will he be happy here?"

"The happiest he has ever been. He spends his days in your Zahiriya, reading ancient manuscripts, talking to the scholars, working with the philosophical instruments. He hardly sleeps, the sooner he might return to the house of learning you built."

"Ah, we must find a strong young slave to comfort you if your cardinal does not spend enough time in your bed."

"I am not the voracious woman you bought from a brothel so many years ago, my lord. Adelberto can satisfy my waning desires."

Baibars laughed, a rumbling sound. "Anything you want, Tilia, in all the sultanate of El Kahira, is yours. You have served me well."

"You took a prisoner and a slave and trusted her. You sent her jewels and gold in a steady stream. You helped her to achieve riches and power in the very heart of Christendom. Why should I not serve you with all my might? Since you sent me from here long ago I have not had the chance to see you with my own eyes and speak aloud my gratitude to you. And now that I am face-to-face with you, words fail me. If I spoke for a thousand and one nights I could not say enough to thank you. To praise you."

Baibars shrugged. "Do you not regret losing it all? You cannot open a brothel here in El Kahira, Tilia. I have closed all the brothels." His eyelids crinkled humorously. "I am a very strict Muslim these days."

"I am ready to retire, my lord. Ready to drop all pretense and come back here, just to be myself."

Baibars's wide mouth drew down, the lips so thin that the line they drew seemed just a slash across the bottom of his face.

"Now that you are here, Tilia, now that we are face-to-face, I want to hear from you the story of Daoud. I want to hear all of it, all that you had no room to tell me in your carrier-pigeon messages. Take as long as you like. Ask for anything that will make you comfortable. My ears are for you and for no one else."

"I am my lord's slave. I shall tell it to you as it happened to me." She settled herself on the cushion. "I first met Daoud ibn Abdallah in the hills outside Orvieto on an afternoon in late summer, three years ago—"

Tilia stopped her tale twice, so that she and Baibars could pray when the muezzins called the faithful to prayer at Maghrib, after the red of sunset had left the sky, and again at 'Isha, when it was dark enough that a white thread could not be told from a black thread.

After the final prayer of the day, a servant brought an oil lamp. Baibars waved the lamp away, then called the servant back and asked for kaviyeh. Tilia drank the sweet, strong kaviyeh of El Kahira with Baibars and devoured a tray of sticky sweets, and then went on with her story.

By the time she was finished, the moon had risen above the courtyard. She sat back and looked at the Victorious King.

"He was to me like my firstborn son." Baibars took a dagger from his sash, held open his shimmering silk kaftan, a costly robe of honor, and slashed a great rent in it.

Tilia wondered what to say. How could she comfort him?

Comfort him? How can anyone offer comfort to a man like Baibars?

"We are Mamelukes," he said. "Slaves. We are slaves of God. We are His instruments. His weapons. I shaped Daoud to be a fine weapon against the enemies of the faith. And it is even as this Simon de Gobignon told the Greek woman Sophia—Daoud succeeded. Abagha Khan still seeks an alliance with the Christians, as his father Hulagu did. But many Tartars have already converted to Islam, and the next Tartar khan of Persia may be a Muslim. I am working to make that possibility a certainty. As for the Christians, my informant at the court of Charles d'Anjou, a certain dwarf named Erculio, tells me that now Charles desires to extend his empire across the Middle Sea into Africa. King Louis is already gathering ships and men for a crusade. But Charles is trying to divert Louis's crusade to Tunisia, which would make it harmless to us. He is a very persuasive man, and I think he will succeed. Truly, this Charles is God's gift to me. He does just what I want. And I do not have to pay him."

Tilia heard no mirth in Baibars's deep laughter.

"And so," Baibars said, "Daoud has won for us the time we needed and changed the fate of nations. And he will be avenged."

"I do not think he would feel a need to be avenged, my lord. He would be happy just to know that he saved his people from destruction."

Baibars nodded. "True. But I, too, am a sword in the hands of God. And if it pleases God to wield me, then in a generation there will not be a crusader left anywhere on the sacred soil of al-Islam.

That will be Daoud's vengeance and his monument. Hear me, O God.''

By the light of the crescent moon hanging over the Multicolored Palace, Tilia watched the Mameluke sultan raise his right hand to heaven. Tears ran down his jutting cheeks. Baibars's tears, she saw, ran as freely from his blind eye as from the eye that could see.

ABOUT THE AUTHOR

Robert Shea is co-author of the famous ILLUMINATUS! trilogy (Dell). His other works include SHIKE and ALL THINGS ARE LIGHTS. He lives in Glencoe, Illinois.